THE
YEARS

ALSO BY NICHOLAS DELBANCO

THE YEARS

A NOVEL

NICHOLAS

DELBANCO

Little
a

Published by Little A, New York

www.apub.com

Amazon, the Amazon logo, and Little A are trademarks of Amazon.com, Inc., or its affiliates.

ISBN-13: 9781477827321
ISBN-10: 1477827323

Cover design by Rex Bonomelli

Library of Congress Control Number: 2014945392

Printed in the United States of America

For Elena, then and now

'Tis time; descend; be stone no more: approach . . .

—William Shakespeare, *The Winter's Tale,* Act 5, Scene 3

BOOK ONE

I
2004

The MS *Diana* set out from the port of Rome, her destination Valletta. Powering south from Civitavecchia, she had stops planned in Sorrento and, on the coast of Sicily, Naxos, Siracusa, and Porto Empedocle. In the old days, under sail, the journey might have taken months; now the trip from Rome to Malta was scheduled for six days. In the old days, in the times of war, these waters had been treacherous; now it was late September, and a pleasure cruise.

The ship's manifest listed fifty-seven cabins and a passenger capacity of 108, not counting crew; she was 87.4 meters long and 13.2 meters wide. Built in 1960, she had been newly refitted. The ship had a Bridge Deck, a Baltic Deck, a Mediterranean Deck, a Caribbean Deck, and, just above the waterline, an Atlantic Deck. Her owner was American, her flag Liberian; her crew came from Croatia. Their names, it seemed to Lawrence, made a kind of music; they introduced themselves as Vinko, Darko, Marko, Ivo, Miho, Vlatka, and Andrea. He tried to remember their names.

Three nights before, he had flown from Detroit and in the morning reached Rome. There he checked into the Grand Hotel Palace, on the Via Veneto, and willed himself to rest. Across the street was the American embassy, fenced in and heavily guarded; up on the next corner loomed the Excelsior, and down the way was the Piazza Barberini, with its Bernini fountain and cascade of loud cars. He was sixty-four years old, recovering from surgery, and his doctor had suggested that he take a trip.

"You're fine," he said. "You've done just fine."

"I don't feel"—Lawrence hesitated—"*ready*, really."

"The risk of stenosis is just about over. It's a statistical possibility, of course—we should wait a year to be certain—but the risk is minimal. And I'm not suggesting you go very far away. It doesn't have to be some third-world country or the slopes of Everest . . ."

"I'm not sure I'm up to traveling."

"Depression," said his doctor, "is a common side effect of angioplasty. In men our age, it's damn near unavoidable. Why don't you take a cruise?"

He knew Tommy Einhorn well. They were neighbors in Ann Arbor, and they played tennis together, and he thought of Tommy as his friend as well as doctor; the advice was kindly meant. "I'm not the type," said Lawrence.

"No?"

"All that forced gaiety. The Princess line. Calisthenics up on deck, the samba by the swimming pool; whatever it is they insist that you do . . ."

"No one's insisting on anything." Dr. Einhorn leaned back in his swivel chair and pressed his fingertips together. "It's only a suggestion. Let me repeat: your heart's just *fine*. It's better now than it has been for years."

"Let's hope so," Lawrence said.

"And these new coated Cypher stents are just the ticket."

"Ticket?"

Einhorn laughed. "The ticket for the ticker: not bad. I should remember that."

———

So he had looked for and then booked a trip to places it seemed safe to go, first stipulating that the cruise ship be small. By "safe," Lawrence told the travel agent, he meant not so much safety from the threat of terror as somewhere where the medical care was adequate and from which, in case of trouble, he could leave. He signed up for travel insurance. The cruise itself had begun in Marseilles, with stops in Nice and Monaco, but he had elected the single-week option and flew instead to Rome.

He had not been there in years. The airport, once so brightly new, seemed overcrowded and shopworn; the train to the Termini reeked. Decades before he had spent time in Italy, studying Renaissance architecture, and he set off for his old haunts—the Spanish Steps, the Borghese gardens, the Campidoglio and backstreets of Trastevere—with a sense of weary duty; to have been young in the Eternal City and to come there now as an aging tourist was bittersweet. He felt not so much nostalgic as aggrieved.

The traffic had increased. The streets were clogged with Vespas, buses, taxis, and the air was rank. Lawrence monitored his breathing and waited for a telltale signal from his chest. It did not come. The Pantheon was ringed by motorcycles, and the Trevi Fountain—past which he could remember wandering at night, and where Anita Ekberg laved herself in *La Dolce Vita*—was a photo op. Everywhere stood groups of sightseers and, waving umbrellas or pennants, their guides.

His sleep was fitful, troubled, and the hotel room too hot. The elegant Italians and the girls in their scant dresses paid him no attention; only beggars waited for him, holding out their hands. The line in front of St. Peter's was so long and daunting that he did not revisit the basilica or the Sistine Chapel but walked by the Tiber instead.

For two days Lawrence wandered. He tried to recapture his old rapt excitement, the fascination of the buildings and the beauty of the hills and the Colosseum and Forum. It did not work. What he focused on instead were pigeons and the dog scat in the paving; by the time he transferred to the MS *Diana*, he was ready—more than willing—to escape.

———

The port of Civitavecchia bustled with tankers at anchor. Lined up by the dock itself were cruise ships in their pastel glory, towering confections like wedding cakes on water. Their names had been emblazoned on their bows and smokestacks: *Marco Polo*, *The Star Princess*, *Island Queen*, *The Attica Swan*. Last and least of this procession was the MS *Diana*, and this pleased him; its scale was small, its aspect self-effacing, and the driver extracted his bags from the taxi trunk with something very like pity.

"*Ecco, signor. Va bene?*"

"*Va bene,*" he said, "*mille grazie,*" and tipped the driver lavishly as if to prove a point.

At the gangplank they were waiting. A man in a white uniform saluted, and a blonde in slacks and sailor's cap said, "Welcome, welcome aboard! I'm your cruise director." She produced a practiced smile, then consulted a passenger list and checked off Lawrence's name. Inside they collected his passport and gave him a key to his cabin and, carrying his luggage, conducted him downstairs. He had a fleeting sense of brightwork, wood, an elevator in its cage, and carpeting and corridors, and then the man who led him to his cabin turned and, half saluting, said in thickly accented English, "Haf a pleazant trip!"

In his room he found a set of thermal clothing and, underneath the portholes, a yellow life preserver. There was a bottle of complimentary red wine on the cabinet between twin beds and a laminated placard asking, *Why Is a Ship called 'She'?* Lawrence read the printed answer:

> A ship is called a she because there is always a great deal of bustle about her; there is usually a gang of man about; she has a waist and stays; it takes a lot of paint to keep her good-looking; it is not the initial expense that brakes you, it is the upkeep; she can be all decked out, but it takes an experienced man to handle her correctly; and without a man at the helm, she is absolutely uncontrollable. She shows her topsides, hides her bottom, and when coming into port always heads for the buoys.

Love her, take good care of her, and she takes good care of you.

He unpacked his clothing first. He hung up his jackets and exercise clothes and stowed the empty suitcase underneath the bed. Then he arranged his medications in the bathroom and laid out his sketch pad and books on the shelf; he liked the cabin's clean enclosure, the wooden containers for stemware and bottles. After the nightlong bustle of the Via Veneto, this organized silence was welcome, and he lay back in his shirtsleeves and attempted to take stock.

———

Before the trouble with his heart he took good health for granted. Lawrence watched what he ate and did not smoke and, although he could have dropped ten pounds and refused a second cocktail, did his best to stay in shape. He looked, he liked to joke, not a day past sixty-three. In truth he did seem youthful, and his students and colleagues in architecture school, when told his actual age, appeared surprised by it; he had retained a wide-eyed and infectious pleasure in teaching, and he paced up and down the studio with spring in his long stride. The profession still compelled him, and although he was no longer a practitioner, New Urbanists still referenced his early work. He had most of his muscle and much of his hair and was known, in Ann Arbor, as a bit of a boulevardier; he had three children and two ex-wives and a series of companions with whom he sometimes slept. For a long time, however, he had lived alone.

When the symptoms of angina came, he at first ignored them, believing the bright pain in his chest was only acid reflux or, maybe, a pulled muscle. Lawrence went to spinning class and worked out on the treadmill three mornings a week, and the shortness of his breath seemed somehow a function of hard exercise; he had always sweated easily. Now he woke up drenched in sweat. The strange taste in his mouth increased—as though he had sucked on tin, then brass—and stairs became a problem; then the band of pain became a vise, extending from shoulder to shoulder. When he begged off from tennis with Tommy Einhorn, Tommy asked him, "Why, what's wrong?"

This was the start of July. In the emergency room they asked for his symptoms and, as soon as he described them, wheeled Lawrence down to the cardiac unit, where white-coated attendants were waiting. They recorded his pulse and blood pressure and temperature and gave him oxygen and heparin and a set of EKGs. It was likely, said the attending cardiologist, he had a blockage in an artery or arteries, and they would perform an angiogram in order to determine where the trouble lay. This was routine procedure, nothing to be concerned about, but he had arrived just in time. An angioplasty or heart bypass might well be indicated, he was told, for he had unstable angina.

Because they did not wish to operate short-staffed on Independence Day, Lawrence waited the long holiday weekend, lying aggrieved in the hospital bed and dealing with visits from residents and interns and Dr. Einhorn and his colleagues. They said he was lucky, very lucky, and if one of his organs was slated for trouble, let it be the heart; we can do much less, these days, about the liver or lungs or the brain. It's a plumbing problem, mostly, and time to fix the pipes.

"You know the first three symptoms of heart trouble?" Tommy Einhorn asked.

"No, what?"

"Denial, denial, denial."

"Very funny."

"Very almost not funny at all, my friend. This is the riot act I'm reading you."

"All right. OK."

"We're prepared to handle it," said Dr. Einhorn, "if you have an infarction. But now you're stable and you're being monitored; only folks in crisis get to go to the theater this weekend."

"All right."

"You have to be patient. A patient patient," Einhorn said. "Hey, not bad. I should remember that."

—

Three bells sounded in his cabin, and a man's voice boomed from a speaker by the porthole. The purser introduced himself. "Good afternoon, ladies and gentlemen, welcome aboard," he said. "On behalf of the captain and crew of the MS *Diana* we wish everyone a most delightful trip." Then over the intercom system all passengers were informed there would be a mandatory life preserver drill before they could depart. They were instructed to report to Level 4 in fifteen minutes, please. "Departure is scheduled for seven o'clock, and in the morning, from Sorrento, we travel to Capri."

Lawrence roused himself. Not sorry to have been interrupted in his meditation on disease—the long wait in the hospital, the procedure itself, its aftermath—he laced on his sneakers and slipped on a jacket and found his way up to the deck. The wind was high. Passengers were milling about, awaiting instructions and laughing together and huddling in corners to hide from the wind. The man beside him on the deck was wearing bracelets on his wrist and an antinausea patch.

"Cold enough for you?" he asked.

The cruise director, smiling, nodding, said, "Everybody, your attention, please!"

Lawrence was provided with a life preserver and shown how to fasten it, then told that in the unlikely event of an emergency he should report to Lifeboat Station #6. He watched a demonstration of the whistle and inflatable flotation device; he was instructed what to carry with him from the cabin and what to leave behind. His concentration flagged, however, the way it drifted in an airplane when flight attendants enacted their preflight pantomime; heart trouble happens to others, he could remember thinking, and most of the time he'd felt fine. Emergencies happen to others, he could remember thinking, and his own was in the past. The document they sent him home with began with the assertion: *Successful PCI of culprit LAD/D1 Lesion . . .*

"You've had," the cardiologist declared, "your last drink of buttermilk and final bite of steak."

"You were lucky," Tommy Einhorn chimed in. "The left anterior descending was ninety percent occluded. But it's just like real estate—what counts is location, location. And yours was in the spot we call the widow-maker."

"I'm not married," Lawrence said.

"You were lucky," his neighbor repeated. "No joke. We caught it just in time."

———

His sons lived in Phoenix and Vail. Ten years before, their mother had remarried, but Janet stayed, it seemed to him, unbending, unforgiving. Lawrence tried to let bygones be bygones, to suggest that their marriage was far in the past and they should—for the sake of the children—be friends. The wound of his old infidelities stayed fresh with her, however; if they met at a concert or the farmers' market, Janet turned away and gave him, pointedly, her back. When John or Andrew brought their wives and children to town, they apportioned the length of their visits and, to keep from playing favorites or offending either parent, stayed in the Campus Inn.

His daughter by his first wife was living in Chicago. As though there had been some contagion, some gene that spawned failed marriages, Catherine too had been divorced and now lived alone. In part as a result of this, she had been very helpful during his time in the hospital and, afterward, at home. His sons had flown to see him and remained in touch by telephone, but Catherine bore the brunt of it—the driving, the grocery shopping, the details of Lawrence's medical leave and then his retirement furlough. It was as though she shared with him the rhythms of domestic life, and he enjoyed the way they did the crossword puzzle together, the way she matched her stride to his during their afternoon walks.

When his daughter returned to Chicago, he found himself regretting it, for he had grown accustomed to her presence by his side. "You've been wonderful," he said. Attempting to show her how grateful he was, he invited Catherine to join him for the trip. "My treat. I'll pay for it."

"Daddy, that isn't the point."

"The point is," he cajoled her, "your father misses you. And you haven't ever been to see—the cruise is billed as—'Treasures of the Western Mediterranean.' Don't you think you need to see them? The Isle of Capri? The temples of Agrigento? Malta?"

"It's called my life, remember? And I need to get back to it."

"I *know* that, sweetheart, I do understand."

Her life, he did not say to her, was something she should try to change: a dead-end job, a bridge game every Monday night, a clutch of other single women living in Hyde Park. How had this happened? he wanted to ask. How had his golden daughter grown so plump and wan? Her husband had taken a business trip and did not return from Atlanta and, as she later discovered, had emptied out their bank account and was living with another lawyer while filing for divorce. Catherine was childless, forty-one, and although she tried to put her best foot forward and a brave face on things, Lawrence knew she too was disappointed; she had been so hopeful once, such an ebullient presence. The laughter was over, the bright light had dimmed, and to the best of his ability he tried to make amends.

"How can I help?" he asked again. "You helped me so much this last summer."

"No problem."

"I *hate* that phrase 'no problem.' It's what everybody says these days. In restaurants, at the Whole Foods checkout line, everybody's telling you, 'No problem.' What they mean, I believe, is *'De nada.'* You're welcome."

"De nada," Catherine said.

———

Before dinner their first night on board the captain offered his passengers a champagne reception in the Elsinore Lounge. There was a bar and wicker furniture and upholstered chairs. Waiters passed trays of hors d'oeuvres. There were portraits of ladies and soldiers and amateurish hunting scenes and one of the goddess Diana covering her nudity with well-positioned boughs. She seemed beguiled by moonlight, and when Lawrence looked more closely at the painting, he saw a man in the moon.

The captain was broad-shouldered, with gold braid and buttons on his coat, and close-cropped black hair. His English was not good. Holding a microphone in one hand and, with the other, his cap to his chest, he shifted on his feet and cleared his throat. The weather was *temps variable*, the captain announced, leetle rain was in the forecast, and the seas were moderate high. He would do everything he could to assurance their comfort, and the *Diana* of course would be entire stable and safety, but he cannot guarantee conditions in the morning and if these waves continue he might have needing to anchor in Naples. "Drink up," he said, "don't worry, for it is always like this on the sea, and we are very glad you joining us this voyage and in a day or three maybe the weather sure be fine."

Lawrence ate with a couple from El Paso and a widow from Des Moines. He did not catch their names. The waiter was called Darko, and he knew this because Darko wore a nameplate and, having introduced himself, served them silently, attentively. The other three had boarded in Marseilles, and they said tonight was the first time their chairs had locked positions on the floor; they pointed to the clips beneath each chair and table, and the fasteners attached; they raised and clicked their glasses, chorusing, "Anchors aweigh!" The lady from Des Moines said she wasn't the least bit concerned; she'd never been seasick a day in her life, and this was her seventeenth trip. Well, only her twelfth cruise, but it *was* her seventeenth trip. She had been to Italy but never Sicily or Malta, and she asked Lawrence if he'd been before to any of their ports of call, and he said not to Malta, no, but Sicily many years ago. She asked how many, and he calculated: forty-one. She said, "How interesting, you can be our expert," and asked him for the salt.

The conversation trailed off. The dining room was full. The sea and sky were dark. He ate in silence—nodding at Darko, who offered more wine—imagining what Catherine would have made of his companions and how she would have handled this and whom she might have found to talk to or dance with later on. Somewhere, a piano played. Lawrence looked around him at the room—the white-haired and the wispy-haired, the ramrod-straight or bent, all elderly—and tried not to regret his choice, this gently pitching vessel that would convey them nowhere in particular and for many thousands of dollars. The men sported striped shirts and blazers; the women wore pantsuits and pearls.

One woman at a corner table arrested his gaze briefly; she was regal-seeming, self-contained, and something in the way she held herself seemed in some way familiar. Her hair, in a chignon, was gray. Her dress was blue. He made a mental note to try to speak to her later, when the meal was done, but the couple from El Paso were discussing immigration and the bridge to Juárez, the difficulty of border patrols, the Mexican families crossing at night, the RV they had purchased and were keeping in Las Cruces, and how America was going to the Democratic dogs. "Don't get me wrong," the man announced. "You all might just be Democrats and as long as we live in this wonderful country, I'll fight for your right to have an opinion. But the opinion's *wrong*."

Lawrence drank decaffeinated coffee and a final glass of wine. He was, he recognized, exhausted and excused himself and made his way down to his cabin and shrugged himself out of his clothes. What he dreamed of was a team of horses cantering, then galloping, and he awakened to the thump of his wineglass filled with water falling and breaking into splinters while the engines thrummed. He spent some minutes on his knees, carefully picking the shards from the carpet, then—when he was sure no glass fragments remained— fell asleep once more. This time he did not dream.

"You used to sing," said Catherine.

"Badly."

"Not so badly, Daddy. It was *fun*, the way we tap-danced."

"I have put off childish things," he said. "I'm an old man, sweetheart. Or haven't you noticed?"

"Not really."

"You know," he said, "last December we put on a skit—the architecture faculty puts on a skit every Christmas, lampooning each other, insulting the dean, looking consciously silly in front of the students—and I've always played a part in it and tried to steal the show. Telling jokes about Philip Johnson & Johnson or Frank Lloyd Wrong—stuff like that. Or Meier to Gehry to Graves being Tinker to Evers to Chance . . ."

She looked at him blankly.

"Forgive me," Lawrence said. "It's a baseball joke, a joke about infielders, famous ones. And Meier and Gehry and Graves— Richard, Frank, and Michael—are big-league architects these days. The point is, I sang. I put on my old baseball cap and found a pair of baseball pants and was standing up there on the stage belting out my tune. 'From Corbusier to Courvoisier, from Libeskind to Liebfraumilch, from Renzo to Piano,' fa la. And suddenly I saw myself the way the students must, an old man being idiotic, and the words just got stuck in my throat."

Catherine reached out her hand to him; he took and pressed and held it.

"There isn't that much music left, is what I'm trying to say."

—

The following morning dawned wetly, and when Lawrence looked out of the porthole, he saw that the MS *Diana* had been made fast to a dock. He dressed and went up to the deck. It was, the purser announced, the Bay of Naples they had sheltered in, and not the more open Sorrento, because tenders in Sorrento Harbor have proved unavailable this morning and the captain has decided not to wait until sufficient tenders for off-loading might be found. "In the meantime, ladies and gentlemen," said the purser, "a bus will take you to the embarkation point for the Isle of Capri, where you will see the sights. In the meantime, ladies and gentlemen, off portside is Vesuvius and behind us the city of Naples, and we wish you all a very pleasant day."

There was a guide called Ettsio who stood at the base of the gangplank and shepherded those passengers who went ashore to a black-and-yellow tour bus with a driver he introduced as "Giovanni, my best friend." There was a round of applause. There was a hurtling drive past piers and storage sheds and garbage dumps to a station where they took a ferry to steep-cliffed Capri. The island loomed ahead. The sky was gray, with threats of rain, and the man beside him in the ferry said, "Hey, if I wanted shitty weather, I could stay home in Seattle, it would cost a whole lot less." At the Marina Grande, where they disembarked, Ettsio handed out tickets for a funicular ride to the village of Capri itself. They boarded, turn by turn, then clattered up the hill.

All this took place in a loud press of bodies, a gaggle of tourists of whom he was one. Bowing his head to the sudden hard rain, he remembered a phrase by Noël Coward—a song about a widow on the Piccola Marina, drinking gin and flirting with Italians. Her name, Lawrence found himself remembering, was Mrs. Wentworth-Brewster, and "hot flushes of delight suffused her," or perhaps it had been *flashes*, hot flashes, instead. Ettsio urged everyone to have a coffee, have a glass of wine, have a look please at these beautiful shops.

The tour group unfurled their umbrellas and loitered in the cobbled streets; Lawrence, however, withdrew. He felt ashamed of having joined in, of being cajoled and organized and told to report to the ferry at noon or he would miss his lunch. *What am I doing here?* he asked himself, and was jostled by a German who said "Vorsicht" sharply, *Careful*, as he stepped back from a ditch. *We then crossed into DI with PT Graphix wire and performed kissing balloon inflations with 3.0-by-15 balloon in LAD and 2.5-by-15 balloon in DI.*

—

Once more that night at dinner he found himself at table with loquacious strangers—this time from Las Vegas and Stamford. The man from Las Vegas had never been out of the country before, and he announced this with pride. "I always say," he said, "you should see America first. We've been to all the fifty states and every single presidential library and figured we'd give Italy a try—but so far, I have to tell you, it's nothing to write home about." Darko glided past them noiselessly, and Lawrence asked for wine. Again he scanned the dining room and saw the gray-haired woman sitting where she sat the night before. Although she was part of a table of six, she seemed to be eating alone. This time he caught the woman's eye, and this time she half smiled at him; she understood, she seemed to say, how little he enjoyed his meal or suffered such company gladly. Again he tried to place her: Had they met before, he asked himself, and if so when and where?

The snatch of song returned to him—*But who knows where and when?*—and he found himself humming the chorus; the man from Stamford said, "Name that tune," and his wife said, "Don't mind Dicky, he's just jealous, he never could carry a tune."

Then she talked about the musical they'd seen last month on Broadway, a lollapalooza of a show called *Wicked*, whose idea was based on *Oz*—that Wicked Witch who used to live in Stamford, which is why the two of them bought tickets in the first place.

He, Lawrence, might maybe remember the actress who played her in the movie version—"I mean to say," the woman said, "*The Wizard of Oz* with Ray Bolger as the Scarecrow and Bert Lahr as the Cowardly Lion and poor unhappy Judy Garland, because who we're talking about is the Wicked Witch of the West, that skinny and pointy-nosed actress by the name of—what was her name, Dicky?—*Margaret*, that's right, that's it, Miss Gulch and the Wicked Witch were *both* the actress Margaret Hamilton, and her life was made just miserable by neighborhood children shrieking every time they saw her. She's dead, of course, but Miss Hamilton was nice as nice could be."

"More wine, sir?" Darko asked, and Lawrence nodded, yes. When the meal was over, he stood again, dispirited; the dining room was nearly empty, and the Elsinore Lounge had a sad clutch of drinkers, and he stepped out on deck to see nothing: the dock, the lights of Naples winking, the cranes and trucks off-loading in the middle distance. In his cabin he did fifty push-ups and tried to read and sleep.

—

Near dawn he dreamed of heedless health and early love; a woman was a statue, and the statue was marmoreal but warmed to his hot touch. When Lawrence woke, he was aroused but there was grief in it also: What had he done or failed to do that left him here alone? What was he dreaming, had he dreamed, that brought him to this pass?

Again the passengers descended and were herded to a tour bus and, at ten o'clock in the morning, conducted to Pompeii. This morning the tour guide was called Gabriela, who spoke English with a German accent; when someone asked how long she'd lived in Naples, she said seven months. She was pursuing, she told them, her doctorate in archaeology, and she knew more by now than ever she needed or—*wirklich, veramente*—wished to know about the business of excavation. Gabriela had red, spiky hair and multicolored plastic bracelets on both arms. She said, "Those of you who wish to be alone should meet me at the kiosk by this entryway at one o'clock for lunch; those of you who wish to listen, come along. We have a special lunch, and it has been ordered already, so I see you later on. It is," she said, "bureaucracy, these Italians are enraptured with bureaucracy, and it is of course the case that everything of any value is in the museum in Naples, but you must imagine what it felt like for people of the city to look up and watch Vesuvius erupt. It's not so much," she told the group, "the popular conception they were caught by lava as they collapse because of smoke; the smoke inhaled, it's—how do you call it?—dying by asphyxiation that makes Pompeii a special place, and nowhere to run to because of the sea, which would be in any case boiling. They could not land the ships. But in every cloud there is—*come se dice?*" she said, "a silver lining also. Because perfect preservation was enabled by the accident—people sitting, people baking bread, people chained to their workplace because they are slaves, and dogs and mosaics discovered intact beneath fifteen meters of ash. You will want to see a rich man's house and also the place of the baths; you will want to see a wine shop and what we call the Luparium, or brothel, and also, naturally, the marketplace; there is more than it is possible in only one visit to see."

Lawrence set out on his own. He studied temple columns and those excavation sites where the work continued: young people with shovels and pails. He wandered for an hour in the increasing sun, consulting his guidebook and looking at the trees and ruins and the ruts in stone where chariots had driven. He thought about Vesuvius, its fecund slopes and lethal ash and how the tethered slaves would have watched death approaching. In a side alley stood a tour guide with a group of tourists, and he stopped to listen. The guide was enjoying himself.

"Signs," he was explaining, "you have—how you say?—McDonald's, and everybody knows what they can order when they see the golden arch; there are pictures showing everybody what McDonald's serves. So you point to *this* one, say, a Big Mac, or *that* one, say, a salad and a coffee, and the people who are serving know what item you prefer." For effect, the tour guide paused. "You don't need to speak the Latin—*spikka da langwich, parler la langue*; you can be, for example, a sailor from a foreign place just off a ship. Well, this building, very popular, very important in Pompeii, is called the Luparium—because women when they were not busy would come out to the corner and howl in the street to make known they are available, although not of course for free. So it is called Luparium, the place of wolves, and they have pictures you will see, explaining what to order. On the *outside* of their rooms is a kind of advertisement, gentlemen and ladies, for what goes on *inside*. The oldest profession, correct? One has such and such a specialty; one has another instead."

There were appreciative titters; people shifted their weight on their feet. The tour guide relished the attention, clearly, and fanned his cheek with his cap. "I will not embarrass you, ladies, by describing what the pictures show, but if you look at them carefully, carefully, you of course can see who prefers to be on top and who is on whose knees. If you were—how do you call it?—a bigwig, a very special customer, you go upstairs and spend the night, but mostly this is—how do you call it?—a quickie, in and out. And so because this is so popular a place to visit, we must take our turn like customers," he smiled, "two at a time. Therefore everybody will have space: enjoy, enjoy. And when you will have had your fill of looking at the pictures"—again he paused, theatrical—"next person has a chance."

Lawrence waited for his turn to enter; then he stepped inside. The Luparium, by contrast with the noontime heat, felt cold. Above the doorless door frames and the entrances to empty rooms, he could indeed see pictures—ancient, faded, but intact—of prostitutes: some lying down, some standing, sitting, others on all fours or leaning openmouthed above priapic men.

He felt not so much excited as bereft. It made a sad display. For centuries, for thousands of years, these same arrangements had been or were being enacted; nothing had changed or would change. Immobile, the plump painted figures aped motion, and someone in the bedroom next to him said, "Hey, baby, look at *that*!"

Lawrence stepped outside. His companion in the dark enclosure touched his sleeve. "Hello."

"Hello."

It was the woman he had noticed in the dining room, then failed to find. "You don't recognize me."

"Excuse me?"

"You don't know me, do you?"

He looked at her. The Luparium had been enshadowed, and the light out here was bright. His eyes adjusted. "Good Christ."

"No, not exactly." She smiled her widemouthed smile at him.

"Hel-*lo*!"

"Hello, yourself. You haven't changed."

"Oh, yes, I have. How *are* you?"

Self-deprecating, dismissive, she made a motion with her hands. "How long has it been?"

"Forty years. Well, forty-two."

"And counting." She put on her dark glasses.

"I *thought* I saw you. Knew you. But you kept disappearing . . ."

"It's not the perfect way to meet again."

"What . . ."

"Here, I mean." She tilted her head to the building behind. "But we're on the *Diana* together. I'm not sure I believe it . . ."

"Good Christ," he repeated.

"No."

"No?"

"Only Hermia," she said.

II
—
1962

When he saw her the first time, she stood in the hallway, her book bag slung over her shoulder. She was talking to another girl, the one he would learn came from Chile, and the way she extracted her hair from the green strap it was snagged by caused her to wriggle, a little. The book bag slid down to the floor. When she saw him, she noticed him watching, his locker half open, a key in his hand. The Fogg Museum had a library he studied in; Lawrence picked up her satchel, then handed it back.

"Thanks," said Hermia, and turned and walked away. They would remember this. He said, "You dropped it on purpose," and she said, "Don't flatter yourself."

It was 1962, and he was a senior at Harvard. He had been driving his mother's Impala, the gray convertible she'd loaned him for use in his final semester; he had a friend on Irving Street with a parking space. On weekends he and Will would drive together to Cape Cod or Walden Pond or Newport or to L.L.Bean's in Maine. There had been a thaw that week, and they took the top down and turned on the heater full blast. Monday morning, returning from Truro, Lawrence had ordered a hot dog for breakfast, and Will respected this. "It's all about freedom," he said.

Hermia was black-haired, tall, and already late for class. The class was on the origins and flowering and decline of the Baroque, and it made no difference that she would be late. Her art history professor stood on a raised platform in front of the screen, using a flashlight as pointer and talking about the meticulous brushwork of a woman's necklace or a soldier's beard. He was an expert on Rubens, and much of the term was devoted to Rubens, whom he labeled "a prince among painters"; he said nobody before or since took such pure pleasure in flesh. "You can practically *feel* it," said the professor, trailing his beam up the nude's outstretched leg. "Just look at the articulation of this ankle and the way the knee enters the sheets."

They met again that afternoon, at Elsie's Sandwich Shop. Lawrence was waiting for his order, the one he always ordered—an Elsie's Special, heavy on the dressing—when she came through the Mt. Auburn Street entrance and took a vacant stool. "Aren't you the one with the book bag?" he asked, and she gazed at him unblinkingly and said yes, hello. "How was your class?" he asked her, and she told him it was dull. Well, not exactly, not really *dull*, but on a spring day like this she just hadn't wanted to *be* in the room, she just couldn't wait to be out in the light, and he said he'd felt that way also and had driven in that early morning from the Cape.

"Oh, where?"

"Truro, you know it? The dunes?"

Hermia nodded. "I do."

She asked herself, and could remember wondering, if she wanted this back-and-forth to continue or the conversation to stop. Did she need to tell him, for instance, that her family summered in Truro and since 1951 had owned a house by Ballston Beach? She loved it there—the weathered shingles and climbing roses by the fence, the path to the sea she could see down the hill—and it was her secret space, the place she prized most in the world. Did she need to tell him her father the painter had had a show in Province-town of dunes in every season, every weather, every time of day, and yes, she did know Truro and had explored each hummock of the beach . . .

"I'm Lawrence," he told her.

"Hermia."

"Art history—is that what you're majoring in?"

"No. English."

"I thought so," he said. "Well, I didn't know it was English, but I did think it wasn't art history."

"Because?"

"Because that's *my* major," said Lawrence. "And I would have noticed."

Her roommate, Silvana, arrived. Silvana came from Valparaíso but had gone to boarding school in Switzerland and her English was formal, precise. The girls spoke about the weather and the group they were part of to memorize slides: two hundred paintings by Peter Paul Rubens they needed to learn for the hour exam.

"He didn't do a lot of them," said Lawrence.

"Are you kidding? Hundreds. *Thousands.*"

"Except his studio apprentices would rough in the sky and the clouds. Or the background figures, often, or the occasional horse."

"Are you a painter?" asked Silvana.

"No."

"Her father's a painter," she said.

Hermia stood. "Well, we've got to start our study group; we memorize them all. We each take forty images and tell the others what to look for. Venus and Adonis. Actaeon and the hunting dogs, the one where he gazes on Artemis—or would Rubens have called her Diana?—and hey, presto, our great hunter turns into a stag."

"What kind of painter?" asked Lawrence. He received his roast beef sandwich and paid his fifty-five cents.

"A good one," said Silvana. "You'd have heard of him."

The girls left.

—

The third time was that Thursday, and again unplanned. He saw her walk down Hilliard Street and recognized her loose-limbed gait, the way she stepped out from the side entrance to the Loeb Drama Center and strode long-legged, the swing of her hips, and how she held her head down. She was wearing a green cape and knee-high polished leather boots and a knitted cap. There was slush in the gutters and snow shoveled in piles at the edge of the pavement; the afternoon was dark.

He followed and caught up to her. Her eyes were a deep brown.

"Hey," Lawrence said, "hello."

Tires screeching, a delivery van rounded the corner of Brattle Street. They stepped back from the spray.

"Strange, isn't it?" said Hermia. "Three times this week."

"They're trying to tell us something."

"Who?"

"The Gods of Coincidence. What were you doing at the Loeb?"

"*The Flies,*" she said. "The play by Jean-Paul Sartre?"

"Rehearsing it? Are you an actress?"

Hermia shook her head. "Stage-managing," she said. "Silvana—you remember her—is playing the part of Electra. I go along for the ride."

"Can I buy you a coffee?"

Her gaze was frank, assessing him. What else was he asking? she wondered. What else would he offer, and should she accept? A fine snow fell. In time to come he would remember standing there, the silence between them extending, and how the pause before she answered made it seem a kind of verdict: "Yes."

They went to Casablanca and drank café au lait. He told her that he planned to be an architect, or an urban designer maybe, because he believed in design; a sense of the shape of the whole is what this country needed more of, *consciousness, coherence,* and not the higgledy-piggledy, every-which-way arrangement of the marketplace. He was going, he assured her, to make trains run on time.

"You're joking, right?"

"Right," Lawrence said, and lit her Pall Mall, and stared at the rise of her breasts.

———

Casablanca was a coffee shop beneath the Brattle Theater; it displayed framed posters of the movie *Casablanca* and large photographs of Humphrey Bogart and Ingrid Bergman and Claude Rains. The space at that hour was dimly lit, empty, and the man behind the bar was setting out glasses in rows. Above them hung a poster of Rick's Café Américain and one of the sheet music for "As Time Goes By."

Upstairs they were showing *L'avventura* and Lawrence asked if she had seen it, and what she thought of Antonioni; he himself had seen *La dolce vita* twice. He thought the final sequence on the beach was astonishing, remarkable, and the scene at Trevi Fountain with Anita Ekberg splashing in the water and summoning Marcello was a hoot.

"But that's Fellini," Hermia corrected him. "Not Antonioni."

Coloring, he asked if she had sisters or brothers and if they all had such names.

She shook her head.

"An only child?"

"Yes." She stubbed out her cigarette. "At least it's not Hermione. That's what my father wanted." Her fingernails were bitten, and her fingers long.

"Your father . . ."

Consciously, she changed the subject. "And you, are you an only child?"

He shook his head. "A sister. Tell me about *The Flies*."

She did. She said *The Flies* was fun to do; apparently the Germans never understood it as a protest play but allowed the director to mount it in occupied Paris. They thought it an update of the *Oresteia*, which was on the surface true, but more importantly it was an attack on fascist rule. The collaborator Aegisthus is a figure out of Vichy and a version of the Nazi stooge Le Maréchal Petain or maybe Pierre Laval. Hermia liked stage-managing in the Experimental Theater, the small black box with risers that they called the Ex. The lighting designer was a friend, and she didn't mind the detail work, the lists of *To Do* and lists of *Done*, but the director was a horse's ass and always putting a move on the dancers. "We open next Thursday," she told him. "Do you want to come?"

He was twenty-one, she twenty, and both of them pretending to a worldliness they had not earned; she had traveled with her family to Italy and France. He had been to Mexico the previous summer and ingested peyote and been violently ill. His hallucinations were multicolored, and the cactus he had focused on seemed ten feet tall. She had had three lovers and he five.

Her first had been in high school. Timmy wanted to be an airplane pilot, then a fighter pilot, and now that JFK had established a space program he would want to be an astronaut. They slept together twice, the week of graduation, and when she thought about him now, she thought mostly about the blood on the couch of his family room, how she had rubbed and scrubbed at it while Timmy said, "Oh, shit." Her next had been in Italy, a gallery owner exhibiting her father's work who took her on a tour of Rome, then back to his apartment, where he seduced her efficiently, saying *"Bella, que bella, bellisima"* while they undressed. The next afternoon, however, when she went with her family to the gallery beneath the Spanish Steps, he acted as though nothing happened, as though they were polite strangers, and she never saw Giovanni again.

Her third affair was serious, and it had lasted all fall. Though Hermia had gotten over it, she sometimes thought that she and Bill were only taking a break from each other, a not-so-romantic vacation, and would date again and marry down the line. Bill was in business school; they'd met at a mixer, and he drove an Austin-Healey and had reddish, curly hair she liked to run her fingers through; at Thanksgiving he had introduced her to his parents and said, "Mom, this is the real deal." After two or three years in business, he explained, he was planning a career in politics; he would make a run for the state house, and was sure he'd be elected, and she'd make an excellent wife.

He had it all planned out. He had no doubts. He had attended Exeter, and his family came from New Hampshire, and there was a seat in the state house that was going to be vacant; with a pedigree like his—his uncle had been governor—and a photogenic Radcliffe woman at his side, it would be a lead-pipe cinch. That was his phrase, "a lead-pipe cinch," and Hermia respected his impermeable self-assurance but disliked it also; when she told him so, he said, "Well, I may have made a mistake. It's possible I'm wrong."

"About getting elected?"

"No. You."

He announced this in his apartment. She felt herself go cold all over, rigid with the shock of it, and got out of bed and walked to the window and covered herself with his blue button-down oxford and stood looking out. There was snow on Boylston Street, and a red light changing to green; a man across the street was walking two dogs at once. He stopped beneath a streetlight while the larger dog—a German shepherd, a husky?—lifted his leg at the pole; then the small one took his turn.

"Come back to bed," said Bill. "You must be freezing, baby."

"No."

"No, you won't come back to bed, or no, you aren't freezing your ass off?"

"The good citizens of New Hampshire," she said, "expect their elected officials to marry a virgin and not to say 'ass.' We both of us made a mistake."

———

Now Lawrence was saying yes to *The Flies*, he'd like to see the production, and what house did she live in? She told him Cabot House. "Should I meet you there?" he asked, and Hermia said, "No, I'll leave a ticket because I'm at the theater *hours* before curtain time." He talked about the dean of architecture at MIT, an Italian called Pietro Belluschi, and how he was more interesting—so Lawrence thought—than the dean at Harvard, José Luis Sert. He talked about the aesthetics of Belluschi and Sert, how they differed yet were similar, and what it would mean to study at Princeton instead. The best of them all was probably Yale, but he just wasn't up for New Haven, and in any case, he told her, he was planning on apprentice work. He needed to be sure of architecture as a profession before committing himself to another course of study; he was tired, *tired*, sick to death of school.

She studied him. His eyes were blue, his mouth was full-lipped, mobile, and his cheekbones were pronounced. He had a way of talking—rapid, allusive—she liked. He was trying to impress her, and though she was unimpressed, she liked how hard he tried. The coffee shop was filling up; music played—"As Time Goes By"—and Hermia felt happy to be sitting at a table with this boy-man in wide-wale corduroys and a black turtleneck sweater and brown Harris Tweed. She picked at her croissant. She had not had a date since Bill—"Bill the pill," Silvana called him—but that was three months ago, and the mournful self-pity had passed.

Looking at her watch, she saw she had an hour left until the cast was scheduled for costume fittings at the Loeb. The costumes were leotards and togas, black or white, and the actors moved a large red crown from head to head when power was transferred. She had been planning to go to her room and maybe get some reading done, or stop in at the Agassiz and check out a monograph she needed for an essay for her Soc. Rel. section. But this coffee together was pleasant; this Lawrence whose last name she realized she did not know was talking about architects, designers, interior designers, advertising and technology, and the city of the future while she shifted in her seat, adrift, and looked at the length of his hair.

"So how did it go?" he asked.

"What?"

"That test of yours. The one on Rubens."

"We haven't got it back," she said. "I did know *Venus and Adonis.*"

He smiled at her. "And Actaeon?"

"You *were* paying attention."

"I was," he said, and smiled again, showing a gap in his teeth.

—

The Loeb Drama Center, newly built, housed a main stage and an experimental theater; *The Flies*, as a student production, had been allocated to the smaller downstairs space. The set was stark, with rocks suggesting both the fields of Argos and its palace. The director had spent the previous summer in Paris, researching Sartre, Artaud, and agitprop theater, and he smoked Gauloises. On opening night Orestes came down with laryngitis, and so the actor used a bullhorn, but everyone agreed the bullhorn was appropriate, a kind of threatful magnifier that made his speech "People of Argos" seem more totalitarian and demagogic-fascist when he incited the mob.

It was the beginning of spring: March 21. The snow gave way to sleet. After the performance, at the cast party in an apartment down the street from Cronin's, the director passed a pipe. It came straight from Jamaica, he said, and on Sunday, when the run was done and they struck the set, he'd pull out all the chemical stops, they'd have an existential no-holds-barred celebration, but tonight they needed just to loosen up and not worry about what the *Crimson* might say. The reviewer from the *Crimson* had given him a thumbs-up sign, and that was a good omen, but as far as he himself was concerned, what mattered was how each of them had played their parts, since—he mimicked Jacques's speech in *As You Like It*, lisping—"'All the world'th a thtage.'"

"But seriously, gang," the director continued, "I'm proud of you, how *everyone* stood up and was counted, and we've"—now he raised the ponytail of the dancer he was sleeping with—"given our damndest, our *all.*" He balanced on a DR stool, holding a bottle of Mateus rosé and slipping into a Southern accent. "*Dang,*" he said, "I'm jes' so dang *proud* of y'all!" Then he declared himself impressed by how they'd pulled together, pulled it off, and the director was, as the French say, if he said so himself, *bouleversée* . . .

"The only other title I know by Sartre," said Lawrence, "is *La nausée.*"

Hermia laughed. "Well, what about *No Exit?*"

"Is that an exit line?"

"It is." She slipped her arm through his.

Parietal hours were over, and they could not go to Cabot Hall or Lawrence's room, a single in Claverly Hall. In any case, she told him, it felt too soon, too sudden, but she pressed against him when they kissed and, disengaging, stared at him wide-eyed; he had an erection she grazed with her palm.

"Maybe we could see each other on Saturday? Sunday?" asked Lawrence, and she answered, "Yes."

The moon was high, the stars emerged, and that promise stayed with him as he walked back to his room. He spent the next day on his thesis, a chapter on Palladio and Palladian influence in Newport, the English manor house and French château adapted for the gentry of America, their ideal of country living by the bay. Will called and said, "We heading out tomorrow?" and Lawrence told him, "No."

—

They became lovers that weekend and slept together all spring. He lived alone in Claverly, in a wood-paneled sitting room with a sleeping alcove on the building's second floor. His windows gave out on an alley, and the light was poor. But Lawrence loved the privacy, the illusion of self-sufficiency, and when he brought Hermia up to his room, he hoped she would approve of it: the reproductions of van Gogh and Mexican bark paintings he had acquired in San Miguel de Allende, the serape on his bed and bookcases he had fashioned out of pine planks and glass bricks.

When he thought of it, years later, he thought of it in pictures: a silent movie played out without language, in scenes. He saw the cowl-neck red sweater she wore, and the brown woolen skirt with the slit to the knee; he saw the mascara and lipstick he smudged and the way that her bra strap had frayed. He saw the two of them embracing by the metal desk. In her leather boots she was taller than he, and when she bent to remove them, he watched the blue vein at her ankle, the curve of her calf and then thigh. He had, and was embarrassed by, pimples on his back. He had a pack of condoms in his bedside table, and when the time arrived to open it, he was clumsy, fumbling; her hair cascaded darkly when she bent across him to help.

They talked; they must have spoken, but what he remembered was silence and the bright whites of her eyes. His pillows were yellow, his blanket green, and the rug on the floor was a full-size flokati his mother had given him: long, tufted lambs' wool dyed blue. He remembered the lamplight, the shadows it cast, and how he turned off the light. He remembered how Hermia paused, emerging from the bathroom, the tilt of her head when she moved to his side, the stretch marks at her hip, the scar along her knee. He remembered in detail the shape of her breasts—the left was a little bit larger—and the tight coils of pubic hair and how her neck arched when she came.

The following Sunday they drove to the Cape, and she took him to her parents' house—still closed down for the winter—and walked the path to Ballston Beach. The wind was blustery, the waves high, and they sat together in the dunes while sand whipped past them, eddying.

"It's beautiful."

"I love it here," said Hermia. "I *love* it," and the word echoed between them; she had not used it before.

Gulls rose and circled, then settled again, and white foam unfurled from the waves. She found the hidden house key where her parents kept it, on the crossbeam of the overhang where the woodpile was stacked. They opened the door to the kitchen— its hanging pots and candles in wine bottles, its dried bunches of herbs tied to nails in the beam. The living room was long and low; she led him past couches in sheets. Bookcases were stuffed with old leather-bound books, and the fireplace had logs laid in it crosswise and ready for burning.

Lawrence recognized, or thought he did, a set of prints by Motherwell, a Kenneth Noland target painting, and a Hans Hofmann oil. There was a landscape by Hopper—a yellow house athwart a green-and-ochre cliff—and later he would understand the value of the art he'd seen so casually displayed, unheated, unprotected, but Hermia was leading him to her small bedroom by the porch. He pulled down his pants, and she pulled off her panties, and they came together standing up. It was quick and sharp and fierce, and in the aftermath she rested her head on his shoulder.

"I've never been with anybody here before," she said.

On the wall of her room, by the west-facing eave, hung a life-size portrait of Hermia herself when young: her skirt spread wide, her black hair splayed about her face, and holding a golden retriever puppy on her lap. The picture had been painted with authority; it was, he guessed, her father's work. The girl on the wall had grown up. Yet the smile on her face then was how she smiled now: a proprietary, ease-filled gaze.

"It isn't too cold for you, is it?" she asked, and he told her, "No."

"Remember how you'd been to Truro that first morning we met?"

"I do."

Wooden shutters with a heart cut out had been fastened at the windows, and through the heart-shaped apertures Lawrence saw the sky. They kissed. He felt, and would remember feeling, as though he had been singled out: so fortunate, luck's shining child, this beauty in his arms.

———

At first the two of them were careful, spacing their encounters, but once a week gave way to twice and then to three meetings or four. By the end of April they met each other daily, drinking coffee at

Hayes-Bick, walking along the Charles River or eating Chinese food and going to movies at night. They saw Bergman and Antonioni and Alfred Hitchcock films, and he told her she looked like Monica Vitti when Monica Vitti wore a black wig. Lawrence completed his thesis on time, and she continued to go to her classes: "Social Relations 10," "The Baroque," "The English Novel," and "Shakespeare: The Late Plays." All through the month of May Hermia left letters in his mailbox, or underneath his pillow, and if they did not see each other at night or over the weekend—if she visited her family or he took a field trip with his art history seminar—they called.

On the telephone he told her he missed her, he couldn't stop thinking about her. The scent of her perfume remained in his room, the smell of their sex on his hands. In early May, with her mother's approval, she was fitted for a diaphragm; they had a joke about "Most Happy Fella" and called it her "Big D." She liked to imagine the child they would have, the way their children would look. Other companions fell away, and Hermia and Lawrence talked about the future: this summer when he would be graduated, the trips they hoped to take and how they would manage to do so, and where he planned to live.

She spoke about her father, the way he drank and unwound with his buddies at cards, playing high-stakes poker all night long and smoking cigars, and how he swore and terrified her as a child. The golden retriever, Tigger, became her pet the year she'd had an operation on her knee and couldn't ride a bike. The knee was fine, completely fixed, but that explained the scar he'd noticed and was tracing with his tongue.

She talked about her father's art, his fame, and how he demanded attention ceaselessly, so everything about dear Dad was *me, me, me, me, me.* Their apartment in Brooklyn was a disaster, with hot water only sometimes when the landlord fixed the plumbing, and a bathtub in the kitchen, and nobody bothering to make the beds or take out the garbage. Still, it had an upstairs studio with a world-class view of Manhattan, and Hermia's mother seemed content to live in what once had been a warehouse, drinking Campari-and-soda and posing for her artist friends and being written about in the *New York Times* and being called a muse.

Lawrence talked about *his* mother, the rigid propriety of his home and how the suburbs seemed the absolute opposite of what she described, Brooklyn Heights. *His* father, a banker, had been a hushed presence all through the years of his childhood, an absence with martinis and the *Wall Street Journal* in the TV room. His father wore bow ties and button-down shirts and was unfailingly polite to strangers, at ease on the golf course and tennis court and the club car in the train. The hedges by their house were clipped, the stones that lined the driveway painted white.

But then his father left when Lawrence turned eighteen. One Friday evening in October he did not return from work, and that was the end of it. There was nothing to do or to say. His father took an apartment on Gramercy Park, filling the closets with his suits and setting out his photographs on the table in the foyer. There was a silver-framed photograph of Lawrence at his high school graduation, a photograph of him and his sister in their tennis whites, and a series of sepia portraits of parents and grandparents standing with horses or at their ease in evening clothes or poised on a ski slope with skis.

Their father, it turned out, was having affairs, and one of the girls in the office got pregnant and wouldn't have an abortion. His father did the "right and honorable thing"—which is how, dripping with sarcasm, his mother chose to describe it; the honorable SOB left his wife and children to marry a teller instead. Well, maybe she wasn't a teller, maybe a branch manager or executive vice president, but Lawrence's mother felt certain she had worked her way up the corporate ladder by choosing to lie down.

The family remained in Scarsdale, in the mock-Tudor gabled house, but all the king's horses and all the king's men—the property transfer and alimony payments—couldn't put them together again. His sister, Allie, turned sixteen and spent hours in her canopy bed, so busy with the telephone she didn't know the time of day or whether it was afternoon or night. The lights switched on or off, the music played, and downstairs in the kitchen his mother beat at scrambled eggs or pounded a veal cutlet flat and scrubbed the kitchen counters in a kind of vengeful fury . . .

They agreed they came from different worlds, but not so far apart the distance was unbridgeable; besides, said Hermia, it's too much fun doing the bridging. He laughed. She had a sense of humor that took him by surprise; she was sly and slantways in her wit, and she liked to tease him. She signed her nightly letters "Huntley/Brinkley" when sending him the day's report; one of the notes she left in his bed was a folded page of paper. On the top half she had written, *I love to suck your great big hard beautiful sweet-tasting,* and, on the inside fold, *ear.*

That season at Harvard, two teachers—Timothy Leary and Richard Alpert—were distributing psilocybin and instructing students to keep journals of their sensations and thoughts and perceptions while high. "The Doors of Perception," as Aldous Huxley called them, had opened wide, and LSD became the drug of choice. At Club 47 on Mt. Auburn Street, Tom Rush and Joan Baez and curly-headed Bob Dylan sang. The world was young, or so it seemed; the world was theirs to conquer, although conquering was not the point, and neither Hermia nor Lawrence wanted to divide and conquer but only to remain together and lie down together in bed.

—

In years to come they were not certain what went wrong. There was no single reason that they broke apart. He was twenty-one, she twenty, and they were not ready for marriage and could not live together in the fall. Lawrence grew restless; he wanted more of the world, he told himself, than the chill insularity of Cambridge. He wanted, he told her, to travel—to look at great examples of civilization's great buildings—and Hermia would not respect it if he just stayed around.

"I'd wait for you," he promised. "Except we're so parochial, so proud of our bad sherry at the Signet and all those people who never leave Boston. It's time to move along . . ."

His friend Will, who lived on Irving Street, was plump and had a high-pitched voice and a cheap guitar. He played the instrument well, however, and at night in his dark basement sang, "'I'm going away, for to stay, a little while. But I'm coming back, if I go ten thousand miles . . .'" He closed his eyes while singing, and rocked back and forth on the chorus while they all joined in.

Hermia was going to be a senior and could not leave Cambridge. Although she and Lawrence promised each other they would stay together and it would make no difference, it did make a difference. He found himself wondering where else to go and what else to do; Will said he was pussy-whipped and *ought* to hit the road. At a party in the carriage barn of a stone house on Fayerweather Street, he got drunk on bad sangria and found himself in a bedroom kissing a girl called Charette, a girl with whom he'd studied the Italian Renaissance, and when he pulled away from her, she said, "Don't stop; why stop?"

Thick-tongued, he explained to her, or tried to, that he was at the party with his girlfriend, Hermia, downstairs, and Charette said, "Why does that matter?" and was stepping out of her Indian-print skirt when Hermia appeared. "You can join us if you want," said Charette, and Lawrence was so shocked he laughed, and that was what, said Hermia, she couldn't forgive: his complicit drunken laughter and the way she felt, oh, not so much insulted as dismissed.

To make him jealous, therefore, or at least to demonstrate what it was like, she called Bill to congratulate him on having finished business school, and Bill said, "Hey, baby, I was *thinking* about you, this is great."

"Great?" she asked, "why, what's so great?" but was flattered, nevertheless, that he was thinking about her, or bothered to lie, and when he asked, "Are you busy, are you free tonight? I've just tuned up the growler and was planning on a spin," she said, "All right, OK."

He arrived in twenty minutes, in the Austin-Healey, looking well, and she got in the passenger seat with the ease of habit and a sense of, if not vindication, relief. She pulled back and tied up her hair. She had been reading *Othello*, and she knew that Shakespeare meant the Moor to love "not wisely but too well," and that the Moor of Venice had been driven half insane. "'Beware, my lord, of jealousy,'" she found herself reciting. "'It is the green-eyed monster.'" Except jealousy was not the point, and she wasn't playing Iago, or the part of Desdemona; she was being driven fast down Storrow Drive, in a convertible with an old boyfriend, catching up . . .

Fidelity meant faithfulness; it meant wanting only one thing. It meant there was no difference between what you had and what you wanted, no space between the space you occupied and where you hoped to be. But if you wanted more than one thing, it could become a problem, and she and Silvana had discussed this; they were living in, said Silvana's European history professor, "the Age of Anxiety," and one of the anxieties engendered by freedom is the problem of multiple choice.

She had planned to be faithful forever; she had wanted to love only Lawrence. But he never did say that he loved her, he never could quite get around to the words, and she was tired not so much of waiting as of his closemouthed caution, his timidity. When she thought about the bedroom on Fayerweather Street, him laughing with that girl upstairs—her eyes like pinwheels and skirt down around her ankles—she thought she could never forgive him, and so she drove away with Bill to the North End for dinner and made herself forget. Hermia's father was a famous man, her mother a great beauty, and she herself was finishing her junior year at Radcliffe. She was tired of multiple choice. Integrity meant oneness; it meant staying faithful forever, and she would return, she told herself, though she went ten thousand miles.

III
1963–1977

Hermia graduated from Radcliffe magna cum laude and moved back to New York. Her thesis "Romance: The Fools of Time in Shakespeare" was, in the end, disappointing; her senior year had been a sad one, and she was ready to leave. If she thought about *The Flies* or, the following fall, the production of *Blood Wedding*, she felt a little embarrassed and even, a little, ashamed. With the Cuban missile crisis, things came into perspective; the world was trouble-filled and dangerous, and it seemed beside the point to arrange for props and costume fittings and check lighting cues. Stage-managing was a diversion, and the diversion passed.

Silvana too said good-bye to the stage; she had played the Bride in García Lorca's play but put off, as they called them, childish things. Instead she got engaged to the son of the ex-ambassador from Chile and returned to Valparaíso, and in her letters every month complained about the plans the wedding planners made and how much fuss and difficulty a formal marriage can be.

At the suggestion of her senior tutor, who knew the managing editor, Hermia applied for and was offered a job in publishing. The job was entry level, at Harry N. Abrams, Publishers, but it paid the rent. As editorial assistant, she had schedules to comply with and deadlines to meet and books about art to produce. Attempting to comply with them, she came to admire the exacting standards of the man she worked for, his attention to the quality of paper and the quality of color in the plates. He wore striped shirts with white collars and a monogram on the pocket and horn-rimmed glasses he wiped on his sleeve. His name was Jack, and he took her out to lunch and, over his second martini, confessed he was infatuated—had been hopelessly in love, in *lust*, for what felt like *forever*, and had to tell *someone* about it—with the editor in chief.

This was, she came to understand, a speech he made to all the young women who worked at Harry Abrams; it was no secret to the interns or staff and had not been news for years. The editor in chief had no interest in Jack, or at least no romantic interest; instead there was an office pool as to which new female arrival the editor in chief would proposition next. Hermia wore miniskirts and white boots by Courrèges. When she herself was propositioned, it was easy to refuse; she lied that she was flattered but had just gotten engaged. He said, "Congratulations, he's a lucky man," and made a mark in his desk calendar and said, "Excuse me a minute, but I have to take a call."

Office politics were fun because she had no stake in them; this would not be a career. She knew she was just marking time; nevertheless, she worked hard. In truth she did enjoy the job and the parties afterward, the art world's ornamental fringe where she was welcome because of her father, his more and more prominent name. Hermia lived alone, on Riverside Drive and Eighty-Seventh Street, and made friends with the doormen and liked to walk downtown.

———

Her parents spent all summer on the Cape. After her second promotion at Abrams, she earned three weeks' vacation, and Hermia rented a car and drove by herself to Bar Harbor, where a weekend with a lawyer turned out to be a mistake. He was recently divorced and obsessed with his Rhodes 19, its rigging and performance, and in bed inert. When they said good-bye, she didn't bother to pretend they would meet or date again; instead she drove to see her family in Truro.

That July, on his fifty-fifth birthday, her father threw a party, and it was a large one: collectors and curators and critics—so her father said, emphasizing the *c*—had been invited, the whole catastrophe of hangers-on, and many of his friends. There was a reception up in Provincetown, and then a dinner at the house and fireworks by the beach.

Her father's black cluster of curls had gone gray, and his beard was white. Lately he had seemed subdued, favoring his left leg when walking and complaining of migraines and gout. But that night he had, again, the manic celebratory energy she remembered from the binges in her childhood, and he sweated profusely and insisted on dancing and made the guests assemble while he tried to do the Charleston. "I used to perform the kazatsky," he mourned. "I used to be a champ." By eleven o'clock he was so drunk—irrevocably, irrecoverably drunk—he passed out on the living room couch.

Her mother stood above him, still seductive and aloof. "Will you look at that," she said. "That's the great man, the birthday boy. My hero, *everyone's* hero. Asleep."

Then she stubbed out her cigarette in the ashtray by Picasso, one of a series of ceramics they had bought that year in Vallauris, and turned to Clement Greenberg and said, "Dreadful sorry, oh my darling Clem, but may I have this dance?"

"Are you all right, Dad?" Hermia asked.

He did not move.

"Can you hear me?"

Slowly, laboringly, his chest rose and faltered and fell.

"Daddy, it's your *party*!"

"Fuck off."

She was shocked, not so much by his language—"fuck" was a word he used often—or that he would swear at her as by the lack of recognition in his wide-eyed stare. Glaring at Hermia he said it again, "Fuck off, fuck *all* of you off," and built himself back to his feet and jostled his way to the porch. Outside, Roman candles exploded. Enfolded in a dancer's arms, her mother was swaying, her slim back arched, ignoring or refusing to acknowledge her husband's bad behavior. The celebration went on.

Then Hermia heard, or thought she did, a truck door slam, an engine roar. "What was *that*?" she asked the room, but nobody replied. "Did anyone hear anything?" she asked. She saw a set of lights ignite and wheel away and veer down the driveway and disappear. "Where's Dad? He shouldn't be driving," she said, but a bodybuilder had asked her to dance, and the music was infectious, and all this had happened before . . .

She heard—she would swear it—the crash. She sensed the collision before she could hear it, could feel it reverberate up through her throat. Then Hermia closed her eyes and *saw* her father's truck accelerating, making for the stand of pine at Pamet Road as though itself enraged . . .

At first she tried to tell herself that what she heard were fireworks: a partygoer out on the beach setting off Catherine wheels.

Her partner asked, "What's wrong, is something wrong?"

She turned from him, made for the door.

All her life she would remember how they learned the news—a gallery owner from Wellfleet who stumbled back to the party, saying, "Help," shouting, "Call the police"—and the crumpled, smoking wreckage, her father slumped over the wheel. She ran to where he had crashed. He had negotiated the driveway but missed the second left turn. She would remember the steam from the engine, the shards of glass, a white pine bent double above the smashed hood as though protective, pitying, and how they could not open the pickup's driver-side door.

He did not die in the truck. He was a tough man, limp from drink, who had somehow remembered to fasten his seat belt; the rescue squad arrived and, using the Jaws of Life, extracted him and drove him down Route 6 to the Cape Cod Hospital. It took him three days to die. Hermia spent the entire time in Hyannis, waiting with her mother and listening to doctors and visiting the ICU and, when permitted, sitting at her father's side. He had become an object attached to machinery, an arrangement of tubing and bottles and monitors with numbers flashing on a screen and lights that went green and then red.

Doctors and technicians bustled past. Men and women with mops and meal carts and wheelchairs were polite to her but made her feel in the way. A little, in the waiting room, she slept. Once, at a nurse's urging, Hermia went for a walk off the hospital grounds. In a nearby sandwich shop she bought a cup of clam chowder and a lobster roll. She could not swallow the sandwich, however, and left it for the gulls.

There were police and journalists. There were many telegrams and telephone calls of support and more bouquets of flowers than the hospital could handle. "In any case," the nurse explained, "on account of how it wrecks the oxygen we don't want no bunches of flowers in the ICU." As always, Hermia felt excluded from the melodramatic spectacle of her father's life, the privacy to which she had no access and the large public display. She had watched throughout her childhood and her adolescence and now was a spectator while her father died. It was as though he ruled some distant seagirt kingdom but had been deposed.

His eyes were shut. He opened them; she watched him try to rise or shift position in the bed—imperceptibly, inwardly, silently—and then again he shut his staring eyes. The monitors registered this; a line of light above his head pulsated, blinked, and went flat.

———

Her mother found consolation. She had always looked her best in black, and the grief was its own kind of diet; in the three months after the funeral, her mother lost ten pounds. The great quantity of work unfinished in the house in Truro and the studio in Brooklyn Heights became a retrospective; *Last Paintings* proved both a critical and commercial success, an "event of the first importance," a "high-water mark of the artist's career." Olitski, Diebenkorn, de Kooning—all these were evoked by way of comparison, as were other such modern masters as Rothko, Gottlieb, Kokoschka, and the range of reference suggested, in and of itself, the wide variety and restless questing of her father's work. In his early years he had been called "derivative," in his middle period, "eclectic"; now he was hailed as an American original, a jack-of-all-painterly-trades. "No other painter of the last decade has tried his hand so daringly at so many forms of expression," wrote one reviewer of the show, "and we can only begin to imagine what he would have undertaken next."

At Harry Abrams they asked Hermia if she would consider introducing a book about her father's work, a personal accounting of the artist's life. When she declined, they commissioned a writer named G. Edson Lattimer to produce the text. G. Edson Lattimer was British-born, raised in Paris and Vienna, and his clothes were perfectly tailored, and his bald head gleamed. He invited the widow and daughter to lunch at Lutèce and appeared to know the owner, referring to him as Andre and returning—there was something wrong with the cork, then the ullage—two bottles of wine. His manners were impeccable, he was courteous during the interview, and though Hermia distrusted him, her mother found him charming.

All along there had been "players," as her parents called them—the assistants and other artists and other people's wives or husbands with whom her parents "played." But this was different, somehow; this seemed too soon, a violation, and when her mother invited the writer to the studio next morning, Hermia felt betrayed. Although she would have been welcome, she did not join the two of them—not in Brooklyn Heights or, the following night, at Quo Vadis—and when Lattimer asked that Saturday what it felt like, in the early years, to sit for her father's sketches and portraits, she said, "I loved it, *loved* it. It was how I got Daddy's attention."

"Undivided," said her mother.

"Right. He used to call me 'Princess.' And then 'Herm the worm.'"

Lattimer laughed.

"The best portrait of all," said her mother, "is the one with Tigger, the dog we gave her when she was—What were you, darling, seven? Eight? Up in Truro. You should see it."

"Absolutely," Lattimer agreed.

Therefore, for the sake of completeness and to provide him with, as he put it, a better sense of "local habitation and a name," her mother took the critic for a weekend to Cape Cod. The house in Truro, after all, would be crucial to the monograph, a major locus of the late artist's art. It was the start of December and time to drain the pipes and put the Adirondack chairs and picnic table away. Her mother said she didn't want to, couldn't *bear* to do the job alone, and would be grateful for company; while she shut the house for winter, her guest could examine the walls.

"Don't you think," she asked Hermia, returning, "he's a charming man?"

"Not really, no."

"*I* do," she said. "He has such a sense of decorum. He knows all the right questions to ask."

"Like what exactly? Like what was Daddy drinking? What happened at the party?"

"Of course not, no. That's not what he's been asking."

"Oh?"

"This is an essay on *painting*, Herm. And not your father's personal habits."

"What was he like in bed?"

"Who?"

"G. Edson Lattimer." She knew even in the asking she had crossed some kind of line. It was not the act itself but the question that seemed indiscreet, a mark of bad behavior that would not be erased. Her mother turned away. But all the anger Hermia was harboring—the shock and guilt and sorrow—made her implacable. "How could you *do* it?" she asked. "How could you value Dad so little, how could you be such a, so . . ."

"Say it!"

"Cheap!"

"We'll be married in the spring."

———

She resigned from Harry Abrams in silent protest at the book; she did not want her father's art to grace the coffee tables or the bookshelves of the rich. At her farewell party—champagne in plastic cups and a wedge of cheese and bagels with smoked salmon—the editor in chief put his hand on her shoulder and, squeezing it, asked, "Are we still, you know, otherwise engaged?"

"No," she said. "I never was."

He frowned and turned away. Then Jack, who had been watching, raised his glass and said, "My beautiful assistant. What will I do without you? How can I ever manage? How will *we*?"

Hermia found a job at Random House, but her heart was no longer in it; it was 1968. The world of art and publishing now seemed as self-indulgent to her as had the stage. The war had gotten serious, and there were marches and demonstrations to join. She stopped using makeup or wearing a bra, but it made no difference; it was a fashion statement like the other fashion statements, and men hit on her anyhow in parties or at bars. She turned twenty-six years old. The "business as usual" attitude of editors and agents seemed corrupt to her, co-opted, and the last best hope of the last best hope of mankind was the protest movement; if "Amerika" did not withdraw from Vietnam, she might have to leave it, and when she was teargassed while marching on the Pentagon, she thought the time had come.

The Pentagon was ringed with troops, smug and dangerous and hateful, and she could not advance past the bridge. Hermia retreated in a press of bodies, and though their presence was a comfort, it felt alarming also; she feared she might be crushed. Her throat was raw; her eyes were streaming; all around her there was screaming and a chorus of "Pigs, pigs!" She did not go to Chicago and the Democratic National Convention, but friends of hers did go and got beaten and arrested, and when they were in New York again, they talked about establishing a safe house in Nova Scotia. One of the men she had slept with that year owned property on Cape Breton; his name was Joe Arnoldi, and he said it was the place to go to, a throwback to the old days and ways, with many more sheep than police.

She and two other women traveled north. They had trouble at the border but did have valid passports and were admitted, finally; the long drive through New Brunswick past the Bay of Fundy and through the empty Maritimes was fun. They drove a VW bus. Hermia and her companions—a filmmaker, a dancer—had become political because everything was political, and you were either part of the problem or part of the solution. This was a mantra and slogan, of course, but also self-evident fact. It was only a question of whether or not you acknowledged the fact or instead chose to ignore it.

For years they *had* ignored it, taking privilege for granted, taking wealth and position for granted in their version of Monopoly, a board game of money and sex. In the original there was no sex; instead there were hotels to buy and properties like Boardwalk and Park Place, and when everyone else had gone bankrupt, you put the board away. But things had gotten serious, not playful now; the soldiers standing at attention with their rifles and gas masks had not arrived to play.

Each afternoon, it rained. When they reached Cape Breton, however, the skies turned a bright blue. This seemed like a good omen, and there was never any trouble finding rooms with three beds in motels. The filmmaker's name was Sally and the dancer's Marian, and they liked to sign the motel register together: *S&M*. Whatever else the movement had accomplished in "Amerika"— and they agreed this was not nothing, this was by definition something—it had changed forever the currency of sex. Sex was not a case of ownership, no longer a commodity to barter for a mortgage and two cars in the garage.

—

They wandered through Antigonish and Ingonish and along the Cabot Trail. They visited a town called Dingwall and, at the outer edge of Cape Breton, a village called Meat Cove. After a week they drove to Inverness, where Joe Arnoldi was living in a trailer, and the friends took turns taking showers in the shower stall Joe had rigged outside. He was renting out his pastureland to the neighboring sheep farmer, or not so much renting it as bartering for help with the house that he was building—he pointed to a wooden frame and pile of lumber down the hill—and smoking this terrific dope; he had hand-lettered posters on the trailer walls: *Turn On; Tune In; Drop Out* and *Make Love, Not War.* Did they know that Richard Alpert was no longer teaching at Harvard and had become Baba Ram Dass?

They bought lobsters for a dollar each and that night prepared a feast. Joe had grown a mustache he was proud of, brown and luxuriant, and he kept smoothing it and saying, "Dynamite you came to see me, what a gas!" He and Hermia had slept together twice, and she remembered how his balls were hairless and his cock bent to the left.

Now, however, he had other plans; he had his hand on Sally's knee and was beating out a rhythm on her thigh. Watching, drinking a glass of white wine, Hermia felt not so much rejected as relieved. She was into abstinence, had been abstinent for weeks and hadn't wanted to sing for their supper by making it with Joe, their host; she ate a second lobster and sopped up the butter with bread.

That night she lay outside. Marian was sleeping on the air mattress in the camper, and Sally and Joe used the trailer, so she took a bedroll and stretched out beneath a tree. Except for the others up here on the hill, nobody who knew her knew where she was lying, and Hermia could not decide if this made her happy or sad. She would call her mother in the morning, she decided; she did not belong in a Volkswagen bus or on a hill in Cape Breton, and her mother ought to know that she was well and safe. She was not in political exile and not among the Wretched of the Earth. Above her, in the pines, a screech owl screeched.

Then there was silence. She felt her heart beat. To calm herself she inhaled to the count of eight and held her breath and, to the count of eight, exhaled. Unable to forget it, she pictured the truck in which her father crashed and how it seemed volitional, hurtling down the driveway as an engine of destruction. Hermia repeated her breathing, exhaling, trying to think about nothing at all until she did feel calm. Faintly, from the trailer, she heard the sound of bedsprings and Sally's rhythmic cries.

And then she too was crying, feeling sorry for herself. She had a sudden memory of lying down with Lawrence in his bed in Claverly Hall; they both had been so young, so tender with each other, but that was very long ago, and she did not feel young or tender. *Where has it gone?* she asked herself. *Where has it disappeared to?—love, my love.*

———

Years passed. G. Edson Lattimer and her mother settled into a routine; they bought a pied-à-terre in Manhattan and spent half the year in England, returning to Lattimer's cottage in Kent every spring. She visited them sometimes, liking her stepfather better each visit and driving his Jaguar, sleeping in the oasthouse they'd converted to a guest house and dating the sons of hunt-club neighbors or musicians on the rise. She and her mother made a truce of sorts, agreeing not to disagree, and profiting together from her father's legacy. The year she turned thirty Hermia was given, by the trust established in her father's will, the house and land in Truro and, with the exception of her father's paintings in storage, its contents; its contents were evaluated—"Surprise, surprise!" her mother said—at two million dollars' worth of art. She sold the Hopper and the Motherwells at auction in order to pay the inheritance tax and, now that she was well enough off not to need to earn a living, lived as she chose, as she pleased.

Edson Lattimer had been married previously, and one winter night in New York she met his son. Paul Lattimer was thirty-four, a correspondent for Reuters on assignment at the UN. To Hermia he seemed a less-polished version of his father, with thinning sandy hair and a pronounced nose and slight stammer she found endearing.

They were introduced at dinner and had, as Paul told her, something in common. "What's that?" she inquired, and he said, "I wasn't any h-h-happier than *you* were when they married." He said this as though he had known her reaction, and she wondered if he had been informed of it or simply had guessed how she felt. In either case she liked his declarative clarity, his way of taking for granted that they would get along.

That evening they discussed Islam, the growing fundamentalism of the Muslim nations, and she was impressed by Paul's knowledge and his prediction that the Third World War would be fought over water and faith. He was in Manhattan on a six-month stint, and leaving soon, and regretted it had taken them this long to meet. At evening's end they shared a taxi, and as he dropped her off at her building, he asked, "Would you permit me to see you again?" Again she was impressed by his formality and courtliness, and she answered, "Yes."

At thirty-two she had grown conscious of the way her right eyelid drooped, the way her breasts were dropping, and the added inches at her waist. She discovered and began to pluck gray hairs above her ear. Men still said she was beautiful, but that was a code word for single and rich, and she had long since lost the illusion that someone she was seeing would tell her the literal truth. She was tired of hypocrisy; sick to death of vanity, and how men had to be flattered, and did not want to think the same held true for her. So when Paul Lattimer confessed he'd been reluctant to meet her, had seen and studied her photo in Kent and thought her a glamorous woman, too glamorous to be an intelligent human being or anything except a model, or possibly an actress, she did not believe him.

"In person you're even more l-l-lovely," he said, and she said, "Stop it, please."

"I mean it," said Paul. "I never say what I d-d-don't mean."

Their courtship was brief. Hermia liked his cultivated stammer, his beak of a nose, the small mound of his belly, and his erudition and wit. She was surprised by her own urgency, her conviction this made sense; she had been jagged-edged before, but now the edges fit. At dinner the next week she felt a wave of *rightness*, and she and Paul Lattimer talked and talked as though they had all evening to converse.

They had, they discovered, a great deal in common; they each liked Brussels sprouts, for instance, and disliked the color purple; they both were impressed by Ella Fitzgerald and unimpressed by Sinatra. His mother had died in a boating accident in foul weather off the Isle of Mull, and this represented another bond between them; they each had lost a parent, and then their parents met. It was as though she'd found a brother, a long-lost relation, except that she could sleep with him and there was no taboo. Paul joked that he and Hermia were sexual relations, enjoying all the advantages of incest and none of the blood taint.

He had traveled widely, spending years in Thailand and Hong Kong, and he told her stories of being in Alaska and chased by a Kodiak bear. He liked the work at the UN and liked his work for Reuters, but lately he had wondered if he shouldn't settle down. He announced this to her carefully, and carefully she asked him, "Where?" and he said, "It doesn't matter, really. Where would you p-prefer?"

They were married without ceremony, by a justice of the peace, and afterward the groom's father gave a dinner at the Explorers Club. Photographs of expeditions and fabled ships and shipwrecks and big-game hunting parties lined the walls. They drank champagne. Hermia felt buoyant, giddy, and she told Paul when he asked her, "Aren't you g-g-glad you waited?" that she wasn't only glad, she was *delighted*, and it was worth the wait. He kissed her hand where the diamond sparkled; he kissed her wedding ring.

"May you be as fortunate in your marriage," said G. Edson Lattimer, "as I have been in mine."

"We hope to be, Papa," said Paul. "We f-follow where you lead."

"Which one of you is Alphonse, and which Gaston?" asked her mother—a flash of her old arrogant impatience visible again. "What's the thing they're always saying, that too-polite pair? 'After you!'"

"More wine, sir?" asked the waiter. They ordered a second bottle and drank a toast to absent friends and agreed that the mousse was too sweet.

Hermia was married now, and thirty-three, and it was as though the whole thing happened when she hadn't quite been watching; one fine day she had a husband, but the whole was a bright blur. She was surprised by how little she'd noticed, how the details of planning the wedding passed her by. She remembered the orchids he gave her, a stuffed bear on the stairwell of the Explorers Club, and how her mother cried. She remembered the blue garter she had borrowed coming undone while they danced. That night Paul fell asleep inside her, and her first reaction was to wake him, shake him, but she had had an orgasm and did not require another and felt a wave of warm, proud tenderness for this sleeping almost-stranger in her arms.

———

Then she discovered she was pregnant. It might have happened the week of her wedding, or the week before, or after; her period had been irregular for years. She did not understand, at first, the way her body felt—the sleeplessness, the queasiness. She had not in particular wanted a child, had certainly not planned for one or believed it would happen so soon. And, because she was no longer young, Hermia worried the baby—her baby, their baby, *the* baby—might not come to term. But throughout her pregnancy—the difficult first trimester and then the easy one and then the final waiting months, the way her body changed and everything was rearranged—she felt that same sense of *rightness*, of comfort; this was the way things should be.

Paul was solicitous and told her he adored her; she was his sacred vessel, and he could not bear it if she felt anxiety or pain.

She felt no pain. It was as though her whole previous life—the pointless jobs and pointless men, the work and play and politics—had been only preparation, only a way of waiting for a child to call her own. She had been idling and now was in gear; she had been lost and was found. When the baby came—a daughter, seven pounds, six ounces, and perfectly formed—they named her Patricia, after Paul's mother, and brought her back from Mount Sinai in a taxicab festooned with flowers. She was healthy and bright-eyed and, from the beginning, good-humored; she had ten toes and fingers and those enchanting rolls of baby fat and enormous eyes.

It was brilliant, said Paul; it was bliss.

But something had been happening, something neither blissful nor brilliant. Again she'd failed to notice and had not quite been watching and, as with her wedding, the details passed her by. She could not put a date to it or say, "It *used* to be this way; it *used* to be different and better." There was no single thing to remember and say, "*Here's* where the trouble began." But the familiar man she married became unfamiliar; the almost-brother who liked Brussels sprouts and Ella Fitzgerald and oral sex was not someone she could predict.

Paul changed. He added a police lock to the apartment's service door and, for good measure—although they lived on the tenth floor—iron grilles on all the windows. In their bedroom he kept the blinds drawn. When he finished his stint at the UN, the management of Reuters asked him to consider a job as bureau chief in Tokyo, and he told them no. They had sufficient money so he had no need to work and instead took a "sabbatical, a time to s-s-s-sit down and think." He was doing research for a book, he claimed, but sat for hours in the living room, staring at the window, not reading or writing. He took amphetamines to stay awake and sleeping pills to sleep; he swallowed tabs of acid in order, he explained, to clarify his thinking on the project he was planning—and sat at his work desk humming, rocking, cradling his head in his hands.

Paul grew jealous of the baby, aggrieved at the amount of time Hermia was spending with their child. When she got out of bed at night, to nurse or comfort Pat-a-cake, he tried to keep her lying down and said, "It's g-g-good for her, helps develop the lungs." When she and Patricia went for a walk—using the baby carriage, and then with the Snugli or stroller—her husband walked beside them as if he were their hired guard, as if he thought a passerby might make off with them instead of ignore them or smile. Once Hermia lost weight again and her breasts stayed full from nursing, he grew even more protective and suspicious—as though the men in elevators or behind a desk in galleries or idling at a traffic light might become her lovers, as though their friends were more than friends and she couldn't be trusted with men.

It was irrational, of course. It made no sense at all. But when she tried to talk to him, he would not discuss it, saying only that he had his reasons, that he hadn't been born yesterday and was nobody's fool. "I've l-lost one Lattimer woman already," he said, "and it w-won't happen again."

His face was red, his eyes were wild, and she thought he might be drinking, though he did not smell of drink. "But I *love* you," Hermia protested. "I don't love anybody else."

"What about P-Patricia?"

"That's different, that doesn't count."

"Who's c-c-counting here?"

"*I'm* not."

"What, s-seven, eight, how many men have you b-been with since our pretty b-b-baby was born?"

She began to be afraid of him, to fear for the child's safety, and when he started breaking things—a teapot handle, a set of Limoges they'd received for the wedding—she tried to find some help. Her mother was in England, and she called the house in Kent, but neither her mother nor stepfather would countenance her fears. It proved difficult to tell G. Edson Lattimer about his son's behavior, and Hermia could not persuade them she needed their support. "Aren't you, are you exaggerating just a little, Herm?" her mother asked. Her friend Silvana came to New York twice a year for shopping, yet when she told Silvana she was frightened of her husband, her old roommate shrugged: "In Chile we are used to it," she said.

—

Pat-a-cake was almost two when Paul fell completely apart. She smiled and clapped her hands and learned to speak and walk, but every time she smiled at a stranger, he grew more agitated. So too with Hermia; if she said "Hello" to the doorman, he ordered her to stop it; when she talked with other mothers in the playground about clothes or weather or how their children were maturing, he warned her—for Paul would accompany them always, standing by the slide or swing, sitting cross-legged on the next bench down, pretending to read the *New York Times* while he glared at men out walking dogs, or tending children of their own—to "S-s-s-stuff it, s-stop it, my last d-duchess, or I'll hang you on the wall."

"Please don't," she said. "Please don't be jealous."

"It isn't jealousy," he said.

"What is it, then?"

"It's making sure what's mine is m-mine."

"We *are*," she said. "We completely are."

"Remember when I said," he said, "I thought you were an actress. Too b-beautiful to be an actual person? A model, my d-duchess. Unreal."

"I'm *not*," she said.

"What?"

"Unfaithful."

"Don't lie to m-me," said her husband. "I s-s-swear I'll make you regret it."

"What? Regret what?"

"If I ever c-c-catch you . . ."

"What? Doing *what?*"

"You know," he said. "And I c-certainly know."

So the evening when he came at her—the wild glint in his eye, the kitchen knife outthrust—she was ready with a can of Mace and blasted him full force. It had been in her handbag for weeks. She had had her suitcase packed, and her daughter's, and while Paul was groaning, collapsed upon the kitchen counter, covering his face and carving patterns in the air, cursing, trying to find water, she picked up Patricia and left.

IV
1962–1963

When Lawrence finished college, he drove home in his mother's Impala. The week of graduation was a week of parties, and he did what he could to enjoy them, drinking and discussing the future of the planet and sleeping with Charette. His parents attended commencement but would not speak to each other. They took turns having meals with him and telling him how proud they were and how they knew the end of school was only a beginning. "The completion of your studies," said his father over breakfast, "is the start of what's to come."

First he returned to Scarsdale, having packed his books and clothes and radio, feeling sentimental but excited to leave Cambridge behind. On his final day in Claverly Hall he surveyed his empty room and found, beneath the mattress, a piece of paper wedged there. It was in Hermia's handwriting, her blue pen and her open scrawl; he unfolded it and read: *I adore you. Adore you. Love. Love.* The note was undated, on yellow lined paper, and he folded and kissed it and threw it away.

In Scarsdale, things had changed. His mother was seeing a doctor, a widower across the street with a prize-winning Pekingese who was, she told him, the reason they'd met; she'd noticed the two of them—Robert and Sam—out walking every morning and again at night. Then one night at nearly midnight she heard the Pekingese barking madly at a tree. She put on her bathrobe and opened the door to see what was happening, but the streetlight showed her nothing and so she went down to the street. Across the hedge the dog was going yap-yap-yap, having cornered a raccoon, and up there on the branch the animal was hissing, spitting, terrified, a pair of eyeballs gleaming from a body twice Sam's size. And there had been something so, so *ridiculous* about it, said his mother, she just had to laugh.

"Can you hold the leash?" her neighbor asked. She could; she held the dog. He hunted for and found a rock and flipped it up sidearm forcefully, and although it fell short of the target, it caused the raccoon to shrink back. "I think you hit him," she declared, and he said, "Think I missed." Then they introduced themselves—she conscious of her bathrobe, and he apologizing for having disturbed her, for the racket Sam was making and how late it was. "Do you always walk this late?" she asked, and he said no, it had been a long day, a difficult procedure at the hospital, and they wished each other good night.

That first conversation had led to another, a third, and now she and the doctor were friends. This was how she described it: "good friends." Her neighbor was, she told Lawrence, an excellent surgeon and father—he had two grown sons in San Diego, both in commercial real estate—and Robert was a decent man, a man who wouldn't lie to you or live a secret life. That was what mattered most to her, his mother said: Robert's cards were on the table and everything was up front and out in the open—how much he missed his dead wife, for example, was a subject they often discussed. She expected Lawrence to like her new companion and be pleased for her, a little, or at least try to be pleased.

He was not so much pleased as relieved. His mother did seem happy, taking pains with her appearance and going to the opera and, before it closed, to *My Fair Lady*, because they'd each enjoyed the show the first time they'd seen it on Broadway and wanted to see it together. In the kitchen his mother hummed snatches of song—"I Could Have Danced All Night," or "On the Street Where You Live"—and busied herself preparing complicated dishes when Robert came over to eat. She was girlish in the surgeon's presence, laughing at his jokes and making sure that Lawrence got the punch line, making sure he understood how carefree she could be.

His sister too seemed happier, caught up in being a racquet club lifeguard and asking for advice about which college to apply to in her senior year. Allie's hair was sun-bleached; she was working on a tan, and when he looked at her, he saw a golden girl with braces, his kid sister growing up. She and a clique of girl-friends were always in her bedroom, cackling together and using the phone and playing the stereo loudly and practicing the Twist. His father had moved to Long Island—remarried now, and with a three-year-old—so Lawrence lazed about the house with a sense of earned inertia, sleeping late and lying shirtless in the hammock, reading books.

At the induction center in Whitehall he was classified 4F. He had had to register, but it was 1962, and there was little pressure on the draft. On the appointed day he showed up for his physical with a letter from his doctor attesting to rheumatic fever, a murmur of the mitral valve contracted during childhood. At nine, he had been ill for months—first with a cold, then with strep throat, and then rheumatic fever. Penicillin and bed rest had cured him, however; there had been no recurrence and the murmur was inaudible. This the letter did not say.

His mother made him breakfast and drove him to the train.

"Don't let's worry, darling." She stubbed out her cigarette in the car's ashtray. "Robert is certain they won't take the risk."

"What risk?"

"Army physicians will reject you; it's the 'cloud's silver lining,' he says. They won't want to deal with an established condition—not 'heart trouble' anyhow."

This proved to be the case. Lawrence waited in a white high-ceilinged room for his turn to be examined while a soldier with a clipboard paced up and down the line. There were names of diseases called out: "flat feet" and "cancer," "epilepsy" and a long list of ailments. When they reached "rheumatic fever," he stepped forward from the line; he was wearing only underpants, and cold. A doctor with crew-cut red hair told him to do fifty push-ups and then listened to his heart, saying, "Breathe . . . breathe deeply . . . hold," and, folding his stethoscope, said, "You're out of here, kid." In a cubicle with a blue curtain, Lawrence dressed himself, then collected his papers and left.

—

That evening he had dinner with his father. They ate at an Italian restaurant, and his father drank dry martinis and over wine confessed he sometimes worried he'd made a mistake: he'd been not so much *railroaded* as *steered*, not so much *forced* as *lured* into being a banker, and sometimes—today was one of them—it felt like his career at work had been only an attempt to meet other people's expectations and other people's needs. It was ancient history, his father said, but he didn't want his oldest child to wake up thirty years from now with the same sense of not so much *failure* as *regret*. He wanted his boy to take time off instead, to not get caught up in the rat race, and now that he had finished college and the army wasn't an issue, he should travel a little and see the wide world. So

Lawrence's graduation gift—he must have noticed, hadn't he, how he'd received nothing at the commencement ceremony?—was an airplane ticket and a blank check.

His father smiled. The circles underneath his eyes were deeper now, and though his hair had been carefully barbered, it looked thin and gray. "Don't think I mean *blank* check exactly," he said. "It's not, I mean, a bottomless well, but there's enough for you to travel with and we'll start with five thousand dollars; that should get you out of here and let you see the world. Don't tell your mother, but I sometimes think if the two of us had had time off the beaten track, we'd still be happy together . . ."

"I'm grateful, Dad."

"Don't mention it."

"No, I *want* to mention it. I'm very grateful to you."

His father's face was pale. "Have some dessert? Zabaglione. *Zuppa inglese.* Everything that starts with *z*. You're a growing boy."

"I'm fine." He shook his head.

"Well, then, the check." He gestured at the waiter, and the waiter came. "I want you to be happy," said his father solemnly, then wiped his mouth with his napkin. "It's the only thing I want."

——

So he was twenty-two and free, intending to be an architect but not this year, not yet. He went to parties in New York and talked to friends from Harvard, and one of them insisted the best way to join the profession was not to think about it but to absorb the way that people lived. "What are you saying?" Lawrence asked, and his host, Dick Silver, plucked a sandwich from the sandwich tray and swallowed an olive and said, "When you travel, you take yourself with you. Except a roof in Africa is a very different thing from Greenland or Nepal."

"Excuse me?"

They drank. The *idea* of "roof" is various, Dick Silver continued, and its function varies greatly, and you have to have some sense of where the variables come from and what different people think of as a "roof." If he himself had hoped to be an architect, he'd work on the distinction between a structure made of, for example, satch or thlate. Thatch and slate . . .

They were at the Players' Club, of which Dick Silver's father was a member. Wearing a double-breasted suit and handlebar mustache, he greeted them. "Glad you could join us, gentlemen," he said. "Can you believe this boy of mine is twenty-four? That must mean I'm over thirty." Then the elder Silver joined his own friends in another room, under oil paintings of actors, saying, "Order whatever you want."

"We were discussing architecture. Food, clothing, and shelter," Dick pronounced. He raised his glass, inclusive.

"And of those three," said Roger, "our Larry here intends to focus on shelter. The last shall not be least."

"The best preparation is looking around," added Allan Silverwhistle. "Just seeing what's out there to see . . ."

This seemed a good idea. Lawrence went to the bathroom and stared at himself in the Players' Club mirror: long-haired, blue-eyed, strong-nosed, drunk. One of his teachers used to say that there are builders and breakers; there are those who worship icons and those who strike them down. "In the future, gentlemen, you will decide which party is the one to which you pledge allegiance—you must cast your lot with nave or knave and not be in between. There's the temple or the wrecking ball, and you will have to choose." His teacher quoted Samuel Beckett:

> *Spend the years of learning squandering*
> *Courage for the years of wandering*

And when he finished the lecture—this had been famous at Harvard, a ritual performance—he would fold his papers at the podium and place them in his briefcase and put on his raincoat and lean into the microphone, completing the quatrain:

> *Through a world politely turning*
> *From the loutishness of learning.*

And exit to applause.

———

As a dog urinates, not completely but in stages, so Lawrence shifted towns. He flew from Idlewild to Orly but was saving Paris for later and took a train to Versailles. There he spent the evening with an ambulance driver's family; he had stopped the ambulance driver to inquire as to hotels, and the man had a cousin in Boston and invited him to dinner. At the hotel he met a man from Glasgow who recited limericks and went "tum-de-tum-de-tum-tum" when he could not remember the words. The man said Glasgow was an awful place, unimaginably horrible, and Lawrence, if he hoped to preserve his sanity, should never go to Glasgow or, for that matter, Edinburgh. "Being impecunious," he said, "you won't have servants there."

He visited the palace. In the Hall of Mirrors he tried to track the sight lines and the effects of perspective; he admired the balconies and stairwells and the long allées. He had read about the Sun King's lush extravagance and the queen who played at being a milkmaid, pretending to work on a farm. Yet Versailles astonished him: the scale of it, the delicate grandeur. He saw the chairs and tapestries reflected in the mirrors, and the way each object was by its own image doubled. When he reached to touch a window, the guard said, "*Défendu.* It is forbidden, *m'sieur.*"

Next morning he proceeded from Versailles to Clermont-Ferrand. Lawrence found a cheap hotel behind the railway station, where a woman in the restaurant said, *"Tiens, les yeux d'un poète."* She sat down at his table and smiled. She was, he came to understand, a prostitute, and she took him to her room and washed his penis carefully and, arousing him, patted it dry. He paid her for an hour but she let him stay two hours, and he flattered himself that she meant it when she said, "The eyes of a poet"; he liked Clermont-Ferrand, its Romanesque cathedral and the plane trees in the streets.

After two days in that city, however, Lawrence took a night train east and north. He made a special pilgrimage to Le Corbusier's Ronchamp. The complicated structure in honor of simplicity, the way the building both belonged to and stood separate from landscape, the proportions and materials and upward-striving thrust of it: all these enthralled him. The chapel seemed a marriage of the ancient and the modern in a way that celebrated both; he studied the shape of the roof.

Next he spent a week near Marseilles. Lawrence moved from town to town with no sense of purpose or hurry, convinced he would profit from travel. He ate and drank and viewed the sights—Arles, Avignon, Saint-Rémy—with diligence, taking pleasure in the trip; he was often alone but not often lonely, and he kept a notebook, noting buildings and facades. His first focus was cathedrals—Gothic, Baroque—and their downspout gargoyles and stained-glass windows and flying buttresses and the carved stone saints. These he drew.

From Aix-en-Provence he took a train to Cannes, where he met a pair of English girls on what they called their hols. When he asked them what they meant by "hols," they said, don't be so thick, it's *holiday*, and the three of them went to a wine bar. They were big-breasted and exuberant, with white skin and red cheeks. They said the Riviera was smashing; they were having a rattling good time. One of the girls, Valerie, confided that her friend Estelle quite fancied him, and Estelle took him aside and said Valerie was frus-*trat*-ed, so he paid for a bottle of *vin rosé* and proposed they empty it as a threesome in his room. "No thanks," they said, "not bloody likely," and linked arms and left.

———

From Nice he took a train to Rome and stayed in the city three weeks. He walked the hills and narrow streets of Trastevere, admiring the monuments and merchandise in shops. He studied work by Brunelleschi and Bernini and decided that his favorite of the "three *B*s" was Borromini; he filled a notebook with the work of Borromini, his use of perspective, the structural components of his windows and ceilings and domes.

At the American Express office in the Piazza di Spagna he found separate letters from his parents saying everything was fine and sending him their love. He sent his parents postcards of the Trevi Fountain and the Spanish Steps. He went to museums and churches and the Vatican and drew several versions of the Pantheon. Again he found a prostitute, this one from Morocco, and relieved himself inside her while she made encouraging noises and swiveled her thin hips.

In December he traveled to Naples and saw the peak of Mount Vesuvius, but it looked bleak, its flanks littered with trash, and he decided he would rather climb Mount Etna. He stayed in Naples two nights. A lawyer bought him dinner at a restaurant by the water, plying him with wine, but when Lawrence rejected the suggestion that they go to his apartment, the lawyer slapped him twice, not lightly. "You have been playing with me, *ragazzo*," said the lawyer, "a game it can be dangerous to play."

Although he was not frightened, he left Naples the next morning. Carrying a duffel bag and knapsack, he reveled in his freedom, the way he could elect to leave a town or stay. Lawrence crossed the Strait of Messina and went to Siracusa and Taormina but found himself disliking Taormina. There were tour buses and curio shops, a self-important quaintness that felt false. He bought a pair of hiking boots and commenced to climb Mount Etna but was turned back before the peak because Etna was erupting. It rained. His hotel in Catania cost the equivalent in lire of eight dollars, and he stayed there for six nights, admiring the black volcanic rock of the buildings of the city. The proprietor of the hotel served a white acidic wine and called it the wine of the Cyclops; if you drink one liter for lunch and another in the evening, he declared, you lose an eye. "According to our legend, the Cyclops's cave," he said, "is very near this part of town, and when Odysseus blinded the Cyclops, he threw a boulder at the ship and it landed here."

After two weeks on the island Lawrence had had enough of Sicily and took the ferry to Piraeus; in Athens he stayed in a hotel beneath the Plaka, and from his window saw a section of the Parthenon itself. Spotlit, it floated on air. At the American Express office in Syntagma Square he collected mail and found letters from his parents and one from Allan Silverwhistle, saying life in the city was dishwater dull. *Wish I were there*, Allan wrote. His father wrote to tell him that the fall had been spectacular, leaf season a real pleasure on Long Island, and his mother wrote she missed him very much, most of all during holiday season, and Allie and Robert sent love.

Lawrence bought a new notebook for Greece. He studied the distinction between Doric and Ionic and Corinthian and drew the base of columns and then their capitals. On the Acropolis he studied details of the temples—how the columns fattened in the middle, and how they angled perceptibly inward but appeared from the ground to be straight.

After ten days in Athens and on impulse he booked passage on a tour boat through the islands. The ship was called *Kalliope* and had scheduled ports of call in Mykonos, Delos, Corfu, Crete, and Rhodes. Because he did not wish to seem too obviously a tourist, he avoided other passengers—the women in seersucker jumpsuits, the men with their hands in their pockets and wearing striped shirts and shorts. But Lawrence was befriended by the cook, a man from Pittsburgh called George Palamis; they shared cigars on deck. He was welcome in the galley and sat there in the afternoons while the cook washed plates and cutlery, then rubbed down the cast-iron pots. Crusts and lettuce leaves floated in the galley sink; when George had finished washing dishes, he would rinse his arms. The other members of the crew pronounced his name as "Iorgo," always saying, "Iasu, Iorgo," and chattering in Greek. George owned a record by Nana Mouskouri and several recordings of Django Reinhardt and Perry Como and Mikis Theodorakis and one of Flatt and Scruggs. He played the records after mealtimes and while he scrubbed the counters, cleaning up.

—

Lawrence disembarked in Rhodes and stayed there for five months. He acquired a taste for retsina wine, its bitter-edged flavor and the way it arrived in open tin tankards; nightly in the tavernas he ordered taramosalata and artichokes and fish. He liked the fort and seawalls and olive trees and lemon groves and the narrow, steep-pitched streets. He liked the people, their bluff warmth, but could not understand them and contented himself with smiling, nodding, speaking pidgin French and English and drinking quantities of coffee in brightly colored cups. He climbed Monte Smith. In February he contracted amoebic dysentery and lay immobile for weeks, unable to keep down the tea and toast and brandy the mustachioed doctor prescribed. An English tourist passing through said, "These should help," and handed him a set of pills called Entero-Vioform. "They're for holiday tummy," he said.

But the pills did not help either. In his rented room near the harbor, Lawrence read *Incidents of Travel in Yucatan* and a guidebook with an appendix of useful phrases in Greek. In a bookshop with a newspaper stall he found a pamphlet by C. A. Doxiadis, called "Dynapolis: The City of the Future," and this he studied with attention. There was no telephone, and the electric lights were fitful; he felt both sick and homesick, remembering his own clean bed and the abundant food and spotless bathrooms at home. He was very far from Scarsdale now and lay by the water, adrift; he tried to remember what he had done for each of the days and weeks and months of his trip, and why he had traveled and what he had wanted to see.

There had been—he was sure of it—snow. The ceiling above him had intricate tiling, and he tried to make sense of the pattern and where the tiles were stained. Dick Silver's face emerged from the floor, making pronouncements about shelter and what his birthday party guests should notice around them in the whirling world, but nothing he said was in English and none of it made sense. Lawrence sweated and shivered and rocked. In his dreams he dreamed of Scarsdale and, wakeful, thought of Truro and his time with Hermia there.

The men of the island were kind. Wearing colored hats and jackets lined with wool, they smoked and played board games with dice and tiles and smiled and nodded at him while he drank his tea or lemon soup and tried to decide what to do. He still had his passport and six hundred dollars folded double in his money belt and in the zippered pocket of his boots. In March he purchased a book on the Bauhaus and the role of Walter Gropius. On the same shelf he found an English-language pamphlet on Le Corbusier and the role of the builder, the technological and social determinants that constitute "New Objectivity," as proclaimed by J. J. P. Oud.

The spring, when it came, was a gift. Fruit trees burst into blossom, and the bougainvillea and bright oleander bloomed. Lawrence had lost weight; his clothes hung on him loosely, but his hallucinations faded and he began to improve. He drew elevations of the harbor and the forts built by Crusaders. He was, he told himself, being aimless for a reason, and his thumbprint on the window showed the whorled striations of a cypress tree or clouds by Van Gogh. By the time that he felt strong enough to travel he had memorized Doxiadis and read *Incidents of Travel in Yucatan* three times.

On the last day of May he flew home and, in the airplane, took stock. He had spent his father's money and traveled through parts of Western Europe and Greece, looking at cities and buildings and learning, a little, to be by himself. He had, or so he assured himself, strengthened his sense of vocation; he was much more certain now he hoped to be an architect. He had visited great structures— Versailles, the chapel at Ronchamp, St. Peter's, the Parthenon— and been moved by them; he had sketched windows and floor plans and facades. During the flight he read Doxiadis on ekistics and fell asleep fitfully, sweating. He had fallen sick and was well.

—

On arrival he informed his mother—who collected him at the airport in Robert's black Mercedes—that societies are shaped in part by the shape of their cities. It makes a difference if the common space sits on a hilltop or instead down by the water, and the great thing about architects, Lawrence maintained, is they build a better mousetrap for the landscape of the future and influence the habitat of generations to come . . .

She told him she was getting married. Next month she and Robert were tying the knot, and she didn't want to be a burden to her children. "There's nothing worse," his mother said, "than a fifty-year-old by herself in the world, and I'm not lonely anymore, you know that, don't you, darling?"

"Congratulations, Mom."

"Your sister too, she's happy for me."

"How's Allie doing?"

"Fine, she's fine."

His mother talked about her wedding plans—well, not so much the *wedding* as the honeymoon thereafter, because all her life she'd wanted to visit New Zealand and the Fiji islands, and she and Robert would travel for two weeks. "It's the most he's been away for *all* his career, the longest they could spare him"—she giggled— "from the hospital.

"'Youth is wasted on the young.' I know you don't believe that, really. I know it's just an expression. But these months you've been in Europe were—what's the word I want?—*remarkable*, a privilege, and I hope you don't take it for granted . . ."

Her voice trailed off. They were crossing the Bronx-Whitestone Bridge. Co-op City loomed ahead, and he asked himself what he had in fact learned, if his talk about landscape and cities made sense, and where he would go next. Lawrence closed his eyes. On the screen of his shut eyelids the book on the Bauhaus appeared. It was rectangular, white. There were diagrams and scale models of buildings and illustrated charts. The image of Walter Gropius— in the photograph the architect was surrounded by disciples, and pointing with his spectacles at drawings on a blackboard— remained. They made the turn to the Hutchinson River Parkway, then Weaver Street, then home.

———

The following day, in Manhattan, he met his father for lunch. They ate at La Toque Blanche. "You're looking well," his father said.

"You too, Dad. Very well."

"You've lost a lot of weight."

"I had whatever they call *la turista* in Greece. I'm fine now."

His father was drinking martinis. He had allowed his side-burns to grow, and hair curled over his collar. He made a show of interest while Lawrence spoke about his time in France and Italy, the months in Rhodes. But it was clear he paid no real attention; he drummed his fingers on the tablecloth and looked around the restaurant at other diners, at the waiters, the walls. "I have something to say to you."

"Yes?"

"Something important."

"All right." Lawrence straightened.

"What I want to say is, your sister is not on my wavelength. Not a person I can talk to anymore. I don't think your mother did it on purpose, but both of them are of the opinion that I'm some-how, oh, I don't know, untrustworthy. The devil in a blue-striped suit. And I wanted to ask you to tell her I'm not."

At the banquette in the corner a couple was laughing, uproari-ous. The girl was in a yellow dress, the man in a seersucker jacket, and they stroked each other's arms.

"All right."

"I *knew* you'd step up to the plate." His father made a swinging motion, wrists cocked, as though he held a baseball bat. "So have you decided?"

"Decided?"

"What comes next. What you're intending to do with your life."

"Is this a change of subject?"

"Yes." His father drank. "It's not like on Tuesday she answers the phone and next day refuses to, but believe me it's not easy when your child decides you're the Antichrist—did I say that already?— in a blue suit. The reason for marriage is to have children," he declared, maudlin, "and now I'm losing one of them. Talk to her, Larry, OK?"

"I'll try."

"It's all we have," his father said. "Time. It's what we don't notice and let slip away and take advantage of, and then one fine morning the alarm clock rings and you wake *up* to it, there's very little left of this commodity you think you've stockpiled and maybe even have too *much* of. Don't waste it, is what I'm trying to tell you, don't let it take you by surprise. Excuse me."

His father stood up from the table and made for the men's room, weaving. The couple in the corner kissed. *"Talk to your sister, OK?"*

V

2004

She recognized him instantly, as soon as he came up on deck. He was gray and thick and stooped, but *Lawrence*, entirely Lawrence—not someone she could ever fail to know. He stood the way he used to stand, wanting to be a part of the party yet wanting also to withdraw from it, holding out his life preserver as though it might protect him and be both shield and badge. He was wearing a windbreaker: black. His shirt was yellow, open-necked, and the tilt of his head was familiar; she *knew* that head, that neck.

Her stomach dropped, heart leapt. Her breath caught in her throat. Those were inaccurate phrases, Hermia knew; a stomach doesn't *drop*; a heart can't *leap*. But that was what it felt like, truly, standing ten feet away from her old lover by Lifeboat Station #6, and it took her a minute to calm herself down and not rush to his side. She forced herself to wait.

It was September 27, 2004. They had not seen each other since 1962. She had Googled him, of course, and found out where he worked and taught, the titles of his books—*Urbanism (Re)considered*, *The Common Place*, the monograph series he edited—and the prizes won. She wrote down his office address. She considered a letter, or e-mail—*everyone* was hunting down lost friends. *Hi, just thought I'd drop a line. Hello, here's a bolt from the blue. A blast from the past, baby, thinking of you.*

But none of that seemed feasible; she did not write him, or e-mail, or call. She thought about him often, as Lawrence no doubt had thought about her, but more than forty years had passed, and there was nothing to do. There was nothing to say to him, nothing to ask, and no way to begin. *Hiya, remember me?*

It took her two full days. At first she wasn't sure she should, or wanted to, or what would happen if she did. How long would it take him, she wondered, to notice her instead? It was not so much the nerve she lacked as certainty; was this a good idea? *Should I? Will I? Won't I? Why not?* Hermia asked herself, and could not decide . . .

She had started the cruise in Marseilles. The Mediterranean looked uninviting; the passengers were loud and dull and hell-for-leather-bent on having a wonderful time. She needed to be left alone; she did not want a wonderful time. Instead she spent days on the MS *Diana* avoiding importunate strangers, reading *The Leopard* and watching the water and wondering what to do next. In Nice, she drank a glass of wine in the Negresco Hotel lobby bar; in Monaco she walked by the harbor and went to the casino when they urged her to, feeling both restless and bored. At Elba, Hermia remained aboard, and when they reached the port of Rome, she more than half considered jumping ship. Therefore, when he came on deck for lifeboat drill, she could not quite believe it: the Gods of Coincidence changing the rules of the game.

She remembered he had said that once, when they first met in Cambridge. They had met three times that week, each time by accident, and Lawrence said he took this as an omen; they saw each other at the Fogg, and then again at Elsie's, and then outside the Loeb. Those encounters, however, had not been surprising; they shared a town and college and were walking the same streets. *This* felt truly accidental: the Gods of Coincidence rattling the dice and inviting her to play . . .

She did not want to bet on things or, again, to play. Watching Lawrence where he stood on deck, she remembered how he'd hurt her, once, and asked herself if he retained that power still. It did not seem likely. She was thicker-skinned by now and had been hurt much more by others since 1962. He shuffled through the lifeboat drill or made conversation in the dining room or sat in his chair in the Elsinore Lounge, looking anything but dangerous, and cloaked in his pale solitude. *Will I, won't I, should I?* Hermia asked herself, and could not decide.

She watched him watching her. She waited a third day. But then, in the Luparium, he'd seemed so lost and lonely, so utterly forlorn, she approached and reached to touch his sleeve. When he stared at her—this grown man gone speechless—it was as though no time had passed, no distance had been traversed. She caught her breath, her stomach dropped, her heart was in her throat. *Ridiculous*, thought Hermia, *I'm sixty-three years old.*

"What are you doing here?"

"What are *you* doing here?"

"The same as you." She tried to smile. "Admiring the view."

He colored. "Dirty pictures."

"Yes."

"The hell of a place to meet up with you, lady."

"Pompeii?"

He gestured. "Here."

"You mean, in a whorehouse?"

"On a guided tour." Lawrence tried a joke. "With, as the man selling postcards said, '*Feelthy* pictures stressing togetherness.'"

She did not laugh. "I mean, what brought you to the *Diana*?"

"My doctor. He said I should travel."

"Your doctor?"

"Wanted me to see the world . . ."

"You *used* to travel, didn't you? Or intended to, at any rate."

"Yes. But that was then." His face was changing as she watched—becoming youthful, softening. "And I've never been to Malta. Or Pompeii."

"Me either. Why a doctor?"

"Do you want lunch? A coffee, maybe?"

"It's good to see you," she ventured.

"And *you*. You look wonderful."

"No. No, I don't."

"You're here alone?"

"Alone," she said. "And you?"

"Not any longer. Not now."

—

That night they ate together at a table set for two. There was much to tell each other, wasn't there, said Lawrence, a deal of explaining to do. Well, not so much *explaining*, Hermia said, as filling in the blanks. She told him a little and kept back a lot, and Lawrence no doubt did the same; they got through the soup and the pasta and fish remembering what they had done in Cambridge and Truro together.

This was easy to talk about—courses of study and houses and friends, what happened to Will and Silvana, for instance, the ones they stayed in touch with and the ones they'd both lost touch with, the graduate school he'd attended, the jobs she'd held and quit. He had read about her father's death and asked about her mother—was she still alive? She said, "Mummy's living in England and a very old lady by now. She doesn't recognize me, or anyone, and hasn't done for years." Hermia asked about his parents, and he said they both were dead; they both had died at seventy-eight when his father had a heart attack and his mother a brain aneurysm later that same day. It was strange, said Lawrence. They hadn't spoken to each other except if it was absolutely necessary; they both had remarried and established other families, but in the end his parents died as though they shared a roof, a *fate*, and were inseparable; his mother had collapsed the night she heard the news.

Darko offered wine. She drank. They avoided the difficult subjects, the disappointment and trouble, the way things fell apart. Lawrence asked if she had children, and she told him yes, a daughter, and he said he had a daughter too and two sons by different wives. "Are you married now?" she asked him, and he answered, "No, are you?" She shook her head. There was, she said, so much to ask, and he said yes, much to tell. And something in the way he said this seemed so familiar she wanted to cry. Where has it gone, she asked him, where did it disappear to, and he asked her what she was talking about, and Hermia said, *"You know."* He did know, he told her, yes; then he advanced his hand and placed it on the tablecloth by the saltshaker and the spoon adjoining hers.

She left it there. It was too soon to take his hand. She remembered it had also been too soon the night of the cast party, although she'd let him kiss her then and promised they would meet that Saturday or Sunday. Then, when the weekend came at last and parietal hours permitted it, he had invited her—so willing, so trustful—to his second-floor bedroom in Claverly Hall, with the bark paintings he was proud of and that atrocious rug . . .

She remembered, she told Lawrence, everything. She remembered his bathtub, the pattern of cracks in the porcelain sink, the shirt he was wearing, the book by his bed. She was blessed, she told him, with a memory for details, cursed with it too; she had forgotten nothing, and he said he also had forgotten nothing, or anyhow nothing important. What day was it, Hermia asked him, and he said March twenty-first, the beginning of spring. "That was opening night," she corrected him, "but not the day we met. What was the name of the play?"

"I haven't forgotten," said Lawrence, "*The Flies* by Jean-Paul Sartre"—and she'd been the stage manager. "Who directed it?" she asked, and Lawrence said, "That's what I mean, I mean he was nothing important."

"We were so innocent," she said, "so hopeful then," and he said yes. "I have to ask you this," she asked. "You're not, are you, Republican?" And he said of course not, no, and she said, well, *that* was a relief. They were—she tried to make a joke of it—in the same boat, weren't they, the two of them both passengers on a ship of fools . . .

"I'm very glad you're here," he said.

"Ships passing in the night. *Colliding* in the night."

"I'll see you tomorrow," he said.

———

The MS *Diana* was scheduled to arrive at Naxos the next morning, via the Strait of Messina, and at two o'clock they passed the isle of Stromboli. The volcano was—so the cruise director informed them on the intercom—a sight to see, and Hermia watched it through her window because she could not sleep. Vesuvius, if not extinct, had been cloud-covered, unremarkable, but this one showed a cone of flame erect in the night sky.

They off-loaded at Giardini Naxos, which was where, their guide announced, the first Greeks in Sicily had settled and prospered, but made the mistake of forming an alliance with their countrymen in the Peloponnesian War. It had been a fatal mistake. Dionysius, the tyrant of Siracusa, had razed the port and killed or sold off all the Greeks, and the few who escaped hid in the hills and only centuries later did their descendants dare once again to make the settlement home. "Here is your third volcano," said the guide. "Here behind you on the left is Mount Etna, where the Titans lie, and these days there is a lava flow to keep us—how do you say?—honest. We have an expression in Sicily: stay mindful of—keep always in your mind the anger of—the gods."

She was sitting next to Lawrence, who made a show of nonchalance. He held out his hand to help her get into and out of the tender, then up the tour bus steps. The bus growled up steep switchbacks to the town of Taormina and disgorged them at the entrance gate; they walked past restaurants and curio shops. This time, however, the sun was out and the village, he said, seemed authentic; had she taken the tour of Capri?

Hermia shook her head. "I stayed aboard. I was having, well, a migraine, and it didn't look like a whole lot of fun, but *this* is better, not too overrun."

"The season's almost over. And there's the amphitheater entrance up ahead"—Lawrence pointed down the street.

"Have you been reading the guidebook," she asked, "or were you here before?"

"Years ago. When I was first in Italy."

"Oh? What year was that?"

He looked at her—one eye closed, his Borsalino tilted jauntily—and said, "I can't remember." He was teasing her, she understood, about her claim at dinner to have forgotten nothing . . .

"It doesn't matter?"

"1962. And the director's name was Greg. The one who did *The Flies.*"

They reached the amphitheater. The night before there must have been a party, or some sort of concert, because teams of workers were cleaning off a raised wooden stage and dismantling loudspeakers and lights. The two of them climbed to the top rank of seats: stone benches cool in the sun. From this vantage they could see the sea, the pillars and brickwork and cypress trees in the distance and the slope of Mount Etna beyond.

Hermia took photographs. They sat. Lawrence pointed to the open space in the high wall opposite and said that was the place the Turks began breaching the structure, knocking it down, but thank heaven for the nineteenth century, its devotion to picturesque ruins, or maybe just a lack of funds, because otherwise some officious someone would have insisted they fill in the gaps and we'd have no such sight line. It's the evidenced *absence* of closure we like; the view *between* pillars intrigues. An incomplete circle compels our attention much more than the one that's complete.

Then he was drawing a distinction between the ancient Greeks and Romans; the Greeks, he said, used such a space for politics and theater, and one informed the other, so when the citizens of Athens or in this case Taormina gathered to witness the Oedipus plays, they were engaged in civic action and democratic governance as well as entertainment. The Romans, though, preferred blood sports, and for obvious reasons—you don't want to let the lions escape or, for that matter, gladiators. You dig a moat and increase the height of the walls that contain them. They were spectacular engineers, the Romans, but this never could have been an authentic colosseum; the real word, Lawrence continued, for colosseum is "circus," Circus Maximus, the one in Rome is called the Theatre of Vespasian, and it isn't all that clear if the sign for mercy would have been a thumbs-up or down. Thumbs-up, he said, is understood to mean "Good news" and thumbs-down "Bad," but it might just as well have been the reverse, signifying "Die," not "Live," because the emperor would have known the crowd was hoping for the chance to see violent death: a slaughter, not reprieve. And so, thumbs-down might well have been a way of saying, "Sorry, folks, I pardon the life of this fighter. I don't give permission to kill."

He went on and on in this fashion, not exactly lecturing but not not-lecturing her either, as though silence between them had become fraught and required the safeguard of speech. She did not require it. She looked at the cords of his throat, the underside of his chin where that morning he'd shaved sloppily and the stubble came in white. She wanted to tell him not to be nervous, not to impress her with all that he knew, and remembered, of a sudden, their first shared coffee in the coffee shop; he'd talked about his hope to be an architect, or maybe an urban designer, attempting to impress her also then . . .

"It's strange," she said.

"What?"

"*The Flies*. I was thinking about it: Orestes."

"Yes, the *Oresteia*. Why?"

"They might have performed it right here way back when."

"That's true," he said. "They probably would have. Not the play by Sartre, though."

"No. Was it the Blue Parrot or Casablanca?"

"Casablanca was the coffee shop. And the Blue Parrot was the bar, I think."

"You do remember, don't you?"

"Yes. You were taking a spot quiz on Rubens."

"I loved you very much," she said. "I don't think I really knew it then. Or understood it, really. But I loved you very much."

This silenced him. He took her hand. She let him hold it, squeeze it, and studied the liver spots and network of veins and his wrinkled knuckles, the fingernails trimmed roughly and the cuticles he bit. A mist was rising from the sea and the light changed register; the construction crew beneath them was sitting, drinking coffee, and somewhere a radio played. She hadn't meant to use the word, had not been thinking *Love, my love*, but the past tense—*I loved you*—afforded a kind of protection, and she was not sorry to have called his chattering bluff. If nothing else, she told herself, it made their conversation serious; she'd altered the rules of the game.

Lawrence looked at her. His pale blue eyes were watering, and hair sprouted from his ears. "Say that again," he said.

"I don't think I really knew it. It was, well, puppy love maybe— not the first time, but the first *real* time. They say you don't ever get over it."

"No."

"No, you don't get over it, or no, you don't agree?"

"No, you don't get over it."

Her temper flared. "Well, *I* did. I got over and over and over it, friend. Don't flatter yourself."

He squeezed her hand. "I was agreeing with you, Hermia. We don't ever really get over it."

"Bullshit. Or, as you Romantics say"—she tried an English accent—"twaddle, poppycock. A *crock*."

"Well"—Lawrence stood—"thanks for the memories."

She'd hurt him, she saw; she had managed after all to pierce his smug assurance. "And that girl of yours upstairs, Charette, I *told* you I remember . . ."

"Bill . . ."

Now Hermia wanted to cry. Where had it come from, this storm of emotion, this idiotic shifting from sorrow to rage? She felt adrift, not tethered; she was veering wildly back and forth between her pleasure in his presence and old anger at his absence, and she did not want or need a lecture on the history of amphitheaters and their reconstruction. Clouds scudded through the sky. She wanted to talk about what had gone wrong, not the architectural distinction between a circus and a colosseum, as if any of that mattered, as if all they were doing was dancing around what neither was willing to say.

"Say it," urged Hermia, "*say* it," and he asked her, "What?"

"Oh, Jesus, I don't know. Say something that *matters*."

"I thought I was dying."

So now it was she who fell silent. The radio bleated beneath them, then squawked.

"When?"

"Not when I saw you," said Lawrence. "This summer. Last July."

"Of what?"

"Heart trouble. Turns out I was wrong. I'm fine, I'll be just fine, the doctors are pleased with themselves."

She rose from the bench to his side. In the middle distance gulls were circling, swooping, and the umbrella pines had turned gray. She willed herself to breathe, to not faint or slap or embrace him or do anything other than stand there on the topmost stair while she fought for composure and found it: a middle-aged woman in Italy, not being stupid, not hysterical, not anything other than calm.

"A transplant? A heart bypass?"

"Not even that." He spread his hands, sheepish. "An angioplasty—you know, the balloon. Ream it out and send the patient home. I'm fine."

"Let's have some lunch," said Hermia. "A great big juicy piece of beefsteak, if they have one here in Sicily, and a hunk of cheese."

He smiled. He touched her arm. They made their way back into town.

—

That afternoon she kept away; her headache returned. That night they ate together again, but this time at a large table; she and Lawrence made conversation about Taormina and Etna and the cities in America where the other couples lived. One man said, "We're from Columbus, Ohio, our names are Dick and Jane. Oh, we know that's just a joke—you remember the movie, don't you, *Fun with*

Dick and Jane—and our real names are Richard and Janet but, hey, nobody's perfect. The point is *everybody* in Ohio has tied yellow ribbons around their trees and wants to bring our boys home. But only after victory, after we've made certain Saddam can't try another 9/11 or ever be able to hit us again."

Lawrence objected. Saddam Hussein had nothing to do with the World Trade Center, he said, or Al Qaeda or Osama bin Laden or WMDs. The whole thing was a put-up job, an act of aggression with blinders. "I hope we can talk about this and not be angry with each other," he told Dick and Jane, "and I know I won't change your opinion about chances of peace in Iraq. But it's getting harder and harder to see a way out, and this has been"—he spread his hands—"a great mistake we've made."

Hermia drained her glass. "You two tree huggers," said Dick, "you're both so scared of progress, but don't be a pair of pessimists, it's not the American way. The American way is be hopeful, is *act*; it's fix a problem when you see it, and there *was* a problem there. Whatever way you cut it, we're making the world better, a safe place for democracy; bottom line is it had to be done. Our boy will win the election and it will turn out fine."

Lawrence was undeterred. "You're right that I'm a pessimist, but you're being optimistic," he told the table over apple crisp. "Iraq has been a hornet's nest, a can of worms. This war has been a terrible mistake, and the thing is to dare to admit it. The whole world was with us on 9/12, completely in America's camp, and now it's completely against . . ."

Hermia went up on deck. The MS *Diana* left Naxos at nine, and the high slopes of Mount Etna glowed, a fulmination in the sky made roseate by smoke. She had been away for ten days. The next port of call would be Siracusa; the next destination was Porto Empedocle, and the day after that would be Malta. They would visit museums and temples and shops; she reminded herself not to return empty-handed but to buy souvenirs. She could envision the end of the trip, the flight from Valletta to Boston, and did not want to play the fool or indulge in a shipboard romance.

That was, she knew, the term for it: "shipboard romance." It was what the widows dreamed of, and the divorcées and unattached: a caricature fueled by yearning and, here on the Mediterranean, wine. Behind her in the Elsinore Lounge stood passengers drinking and laughing. They were playing Parcheesi, or Scrabble, or hearts, and asking Marko the bartender if he knew the words to "Melancholy Baby" or could play "Hail to the Victors" on his acoustic guitar. They were tapping their sandals and snapping their fingers and chorusing "One for the Road."

She could not bear it, not abide it; she had been alone too long to yield her hard-earned privacy. From her safe vantage on the deck the lava flow looked beautiful; it would not look that way, she knew, if near at hand. She went to bed at nine o'clock and slept a dreamless sleep.

—

In the morning, however, the sun was bright and the port of Siracusa—with its seawalls and churches and sailboats, the busy hum of commerce—made Hermia, though stalled in traffic, happy; once more they sat together on the bus. Once more they had a tour guide, a short plump man named Luigi, who spoke through a microphone about the history of ruins and apartment buildings and the rock quarries they passed. In heavily accented English he joked about the Jolly Hotel and the way it earned its name; he pointed to a church and said it resembled an orange; then he made jokes about the Mafia and bad Italian drivers and the *dolce farniente* of traffic police.

He looked just like Danny DeVito, said Lawrence, a dead

ringer for Danny DeVito, and Hermia agreed. Then in the cave where, rumor had it, the ancient tyrant Dionysius could hear each whispered secret because the acoustics were perfect and the echoes carried, Luigi sang "Santa Lucia." He took off his hat and fanned himself with a white crumpled handkerchief and held the high notes tremblingly, then bowed. "I am," he said, "not Pavarotti but *Povarotti*; the other one is big and rich, and I am small and poor. But you see we both are fat."

They drove to the old part of town, then left the tour bus and walked. Luigi showed them the cathedral that had also been a temple, and how the Greek pillars supported the roof of the church; it first had been a temple, next a Byzantine church, next a Muslim mosque; then, when it was a church again, the motif was Baroque. "In here I must not sing," said Luigi. "In here I must be quiet, and we must be grateful everyone still worships. Otherwise this building would be pillaged like the world."

"Did he say 'pillaged like the world'?" asked Hermia.

Lawrence took her hand. "It's not," he said, "so terrifying."

"What?"

"Beginning again. People do it, you know."

"Begin again?"

He nodded. "I mean, every time I turn around I hear a story about high school sweethearts who meet after many years— *decades*—at their high school reunion. Or at kindergarten on grandparents' day. Or they call each other up after failed marriages. Or they're widowers or widowed and meet again at the funeral home—you know."

"I don't know, no."

"They hunt each other on the Internet. They subscribe to the same dating service, or use the same search engine; they meet each other at the retirement party of friends. Or somebody's birthday party. I hear about it all the time . . ."

"All right," she admitted. "I Googled you."

He smiled. "Is that a verb?"

"I did," she said. "I looked you up."

"And what did you find there?"

"Your picture. Your address. A faculty blurb from the School of Art and Design. A list of your prizes and books."

"I know what Google means," he said. "And I thought about tracking you also that way, and wanted to write you often."

"You're not a very good liar."

"What I'm trying to say," Lawrence said, "is there's nothing surprising about reconnecting. Connecting. It's a thing you don't get over—or at least *I* don't, I never did—having been together way back when."

Now, without warning, her anger returned. "'Been together,' what's that mean?"

He flushed. "You know what I'm trying to say."

"No, Lawrence. *Say* it. I *know* you, remember. You mean you spend your nights remembering women you slept with . . ."

"Is that what it sounds like?"

"It is. It does." She mimicked him. "'. . . *having been together way back when.'* Well, la-di-da."

They were walking now back to the ship. "You're a difficult person to talk to," he said. "You're not, are you, making this easy."

"And exactly why should I?" she asked. "'Connecting, reconnecting' . . . Oh, give me a break, Lawrence."

The MS *Diana* came into view. She took photographs. There was a gangplank, a potted palm in front of it, a roped enclosure through which they both passed.

"So why *did* you Google me?"

"I told you," said Hermia. "Love."

———

There was, she knew, no way around it; the only way was through. It was a thicket, a dark wood; it was undiscovered country, and she did not know the way. This courtship—if it was a courtship, if what they were doing was courting each other—had caught her completely off guard. She went to her cabin alone.

The night before, at dinner, when Lawrence had been saying what Hermia also thought, it was as if their solidarity had needed no explaining: he'd spoken for them both. Dick and Jane, she understood, had seen them as a couple and believed them to be partners and, at least in terms of politics, allied. She knew next to nothing about him, as Lawrence knew little or nothing about her present life. But of *course* he would think the war was misguided; of *course* he was a liberal and not conservative, a Democrat and not Republican. The boy she used to sleep with was someone she had recognized and with whom she had belonged.

In the Valley of the Temples they walked together next morning; Porto Empedocle and Agrigento took her breath away. Again the day dawned brightly; again they disembarked and sat together on the bus and were herded by a tour guide through a field of ruins and temples and rock. Once more Lawrence tried to impress her, pointing out the plinths and capitals, describing the tricks of perspective that Greek architects had utilized: the way the columns appear of a uniform width, for example, but bulk slightly in the middle—the word for it's "entasis," he said—the way the columns lean but look perpendicular.

She let him talk. To silence him, she took his hand. When he asked what she was thinking, she said, oh, how long ago the people came to worship here, how many centuries ago they stared at the same sea.

And the water was much nearer then, said Lawrence. It's been withdrawing since time out of mind, and ebbing away from— what's that word in "Dover Beach" . . . ?

"The shingle. I *am* glad to see you again."

"I thought about you often, and I know it sounds romantic but I did think about it. Us."

"You kiss me at this point, I think. We're staging a scene, and we kiss."

Now it was Lawrence who drew back. "You're joking, right?"

"I'm joking, right."

"Well, wait till I adjust my teeth. Or brush them, anyway."

"All right," she said. "We're not staging a scene."

"I didn't think so, no."

She kissed him then, but briefly, on the cheek. He smelled of—what was it?—Paco Rabanne and what he had eaten for breakfast and a compound of toothpaste and sweat. He smelled of caution and age. With her lips she brushed his other cheek and trailed her fingertips across the rough white stubble and, stepping back, smiled. "Oh, but you do feel familiar."

———

That night the captain gave his farewell banquet; Hermia had eaten it before. The meal repeated, course for course, what she was served the night they docked in Rome, when passengers were disembarking at Civitavecchia. The waiters dressed in native costumes and sang drinking songs. They wore skirts and brightly colored caps and played what sounded to her like the ukulele; they said these melodies come from the Carpathian Mountains and villages in Croatia, and the captain wished everyone wonderful trip and said, well, the weather was fine. "You everybody did your best," he said, "to wish for perfect weather, and I am perfectly happy tonight because the moon is shining so my heart is also full." They ate lobster bisque and caviar and fish, and by this stage in the journey Darko knew his customers; he poured Lawrence glass after glass of red wine.

She herself was drinking white. "Between the two of us," he said, "we lick the platter clean."

"Between the two of us," she said, "except for meeting you, of course, I more or less hated this cruise."

"No."

"Veramente."

"But think of all you've learned," he said, "about Greek and Roman architecture. The difference between Doric and Ionic and Corinthian . . ."

"Don't start. I'm being serious."

"Do you think we would have met again in some other context?" He raised his glass. "Or in any other way?"

"Does it matter?"

"Not really, no."

"Let's dance."

So they took their places on the cleared floor of the Elsinore Lounge, where couples were doing the fox-trot; others remained at the bar. One of the waiters was playing guitar, and one of them sat at the keyboard, with fixed smiles on their faces and their feet tapping the beat. Lawrence bowed. He held out his arms; they embraced. At first they were clumsy together, then less clumsy, then assured. She gave herself over to music, the tinny percussive mechanical tune, and something in Hermia quickened, and she twitched her hips. It was, she knew, the moonlight, the wine, the pleasure of dancing and all the old rhythmic enticements: the way his hand felt on the small of her back, the way he focused, frowning, guiding her, one, *two*, and three, and *four*. Then Dick and Jane were next to them and smiling, sweating, thumping up and down, and then they were out on the deck.

"Do you remember," Lawrence asked, "'As Time Goes By'?"

"Of course I do."

"Your cabin or mine?"

She stared at him: he was making a joke. He was, she saw, as uncertain as she; he did not know what to do next. The MS *Diana* was making for Malta, its engines thrumming, its wake white, and she was staring out to sea and having her shipboard romance. For an instant, Hermia shut her eyes and leaned against him, hip to hip, and he put his arm around her waist. It was, she knew, the thing to do; it was what she'd expected since she'd first seen Lawrence days before when he stood across from her by Lifeboat Station #6. She lifted her head for a kiss.

And then she saw Patricia. Her daughter danced along the waves; her daughter rode beside her, skimming the bright spume. The girl was dressed in black, as if for a recital, and her hair was cropped yet billowing, arms outstretched as if to play. Her feet in patent leather pumps kept pace effortlessly on the water—suspended there, mouth pursed in concentration. Her neck was bent. As though she were a seabird and the *Diana* a part of the flock, her daughter glided a hundred yards off—dipping, swooping, hovering—and would not go away.

She screamed; she could hear herself scream.

"What is it?" Lawrence asked. "What's wrong?"

"I've seen a ghost," Hermia said.

VI
—
1977–1987

Where she went was down the street. Her friends Ellen and Robert Oppenheim had known about her trouble, and they were ready to help. The couple made her welcome, with a room prepared for her and her daughter; they offered Hermia Valium and waited by the bedside until she fell asleep. That night she dreamed of Truro, of the time when she was young, and free, and there had been no damage. When she awoke in the morning, with Patricia safely next to her, thumb in her mouth, her black curls damp from sleep sweat, she felt as though they had escaped from a looming danger, and her own cheeks were wet.

On Friday they drove to Vermont. Their house in Arlington was Hermia's to use, the Oppenheims assured her, a place she could be safe. Robert was a therapist, a specialist in family counseling, and he repeated she'd done the right thing. A psychotic break has long-term implications, and recovery takes time; although he would no doubt apologize and try to win her back, her husband had entered a fugue state; Paul was taking acid—wasn't he?—and had had a bad trip. Ellen agreed with this, nodding her head; they all had seen it coming, and Hermia had been at risk. Right now the man was dangerous, said Ellen, and she should stay away.

And so her long exile began. After the first weekend the Oppenheims left her alone with keys to the house and a Jeep they kept in the garage and, repeating that Hermia had no reason to worry, returned to their jobs in New York. There was, they insisted, no way Paul could track her down, and anyhow he posed no present threat. "This whole episode was bound to happen," said Robert. "It's been in the cards for years, and you mustn't blame yourself. We'll make certain he gets help."

She and Patsy stayed in their benefactors' farmhouse off the River Road. The building was white clapboard, with green shutters and four chimneys and a picket fence; its front door displayed the number 1828. The antique furniture was good, the wide pine floors had been burnished with wax, and the cupboards and closets were full. Split-leaf maples flared above the gray slate roof. To Hermia it seemed as though she'd stepped into a canvas straight out of Grandma Moses: steep-pitched hills, the rock-rimmed pasture where the neighbors' horses grazed, the plumes of chimney smoke.

She did try not to worry. She drove to the Enchanted Garden ten miles north in Manchester and bought her daughter a dollhouse and elaborate series of dolls. She bought a television so they could watch *Sesame Street* together, and *Mister Rogers' Neighborhood*; when Mister Rogers declared how pleased he was to be their neighbor—taking off his shoes and putting on his slippers and buttoning his cardigan—Patsy sang along with him, in perfect pitch, clapping her hands when he clapped. The child was a glad chatterbox, burbling to herself all day and busy with crayons or dolls. She peered at books intently and loved to turn their pages and knew *Goodnight Moon* and *The Runaway Bunny* by heart.

Still, Hermia did worry. She wanted to forget the past; she could not believe Paul would leave them alone or just let her live. In the beginning she was always frightened—afraid of the doorbell or sudden night noise, convinced that he had followed her; outside, she wore dark glasses and a hat. She saw him, she was certain, at the post office or gas station or the convenience store. When she closed her eyes at night, she saw her husband glaring at her, spittle on his lips. All that first autumn she feared he would find them, his knife outthrust and jealousy intact.

But the Oppenheims assured her Paul was getting help. He had been hospitalized. He was heavily sedated and on medication when released, and then she learned he had returned to England and resumed his employment at Reuters. In February, from London, he wrote to apologize. Paul sent the letter to her lawyer, not asking for forgiveness because—or so he wrote—what he'd done was unforgivable, but he had come to understand their marriage had been ill-advised. He wasn't, he understood finally, the marrying kind or cut out to be a father, and he hoped she would forgive him and perhaps think kindly of him or at least a little better. He wished the two of them well.

There was a legal injunction, a series of letters from doctors and lawyers, and, in the end, a divorce. This procedure took two years. During that time she and her daughter did everything together and went everywhere together and slept in the same room. She told her stepfather and mother often, on the telephone, how hard she'd tried to make the marriage work, but anyhow had failed. By the time Paul moved to Tokyo and Hermia felt safe again, there was a playgroup for Patricia and, the next September, a nursery school down the road.

———

Time passed. Unwilling to relinquish it, she rented out the house in Truro but gave up her apartment in New York. Because she could not stay at the Oppenheims' indefinitely, she rented and then purchased her own home. It was half a mile from her friends' house, across from riding stables, and Hermia began to think of Arlington less as a place of refuge than as a place to remain.

The village was quiet; fishermen fished there for trout. More farm machines and pickup trucks than cars drove past the house. The Battenkill River was famous, and there was a covered bridge and sugaring house: scene after scene of country life untroubled and unchanged. What changed was the weather, the wind.

On a level patch of lawn behind the porch, she installed a ChildLife jungle gym.

She pushed Patsy on the swing and raised her up and dropped her down on the wooden seesaw and watched her daughter clamber up the ladders and dangle from the balance bars and slide down the slide. The spokes were green, the platforms brown, and it felt as though they had established a shared playground by the rhubarb bed. When autumn came, they raked and raked, and Patsy loved to jump into the maple-leaf piles and be buried there.

Men and women of the village were polite but not intrusive; they plowed her drive and fixed the furnace when the heat shut down. They smiled at her and waved from the front stoop when she drove by or, if they passed her on a tractor, tipped their Agway caps. Mother and daughter bought strawberries and blueberries and fresh-picked corn from roadside stands; they bought doughnuts and apple cider from the cider mill. Hermia planted a garden and had the house painted and, as before in Truro, trained pink climbing roses along the picket fence.

She reveled in the silence. She had had enough of noise, the whir and bustle of machinery, the sirens and traffic sounds all through the night. She had had more than enough of Manhattan, the "players"—in her parents' word—and the runners-up and also-rans and the getting and spending and sex. It was not so much the isolation as the privacy that suited her, a New England reticence she liked. She wanted to be with her daughter, only her daughter;

they could shuck peas or corn, not speaking, or watch the sunset or TV together in a companionable absence of speech, a silence that made her feel calm.

People left the two of them alone. She and Patricia had a private language, a way of knowing without asking how the other one was feeling and what the other was thinking—a sigh or a smile meant "I'm hungry," a tilt of the head meant "I'm full." They had an unspoken system of signs: "Let's go for a walk. Let's go home." And even when they disagreed—if Pat-a-cake wanted to watch cartoons but Hermia wanted to go to the pond or, the other way around, when she just felt like staying home but the girl preferred bike riding—the disagreement was minor, a momentary shift of balance until balance was restored.

From time to time she felt her daughter should have someone else to play with, or that she herself required adult company and was growing old and dull, but then a playmate of Patsy's would come to the house after nursery school and the visit would suffice. It was astonishing how long a conversation lasted at the butcher's, or at the post office counter. An exchange about the weather—about the heat or rain or need for rain, about the snow or lack of snow—could slake her desire for talk. Most weekends the Oppenheims drove up from New York, and Hermia would see them and their company for lunch or at a picnic, and the social interaction would last her the whole week.

"Are you still happy here?" asked Ellen. "Are you getting enough stimulation?"

"Do you mean am I lonely? No."

"I'm not talking about, oh, the movies. Or Broadway or museums . . ."

"Then what *are* you talking about?" Lately she could hear in her own voice her mother's forthright bluntness, the old arrogant directness.

"Nothing special." Ellen spread her hands. "Just I myself would go crazy here. Without, you know . . ."

"I don't, no, know. Without a lover? A vibrator?"

Her friend looked shocked. Then Ellen collected herself: "Next weekend we're bringing a guest. You remember him, Harrison Laughlin. He's just been divorced and is dreaming of the country in leaf season—they're all leaf peekers in October, aren't they?—and owns two of your dad's paintings of the dunes and asked, specifically asked me, if maybe you would come to dinner."

"The two of us? Can I bring Patsy?"

"If you prefer . . ."

"I haven't found a babysitter yet."

"Oh?"

"Let me try to explain it," Hermia said. "This morning we were making pies—because Patsy likes to roll the dough, she's getting good at it—and she looks up at me and says, this five-year-old, 'Mommy, I love doing this, because it starts out one thing and it ends up another thing, but both of them are tasty. They change but they're really the same.' And I thought to myself, 'Hey, that's not bad, that's quite an observation,' and she said, 'But the *real* thing is I watched these apples since they were blossoms, just part of a tree.' And I said, 'You're Golden Delicious, you're good enough to eat,' and we laughed and laughed together, and so no, I don't need company and don't feel alone."

"Still . . ." Ellen said.

"All right. You're kind to ask. We'll come."

—

Harrison Laughlin was forty, an associate professor of English at Columbia, and when she told him she had written her thesis, way back when, on *The Winter's Tale* and *Cymbeline*, he took out his pipe and filled it with a pinch of nonexistent tobacco and said, "Good for you." He was attempting, he told her, to stop smoking, and he had a new system and was certain it would work. His strategy was to go through the motions of cleaning out his pipe stem and filling his pipe bowl and tamping it down and lighting a match but only in mimicry, only as a way of imitating the procedure and calling up the memory without any tobacco involved. This provided, he told Hermia, the satisfaction of reenactment, and he felt he got a smoker's rush by going through the motions and inhaling air. So too with Shakespeare, Harrison said, there were ritual observances in the late plays and romances that were mostly gestural—"Think of the masque, for example, in *The Tempest* or the pageantry of *Pericles* and you'll perhaps see what I mean."

She did not see. She told herself that this was why she avoided company—the babble and prattle and *me me me me*. For Ellen's sake, and Robert's, she had taken some trouble with her appearance; she had used lipstick and mascara for the first time since August, and she wore the purple shot-silk scoop-neck blouse Ellen had given her for her birthday. She could see the impression she made on their guest, the masculine *quack-quack* and *me me me*, and wished she had not bothered, had decided not to come.

The dinner, however, was good. Ellen was a first-rate cook, and she produced *coquilles St. Jacques* and then *truite amandine*; they drank two bottles of Pouilly-Fumé. As always, the Oppenheims talked about retirement, what it would mean to live full-time in Arlington, and as always concluded that they loved the city and their work—Robert more so than Ellen, who could take her job or leave it—and weren't yet ready to move.

"And you?" asked Laughlin, "any regrets?"

She shook her head.

"Hiding your light," he said, "under a bushel." He laughed.

Though she had trained herself to not talk about her father, Hermia found herself discussing him nonetheless: her dinner partner flattered her because of her last name. He spoke about the oils he owned, the two renditions of the dunes her father had made in 1957, and how much he admired them. The impasto of the beach, the very *essence* of the beach, was something he consulted daily and could not imagine not seeing, that column of light bisecting the dunes, the thick white line perpendicular to green and yellow waves, and he had fairly *bankrupted* himself acquiring them at André Emmerich. But it had been, of course, an excellent purchase, a spectacular investment, and if Hermia felt the need or desire to see them again, he would be delighted to invite her for a viewing the next time she came to the city; it would be a pleasure and they could have lunch.

Patsy was sleeping in front of the fire, holding her blanket and sprawled on the Oppenheims' couch; they would be going home soon. She had fallen asleep with a great noiseless crash, turning the pages of her Dr. Seuss book and then no longer turning them but stretched spread-eagle on the pillow, her blanket at the corner of her mouth.

Robert offered his dinner guests cognac and *poiré*. Hermia drank *poiré*. They talked about the traffic in leaf season; this afternoon, driving up from the city had taken them six hours, though on an average weekend they required only four. But it was worth it, said Harrison Laughlin, every minute has been worth it, and that last hour on Route 7 had been just spectacular. Was the term for it "leaf peeper" or "leaf peeker" or "leaf peaker," *p-e-a*?

The Oppenheims retreated to the kitchen, insisting they would do the cleaning up, they preferred to finish together, they had their own private system, and it had been a long day. "I'll take Patricia home in a minute," said Hermia, "but I do hate to wake her," and Ellen said, "Just let her sleep."

In the fireplace logs crackled and a piece of birch bark flared. "Good night, you two," said Robert, yawning, stretching ostentatiously, and Hermia said the trout was excellent, thanks for everything, everything, and "I'll drive home soon, I promise." Harrison Laughlin was saying, "I don't know if you've ever seen the trees in France with bottles tied over the blossoms—a ship in a bottle, so to speak, except the masts are growing fruit and it's beautiful, spectacular. An orchard full of glass. And then of course once the apple or pear is safely in the bottle they add what we're drinking, a brandy. *Santé.*" He raised his snifter and drank.

It was, she knew, her decision; he would take no for an answer. She could gather up Patsy and leave. She would not bring this noisy stranger home or permit him in their private space, but it was tempting anyhow to let the flirtation continue. If she did continue—listening to Laughlin and encouraging his talk about the English department, his prospect of tenure, his colleagues, his hopes for publication, his windfall from a bachelor uncle with which he'd bought her father's oils at Emmerich, his Columbia-owned apartment on Claremont Avenue now suddenly too big for him; then waiting for him to explain what had gone wrong with his marriage, how the ex-wife was not a subject he wanted to discuss, and then discussing it anyhow, her arrogance, her self-regard, how he himself refused to make aspersions or be negative and then making aspersions, being negative—she could foresee the result. There would, she knew, be a third glass of *poiré;* there would be his hand on her knee. Hermia could predict it all: the fireplace embers, the closed door of the library, the furtive grappling and clothes on the floor, the way the Oppenheims next morning would studiously avoid the subject of her behavior and offer her coffee and toast. Her home was inviolate, half a mile off, and all she had to do, she knew, was lift her daughter from the couch and say good night and go.

Nonetheless she fucked him. It seemed the thing to do. There was a friction, an itch to be rubbed, and though he himself was unfamiliar, the procedure felt familiar. It was over rapidly—a quick ejaculation, a small hot spurt along her legs—and then there were the sighs, the smiles, the protestations of devotion while she collected her clothing and woke her child and left.

—

That was the end of it, however; she had had enough. He did call in the morning, but Hermia claimed a headache, one of her migraines, and spent the afternoon in Manchester, buying a sweater for Patsy, avoiding the prospect of company and, when they came home again, not answering the phone. The next day they drove to Albany, watching *Snow White* and *Cinderella* and *Bambi* all in the same afternoon for a Disney children's special, and having dinner afterward and not returning to Arlington till night. By that time Laughlin and the Oppenheims had had to leave, and when Ellen returned the next weekend, she said, "You made quite an impression. He couldn't stop talking about you," and Hermia said apparently he likes to talk but please let's not discuss him, or what he wants, OK? and Ellen said OK.

It was 1981; she was thirty-nine years old. The countryside was changing, a place she no longer belonged. The more time she spent in Arlington, the more she saw its bigotry, the limits to the tolerance of those who mowed her lawn. What first had seemed a picturesque backwater now seemed merely backward, and cruel. This place, she told the Oppenheims, has come to feel provincial, and she did not like to think that she herself was living in the provinces or Pat had no friends. Therefore Hermia drove her daughter every morning to the village of North Bennington, fifteen minutes south, where education was progressive. The founders of the

Prospect School encouraged free expression, and the water table and the turtles were as important as arithmetic; during "quiet time" the students wrote down stories in their journals or built things out of clay. The teachers at the Prospect School wore homemade clothes and headbands and encouraged empathy with inanimate things; they would tell Pat the "hot water wants to be turned off" or, at the end of quiet time, that her cubbyhole "wants to be cleaned."

One of the teachers, Anne Martineau, lived in a commune in Pownal. She had long blond hair and sturdy legs and a German shepherd called Max who went with her everywhere; she said Pat had a special gift for music and had her mother noticed how she never missed a note or forgot a tune? Anne had been teaching for seventeen years, and she was certain, she told Hermia, this particular child has a gift.

Pat began to study piano, and Betsy Harrington, her piano teacher, also was impressed. The girl could memorize music, not taking any trouble over it; the notes stayed, she said, in her head. She played with concentration hour after hour: first improvising freely and then practicing her lesson book or the Czerny exercises, long arpeggios and plangent chords and, by her second year of study, Mozart. Hermia loved to listen and, just as important, to watch her straight-backed child enraptured on the piano stool, arms out and nimble-fingered. It was as though their silence had transposed itself to harmony, and Brahms or Grieg were visiting this child in thrall to song . . .

Betsy Harrington arranged a recital. There was a converted carriage barn across the street from the Prospect School, and it contained a Steinway grand; five piano students performed. The Carruthers twins played a thumping four-hand polka, the Cohen boy played a thick-fingered nocturne by Chopin, and teenage Katharine Spencer played a sonata by Liszt. A composer from Bennington College arrived and joined the audience; he was

Katharine Spencer's uncle and made a show of settling in—smiling, shaking hands. Anne Martineau and Max were also there, the great dog lying at his mistress's feet. It was a fine September afternoon, rain-rinsed and with a hint of chill, but Hermia was sweating; there were wooden folding chairs and a head-high vase of flowers and a table with cookies and punch.

Patricia came out and sat down. She wore a pearl necklace, a spray of roses in her hair, black pumps, and a white wide-skirted dress that buttoned in the front. She did not carry sheet music; stiffly she stared at the keyboard, then adjusted the height of the stool. For her part in the recital, she had selected Robert Schumann's *Kinderszenen*, and played with emphatic restraint. "Scenes from Childhood" filled the hall—the sweet simplicities and hints of sorrow yet to come. Swaying lightly to her own engendered rhythms, eyes halfway closed, head nodding, her daughter seemed to Hermia a creature from another world, a better world, a place where melody was everywhere and there could be no discord; when Patricia stood and curtsied, there was prolonged applause.

Afterward, they praised her. "So poised," said the composer from the college, "so self-assured and yet so young."

"It's not assurance," said his partner. "To me it's the reverse."

The two men faced each other—one white-haired and flamboyant, the other with a close-cropped head and wearing a black suit. "What are you saying, George? Don't be so utterly *runic*."

"It's a *lack* of self-awareness." George appealed to Hermia. "That's what's so charming, correct?"

"Vladimir Horowitz," said the composer, "called *Kinderszenen* the hardest piece in the repertoire to perform—not because of technical complexities but because of its emotional demands."

"Your daughter was splendid," said Betsy Harrington.

"Yes," said the men from the college. "She *must* continue her studies. She *must* be properly trained."

—

The following summer, therefore, Hermia sent her daughter off to camp. She did so with a heavy heart, a fear she both could name and not name that Patricia would be lost. She tried to hide this from the child and be enthusiastic because the piano teacher promised music camp would be just the thing. The Interlochen Arts Academy was on a lake in Michigan, and Betsy Harrington had sent young people there before; Hermia should think of this as a great opportunity and could be pleased and proud.

She did feel pleased and proud. She had produced this gifted girl, had done so by herself, and sooner or later it was bound to happen that her daughter would take wing. But it felt too soon, too rushed, and all spring Hermia was terrified, as she had been when first they moved and she feared her husband would find them. They had lived alone so long together in the house she could not bear to think about the prospect of true isolation when Patricia went to camp. She looked at maps of Michigan, at a place called Traverse City near enough to Interlochen so she could pay a visit, not just on parents' weekend but every other day. She imagined sitting outside the practice rooms, or in the hall where students played, or by the lake listening to and watching over the piano, not being in the way . . .

This would not, she knew, be possible. Their sanctuary had been breached; the place of their shared privacy was no longer private, or shared. As the date for departure approached, she felt her heart would crack. Having stitched her daughter's name into her shorts and towels and shirts and even on her bathing suit, for fear it would be lost, she packed Patricia's bags meticulously. She folded and refolded skirts and sweatshirts and a knitted cap for the cold nights, and Patricia's music books and the book about pioneer women and, for reassurance, her "blankety" with its frayed silk strip and wool worn thin from washing. She prepared a stack of postcards and envelopes with stamps, all preaddressed, and put them in a folder and the folder in the suitcase, with an *I Love You* sticker and her stuffed embroidered heart with the yellow *P*.

For breakfast on their final day she fixed everything her daughter liked—French toast and bacon, orange juice, hot chocolate—but neither of them ate a thing and, after twenty minutes, Hermia stopped pretending that they could. They walked across the meadow to the pond to say good-bye to the Muscovy ducks, and there were wildflowers everywhere and a groundhog and the blue sky she could not now take for granted. Making the drive to Albany, they arrived at the airport an hour early, in a thunderstorm, but the plane remained on schedule and there was no reprieve.

Patricia flew the first leg of the journey alone. The girl was traveling to Detroit Metro Airport, where she would meet a dozen other campers and a counselor, and they would proceed to Traverse City. A flight attendant greeted them at the US Airways counter and fastened a red ID tag and ribbon to her wrist.

"Don't worry, Mom," she said, voice quavering. "I'll be OK."

"Of course you will."

"I will."

"I worry anyhow," said Hermia. "I have to keep the airplane up."

"You're joking, right?" the flight attendant asked.

"I'm joking, right."

"I love you, Mom."

"Oh, I *adore* you, darling. Have a wonderful, wonderful time out there."

"I'll write."

"And I'll write *you*, I promise. Every day."

They embraced. It was, she knew, the end of the beginning, but it felt like the beginning of the end. She watched her daughter—so small, so young, so determined—walk to the door of the plane, then wave and disappear. Hermia waited while the airplane taxied to the runway and watched till it was airborne and made her way back to the parking lot, bereft.

Until she stopped sobbing, she sat in the car, resting her head on the wheel. Then, avoiding Route 7 and traffic, she drove the long way back to Arlington—leaving the Northway and winding through Mechanicville and Buskirk and Cambridge and along the Battenkill on Route 313. The skies had cleared, the river gleamed, but it made no difference; the passenger seat was empty where at noon it had been full.

At four o'clock she reached her house and walked through the rooms, arranging, rearranging things, keeping the airplane in the air and landing it safely on time. She called to make certain the plane was on time. For no reason she could understand she pictured herself a beginner, a girl studying in Cambridge all those years ago. In her head she heard plump Will again, his head thrown back, eyes shut, warbling, picking out the minor chords on his guitar in Irving Street. There had been a party; there was beer and marijuana and their host was singing mournfully:

> *I'm going away,*
> *For to stay,*
> *A little while . . .*

Anne Martineau called. She asked for a meeting with Hermia, a coffee at the Villager, where she confided there was trouble in the commune and she might need to move. There were these power players—"Well," Anne said, attempting to smile, "that's *my* side of the story, you might hear something different if you asked somebody else"—and they had made a grab for power. "But our whole idea, our *charter*, is that that's not acceptable, because if you stack a cord of wood, it doesn't mean you keep it for your own use only, and if you're working as a bookkeeper at the tanning factory in Pownal, you don't cook the books." She went on and on about the bad behavior of the man who owned the orchard, Mel, and how they used to live together but he'd become impossible, a kind of petty tyrant, a macrobiotic protofascist, and the point was, she admitted, that they had had the kind of set-to that required cooling down; she and Max were *personae non gratae*—well, Max wasn't a person, of course. They would probably want to keep Max. Anne rubbed her left wrist and wondered if, just for a day or two, while she was getting her feet on the ground and looking for a place to rent, she could borrow the spare room and crash in Arlington, out of harm's way for a while. The dog, she promised, would be no trouble, and she had her own station wagon and cooking utensils, and it was no emergency but she'd rather not sleep in the Ford.

Hermia said yes. She remembered how she too had needed sanctuary once, how the Oppenheims assisted her when she fled New York. Now it seemed her turn to help. Anne Martineau was grateful and arrived that evening, her station wagon stuffed with clothes and pots and pans, and she and Max moved into the house and made a welcome diversion. The day or two became a week; the week became a month.

Anne cooked. She made elaborate stews of vegetables and lentils, discoursing on each ingredient and their healthful properties and how the juice and spices interacted. She said, "You don't mind, do you?" and lit joss sticks in the living room and positioned her tin Buddha in the hall. When the mail was delivered, if there was news from Patricia—after Hermia had read the letter to herself twice, silently—the women discussed it and remembered being young, and how much they'd missed their mothers; if no postcard or letter arrived, they spoke about the heedlessness of youth.

As time wore on, they talked about their pasts. Anne was forthright, unabashed; she talked about the boys and, later on, the girls she'd had affairs with, the choices she'd made, and mistakes. Mel, for example, had been a mistake, with an ego that needed massaging nonstop, and this delusional sense of himself as a leader, a savior, this series of edicts he issued in Pownal—here she mimicked him—"'Don't worship Mammon or shave your legs or eat shellfish or *tref* and do everything just as I say . . .'"

The Martineau family came from East Lansing, and Anne herself had attended Interlochen Arts Academy, which is why she'd known Patricia belonged there, and agreed with Betsy Harrington— it was a dynamite place. "The north of Michigan is worth a visit, and you'll be glad to go; the thumb, they call it"—Anne spread her hand out and stuck up her thumb—"and Interlochen's right here. You'll *love* it," she told Hermia, "just the way Patricia does, a place where everyone believes their art's the only thing that matters."

"It's strange," mused Hermia. "My father was a painter, and my daughter's a musician, but I'm just a go-between, a necessary interval between the generation that produced me and the one I produced . . ."

They sat together at the kitchen table or on the west-facing porch, drinking tea and eating apples while the long days waned. Anne spoke about the pines and lake at Interlochen, how winters there are difficult and how much fun Hermia was going to have on her scheduled visit. Two nights before parents' weekend, however, she contracted a bad case of flu and was so violently sick to her stomach she could not leave her bed. Her fever climbed to 102; she sweated and shivered and was unable to fly and had to cancel the trip. Uncontrollably, she wept.

But Anne stayed by her bedside, nursing and consoling her, assuring her Patricia would be fine, just fine, and explaining to the counselors why Hermia had to stay home. When her daughter did return at last, at August's end—full of stories about water fights and bunk mates and new best friends from Chicago—she listened with amusement and, because her prodigy was still a child, relief. And when the Prospect School began, and Anne and Patricia and Max the German shepherd drove together every morning and back again each afternoon, Hermia remained at home, preparing dinner for the three of them, for only those hours alone.

VII
—
1964-1973

Lawrence applied to architecture schools and was accepted by three of them and, after some uncertainty, accepted the offer from Harvard; he had not planned to live again in Cambridge, but the terms of the offer were generous and the curriculum good. He found an apartment on Linnaean Street, behind the Radcliffe campus, and walked every morning to Robinson Hall, the Graduate School of Design. Making his way past Cambridge Common, he cut through Harvard Square and then Harvard Yard. On those mornings he had time to spare, he took the route through Radcliffe and looked up at what had been Hermia's window and asked himself idly where she might have gone and what she might be doing now and if he should try to find out.

The walk took eighteen minutes. The reek of tradition filled Robinson Hall: the names of great designers incised above the portals, the gooseneck lamps bent low above scarred wooden desks. Portraits of retired deans stared out at the corridors sightlessly; blueprints of gardens and buildings hung framed and preserved on the walls. He examined the school's history in glass-fronted freestanding cases: the drawings and scale models of what had been built before. When he had time, between classes, he walked across the street and visited the Fogg.

Lawrence lived alone. White-haired professors, girls with their book bags, Cambridge matrons with leashed dogs and plastic rain hats: all hurried by him in the morning and again at night. At times he saw Hermia coming toward him, or pedaling a bicycle, or lying down, sunning herself by the Charles—but it was never truly Hermia, her long-legged, dark-haired actual self, and he walked away.

In the pre-Classical period, he came to admire the Incas, the Egyptians, the Etruscans, and their methods of construction: their palaces and pyramids and tombs. Having learned the history of ancient Greece in terms of the terms of its structures, he absorbed the role of roof beams and the lintels and entablature. From his glossary he learned the definitions of such sequences as "narthex," "nave," and "niche."

But Lawrence focused much more closely on examples of modernist architecture; his studies at the GSD were future-facing ones. He took pleasure in technical drawings, the making of models and diazo prints; he studied the details of wiring and heat. In his class on urban design, he was compelled by the charged interaction between the three professions of architecture, landscape architecture, and urban planning itself. Le Corbusier's Carpenter Center for the Visual Arts loomed like a promise down the street: *Abandon all your ancient ways, ye who enter here.*

Those were the years at Harvard when the cutting edge that sliced through Cambridge seemed, in Dean Sert's curriculum, keen. Lawrence worked hard. He spent most of his time in studio, considering space *between* structures and learning to configure floor plans and develop a *parti*. The fruitful interaction of his three fields of study argued a pluralist agenda; painting and systems analysis could share a common roof.

One of his professors, Serge Chermayeff, had a house in Wellfleet, on a freshwater pond. In April he invited a handful of students to look at the modernist cottages of Breuer, Saltonstall, and Morton—their attention to siting and landscape, their methods of construction. The group drove to the Cape in three cars.

Chermayeff himself was an imposing presence, lean and aquiline. An associate of Gropius, he spoke with a strong Russian accent and somehow made their field trip feel like a favor conferred. His *Community and Privacy: Toward a New Architecture of Humanism*—written with Christopher Alexander—examined those configurations that distinguished the public from the private realm; he discoursed on the Bauhaus while they walked along the beach.

The day was bright and cold. One of the other students, in answer to a question from Chermayeff, spoke of the flotsam that defines society, the intersection of climate and topography of which settlements are made. A trading post, for instance, will become a city so long as the commodity it trades in proves of value, and so long as the supply continues. Or fails to meet demand, offered Lawrence; it has to be—or give the *impression* of being—scarce. Explain your point, Chermayeff said, and he found himself discussing diamonds, the way that the De Beers cartel, if he understood it correctly, had convinced the world that diamonds were rare, not plentiful, and therefore should be prized. In *fact* a diamond is no more precious than, say, a garnet or turquoise, but if you manage the market correctly, you can persuade the public it's a gem to treasure, a commodity to hoard. It's not so much the eye of the beholder as the bank account that counts. What does all this have to do with architecture, asked the professor, impatient, and Lawrence admitted: not much.

Gulls scattered, then settled behind him; a great blue heron flew past. There was driftwood on the beach. He was, he knew, near Truro, and he thought about his time with Hermia, the weekends they had spent nearby in 1962. He would continue his studies and, in time, complete them; he would become an architect and, in time, successful. But often, in the years to come, Lawrence remembered this landscape, the rotting weed and tide spawn, the students walking on ahead and cold wind in his hair.

———

He met Annie Gunderson at dinner at the Sievers'. She was blond and pert and committed, she informed the table, to social engineering—not B. F. Skinner or Karl Marx or any of those patriarch-determinist-authority types, but *voluntary* innovation, *voluntary* reconfiguration of the social contract. All social behavior is rooted, said Annie, in biological need.

"I'm not so sure," said Warren Anderson. "My own opinion is the reverse."

"Example?" asked Rick Herrick.

"Our society is organized to *counter* biological need. *That's* the social contract; it's what we agreed to when we came to this party in clothes."

"Speak for yourself," Annie said.

"If everyone followed their instinct"—Warren appealed to the table—"we'd be having food fights; we'd be jumping each other and humping each other and wiping ourselves with the tablecloth and stealing the silver instead."

"I *told* you we shouldn't invite him," said John Siever.

They laughed. These people were accustomed, or so it seemed to Lawrence, to debate. Over pasta and then spare ribs they argued politics, the sincerity of Lyndon Johnson, the "single gunman" theory offered up by the Warren Commission, and the management and prospects of war in Vietnam.

"Dystopia," Warren was saying. "It's not—by any stretch of the imagination—utopia. The social contract, I mean."

"But the female of the species"—Annie nodded at her hostess's dress—"may require multiple partners to ensure fertility. A stranger: a new male arrival, let's say, who doesn't belong to the pack. So the point of all our plumage is to cast it off."

"'Off, off, you lendings,'" said Brittany Siever. "That's *Lear.*"

"The heath scene, isn't it?" asked Rick. "'Pray you, undo this button . . .'"

"Did we finish the Chablis?"

"Don't get me wrong," continued Annie, smiling down the table at Brittany in her black dress. "I do, I just adore chiffon—the way the sleeves billow, the collar. All your decorative finery, the things we wear tonight. But it has more to do with Darwin: *un*natural selection . . ."

When Lawrence asked her what she meant, she smiled at him: "You'll see."

"Are we imagining the Great Society?" asked John Siever, serving apple pie.

"No, thank you," Annie said.

"Sex," announced Brittany Siever. "That's what she's been discussing. The politics of mating—the games people play, am I right?"

Lawrence accepted a slice.

"What else is new?" asked Warren Anderson. "It's what she's *always* discussing." He passed his plate.

"The social utility of attraction." Annie smiled again. Her teeth were white, her lipstick a bright pink. "Attractiveness. It's preening and planning and making the male of the species provide us with successors. So we can guarantee the next generation of women . . ."

"Bingo," agreed Julie Herrick. "You hit the nail on the head."

—

Annie lived off Central Square, in a second-floor apartment. There were kilim pillows on the floor and photographs of elephants and warriors in war paint hanging on the walls. There were photographs of her as a girl in what she said was Denmark, on a hillside surrounded by sheep. There was a photo also of her face enlarged to full-length mirror size, so the pores of her nose looked like craters and her cheeks a snowfield down which—when he focused on it—he saw minuscule skiers descending the slope. These had been added to the blown-up image with a fine-tipped pen, and there were dates on the skis: 7/12/66, 8/17/66, 9/5/66, 11/11/66 . . . beginning at her eyelashes and down to the top of her lip.

It was December twelfth, and cold; the radiators clanked. "You should bleed them," Lawrence said.

"Bleed?"

"At your service, ma'am." With his pocketknife he turned a set-screw, and the steam valve of the radiator hissed.

"That's very impressive," she said. She had moved to Cambridge from Chicago, where her family owned real estate, and was working for a partner of her father's. She was twenty-five, high-breasted, and described the work as boring, though it helped to pass the time; it's what we're after, isn't it, said Annie, a way to fill the week.

She offered him hash brownies, and he swallowed two. She was on the pill, she told him, and asked if he minded that she had had herpes; she was, she was sure of it, cured. The son of a bitch who had given her herpes worked in her real estate office, and she'd made certain he'd gotten the axe. "Not literally." She smiled. "But Daddy fired him after I asked."

"You're serious?"

"I'm serious." And then she laughed and laughed.

They drank. Annie asked, "What are you doing here, what are *we* doing here, not, I mean, in this apartment but walking up and down upon the earth?" Lawrence talked about design, his dream of building something that might make a difference, *would* make a difference to how people lived, our human impact on the planet and the way to contain urban sprawl.

The drugs were having their effect; he heard himself breathing as if underwater and what he said seemed profound. "Imagine for a moment you were living in a round house and not a square or rectangular space," Lawrence said. "Imagine what that does to physical orientation, the *shape* of social behavior: interaction, intercourse . . ."

"Interaction, is that what you call it?"

He smiled. "Why not?"

Sitting beside him on the couch, Annie leaned down and kicked off her shoes.

"It's maybe the hash talking," she said, "but I believe we've got something going, I thought so the minute I saw you. I saw the ring around your head, the light I mean, the *halo*."

"Not really a halo," said Lawrence, and she said, "That's good, that's a relief, I like the way you wear those pants, why don't you take them off?"

"With all those ski bums watching?"

"You noticed, didn't you, you're a noticing person, I like that." She leaned toward him and stuck out her tongue and wetly licked his ear. "The dates are my own private record, a way of keeping track. I can add you in the morning if you want."

———

In the morning, however, she seemed subdued, and when he asked her if she felt all right, she shook her head.

"What's wrong?" he asked, and she said, "It felt automatic, didn't it, it all seemed so predictable."

"What?"

"The way we got together. What we're going to do together."

"How do you mean?"

"Get married. Have a child."

"Excuse me?"

"Were you listening to me last night? *Weren't* you?"

He nodded.

"I saw it the minute you came in the room. And when you sat down at the table, their table, that terrible table, just listen to me—" She counted it out on her fingers. "Six *T*s in a row at the start of a word—no, *seven*, that *terrible* table—I felt, hey, whoa, wait just a minute, girl, hold on to your horses, he's *yours*. *Mine*. It's what I mean by a halo, it's what I saw when you walked in the room. Our marriage, the result of it, a baby girl . . ."

He wondered, was she joking? then understood that she was serious and wondered, was she sane? Annie stared at her fingernails, tears in her eyes. "Blue Mountain Coffee?" she inquired, mimicking John Siever. "Or would you prefer Purple Hill? Turquoise Valley? Myself, I serve Sanka, OK?"

She was the youngest child of three, and by the time that she was born, said Annie, her parents had a warring truce, a household arrangement as to who would be responsible for what. Both her parents had agreed she needed some other someone's attention, so she had a succession of nannies—"That's what Mummy called them," she told Lawrence, "*nannies, ninnies, nincompoops*"—and then a crew of gardeners who worked around the house. One afternoon when she was fourteen a carpenter called Brian—he came from Dublin, she remembered, and had a thick Irish accent, a brogue—raped her; she'd just come home from school. "Don't look so shocked," said Annie. "It happens all the time." It had been, she said, predictable:

a kind of fondling—a kiss in the pantry, a hand on her ass—a flirtation she'd been proud of and been flattered by and had in a way invited until suddenly it wasn't flirting, wasn't friendly harmless petting anymore. That afternoon when she got home, there was nobody else in the garden or house, and she let him kiss her like she liked him to, then said, "No, stop, OK? You're hurting me." But Brian had not taken no for an answer and fucked her there, down on the floor. The *greenhouse* floor, she remembered the tile, because they had had a greenhouse full of orchids by the living room.

"Were you hurt badly?" Lawrence asked, and she shook her head. "What did your parents do?" he asked. "Whatever happened to *him*?" Brian too, she said, he got the axe, only this time the literal version—again she laughed—what you'd call a dickless Mick. "But anyhow and since that afternoon I've never been able to appreciate orchids; Mummy kept orchids," she said.

He wondered if he should believe her. He wondered how much of what Annie told him—lying naked on the bed, her thigh across his knees—was true. She was self-assured, shored up by wealth, and at the edge of coherence. With her fingernails she raked his chest, speaking in a monotone, saying he was, wasn't he, a Virgo, she could tell it from the way he walked, the way he matched his tie and shirt: a search for perfection in others and precision in the self. "It's why you'll be an architect, you *are* a Virgo, aren't you," she said, "a kind of innocent with Lincoln Logs who dreams of building things. The risk is"—she walked her fingers down his stomach—"well, rigidity, but that's a risk we'll take. Let's take it again right now, OK, before you have to leave . . ."

In years to come he wondered what had in fact occurred. He never knew how much she lied or if she believed what she said. He never knew, for instance, if there had been a carpenter called Brian and some sort of rape. When she described her time at Smith, it did seem pure invention, or at least exaggeration: the affair she had had with her history teacher, the way the old museum guard had caught them in—Annie laughed her high-pitched laugh—the phrase the dean used was *flagrante delicto* after museum hours on an eighteenth-century sofa in the upstairs gallery. They had been trying out positions on the furniture, and the whole thing was recorded on surveillance tape. She herself had been suspended, but her professor became—again she laughed—dean of the Office of Student *Affairs* . . .

Perhaps all this did happen, and perhaps it had not happened; Lawrence did not know. She lied about her pregnancy, the pill she told him she was on but had not in fact been taking, the diamond earrings she'd examined in a jewelry store and found for some reason one night in her purse. She'd not told the truth about Denmark, she confessed to him much later; the photo of the hillside was of a farm in Wisconsin, the place where her uncle kept sheep. When, seven months after the wedding, their daughter, Catherine, was born and her postpartum depression was at its worst, Annie lied about the drugs she took, their quantity, their origin, the way her body changed and how it was *his* fault.

The marriage was brief, a mismatch from the start, and if she hadn't been pregnant, she wouldn't have considered it. But she *did* want the child. "What *you* were," Annie told him, "was a necessary evil. I couldn't have done it without you, *we* couldn't have done it without you, but thanks a lot and no hard feelings and good luck. Katy and I are going home to Chicago, and you can kiss her good-bye."

At first he had been angry, then unhappy, then relieved. There was a phalanx of lawyers, a series of discussions, and, finally, agreement. By the time he moved to San Francisco and his job at Skidmore, Owings & Merrill—a job in part arranged for him by Annie's family—he found himself disposed of; he was twenty-seven years old with an ex-wife and daughter and visiting rights in the summer, as well as one weekend per month.

Warren Anderson, it turned out, had been Annie's lover; the two of them resumed their old affair and moved to Winnetka. "Do you remember," asked Warren, "the night we met, that dinner at the Sievers'? It was when she decided she wanted a baby, but *I* didn't want one or want to adopt, and you were the stand-in. That's what Annie told me, anyhow, when we got back together, and the thing to do is believe what she says. Or pretend to, anyhow . . ."

Lawrence did his best to stay in touch. For the first years he did visit, playing badminton and checkers with his daughter; they went to the mall and the Field Museum together. His best, however—so Annie told him—wasn't anything like good enough, and thank you very much, "We're all entitled to mistakes, and I was your mistake." She married Warren and divorced him and married again, in rapid succession, and by the time that she turned thirty and had divorced a third time was a Buddhist. *The truth of life is suffering*, she wrote Lawrence from an ashram in Colorado, *and existence is a wheel.*

For the three years of apprenticeship he worked at SOM in their San Francisco office, moving from position to position and being supervised. He liked the city and the job, the feel of being entrusted with tasks both "hands-on" and conceptual while watching skyscrapers rise. Nat Owings himself would sometimes appear, and Chuck Bassett, the head designer, took the idea of apprenticeship seriously, preparing new arrivals for licensing exams and assigning each of them a partner to whom to report. Lawrence wrote a paper on Constantinos Doxiadis and the theory of ekistics, then a paper on Buckminster Fuller and the Dymaxion House. These were outtakes from the work undertaken at Harvard, but they seemed suited to the time and place—San Francisco burgeoning, a city conscious of its past and enlarging future or, as his supervisor Ted Hutchins put it, "Westward ho!"

There was nowhere, of course, to expand due west, and the fault lines from the earthquake seemed a stark reminder of the limits of expansion; the idea of urban renewal had gained widespread currency. Lawrence lived in a garden apartment on the east-facing slope of Nob Hill. He joined a dojo and studied karate and judo and yoga as a form of discipline; he taught himself to cook. On weekends he would drive past Tiburon and Belvedere, the still-racy Sausalito and the slopes of Mount Tamalpais and the flats of Stinson Beach. He told Ted Hutchins he was drawing up a master plan for Inverness: a small-scale version of Sun City or Reston for the rural working class.

His mother called. She and Robert had a proposition for him, she said, or not so much a proposition as a *proposal*. She was sad about how far away she felt from her children, how little they saw of each other, but she and Robert had just now completed the purchase of five acres of farmland on the shores of Lake Champlain. They were hoping for a summerhouse, as well as a place to escape to in winter, and they wondered if Lawrence would like to design it; this had been Robert's idea. "That's the sort of man he is," she said, "and money's no object, or not an *objection*, and we think of it as a retirement home. We aren't ready for retirement, we're not talking ramps and wheelchairs, but it's a *beautiful* property, we can't wait for you to see it. Darling, do say yes."

He did. He had no license to practice, but one of his classmates from Harvard was licensed as an architect in Vermont and could sign off on the plans. Lawrence flew to Burlington and met his mother and stepfather there, and they drove him to and walked him through the site. It had been well chosen: a meadow sloping gently down, a rise with wide views west and south, the great blue lake beneath.

"We think of this," said Robert, "as a new chapter for us both—you see what I'm saying, no *baggage*, no *history*, nothing except what the two of us bring to it, your mother and me, and you too are starting out, so let's do this together, OK? I see it as win-win."

He designed a multilevel house. The living quarters were at entry level, so they did not need to climb, and the upstairs was a steep-roofed sitting room with views in the four directions and a sleeping balcony for guests. The master bedroom suite and balcony faced west, and the second floor could be sealed off when not in use. His "clients" wanted the feel of a farmhouse, a contemporary structure with rough-hewn wooden beams that nonetheless might seem as though it had been standing in the field for generations. Lawrence convinced his mother and Robert to clad the whole in Cor-ten steel. It was expensive to install, but there would be no maintenance, and the rusting siding would look, from a distance, like wood. The roof was corrugated tin.

This juxtaposition of modern and old was the organizing principle for what became his first commission and completed house. "What we can do with steel these days," he remembered a teacher declaring, "makes the imagination of even Piranesi look a little hidebound. If it's *doable*, do it, why not?"

He added a silo for storage. This cylindrical structure was sided in corrugated tin, and the local workmen—taciturn but skillful—treated him as though he were a well-heeled madman, warily. The house was sixteen hundred square feet, but the twelve-foot ceilings made it feel more spacious, and both the middle-distance views and those of Lake Champlain seemed somehow a part of the interior space. In private, though he did not tell his mother this, he felt the whole to be derivative of—or, to put it generously, an act of homage to—Le Corbusier. On a whim he sent a set of photographs and plans to the National AIA Honor awards program and heard nothing for six months; then he received a letter of congratulations and an official citation.

This pleased them in the office, but he designed a second house—this time for his father, on Long Island—and his supervisor warned him not to spend too much energy on private commissions. "We're glad to see you working hard," said Ted Hutchins, "but remember you work *here*, at SOM, and at *least* forty hours each week."

Ted Hutchins was affable, plump. He wore a goatee and suspenders and had crescent sweat stains in the armpits of his shirt. He was proud of his young protégé; he wanted Lawrence to be clear this wasn't a reproach but a statement of fact: "Sooner or later, not yet but someday, there might be a conflict of interest, and we'd like to keep you here or send you to the office in Chicago. You're doing fine now, you're part of the team, and let's keep it that way, OK?" Having completed his apprenticeship, Lawrence took the three-part exam and did receive board certification as an architect in California; licensed, he entered the profession and asked himself what would come next.

What came next was the Mason house in Inverness—this one solar-heated and facing out on a fenced pasture with Black Angus cows. Here the material was redwood and old railroad ties, and the second-story windows were a set of salvaged portholes from a Port Townsend tug. That motif—his client owned a mail-order "nautical supply shoppe"—was reinforced by outsize anchors framing the entry drive and a series of hurricane lamps. There was a three-page pictorial spread in *California Living*, and the house photographed well. It too was carefully sited, and it too received an award.

Henry Mason, however, was not a relative, and although his wife, Denise, seemed pleased, he himself proved querulous. Mason complained about the expense of the construction and the shadow of the overhang and a problem with the fireplace draw, once the mason had laid in the smoke shelf. "It's *my* nickel," he was fond of saying, "*I'm* the one who earned it, and it's me who decides what to spend . . ."

"Well, sort of," Lawrence said.

"They told me—everybody told me—that you double the cost estimate; you should plan on twice as long and twice as much as the architect says. But I'm damned if I expected to multiply by three!"

"I'm sorry."

"Bullshit you are."

"It was *you* who kept adding things, Henry. The rear deck. The hot tub. The wine cellar just last week . . ."

"It's *my* nickel," Mason repeated. "And it was Denise who wanted the hot tub, not me."

There was a threatened lawsuit, and although it never went to court, the specter of a lawsuit troubled Lawrence greatly; his client belonged to a different world. The state of California had real estate developers and conservationists in almost equal measure, and if the car you drove or clothes you wore made a political statement, then certainly the house you lived in also staked out a position: "By their dwellings ye shall know them," as Ted Hutchins liked to say. "Bullshit," said Henry Mason, "we're talking cost overruns here."

His client's wife was seductive; she poured Lawrence wine while they studied the drawings together. Denise threw back her head and, laughing throatily, let her fingers graze his thigh. She complained about her husband, his lack of taste and—"let's be honest about it"—imagination. But Lawrence felt uneasy, unable to reconcile what he had hoped might prove to be a visionary modular system with the need to turn a profit: high-end custom structures, although a challenge to design, were not now the point.

—

What *was* the point? he asked himself, and bought a white Volvo P1800 with red leather seats. He liked the car, its handling, its solidity, and the fact—although he had not known this when he purchased it—that the Volvo once was featured on a television series called *The Saint*. Strangers would point at him, smiling, and sometimes they asked for his autograph; he assured them he was not a star, not a TV celebrity, but nonetheless liked the attention.

On weekends, he took trips. The woman he was seeing, Marisa, joined him for dinner at Nepenthe, and they spent the night together at the Big Sur Lodge. Marisa herself had a home in Carmel, and she had driven to meet him; they drank scotch and watched the sunset and made love and, over coffee and croissants and homemade jam in the morning, discussed the future: if he was free to join her next weekend and make a commitment or not.

"Do we have to decide?"

"It's not," she said, "irrevocable. I don't mean *that* kind of commitment."

"No?"

"I'm not your jailer, Larry. It isn't a *prison*, commitment."

"I thought we were discussing next weekend. Sonoma, San Simeon, whatever."

Marisa was a child psychologist, and when they argued—which was often—she said his was a case of arrested development: he was a perfect example of an American boy-man, the type who refused to grow up. It isn't refusal exactly, she said; it's more an inability or deficit; it's being fixated on actualization but not *self*-actualization, and he should read Abraham Maslow and try, just a little, to act like an adult, all right?

"Does that mean making choices?" he asked. "And abiding by them?"

She nodded; she patted his cheek.

"Can I choose to get out of here?"

Marisa paled. "If it's what you need to do, yes."

Lawrence pulled on his sweater and left.

———

He moved to a larger apartment that was half a house on Filbert Street and remained at SOM, working on regional projects, writing articles, and practicing karate at the dojo each Tuesday after work. His sister came to visit. Allie had earned an MBA and was being recruited by a firm in San Francisco, but there were competing offers and she was planning to accept instead the one from Philadelphia. "I'm an East Coast gal," she said.

They went out to dinner at Ernie's, and the headwaiter treated them as though they were a couple, romantically involved and not brother and sister. This amused her, and she said so, and they spent the evening discussing their childhoods, the new families their parents had acquired, and the houses he had built. Allie was wearing pearls, a tailored suit, and in the years of business school had acquired a hard-edged authority; her fingernails and lips were crimson and her gestures brusque.

"What I don't understand," she said, "is how we all got through it. The years and *years* of bickering. The endless arguments."

"What I mostly remember," said Lawrence, "is silence."

"You mostly weren't home by then, brother."

He smiled at her. "That's true."

"Can I ask you," Allie asked, "what it felt like to repeat it? Divorce."

"Excuse me?"

"Did you ever believe you were copying them, repeating a failed marriage? Or being *influenced* by them—our parents?"

"No."

"No?"

He heard himself saying that what he had gone through was mostly denial, mostly a way of ignoring the past: "Who I miss is my daughter, not my wife." When she asked about the divorce, said Lawrence, he'd not made the connection to their shared family history; "I do believe in marriage, except not the one I had . . ."

She was blushing, he noticed, and biting her lip. He drank. Then his sister said something that shocked him: "You fall in love

once only, or anyhow that's what I think, and all the rest is playact-
ing, a way to pass the time. And I've done it," admitted Allie, "I've
gone and *done* it, goddammit, except it's a kind of addiction and
I've been trying to quit." The best reason, she confessed, to come to
California was to put a continent between herself and Mr. Wrong
since her own love affair wasn't working and was, it turned out,
hopeless, the oldest cliché in the marital book. The man she was
seeing was married and had two children of his own and wasn't
planning to leave them; there was only so often she could answer
the phone and be disappointed or come running at his say-so, only
so many hotels and motels, because he was fifteen years older, a
kind of daddy substitute, a sorry excuse for their own absent father,
or that's what her doctor suggested, and maybe her doctor was
right. For the longest time—for three *years* now—she had refused
to believe it, had not taken no for an answer but convinced herself,
or tried to, that maybe tomorrow or next week or month they'd
turn a corner together and he'd wake up and see the light and the
two of them would live together happily forever and ever amen.

She continued in this fashion, looking down at her plate, describing her trouble in detail, her new resolution to end the affair and
not pretend there'd be a happy ending, no wedding band or bed of
roses or full moon in June. The waiter, hovering, inquired, "Another
bottle, sir?" and he looked at his sister questioningly. She shook her
head, eyes misting, and Lawrence asked for and paid the check. Allie
scraped back her chair and, standing, linked her arm with his, saying, "It's excellent to see you, brother, and have someone to complain
to. Someone who knew me way back when . . ."

But he had become inattentive, adrift, remembering what she had
said—"You fall in love once only, or anyhow that's what I think"—
repeating the one word in silence: *Hermia,* his name for what was lost.

VIII
—
2004

"The harbor of Valletta is," their tour guide said, "impregnable. These seawalls has never been breached. The Knights of Malta from earliest times are warriors and healers; they have always been Crusaders and ministered the sick. They has, you see, two duties: they are soldiers and hospitallers both. When the Knights were driven out of Rhodes because of Arab siege," the tour guide continued, her voice high-pitched, "they settle here in Malta to make of the island a stronghold—which it is remaining until the present day."

They walked beneath an arch. The town of Valletta, their guide said, had been founded in the sixteenth century by the Grand Master of the Knights, Jean Parisot de Valette. "He make a stronghold for his peoples commanding in position. Is a military community," she told the passengers from the *Diana*, "according to the Roman model."

"What's that?" asked the man from El Paso.

"Streets slope from down the heights for soldiers to keep watch from, see? And also the architects bring us fresh water. This one is not a town by accident, not just something that arrange itself—how do you say?—by circumstance but *planned*."

A bell chimed eleven o'clock. In contrast to the negligent clutter of Sicily, the streets of Valletta, though crowded, were clean; the traffic too was orderly, and there were traffic police. This town seemed less a tourist destination than a place where people lived and worked; young men with leather briefcases and women swinging handbags bustled past.

"Here is a very ancient place, a very ancient peoples and civilization," resumed their guide. "You will see in the museum the goddess of fertility, and the peoples from the Stone Age are excellent workers with stone. In our entire history only the little Napoleon succeeded to conquer the island, and only when our soldiers decided not to fight. This was because the Knights of Malta elected from France refuse to battle with their emperor, and the Grand Master of the Knights say, well, in that case, *seigneurs*, we make him welcome; if we do not lift arms together, we lay them together all down."

The tour guide was petite, and trim, wearing a yellow beret. She walked with an umbrella and used it to extend her arm, pointing at buildings. The sky was bright.

"Are you all right?"

"Not really, no," Hermia said.

"What's wrong?"

She shook her head. For what in fact was there to say; how could she explain? Last night she'd clung to Lawrence, but it had not helped. "I've seen a ghost," she said to him, and when he asked her what that meant, she shut her eyes.

"What's wrong?" he persisted. "What sort of ghost?"

Her daughter rode ten feet away, suspended on the wave spume by the railing where they stood. The dress was diaphanous, flesh only bones. The face, however, was unchanged: near and dear and intimate, mouth pursed in concentration. "Take no for an answer," her daughter had said, the final time they argued, and slammed the kitchen door.

Behind them in the Elsinore Lounge, someone was playing a polka. Hermia trailed her fingers down Lawrence's cheek and, shivering, left him on deck.

—

So now it was bright day again, the last day of their trip. "My name is Amelie," their guide announced, "and I pass my whole entire life on the islands of Gozo and Malta, except for two years in Scotland—are any of you Scottish? No? In that case I confess to you because of Edinburgh I very much esteem the weather here, the lack of soot. We have, in the dry season, dust."

Her English was inaccurate, her accent strong, and yet she managed to suggest they had been strolling down Bond Street or through Piccadilly Circus in the rain. The sun was hot.

"Except just now we were discussing the little Napoleon," said Amelie. "That is how we call him in these parts, the Corsican Buonaparte, who was presented the keys to the city, and he assure the Knights they would no one be harmed. Indeed, he keep his word. But after three days he collected the plate—all the silver and gold from the church, the *auberges* and the palaces—and melted it to bullion to pay for the campaign in Egypt with ill-gotten gains that had been the Knights' treasure. This is the one time Valletta was taken, and for the reason only that we do not choose to fight."

Lawrence and Hermia smiled. They did so at the same moment, and Amelie noticed. "It took your great Admiral Nelson," she said, "to be blockading the harbor and force away the French, because by that time the Corsican he understands this is not a hospitable place. Since then we have been English or belonging to the Commonwealth, and King George in the Second War was grateful to us all. The Maltese people refuse to be beaten by Germans who besiege us and afterwards he honor every person on the island fortress for their suffering and steadfast ways. You see here the George Cross."

They were standing in a courtyard, by statues of Crusaders. Jane from Columbus asked about the agriculture on the island, and what the people grew. Their tour guide discussed the crops of Malta, the density of population, the balance of payment problems and desalinization plants, and the question of the European Union. She was enthusiastic, voluble. The language here was half Sicilian and half Arabic, she explained. "Not many people speak Maltese, but it is a beautiful language; you must listen when you walk. And visit the elegant shops."

Next she described the Knights of Malta—their chastity, their vows and power and crusading zeal. "One hand the sword, one hand the bandage, see? There are three categories," said Amelie, "and every member of the knighthood is a candidate from one of these—the nobility, the wealthy, and the serving men.

"By serving men I do not mean," she explained, "a servant; I mean only they has some particular skill and use it for the profit of the Order. The painter Caravaggio, for example, take refuge here and became a Knight of Malta but could not offer money because at the time he has none. Caravaggio could claim of course no previous nobility; instead he offer what he promise is his largest and would be most important painting—the only one he sign. In the Cathedral of St. John you will see it when you go."

Brandishing her umbrella, she continued down the street. There were many people shopping, striding purposefully, but Lawrence and Hermia lagged behind. The gaily decorated shops and stone houses made a maze they wandered in; he took her hand.

"Let's let them go, all right?"

"All right."

"We've elected the privacy option."

"You don't want to see the Knights' armor?" she asked. "Or, in the museum, the goddess of fertility?"

He shook his head. They descended an alley with boutiques, a bank, a travel agency, and, at the corner, a café; he ordered them both cappuccino, and they sat to drink it at a table with an umbrella. The chairs were green, with red wooden slats, and the tablecloth had brightly colored variations of the eight-pointed Maltese cross. She remarked upon this, and he asked, "Do you want pastry, a croissant?"

"Coffee's fine," said Hermia. She pressed her lips together; her single dimple showed. "They stuff us, don't they, on the ship, I'm still digesting dinner. And must have gained five pounds since Rome . . ."

"Not so I've noticed."

"Well, three . . ."

"You're fishing for compliments, ma'am."

"Yes. But I don't want a pastry."

"I want to know," said Lawrence, "if you're angry at me." He drank. "And if you're angry, which you are, I think, what I can do about it, why . . ."

"This isn't about you. Not really."

"Oh?"

"Except you've been so eager. You were always so, so *eager*—that's the word for it—so puppy dog ready to please."

"Is that what it looks like? Is that how I seem?"

Now it was she who raised her cup. There was froth at the rim of it; Hermia drank. "You're right," she said. "I'm being dismissive. But not unfair, exactly. You've been thrusting yourself at me all through the trip—or, anyhow, since Pompeii. And I'm not a college girl and things are not the way they were, and we can't pretend we're children—we've *got* children—and it isn't just a matter now of—what did we call it?—wham, bam, thank you, ma'am. I'm sixty-three years old."

"I know that. Remember, I'm sixty-four."

"Old enough to know better," she said.

———

So the mood between them lightened and the tension lessened. They finished their coffees; he paid. She took photographs. They made their way through little squares and thoroughfares into a public garden, then found a bench and sat together in the sunlight, watching children playing, watching the elderly walking their dogs.

"Do you want lunch?" Lawrence inquired, and she shook her head. "Your cabin or mine?" he asked again, and this time Hermia laughed. They found the road down to the harbor and walked together past the customhouse, smiling at the men in uniform who sat smoking by the seawall, and past the potted palm until the roped enclosure of the MS *Diana*.

The ship had numbered brass medallions for the passengers, a system by which the cruise director kept track. A board hung by the gangway with a list of names beside it; when disembarking, those who went ashore would lift off and pocket their numbers and, when returning, replace them. "That way," the cruise director explained, "we know who is here and who's not."

He returned his number, 63, and hers, 71, to the registry board. Most of the medallions were missing, since the excursion to Valletta was the last one of the cruise, and only a few passengers had chosen to stay on the ship. Sailors were polishing brightwork; sailors were mopping the deck. By the purser's desk she told him, "I'm in the Owner's Stateroom."

"Oh?"

"They rent it out if he's not aboard; it's on the upper deck and does have views." She smiled. "Etchings. Would you like to come on up and see them?"

Lawrence nodded yes. His own quarters down below were cramped and unforgiving, with exercise clothes on a hook. So he followed her upstairs and waited in the hallway while she fumbled in her handbag for a key.

—

There were wraparound windows that gave on the harbor, a seating area, a chaise longue. The curtains were of watered silk, and Oriental carpets festooned the hardwood floor. This gave him pause. It altered the equation, somehow; it made him feel foolish, a little, as though he'd been pursuing her the way a passenger in steerage might chase some great bejeweled lady in first class. The captain's bridge was just above; she had a private balcony, and during their absence that morning, the bed had been made up. Silk pillows with the name *Diana* lay plumped along the headboard, and the bedspread was embroidered with a clipper ship, sails furled.

Years before he'd seen *Titanic*, the movie of a street-brawling boy and rich girl who fall in love aboard ship. She had been carrying Picassos and Cézannes and was supposed to marry an arrogant aristocrat but in her heart of hearts adored the boy instead. There was, of course, a storm at sea; there was an iceberg and a rending crash and great catastrophe; there was an orchestra playing "Nearer, My God, to Thee."

"I'd forgotten," Lawrence said. "Well, not forgotten, really . . ."

"What?"

"You're an heiress, aren't you? You always take the penthouse suite."

"Don't be unkind," she said.

"I mean it as a compliment. I'm being respectful, ma'am."

"Bullshit. All it is, is money."

"Yes."

She moved to him, half teasing. "Would you like to close the curtains?"

He did.

"That's better. Thank you, Jeeves."

They were enveloped, of a sudden, in the protective dark. Hermia kicked off her shoes and therefore was less tall than he; he straightened his shoulders and held out his arms. A bouquet of white lilies had been arranged on the bureau. Their odor was pungent, suffusing the room.

"Well?" he said.

"Well."

"Would you, wouldn't you, like to kiss me?"

She moved against him yieldingly and pressed her lips to his. At last the moment had arrived—in this romantic setting, this Owner's Stateroom on the topmost deck—but Lawrence felt constrained. They stood by the armchair together. While he was touching her and holding her, he told himself he could continue or not; he could proceed with these maneuvers or stop kissing her; it did remain a choice. He coughed. She stepped away. Hermia found herself remembering, long years before, that time she'd slept with the Oppenheims' friend—what was his name, the one who owned her father's paintings and taught English at Columbia?—and how she asked herself then also if the game was worth the candle and if she was willing to play . . .

Again, he cleared his throat. They leaned toward each other, pressed against each other, and she wondered what her breasts would feel like if he kissed them as he used to, and what would happen next. She saw them in the mirror, two bent gray heads adjacent in the ornate gilt-framed glass, saw them touching lips and cheeks as though performing for the camera in some sort of time-lapse photograph, a present overlay upon the past. The stubble at his chin was white. The folds of his neck were—what was the word for it?—"wattles," and they were going through the motions clumsily, anxiously, feeling their way past the layers of clothing and flesh. It was as though the mirror became a movie camera, and she was her own director, holding the viewfinder, watching. *Take one,* she told herself. *Take two, all right, try that again . . .*

They sat at the bed's edge, his arm at her waist and her head on his shoulder, and the muted light through the curtains illumined the wall opposite: the bureau, the mirror, a painting of a shepherd with his flock and sheepdog and flute. Briefly, Lawrence shut his eyes. Briefly, she closed her eyes also. In the ensuing silence she could hear machinery: the hum of idling engines, the system for heating and cooling, the tick of the clock.

"Do I . . ." Hermia began to ask, then stopped.

"Look beautiful?" He smiled at her, gallant. "The answer is yes."

She blushed. "That's not what I wanted to ask you."

"Well, what?"

"Do you feel up to this? Oh, it's so embarrassing, I don't mean *up* but ready."

"We don't require Viagra," said Lawrence. "If that's what you're asking . . ."

"No." And now she did feel safe with him and took his hand and pressed his fingers one by one and traced the deep lines of his palm. Haltingly at first, and then with a sense of rising relief, she spoke about Patricia. She told him what they'd fought about and how they argued and flailed at each other till the girl walked out in anger and did not return. She'd slammed the kitchen door so hard the calendar had fallen—Hermia could *see* it, *hear* it crumple—to the floor.

This was the day she paid taxes, and there were tax forms awaiting her signature and checks to write and envelopes to send them in; her accountant had filled out the forms. She could remember her anger, and every single thing the two of them had fought about all winter. She could recall each hurtful word and what was in the oven and where, above the radiator in the sunlight by the south-facing window, bread loaves rose. The kitchen door had slammed before; the disappearing act was one that she herself had performed. For there had been another kitchen, she explained to Lawrence, another fight and rapid flight when she and her young child escaped New York. It was too obvious, too neat by half to think that Patsy—Pat-a-cake, Patricia—did what she herself had done, and all of this was preordained, some sort of blood taint or DNA for retribution implanted by her husband. She could not bear to think the wheel had come full circle and could not be reversed.

Therefore she had waited for her daughter to return. It was April 14, 1992. Since then, she'd lived alone. The first weeks Hermia was hopeful, then fearful, and at last had understood—with a deep blank certainty, an icy recognition—her girl had left for good. She waited all that spring. Now, weeping, she stood at the porthole and stared at the white harbor walls.

———

Lawrence disembarked at three o'clock, too restless to remain aboard and needing open air. He walked by himself into town. The scene in her cabin stayed with him, however: her cheek on his shoulder, her tears. Leaving, he had offered, "If you want me to, I'll stay," and she forced a smile and said, "I'll be all right, I promise, I'll see you later on."

He took the road they'd walked before, and in the center of Valletta found the Cathedral of St. John. There he made his way through heavy doors and, entering, was shocked; the austere facade of the building had not prepared him for the pomp within, the splendor of the windows and ceilings and multicolored floors. Beneath his feet the Knights were buried, square by inlaid square. Triumphal death was signaled everywhere: the skulls that grinned at him, the portraits of Grand Masters and bones crisscrossed on marble crypts were baroque in their exuberance. *Step lightly,* they seemed to be saying. *We too were fleet of foot.*

After some time he located and sat in front of *The Beheading of Saint John the Baptist.* It moved him very much. The red of the saint's cape, the red blood pooling under his neck, the doorway's arch, the elderly couple recoiling: all these signaled mastery. A muscular killer leaned down with a knife while a maiden at the painting's left leaned forward with a basin; was she a servant come to fetch the head or perhaps the princess, implacable Salome?

Lawrence was sweating; with his sleeve he wiped his face. Every afternoon of the journey except for this one he had used the treadmill on the MS *Diana*, and fleetingly he wondered if the twinge in his chest were a warning. He had not made love since June. He had not wanted to. But Hermia had challenged his long abstinence by offering her story, and he asked himself and did not know if he could start again . . .

"*The Beheading of Saint John,*" a nearby tour guide was saying, "is Michelangelo Merisi's gift to this cathedral and his masterpiece. A large composition—the largest he painted, the only one we know he signed, and here he use his pen name: Caravaggio. What he was doing in Malta, eh?" the guide inquired of a listening group. "Because he flee from Rome to Naples and then from here to Sicily and then again he quarreled, this man was always quarreling, he was a very great painter but difficult person, I think.

"Consider the men in the window; they are watching this terrible scene? Do you think they like to see the blood or fear because their turn come next; are they prisoners perhaps? Caravaggio of course is famous for how he paint light, the Einstein of the period, the one who first invented what we call chiaroscuro, yes, and though the saint himself is brightly—how you say?—illuminated, the painting here is dark. It is in honor of the patron saint for whom we name this building; St. John had a shipwreck on Gozo, the island next to Malta, and pray for safe deliverance, which he discover in this place.

"Caravaggio is telling everybodies, I believe—the Knights, the Grand Master of the Knights of Malta to whom he offer this picture—we live in darkness and die in the light. We must be prepared, the artist say, for the girl with a basin and blood on the floor, the one who studies sacrifice, and she is standing at the picture's side for both our beginning and end."

—

"How was your walk?"

"I missed you," Lawrence said.

"I'm sorry I didn't come. Come with you, I mean. Oh, Jesus"— she spread her hands—"why does *everything* have to sound so, oh, I don't know, suggestive? I feel like I'm a kid again."

He sat. "You're right: Since the day you found me in Pompeii, I've been behaving like an adolescent. Or just pretending to be grown-up, the way I did at Harvard. But it isn't all that bad, I think; it makes me feel so *hopeful*."

"Really?"

"Hopeful, I mean, that the future is bright. And you should *see* the Caravaggio. The whole cathedral, Hermia, the way the Knights filled it to bursting: how ornate the carvings are, the skeletons and all those skulls and bones."

"Cheery little business."

"What I'm trying to say," said Lawrence, "is I'm back to being optimistic. To thinking things are *possible*, not over . . ."

"Not over, no. Except we've waited forty years."

"Who's counting? Forty-two."

"I've given up arithmetic." She leaned across and kissed his cheek. "That too."

At dinner Lawrence and Hermia joined an elderly couple from Boston and a pair of newlyweds. The gentleman from Boston was distinguished-looking, with a mop of white unruly hair and a carefully tied bow tie; he patted his lips with his napkin each time he started to speak. He had worked as a geologist, and he regaled the company with stories of eruptions throughout the Mediterranean, the recent behavior of Stromboli and Etna, as well as the more famous eruption of Vesuvius and the kinds of volcanic activity one might hereafter expect.

His wife picked at her chicken and played with her carrots as though herself a child. She was, she confessed to the table, a little hard of hearing; they lived on Beacon Hill. Lawrence knew the street, he said, and in architecture school did a set of elevations of the rooflines of Newbury Street. "The chimneys in particular," he said, "I remember the chimneys." "You *must* come and see us," said the geologist, "you and your wife will be welcome," and Hermia began to correct him and declare they were not married. Then she decided not to; it would have been no kindness to tell these old people the truth. Lawrence smiled and said, "We'd love to. Next time we're in Boston, we promise."

The younger couple worked in advertising. Bruce and Judy lived in Connecticut; did Hermia know Westport? They lived in the center of town but had met each other, Judy explained over salad, at a copywriters' convention in North Carolina this spring. All blessings—she fashioned a cross in the air—upon the Grove Park Inn. She had lost her husband six months before in a car crash on an icy road, and though she did feel *terrible* about it, the truth was their marriage had been going nowhere and was heading for divorce court that same week. Bruce himself had been divorced, and when they met in Asheville, they knew they were made for each other, had been very lucky, if you can call it luck when there's divorce and death. So this was their honeymoon voyage, their chance to get it right for once, and she was bound and determined now to get it right. Had Hermia been to Asheville, and did she know the Biltmore House and how romantic the gardens could be? Judy proposed a toast to everyone's good fortune and, gesturing at Darko, held out her glass for more wine.

So they were one of a group of three couples, and talked about the trip. The best parts, they could all agree, were Malta and Agrigento; the worst was the Isle of Capri. "It has to do with weather," said the elderly geologist; Hermia tried to remember his name. It was too late in the evening for her to ask his name again; his wife said, "Yes, but there is inner weather also, inner temperature. Isn't that so?"

She was wearing bracelets with large turquoise stones embedded in the silver; her husband patted her arm.

"Indeed," he said. "We're ninety-eight point six . . ."

After dinner Lawrence and Hermia stood at the railing, and the moon was high. She steeled herself to look over the bowsprit, but there were no ghosts. The fort of the Crusaders and the high stone battlements loomed floodlit and imposing.

"Did you enjoy yourself?" he asked. Flags fluttered in the breeze.

"When?"

"At dinner?"

"I've been having a wonderful time."

He gestured at the seawall. "Hard men, the Knights."

She was feeling happy now, alone with him, loose-tongued a little because of the wine. "Hard?"

"Yes, unyielding. Famous for their discipline . . ."

"Then what a shame," said Hermia, "they took those vows of chastity."

He smiled. "I don't imagine they kept them . . ."

"And you," she asked, "are you still being courtly?"

"I do repent me," he said.

They went up again to her cabin, and this time the curtains were drawn; a pink lamp glowed softly by the bed, and the bed linen had been turned back. They kissed, and this time meant it, and she felt Lawrence stiffen against her. The darkness aided both of them; in silence they took off their clothes. Time stopped.

———

The morning's departure was scheduled for six. In separate cabins they packed their suitcases and set them out in hallways for off-loading. Then, having collected their passports from the ship's purser, they left tips for the personnel and took a taxi to the airport; there they stood on numbered lines—he for the plane to Amsterdam and she for Rome. He would fly from Schiphol to Detroit Metro and she from Fiumicino to Boston Logan; he would return to Ann Arbor and she to the house on Cape Cod. Once their tickets had been processed and their luggage checked, they went through the procedures of security together.

The officials were polite. Nonetheless he divested himself of his jacket; she smiled at him as though again in her cabin, unclothed, but this time on public display. Courtly, Lawrence took her carry-on and offered his arm for balance while Hermia stepped out of her shoes. She removed her coat, he his belt. They passed through the metal detector; she raised her arms, he his. Once they had dressed and collected their coats, they walked into the waiting room and found an unoccupied corner beneath a plate glass window and sat down.

A fine mist cloaked the runway. "Do you want a coffee?" he asked.

She shook her head. He had asked the same thing yesterday, but somehow this morning the question seemed changed. It was the identical question, but everything had changed. She wondered if she could say this out loud, and if he would agree. The banality of travel, Lawrence was saying: a thousand years ago this would have been astonishing, a hundred years ago worth noting; now we travel for a day and cross continents or oceans and the airport is a modern common denominator for what feels like symbolic transport and no actual journey at all.

"Do we have to keep talking like this?"

"No, we don't have to, I'd much rather talk about *us*."

"That's good," she said, "that's better."

"Will I see you again?" Lawrence asked.

"I've changed my mind, I could use a coffee. Do we have time?"

"Will I see you again?"

"With milk, please. And no sugar."

"In the ancient stories they ask this question three times. Will I see you again?"

She smiled at him. "Just Google me."

"In Truro? Should I come to Truro?"

"Do you want to?"

"Yes."

IX

1985–2003

When Pat became Patricia, at ten, she went to the Pine Cobble School, and then high school in Manchester. She attended Burr and Burton for four years. Her friends were the children of lawyers and doctors; her grades were good. Yet something secretive arose in her, something both guarded and inward, and Hermia felt she was raising a stranger—well, not a *stranger* exactly, she said to Anne, but someone she couldn't predict. There was a time she had known without asking the things her daughter thought.

"It's called adolescence," said Anne, "and nothing to worry about."

"No?"

They were in the kitchen, stacking plates and cups.

"Or what I mean to say is *everyone* goes through it, and though you're right to notice, there's nothing to be done."

"Of *course* there is," said Hermia, "or anyhow there ought to be; do you think she's doing drugs?"

Anne laughed. "I don't, no."

"Are you sure?"

"I'd recognize the smell of pot. And so would you."

"I didn't mean she's smoking in the house . . ."

"She's just restless."

"Restless?"

"The music," Anne said. "Have you noticed what she's playing?"

"Bach? Busoni?"

"I don't mean what she's practicing, I mean the stuff she listens to."

"Oh, *that*," said Hermia.

They laughed. They reminded each other what it had felt like long ago—the wakeful nights, the nameless yearning to escape, the posters of Brando and Newman and Dean, all those hormones raging. They were relieved, they agreed, to have put adolescence behind them and become middle-aged. Hermia scraped the table leavings into the pail of compost and rinsed out the bottle of wine. This was, they told each other, only a phase, something everybody goes through, and it would level out.

But it was a slope that grew steeper, not flat; it grew worse and not better with time. Patricia rarely said these words aloud, but what she said each time she spoke was *No. No way, not ever. What you want from me is not what I want, and whatever you're asking, the answer is no.* In Interlochen, Hermia knew, something had happened to her child and was happening again in school; when Patricia turned fifteen, she brought home friends called Rain and Perdita and Ocean and announced they were a band. "You'll like our name," proclaimed the girl. "We're the G-String Quartet."

Max the dog turned fifteen too; he hobbled, and one eye went blind. If Hermia encouraged him to join her on a morning walk, he built himself to his feet with difficulty, wheezing, spittle hanging from his muzzle, and after a few hundred yards would look at her with what she felt as reproach and lie down in the shade. Rain and Perdita and Ocean complained: *He smells, he stinks!* Squealing together throatily, they wrinkled up their noses like the girls they pretended no longer to be; they sang "Manic Monday" and "Eternal Flame." They wore beads and bandanas and miniskirts with fringes and vests with patches saying *LOVE*.

"She has a head on her shoulders," said Anne. "I know it doesn't look like it, but the girl does have a brain . . ."

"Yes, where?"

"Don't be so hard on her."

"I'm not. I'm *not* being hard. I adore her, you know that, I'm just disappointed."

"Well, don't be. Or, at any rate, don't let her know you are."

Hermia began to say, and stopped herself, that Anne, who had no children, couldn't understand the way it felt to be going through this: the flesh of her flesh growing up and away, growing separate, *scornful*, aloof. If she reached out for a touch or hug, it was as though she were contagious, and Patricia shrank away. She remembered the time at the Albany Airport when she'd consigned her child to a uniformed attendant and watched them while they walked together down the Jetway, disappearing: the brave face her daughter put on.

This new face was a blank. It wore purple lipstick, then black. The Bangles gave way to other models and were declared passé; the G-String Quartet, next summer, patterned themselves on bands with names like Pussy-Posse and T-N-A and Slot. They wired the milk shed for sound. Rain and Ocean, who had dyed their hair, said politics was where it's at—"Let's change our name to Molly Stark, because she was a hero of the revolution way back when."

They were changing attitude; they tried punk on for size. They called themselves the Indie Go-Girls and Green Mountainettes and Glastonbury Pass. When Hermia and Anne approached, they said, "Listen to *this*," and played a progression that they said would be their signature: three majors, then a minor chord, the final note

B-flat. After breakfast every afternoon the girls clumped out of the
kitchen and beat a path up through burdock and thistle, carrying
their instruments and saying, "Whoa, it's *hot!*"

Soon an eardrum-threatening cacophony would thump across
the pasture: a bass, a drum, a saxophone, with Patricia playing keyboard, pounding away in a frenzy of elbows and tossing her dark
hair down over her eyes like a creature in pain or possessed. Max
followed them, then fled. "I got to get *out* of here, got to get *out*"
was the only lyric Hermia could understand: all the rest was *wa wa
wawaaa* . . .

—

In the spring of 1991, Ryan Joffrey arrived. He did so on a motorcy-
cle, roaring up the River Road, wearing goggles and a ponytail and
reeking of patchouli and Old Spice. He played the acoustic guitar.
She and Anne were horrified, but the girls admired him, and they
sat together on the porch or drove the roads of Arlington or practiced in the milk house and talked about Bob Marley and Jimi
Hendrix and Jim Croce and Otis Redding, the great dead. "What
about Janis Joplin?" Hermia inquired, and Ryan said, "What about
her?" and she said, "I was only asking," and he turned away.

His earring was a cross. He braided his ponytail thickly and
had pimples all over his chin. She could not bear to picture him
pawing at her daughter, her lovely corruptible child. When she did
the laundry and found blood on Patricia's underwear, she said,
"Honey, do you want to—don't you want to—talk to me?"

The girl shook her head.

"We need to talk," said Hermia.

"There's nothing to talk about, Mom."

"That can't be true."

Patricia turned back to her book; it was, she saw, *Lolita*.

"OK. Except I have a question. Do you miss your father?"

"Whoa. Where'd *that* come from? I don't even *know* him."

"Me either," Hermia said. "I'm not sure I would recognize the man, in an airport, I mean, if he were alive. And the two of us got along fine, I think, or thought, or used to, you and me, not your f-father and me"—she could hear herself stuttering, making no sense—"before all this, oh, what would you call it, *disruption.* But sometimes I wonder if there ought to be, should have been someone, a man in the house. Some adult to stand at the door."

"What are you *talking* about?"

"Ryan. Protection. I don't want you pregnant . . ."

The look she got was withering; Patricia stalked out of the room. As if on cue and by way of an answer she heard the staccato bleat of the machine in the driveway, scattering gravel and clearing its steel throat. There was a pause, an idling, and then they roared away.

Max died. One morning Anne discovered him, in the kitchen, on his pillow bed, motionless and stiff already, with his sightless eye unblinking and pink tongue hanging down. She screamed.

Hermia came running; she had been brushing her teeth. The friends clung to each other, crying, trying to comfort each other and failing, until finally they knelt and stroked the shepherd's lifeless fur and placed a biscuit near his mouth as a propitiatory offering and covered him with a sheet.

They buried him that afternoon, in a trench Ryan dug by the pond. He worked uncomplainingly, and for this the women were grateful; he dug deep. The four of them stood by the grave for some minutes, burying the dog's leash and collar and a box of biscuits, taking turns with the shovel and the clumps of clay and topsoil. Then Ryan finished the job.

———

Afterward, the house on River Road seemed less and less a haven. If Patricia did come home alone, she stayed in her room or on the phone; the Steinway gathered dust, unplayed, and when Hermia asked if she wanted it tuned, her daughter only shrugged. The four girls ceased playing together; Perdita and Rain and Ocean went their separate ways. Patricia herself seemed not to care; she said, "We weren't that good, *they* weren't that good, and it was going nowhere, *we* were going nowhere, and Rain thought she was, like, God's gift to music, but it was like this ego trip and had nothing to do with what we were doing, OK?" When it was time to talk about college, which ones to apply to and which ones to visit, she said, "That's *your* scene, Mom."

"But everyone—"

"Not *everyone* . . ."

"Well, what else would you be doing?"

"Lots of stuff."

"Is that an answer?"

"It didn't sound like a question. You weren't, like, *asking* me anything, you were just making assumptions. Me and Ryan—"

"Ryan?"

Patricia nodded.

"What's *he* got to do with it?"

"You asked me, right? You were asking a question."

"What I wanted to know about is what *you're* thinking. If we should be planning, oh, campus visits; you've got a counselor, don't you, an adviser with suggestions?"

"Radcliffe. Your precious Radcliffe. The place you went and expect me to go . . ."

Hermia stiffened. "I never said that."

"You didn't have to, Mom . . ."

151

"Never *thought* about Radcliffe," she lied. "I couldn't care less where you go."

"Then let's just forget it. Cool."

"Well, this is fun."

"What?"

"Trying to talk. It *used* to be so easy."

"Right."

"Oh, what's the use. Have it your way. Let Ryan be the expert here . . ."

But Ryan too stopped visiting, and soon there was someone called Danny who went to Keene Valley Community College, then someone called Pete, then Jimbo, great hulking boys who thumped up the stairs of the porch. She tried to tell them apart. She wanted to ask what had happened to Ryan and to have a conversation with her daughter, or just to be easy with silence. But it felt impossible; the silence was not easy, and she couldn't bring herself to ask about Danny or Pete or Jimbo, their interchangeable bodies, their faces like boxes, their lives in the workaday world.

That autumn Anne moved out. She rented the top floor of a two-family home in North Bennington, down the street from Prospect School. She was bone-weary, she told Hermia, from driving back and forth to work—especially in winter, especially alone. "I can't handle it," said Anne, "not being with him in the house, not having him here—Max, I mean. It's just too sad, too much a reminder. I need not to be here, OK?"

"OK."

"Try to understand," said Anne, and explained herself at length. She didn't want to be the uninvited guest, the one who came to dinner who moved in all those years ago, and needed to move on. It was 1992. She had planned to stay maybe a weekend, a week; "*now* look at us," she said. Those car trips with Patricia, when she was at the Prospect School, well, it wasn't exactly *commuting*, but it had felt like company, and now she drove to work and back alone. She was forty-nine years old and needed her own private space.

Hermia too felt ready for a change. And though the women stayed in touch, they were no longer intimate; the things that had united them—a dog to walk, a child to raise—no longer could be shared. It was, she told herself, a period to get through, and Patricia would come to her senses and return to her old ways. It was, she thought, a long wakeful nightmare, a dream she would have to endure.

But this was a dream she couldn't stop dreaming, a nightmare she failed to escape. One afternoon in the kitchen, when Hermia was baking bread—the loaves rising in their pans—her seventeen-year-old brushed past, wearing boots with so much mud in the treads that everywhere she stepped turned brown, and there were pebbles and straw on the rug.

"You could, couldn't you, take off your shoes? Would it be too much trouble?"

"Yeah."

"Yeah, what?"

"I could."

"Well, all right, take them off."

"Except I'm heading out again."

"Oh, where?"

"Out."

"Don't overdo it, darling, don't be *too* much a caricature. You sound like you've been practicing."

"For what?"

"For the part of the insolent child. The one with no manners . . ."

"Fuck manners."

"Excuse me?"

"You *heard* me. Fuck manners."

She could hear herself breathing. "And why?"

"Because I *live* here," said the girl. "It has nothing to do with good manners."

"The mud . . ."

"If housekeeping's *your* thing, Mom, why don't you clean it up?"

She gripped the tabletop. "You're doing this on purpose, right?"

"Not *purpose*. I walked into the kitchen, that's all."

"And can walk right out again."

"You mean it? Take no for an answer?"

"Yes."

"You hear what you're saying? You won't, like, try to stop me?"

Hermia shook her head.

—

That was the end of it. Patricia grabbed her hat and parka from the hook in the pantry—the straw hat with the turkey feather and green parka stitched with a Toxin sign and *PEACE*—and slammed the door and clattered away down the steps. There was the now-familiar noise of an engine starting, a spray of driveway gravel and music thumping, blaring, then the perforated muffler of the car that bore her off. Hermia barely saw it disappear—big, dented, maybe ten years old—and did not go outside but stayed in the kitchen and watched through the window, where there were muslin curtains and a pot of geraniums blooming; she'd been so furious she wouldn't, *couldn't*, trust her memory for details, but was certain the car had been brown.

When policemen asked her, later, if she had noticed the make of the car, or the license plate number, or state, she shook her head. She hadn't been paying attention, or paying *that* kind of attention; she had been dealing with anger and cleaning the mud off the floor.

She could describe Patricia. She did this with precision, and also the hat and the parka and the stonewashed jeans and boots.

The parka was dark green, from L.L.Bean. The letters *PEACE* were yellow, maybe six inches tall, and had been stitched across her daughter's chest, with *PE* on one side of the zipper and *ACE* on the other; her daughter stood five-foot-ten. Her daughter had black hair.

But Hermia waited to file a report. The first night felt no different from other nights of waiting, of staying awake and falling asleep exhausted and waking up at two a.m. when a car rumbled into the drive. The morning was only a little bit different—a list of grievances, a mounting rage—and she in fact expected Patricia to come back. All next day she pursued the argument—those tracks on the floor, the heedless self-absorption, that "Fuck *manners*, Mom"—and came up with things to say, a way to deal with accusation and make her answer clear.

It was then she most missed Max, and Anne. Always before she'd had company waiting, and someone to complain to or sit up with through the night. Anne would have distracted her; they would have talked and shared herb tea and built a fire in the winter if the living room felt cold. Max had been a watchdog, and he would hear a car on River Road a long time before its arrival. His tail would wag or he would bark in welcome or in warning, and all his life—even near the end of it, even fat and blind—make his loud way to the door. Now Hermia sat by herself, by the window and the telephone, while her daughter refused to come back.

The second night *was* different, and she had trouble sleeping, sitting in the rocking chair and waiting for a car, or call, or any sort of sign, and hearing the house silence envelop her like noise. Then it became the weekend, but often before on a weekend Patricia had what she said was a sleepover date, with friends at whose houses she slept. Fingernail parings and discarded clothes seemed proof of continuity: her daughter might return. Her child was not a missing person, Hermia assured herself, not yet.

The police were dutiful. They came to the house and answered her questions and took her deposition at their headquarters out on Route 7 and distributed fliers in Bennington and Manchester. But it was clear this had happened before: a runaway girl is no sort of news, and there are teenagers all over the county who leave home, then show up again. Odds are—they tried to comfort her—her daughter was just fine. They would file a report, of course, but she should try not to worry; there was no evidence of kidnapping or violence. They would, they promised, stay on the case and update, on a weekly basis, the Missing Persons list.

Night after night she waited; day after day she drove the streets of Manchester and parked at the entrance to Burr and Burton, or went inside and interviewed Patricia's teachers and college guidance counselor. Not one of them had anything important to report. She drove to Williamstown and Rutland, and managed to find Ryan there and ask what he'd heard; he could offer no help. He always had been a know-nothing, and now he knew nothing at all.

On Memorial Day the telephone rang. Hermia was gardening, dealing with the first spring peas, which needed to be thinned and staked; then, when she came inside, there was a message from Patricia, saying, "Mom, it's me, don't worry, I'm OK." The red message light on the machine was blinking; the call had been made seven minutes before. She pressed Star 69 because she had been told Star 69 would reconnect to a previous number and return a call. But there was only a buzzing, a blankness, and then a mechanical voice announcing, "If you'd like to make a call . . ."

Next week another message came: "Hello, it's me, don't worry, OK." The week after that: "Mom, I'm fine." It was uncanny, nearly, the way the girl would telephone the few times Hermia left the house, or hang up if she answered—just a pause, a breath, a click. The relief was enormous, of course. The relief was the important thing, and she tried to tell herself her daughter would return. She recorded a new message of her own—"Patricia, please tell me the best way to reach you"—but decided not to offer money or to ask for a telephone number or to plead "Come home!"

There were five calls by September, and then a postcard with a postmark out of Santa Fe, and by the time the card arrived, Hermia was angry. What had she done to deserve this, she wondered; why hadn't her daughter just come out and said it: *Mom, I don't want to be a musician, I'm not good enough for Radcliffe*—or however she'd explain herself. Why couldn't the girl be straightforward, she wondered; what was this need for secrecy? *I need my space*, Patricia wrote. *I need to not be anybody's family for a little while.*

The autumn leaves were dull, and fell, and winter came early and stayed. The cold was unremitting. When her horoscope read, *A person very dear to you will come into your life again*, she cut this out of the paper and pasted it on the refrigerator door. *All is not lost*, her next horoscope read. This too she cut out and kept.

As the months crept past, she stopped awaiting daily news; the police said the same thing always: they had no tips, no leads. In December she hired a private detective with an office down in Bennington who turned out to be incompetent, a waste of time and money. She did not begrudge the money but hated the way he made his report: the lewd suggestiveness and back-alley insinuation there were drug dealers involved. She posted a reward. It too proved unavailing: the post office box she rented was soon stuffed with misery—requests for help, long rambling letters from strangers blaming Jews or godlessness or crack cocaine, advice that she *Trust in the Lord*. The detective said the trail was cold, but the pattern of the postcards and calls was a pattern he could follow if she wanted him to travel and track Patricia down. She did not renew his contract, and in March she withdrew the reward.

—

When a year had gone completely by and April fourteenth arrived once more, Hermia decided she had to leave Vermont. The house had seemed a refuge once, a place of safety and escape, but now it offered no solace. She did not sell the property because her daughter might return, but could not bear to live alone through spring and summer, fall and winter in this empty place. The year she'd waited felt like ten, the seasons were interminable, and she knew she could not last through 1993. Instead she thought about the home in Truro, empty all this time except for summer rentals, and where she had been happy once when young.

Anne called. "You're leaving?"

"Yes."

"How long?"

"I don't really know yet . . ."

"I don't blame you."

"Blame?"

"You know what I mean, Herm, it's like when Max died. *I* myself just couldn't hack it."

"She's not dead."

The receiver crackled; there was static on the line.

"Would you rent the house out, maybe?"

"No."

It surprised her how easy it was just to leave. She arranged for the mail to be forwarded and changed the telephone message to say, "I'm on the Cape." She took more than a parka and rain hat, of course, but what she packed for Truro barely filled the Volvo, and Robin the caretaker promised to check on the furnace. He drained the pipes and lowered the heat and fastened the shutters upstairs. Robin stopped by once a week to check the lights and windows; he mowed the lawn and raked the leaves in autumn and kept the driveway plowed. The house on River Road had lasted, Hermia told herself, two hundred years without her, and it could last a few more.

She called her mother in England to explain about the move. Her mother was a widow now, and inattentive, fading, saying "That's nice, dear" routinely. She was growing deaf as well, and complained about the phone. She kept saying, "What? Speak up, don't *mumble*," and it was hard to know for certain what she understood or failed to. Hermia did not discuss Patricia, nor did her mother ask. "Give my best to the Baileys," she said. The Baileys—Frank and Annabelle—had been their neighbors in Truro in 1959, and were long since divorced. Frank Bailey had remarried, and Annabelle Bailey was dead.

After the first shock of it—on arrival, Hermia thought, *How small, how dark*—the house in Truro proved simple to arrange. She unpacked and stocked the pantry shelves with what she'd brought from Arlington. Fortunately, she had had the interior painted, and the walls were freshly white and the wood floors of the living room and parlor and the staircase gleamed. Her father's presence filled the place—his paintings on the walls, the Dogon mask above the fireplace, and even an unopened case of Jack Daniel's on his studio closet floor. These totems of her youth were familiar; there was a great deal to cherish, and she felt her spirits lift. As though she were a child again, she remembered dinner parties, dancing parties, the ruckus of celebration when her father finished work.

The ghost of Lawrence welcomed her also, waiting on the couch. The braided rug, the trundle bed, the bathtub each revealed him; as before, he raised his arms. She remembered making love with him that first time he had visited, in her childhood bedroom, standing up. Now she was fifty-one. It all had happened years ago but still felt like yesterday: the key on the nail by the woodpile, the way they'd warmed each other, flesh on flesh . . .

The chimney needed pointing, and a mason came and dealt with it; his cousin pruned the apple trees and left a stack of applewood to season for the winter. She trimmed the climbing roses and had someone from Consider the Lilies clear the flower beds. The house began to breathe again, to feel lived in and welcoming, and she kept a lamp lit in the living room and played music while she cooked.

She joined a reading group. She volunteered for Meals on Wheels, and the Safe House Auxiliary Service, and marveled at how rapidly the weeks and years went by. People offered her five hundred thousand dollars for the house. Then they offered her a million dollars, and then the real estate agent said, "Just name your price." "You don't understand," said Hermia. "I *live* here, I don't plan to sell." When the days and weeks felt empty, it was easy enough to fill them, and she was astonished, a little, by how easily she'd settled in and down.

At the grocery store and the post office Hermia met old friends. Time had bent and altered them, but not beyond recognition. There were sculptors and poets and retired airplane pilots and State Department officials from the Kennedy administration; there were, it seemed, psychiatrists and psychoanalysts in every house on Bound Brook Island or on the rise of Corn Hill. One man, Arturo Tucci, had been a colleague of her father's, and he said, "My dear, I'd like to paint you. If you're able to sit still, that is. I'm a creature of habit and cannot be rushed."

Arturo was seventy-six. After years of landscapes, he said, he was doing only portraits because only faces continued to be interesting; did Hermia agree? He had done a series of studies—line drawings, charcoal sketches, watercolors, oils—of his wife, Irene, and when she died three years ago, he'd been, he said, unable to keep working. He could not paint for months. He hated his easel, his studio, *everything*; he couldn't hold a brush. He turned the series of portraits of his wife's face to the wall.

But now again, Arturo said, the only important thing was faces, and he wanted to paint hers. She took this as a compliment and drove to his studio daily; he greeted her with a piece of shortbread and a cup of tea and sat her down in Irene's chair and said, "No more talking."

Then he commenced to draw. In the chair, in the north-facing light and the embrasure of the window, with this elderly painter observing her, his hand moving over the canvas as though disembodied, Hermia felt young once more, and wished she had a dog to pet, a blanket on her knees. He squinted, frowned; he shut first one eye, then the other; he peered at her intensely. But he was dissatisfied, he told her; there was something missing in the face, some expression he couldn't get right.

Often, she would return for a sitting to find the canvas painted over or a new one waiting, blank. When he finished the day's labor, he would shake himself free as though from a dream, and say, "Another cup of tea?" and she would make it for him, at ease in his old kitchen. Then they would talk. White-haired Arturo knew many people on the Outer Cape, and he regaled her with gossip: who was well or ill or who had gone bankrupt or mad.

—

The open wound of her daughter's disappearance closed over, a little, with time. It did not truly heal, of course, but when she thought about it now, she thought of Patricia as someone in childhood, not a woman turning twenty and then twenty-five. To think of her lost darling was like fingering scar tissue or pressing on a bruise. She rented out, then sold the house on River Road. Hermia entered into the community of Truro—its close-knit residents, its summer celebrants—as she had never, quite, in Arlington; her parents had been famous here, and she'd learned to ride a bike and drive a car down the side roads by the beach. And when the letters and postcards came each year—on her birthday or at Christmas—she read the nothing they told her as if the lines came from a stranger (*I'm*

*fine, I like it in this town, I've been working as a temp and sometimes
I borrow a piano; I know you're on the Cape, I hope you're OK, I'll be
in touch*) and preserved the letters in a leather folder on her writing
desk. There was no way to answer and no return address.

Her neighbors Bill and Helen Watts returned from a cruise of
the Mediterranean, and had had a wonderful time. They invited
her to dinner, along with the Wilsons and Banners and Arturo, and
bored everyone all evening with the details of their itinerary, the
cities and sites they visited. Returning with a bottle of grappa purchased duty-free in Fiumicino, they poured everyone a glass and set
up a screen in the living room and showed an assortment of slides.
"*This* is Vesuvius," said Bill, "and *this* is the town of Pompeii; *this* is
where we had that guide—what was his name, Helen?—who kept
announcing, remember, 'We are making refreshments out of antiq-
uity.' Remember how much fun we had in Naples, how we had perfect weather every single day?"

Arturo had fallen asleep. The Wilsons and the Banners too sat
stuporous in armchairs, nodding, and so Bill and Helen turned to
Hermia, insisting that she take the trip. They talked about Sardinia
and Sicily; they believed a trip like theirs would be just the thing
for Hermia, exactly what she needed, and they went on and on
about the excitement of sightseeing, the value of a change of scene.
"Are you auditioning for the job of cruise director?" She wanted to
ask. "Do you get a commission?"

But Bill and Helen were unstoppable, laughing together and
reminding each other about what they'd eaten and done. The
two of them meant well, she knew, and poured out the last of the
grappa and continued to show slides of blue-green water and white
temples and each other smiling in front of every "bella vista." Bill
translated the phrase repeatedly, saying it meant "pretty view," and
they'd had a spectacular time.

At evening's end, to silence them, she promised to look into it, and the next day a travel agent in Orleans called her, saying, "Your friends the Wattses suggested I should get in touch and send you some details, OK?"

"OK," said Hermia, and two days later a brochure arrived. To her own surprise she found herself reading it with interest: the cruise would last two weeks. Except for visits to her mother in England—who no longer recognized her and to whom it made no difference, seemingly, if she were in the room—she'd not left the country. It would be a change of pace, a change of landscape mostly, and Hermia reserved a cabin for the trip.

X

1974–2003

When he took the job in Ann Arbor, he rented an apartment near the farmers' market. Lawrence liked the town, its coffee shops and jazz bars and, everywhere, its low-key affability. As half-time adjunct assistant professor in the architecture program, he made friends on the faculty and with those who worked downtown— designers and lawyers and real estate developers who asked him to join them at lunch. There were concerts and basketball games to attend; there were parties to go to and give. On his thirty-fifth birthday he joined a health club and started to work out four days a week; he enjoyed the anonymity, the nodding acquaintance with men on adjacent machines.

Again, he wrote steadily, liking his classes and liking the students, preparing his lectures with care. They would, he believed, make a book. His course "Public and Private Space" was popular, and his editorial "Urbanism and the Public Realm" was published in *Architectural Record*; this pleased him very much. Lawrence divided his time between the Art and Architecture Building and the local firm of Spence & Mills Design Group, spending Monday, Wednesday, and Friday afternoons on North Campus and the rest of the workweek downtown. At times—consulting on a shopping mall or a condominium complex adjacent to the golf course—he wondered what had happened to ambition. Early on he'd hoped to change the shape of things, to be a kind of Frank Lloyd Wright or Buckminster Fuller for his own generation; now he was producing drawings for a downtown four-story garage . . .

Still, he felt at home in Ann Arbor; the city paid attention to its common space and parks. There were walkways by the river and playing fields and bridges where the students clustered, a pond near his North Campus office where he could sit and smoke. On fair days he would walk or jog through Gallup Park, and sometimes he drove out to Baseline Lake and rented a canoe. He met his second wife in the Nichols Arboretum, one afternoon in June. She was sitting on a blanket, drawing, and he praised the way she rendered sprigs of willow leaves.

The woman smiled and returned to her work. She was wearing a tie-dyed wraparound skirt and drawing willow roots exposed on the bank of the river.

"Do you do this for a living?" Lawrence introduced himself.

Squinting, she looked up at him; he was standing in the sun. She had a clipboard and a sketch pad and set of drawing pencils.

"I'm sorry, I don't want to interrupt . . ."

"But you're interrupting anyway," she said. "Janet. Janet Atwan."

"I mean, you're very good at this."

"You're standing in my light."

"Oh, sorry. Is that a suggestion?"

"It is." Again, she bent back to her work.

———

In years to come he remembered the line, the way she instructed him to step aside. It was, Janet told him, a quote. Alexander the

Great once made a pilgrimage to the beggar-cynic Diogenes, asking the seated man what he desired. "You have only to ask a favor," said the reverential emperor, and "it will be conferred." The philosopher answered—or so the story went—with the phrase she repeated to Lawrence: "Get out of my light, lord, I'm cold."

All through their marriage it felt the same way: he standing, smiling, praising her, and she beneath him, elsewhere-focused, saying what bitter Diogenes said: *You're casting a shadow. Move on.*

Janet had her own career and proved successful at it, working as a bookkeeper for an insurance firm, and then as a certified public accountant, and then preparing taxes for well-heeled individuals and corporations in town. There were years she earned as much as he, and years when she earned more. But always she seemed to be nursing a grievance, always reminding him how much things cost—not in financial so much as emotional terms—and what she gave up to have sons.

They produced two of them—Andrew, then John—and in 1979 purchased a one-story home on a two-acre lot in Ann Arbor Hills. As the children grew, so did the house; Lawrence remodeled it, building a wing to the rear. He designed a series of glass-fronted bedrooms facing the woodlot, gesturing at Philip Johnson's Glass House but from a respectful distance—as Johnson had gestured at Mies. There were skylights and freestanding chimneys and a wraparound Florida porch.

At Janet's urging, when Andrew turned three, they acquired a Labrador retriever the family named Daisy, and then a cat named Peek-a-Boo and hamsters and a parakeet and, until it grew too large to keep, an alligator called Rex. When the boys were old enough for school, and if the weather was pleasant, he and Daisy walked them there, through tree-shaded winding streets. The neighborhood children cried "Daisy" and ran to pet her fearlessly;

she wagged her tail and rolled on the ground and let them scratch her belly and pull at her soft ears.

Lawrence liked being "Dad." He had many happy memories—games of Frisbee on the lawn, the barbecue he built himself, springtime dinners at the picnic table where white azalea bushes and rhododendron bloomed. When he collected his children from school, they were always glad to see him and hurtled out the door. He liked helping with their homework: the spelling and arithmetic and the building projects with cardboard and construction paper; he fashioned a platform for Lionel Trains. Fixing lunch for his sons was a pleasant routine: the peanut-butter sandwiches and potato chips and chocolate-chip cookies and boxes of fruit juice he packed into brown bags. They drove to the Toledo Zoo and the Henry Ford Museum when Catherine came to visit, on those rare occasions Annie sent her east. He tried very hard to be faithful, and to make his marriage a success.

But there were women everywhere: the lighting designer from Cleveland, the client from Grosse Pointe Shores in the throes of a divorce, the secretary in the office of the dean of engineering who wore tight skirts to work. Over time, it seemed to him, Janet grew more and more distant—preferring her Monday quilting club or Saturday morning live-model class to staying home with him at night or staying, on weekends, in bed. He told himself he needed sex more often and more urgently; if he lived in France or Argentina, there would have been no stigma in acquiring a mistress. It would have been *expected*, and not an issue at home.

The woman from Grosse Pointe Shores owned a building site in Bay City and asked him to design a lakefront house. She had been referred to him because of his experience with solar panels and the Breuer house in Wellfleet, of which he'd made a model and on which he'd lectured in class. She came to his office in North

Campus, saying, "Money's not an issue, not *at* issue anyhow, the main thing is getting it right. Don't you agree?"

He agreed. He asked her what she wanted, and she told him what she did and did not want—how she thought of the new structure as a getaway, a place to be alone. They made a site visit together, driving north, and that night she came to his hotel room with a bottle of white wine and said, "I'm lonely, aren't you lonely?" and undid her blouse. Her name was Marianne, and her husband, she confessed, had a marked preference for men. It undermined her self-esteem to be so obviously not the partner he wanted; did Lawrence find her attractive, and would he object if she took off the rest of her clothes?

He did find her attractive and did not object. She was passionate beneath him, scratching at his neck and back, and he felt young again and somehow deserving, as though all of those days making breakfast for the children and all those nights doing homework had earned him this session with reckless Marianne in bed. In the morning he visited her hotel room, which was two doors down the hall; they took a shower together, and she turned around and soaped herself and fitted him inside her, saying, "This is what Nathaniel likes."

"Nathaniel?"

"Nat. Mr. Soon-to-Be-Ex."

When he returned to Ann Arbor, Janet appeared not to notice the welts on his neck, and he settled back to his routine with a briefly slaked desire; he was solicitous with the boys and did the grocery shopping when tax time approached and his wife worked overtime. Lawrence remodeled the home of the man who owned the Porsche and Volkswagen dealership and then the loft of a couple who owned Main Street Music; he too spent long hours at work. But often he pictured Marianne beneath him, her brazen nakedness, and although she decided not to pursue the beach house project, he did try to see her again.

She refused. When he called from the office, she said, "It's a bad idea, it would be too damn confusing, and anyhow we've gotten back together. Me and Nat, I mean, we're going to give it the old college try." To solace himself he slept with Dana the lighting designer, after her presentation on North Campus, in the motel she was staying in off Plymouth Road. She too was ardent, unrestrained, and when she left for Cleveland, she said that she'd had a good time. "I'll see you next fall," Dana said. "Or you could visit me in Cleveland, if you want . . ."

Again for a month he felt happy at home, and that spring he planted a vegetable garden on the flat lawn up above the barbecue. He did not fence it, however, and rabbits and groundhogs ravaged the lettuce and beans. Daisy ran after them fruitlessly, too fat and slow to catch her prey but enthusiastic nevertheless at the prospect of the chase. While John and Andrew watched TV, he sat out at the picnic table, sketching a plan for a sauna; Janet joined him with a gin-and-tonic and a plate of cheese.

"This isn't working, is it?"

"What?"

"Our marriage," she said.

"Excuse me?"

"You know what I'm saying. You heard me."

"No."

"No, you didn't hear me, or no, it isn't working?"

"No, I'm not certain I know what you mean."

She offered cheese. There was Stilton on crackers, a wedge of Emmenthaler, and sliced Brie. "Dana called."

"Who?"

"Dana. She seemed surprised you had a wife. She tried to pretend the number was wrong, but I told her she was right. Correct, I mean, to think you won't be married much longer."

"What are you *talking* about?" He looked at his sketch.

Janet took his pencil from the picnic table and reached across and X-ed out the drawing thickly, twice.

"You don't want a sauna?"

"Denial. You've been into denial for *years*. Just because we don't discuss it doesn't mean I haven't noticed."

"What?"

"How unhappy you are, Lawrence. And how unhappy you make me."

"I do?"

"How we don't belong together, never did . . ."

Janet drained her glass, then emptied the ice on the grass. She seemed matter-of-fact and bemused by his shock, explaining herself to him as to a child; she had known about his escapades, his little adventures, his— The word for it was "flings." Ann Arbor was too small a town for him to keep behavior hidden, and she didn't love him, hadn't ever loved him maybe, didn't think she could forgive him, and wanted a divorce. They had done what they could to pretend the marriage worked and they belonged together, but should have stayed apart. She should have known from the beginning they were making a mistake, and for a while, for the sake of the children, she'd tried very hard to ignore her unhappiness and hope things would improve. But it wasn't working, wouldn't work, it was no favor to the children, and they'd all get over it; she wanted him out of the house. "This is," she said, "the end of it; I need to get on with my life."

—

His own, he decided, had gone wrong. The schedules that his children kept no longer seemed to require him, the noise that once seemed a distraction now was a fuss he missed. Lawrence drank. He mourned the clattering ruckus of domesticity, the busy jumble of the house. In his furnished apartment on Ann Street, he tried to focus on his work, writing an essay on postmodernism in which he praised Moore, Graves, and Tigerman, also acknowledging Venturi in "this rejection of the Modern Movement." Watching his sons play baseball or soccer, he kept his distance in the stands; he slept again with Dana, but the edge of desire had dulled. He was forty-eight years old, a bachelor, assailed by a sense of the passage of time and how it was passing him by; he consulted a therapist, twice.

The sessions were not a success. He positioned himself on a brown leather couch while the therapist—Alan McDiarmid, who had been recommended by a colleague—sat in a Barcalounger. McDiarmid had a close-shaved head but thick black eyebrows and a white mustache; during the second visit he interrupted Lawrence, saying, "Let's get to the point."

"I'm not sure I know what you mean . . ."

"Meaning?"

"*Point.* Does there *have* to be something I'm after? Some problem I'm supposed to solve?"

"Well, why else are you here? Why did you make an appointment?"

"I thought maybe . . ."

The therapist seemed impatient. "Yes?"

"Maybe what I'm going through is, you know, representative? A predictable pattern in middle-aged men? A rite of passage, somehow . . ."

The wall clock audibly ticked. There were leather-bound books and a gaslit fireplace and above it a framed painting of a stag bending down at the edge of a lake. Traffic rumbled down Liberty Street. Lawrence coughed; he needed to decide, he said, if he wanted a permanent teaching position, if he should go up for tenure or be mainly a practitioner. He was at a turning point, a fork in the road, and could use help with directions.

"Oh?"

"What I'm trying to describe," he said, "is everything feels out of sync—like one of those movies with bad splicing. Bad *editing*, maybe. I open my mouth and language comes out, except the audio is poorly dubbed, and there's a difference—a split-second pause—between what the character says and how his mouth moves, it just isn't right . . ."

"You called yourself a 'character.'"

"Did I?"

"Why?" McDiarmid made a note. "Why would you do that, I wonder."

"Do what?"

"Why do you *think* you use the third person? Or talk about bad editing? You mean you're not able to say what you mean?"

He shook his head. "It's just I feel so far away from what I dreamed of early on, from who I thought I'd be, or be with."

"And this feels like a problem?"

"Almost everything feels like a problem, but none of it touches me really. I'm not really here, if you know what I mean."

"No . . ."

McDiarmid's clinical style, he recognized at last, was confrontational. "No *what?*" Lawrence asked.

"Who did you think you'd be with?"

"Does it matter?"

"If you think it does."

"This conversation makes no sense. All I do these days is work, and even the work isn't working . . ."

"Oh?"

Now he repeated what Janet had said: "We don't belong together, never did."

———

Still, his time with the therapist clarified things; he decided to stay in Ann Arbor. On the basis of two P/A Awards and *The Common Space*, the College of Architecture and Urban Planning proposed him for tenure; in 1991, he became a full professor. This promotion gratified him to a degree he found surprising, and he told the dean how thankful he was for the vote of confidence. "It's a slam dunk," said the dean.

While the boys remained in town, he tried to be an active father, attending practice sessions and tournaments and concerts and carpooling with the other parents and paying the Greenhills tuition. With Janet's grudging permission he took them out on rafting trips and, for Tigers games, to Detroit. They liked the Detroit Lions also, and he bought a set of tickets, but the games were cold, and long, and the Lions rarely won. Lawrence solaced himself with the notion that all children sooner or later leave their parents behind, but in the case of *his* children the process had been reversed.

While his daughter was in college, they saw each other often; Catherine enrolled in Oberlin, a three-hour drive away. She and her friends spent weekends in Ann Arbor, and if he himself went out of town, he left her the key to the place. By junior year she began to display her mother's pampered recklessness; he worried for her safety and what he thought of as poor judgment. "Please be careful," he would say, watching irritation play across his daughter's face. "Don't think I'm being . . ."

"Being what?"

"Oh, I don't know. Censorious?"

"A censor. Why would I think that?" Catherine shook her golden mane at him and shrugged and turned away.

Then the boys too left for college and ceased being in regular contact. How did it happen, Lawrence wondered, that the person in the mirror was sprouting liver spots and wrinkles and hair in his nostrils and ears? How did it happen that his wives and children found him an irrelevance, a stranger to be tolerated and, when possible, avoided? His waistline had thickened, his neck too, and he found himself comparing the price of real estate and cars and clothes with prices he remembered from a quarter of a century before.

He went to his thirtieth Harvard reunion and reported to the tent where classmates gathered, putting on badges and hats. They seemed old and fat or wizened and bald; at first he believed he had made a mistake and gone to the wrong tent. The class representatives had no difficulty recognizing him, however, and handed him his welcome folder and slapped him on the back.

There were panels and speeches and parties; on Friday night there was a dance. Turn by turn he danced with classmates' wives and trophy wives and old Radcliffe classmates, trying to enjoy himself, full of self-pity and scotch. Next morning, nursing a headache, he sat on a panel on "urban revitalization," comparing Newark and Atlanta and Birmingham and dealing with the three cities in terms of city planning, the shift in profile of their population base. When it came his turn to talk, he reached for the microphone and, remembering the couplet from Samuel Beckett, recited it: "'Spend the years of learning squandering courage for the years of wandering . . .'"

"That girl of yours," someone asked him at lunch. "Whatever happened to her?"

"Who?"

"What *was* she called, I can't remember. The one with long black hair and the weird name. Hannah? Henrietta?"

"Hermia?"

"*Hermia*. Right."

"I don't know," Lawrence admitted. "We've dropped out of touch."

"Me, I've got grandchildren," said the man. "Five of them. Amazing, isn't it—remember that old Latin saying, 'Tempus fugit.'" He laughed. "Bottoms up. It's what I tell my grandsons, bottoms up."

"Where are you living, Larry?" asked Tim Bell. Tim Bell wore a blazer and wide crimson tie.

"Ann Arbor."

"Oh. Retired yet?"

"Not yet."

"We've just done it," said Tim Bell. "The missus and me and *Betty* makes three." He smiled. Then he explained that *Betty* was a forty-foot sloop, a rig he had brought up to Camden and was planning to sail to Tortola before hurricane season, then winter over in the Virgins, and he told the others at the table there was nothing like it—Tortola, Virgin Gorda, and the rest—for pleasure cruising, push come to shove; the Drake Channel made everything worth it, those *years* at the office spent sucking it up.

"I never would have figured you for the retiring type," said Sammy Lax, and everybody laughed.

"Did you say *Virgin* Gorda?" asked a man whose name he did not recognize. "Is that the one where the resort is Little Dix? No *wonder* it's still virgin—get it?—the Rock Resort is only Little *Dix?*"

Lawrence tried to join in the general merriment but could not. The men were wearing crimson caps, the women crimson scarves. He looked around him at the dining tent—this herd of well-dressed, well-fed citizens—and asked himself how he arrived at this place and how youth had drifted away . . .

———

For three years he served as chair of the architecture program, dealing with issues of recruitment and curricular reform and retention of lecturers and the President's Planning Advisory Commission for the allocation of campus space. There was a kind of comfort in the imperatives of detail work, a sense that something was expected of him hourly, daily, weekly, via the printout of appointments and committee meetings his secretary compiled. He was sitting at lunch in the Michigan League, working on arrangements for a joint exhibition with the faculty of Art and Design at the newly constituted ArtSpace, feeling tired, feeling restless and, although he tried to hide it, bored. Once the discussion was over, Lawrence paid and left. But his progress was impeded; a crowd of young people appeared. Great clusters of them filled the hall. Exuberant, wearing dreadlocks and caps and denim jackets, they cascaded through the lobby doors and blocked the exit stairs.

He could not move. He tried; there was nowhere to go. Streams, then a river of children poured past: laughing, shouting. "One aspect of increasing age," he told the associate dean at his side, "is how hard it is to guess the ages of young people; these are high school students, aren't they, not college level yet? Remember how, when we were young, we couldn't tell about old people—if they were forty or sixty or eighty; well, now it's become the reverse. Who are they; why are they here?"

Why they were there, it developed, was for a talent show. This was, Lawrence discovered, the Midwestern regionals of a performing arts consortium, and there were high school students from the area as well as teams from Ohio, Indiana, Illinois, and the Upper Peninsula of Michigan. They wore insignias and headbands and T-shirts emblazoned with logos and jostled each other happily; they wore earrings and nose rings and metal in their eyebrows and cheeks. They were high-fiving each other and adjusting their Walkmans and drinking water from small plastic bottles and angling for position in the hall.

He checked his watch. He had, he realized, less than an hour until his next appointment—too little time to return to his office. So Lawrence found a chair at the edge of the room, just inside the paneled door, and watched and waited for the crowd to thin. It did not thin. It packed the room and aisles and hallway, and there was an insistent beat, a jubilation everywhere. A platform stage had been erected, with a podium and microphones; groups of young people were twirling their arms and punching the air in near unison, shouting. The beat of the music was loud. The rules were five minutes a performance, and a timekeeper stood at the edge of the stage. The microphones hummed, thrummed.

A series of poets recited their verses and, watching the clock, took turns. They did dance steps or shuffled and shrugged. Three guitarists played flamenco; two girls played a transcription of the Pachelbel Canon for flute. A boy with a cherubic face and rolls of baby fat declaimed, "I got a song to play ain't got all day it's catch and throw, I gotta go and so let's get it ON ON ON. Because what's the point let's blow this joint, our gov-uh-ment is up for rent and everythin' is stinkin' in this land of Ford and Lincoln." Three more boys joined in the chorus, shouting it together: "The game of fame is pitch and catch, I gotta go and so let's get it ON!"

A girl walked out on stage. She was tall and thin and black-haired, in a tank top and black jeans. She was older than the others, Lawrence saw, and moved with the coordination of a dancer, rangily, snaking the microphone wire behind her, tapping her heels and the hand on her hip. He was too far away to see her well, but she possessed authority and the seated audience knew it; they shouted out approval while she stood and stared. If this had been a show, she would have stolen it; if this had been a chorus line, she would have been the star. Then, in a pure contralto, and meditative somehow in the middle of this public space, she sang a cappella:

> *You say you'll wait another day—*
> *eternity for me, you say—*
> *and that you're near though far away.*
> *But when I left I was bereft*
> *and what I do is take you too.*

Your heart comes with me on this ride,
the seat belt cinched across my side,
each breath I breathe is You!

Lawrence left. He had twenty minutes now to make his meeting at OVPR, and he started walking. The figure of that black-haired girl remained with him, however. On State Street and in the Fleming Building while they wrangled over space, and cost, and the proposed center for information technology; all during the afternoon seminar he led on "Post-Urbanism and Re-Urbanism"—an unlikely pairing, but conjoined in a repudiation yet guarded embrace of Everyday Urbanism—and at the reception for the lecturer that evening, a "green" architect visiting the program from Seattle, and dinner afterward; she stayed with him. Then, when finally the day was done and he was back in Ann Street, kicking off his shoes and taking off his tie and finishing a scotch-and-water as he sorted through the mail, he understood at last what memory had been aroused and what he had responded to: the image of Hermia, young.

—

Catherine announced she would marry a lawyer, and did so in September 1996. At the wedding he sat next to Annie and was shocked to see the change in his ex-wife: wan and thin and wearing strong perfume. The minister described the young couple as selfless, devoted to each other, and spoke at length about Catherine, describing someone Lawrence failed to recognize: his daughter as Samaritan, generous to those in need and unstinting as a volunteer and always ready with a helping hand to anyone who asked for help. On the dance floor afterward, while he was piloting her back and forth, she said, "Oh, Daddy, I'm so lucky. So grateful for all that you've done."

What had he done, he asked himself, what could she be grateful for, and who was this man she had married?—fair-haired Philip fresh from law school and earning six figures already. The wedding party was boisterous, lawyers and doctors and account managers and Catherine's college friends. But Lawrence felt unsettled, and Annie in this incarnation was a stranger totally. "Isn't it amazing," she asked him over wedding cake, "we produced this girl together? How did we *do* it, I wonder?"

"By interaction," he wanted to say. Once this would have amused her, or provoked a response, but the matron at his side was picking at her wedding cake and drinking sparkling water with a slice of lemon, then a cup of decaf coffee, and would not relish the reminder of her old recklessness. She had become the very image of propriety, and he held his tongue. "*We* didn't do it," he managed instead. "The credit's entirely yours."

Annie patted his hand. "That's sweet."

"Sweet?"

She nodded. "I *will* take the credit. She's sweet."

Then his sons too got engaged—Andrew to a friend from college and John to a high school history teacher who was half Korean. The three weddings happened in rapid succession, as though his children were competing to establish separate families and see who could move away farther and faster; by 2001, when he turned sixty, Lawrence had grandchildren whose birthdays he registered dutifully and of whom he was fond. Andrew's wife, Vanessa, was an ebullient redhead, and John's wife, Irene, a solemn dark-eyed presence, and everyone seemed happy and got along well together. Andrew settled in Phoenix and John in Vail, and when he had business in the Southwest, he made a point of visiting, and if they came to visit him, he made a point of "treats." But year after year, when the visits were done, he had a sense of exhausted relief; his children and their families felt very far removed.

Once more he shared meals with women and was their companion at concerts, and once or twice he slept with them, attempting to enjoy himself as he had done when young. But it all seemed automatic, a bodily memory, like walking or breathing, that he performed from habit and without conscious application. Elise Aronoff, for example, was smart and fierce and, as he was, twice divorced; she had a brittle energy Lawrence found attractive.

She owned and operated the Artists' Collaborative Space on South Main Street, a three-story brick building with studios and galleries and, in the lobby, a shop. He met her at the display case while buying earrings for Catherine, and he confessed that, after all these years, he couldn't quite remember if his daughter had pierced ears or not; she said it wasn't a problem, he had a fifty percent chance of getting it right, and they could adjust the clip-ons if he got it wrong. Therefore he purchased the earrings—amethysts in the shape of a teardrop, with a thin gold coil suspending a second, smaller stone beneath—and Elise commended his choice. She gift wrapped the box carefully and added a black bow.

They had coffee together and, later that same week, a drink. She invited him for dinner and prepared a cassoulet, first having determined that he was not a vegetarian or allergic to the ingredients, and he admired the style of the meal and praised her for it lavishly. They drank a bottle of rosé and, for dessert, Muscat de Beaumes de Venise; Elise caressed his cheek and shoulders while they were sitting on the couch. They talked about their children, where they lived and worked and how rarely anyone *saw* anyone these days, how the geography of distance had grown commonplace for families. "It's much too fast," she warned him, "don't you think we're rushing things?" but he folded her into his arms.

The affair lasted six months. He enjoyed her passionate convictions—the way she hated Cheney, Bush, and Rumsfeld, for example—and how meticulous she was about arranging the flowers when he brought her a bouquet, or how she insisted on shopping at the farmers' market instead of at Whole Foods. Her body was firm-toned from yoga, and she enjoyed herself, or appeared to, in bed. The prospect of sustained companionship no longer felt welcome, however; he preferred his private space, he told her when she suggested a week together up north, and the idea of starting out anew with Elise Aronoff did not excite him. At the Artists' Collaborative party in June, he threw a pass at Susan Ward, one of the ceramists exhibiting pots, and made certain that Elise was watching, so later that night, when she complained about his embarrassing behavior, Lawrence told her he himself had been embarrassed only by Susan's refusal, because he was a free agent—just as she, Elise, was a free agent—and would remain that way.

—

It was time once again to take stock. He was a tenured professor of architecture, a published presence in the field now nearing the age of retirement; he looked often at the size of his portfolio with TIAA-CREF. He had, he decided, thrown away—or in truth had never been presented with—the possibility of a career as an architect; what he nibbled on were table scraps from other men's accomplishments, Piano and Pelli and Eisenman and Foster, the long list of those who were doing what he had hoped to do. He ceased practicing karate and took catnaps when he could, but mostly he conducted business as usual and, more and more often, was bored. He was a father and grandfather, twice divorced, a solitary man who read the *New York Times* with attention, then did the crossword puzzle. Lawrence signed a living will, directing his survivors not to take extraordinary measures to resuscitate or keep him alive if impaired.

XI

—

2004

At the start of December he drove to Cape Cod. They had called each other often, e-mailed daily, written letters; her handwriting, he told her, was unchanged. She signed her letters: *Love.* In e-mails they discussed the weather, the tasks of the day, the trivia of plumbing problems, or the lack of progress in a local murder mystery, a woman killed the year before whom Hermia had known. The police were asking everyone—all the men of the area, anyhow—to provide them on a voluntary basis with DNA samples; this might or might not prove useful, she wrote, but it's a civil liberties issue, and everyone in Truro has an opinion one way or another; should the government be adding evidence to what they compile already as a dossier on their citizens? The dead woman had had several lovers, but they each had alibis, and what bothered her, wrote Hermia, was the cloud of suspicion that hung over Truro, the fear that had settled in town.

Ann Arbor seemed, to Lawrence now, full of senior citizens. On sunny days he passed them in the park. He saw them at the farmers' market, or doing tai chi at the gym. He was finishing an article, "(Un)intentional Planning," with a focus on the distinction between anticipated and preexistent conditions—as in, for example, what General Oglethorpe designed for Savannah and Baron Haussmann for Paris. Is it easier to start with a blank slate or work with the existing urban fabric? What have the City Beautiful movement and Urban Renewal done—or failed to do—with the American town-and-cityscape? There were case studies on Brasília and what "Corbu" had achieved in Chandigarh.

The prospect of Thanksgiving made him, as always, uneasy; he had insufficient space for his children and did not invite himself to visit them instead. His sons' wives had families also, and he would have been welcome in Phoenix or Vail, but the idea of travel that weekend was daunting. He was fine, he told them when they asked, just weary a little from the cruise and ready to stay home.

Halfheartedly Catherine inquired, "Dad, what are you doing?"

"When?"

"For Thanksgiving. Your dinner, where will you be eating it?"

"Spence & Mills," he lied, "has an office party and we're all invited."

"Really? Who's cooking?"

"The Moveable Feast, their catering service. I'm fine."

So Lawrence remained in Ann Arbor. On Thanksgiving Day he watched the Lions game on TV, then went by himself to a movie—a holiday screening of *Bringing Up Baby*—watching Cary Grant and Katharine Hepburn and Charlie Ruggles disport themselves enchantingly with leopards and puppies and dinosaur bones. When the hero and heroine kissed at film's end, he joined in the applause. What he hoped for, he told Hermia on the phone, was to spend more time with her, and with her alone.

"You mean it?"

"Yes."

"You're not being polite?"

"No. Yes, I'm not being polite."

"Are we rushing this?" she wondered.

"You *asked* me, remember?" There was static on the line. "The day we left from Malta."

"Of course I remember. And it's a straight shot from Boston. Or T. F. Green in Providence, and then you rent a car. Or you could fly to Provincetown and I'd collect you there."

"I'll drive," he said. "It's time for a visit. And I'm not bringing a moving van or planning to turn into fish."

"Fish?"

"It's an old expression: After three days, all guests smell like fish. I promise to shower."

She laughed. "You're welcome whenever you want to . . ."

"What, shower?"

"No, visit. Do come."

They agreed he would come in December, before serious winter set in. He would drive from Ann Arbor to Truro, spending the night in the Finger Lakes maybe, or Buffalo or Albany or one of the towns in between. "I'll be driving my mother's Impala," he said. "You know, the gray convertible. The horse does know the way."

"You're joking . . ."

"Yes."

"I remember that car."

"I remember the backseat," he said.

"Come ahead," she told him before they hung up. "I'm ready, I can't wait."

Yet Hermia did worry, fearful she'd made a mistake. What did she really know, she asked herself, about this man and how he would behave? She had trusted him in Malta, and years before in Cambridge, but more than forty years had passed, and who he was in 2004 was a person she no longer knew. A night on shipboard in a foreign country is a night on shipboard in a foreign country, nothing more. And *that* was not her life or world; she hoped inviting him to Truro had not been a mistake. Everywhere, or so it seemed, she read or heard stories of courtship: old high school classmates tracking each other down on the Internet, then meeting again after years. "Should auld acquaintance be forgot . . ." was the theme song of such stories, and they ended with a kiss. Old friends were reunited; old friends would meet and marry and their love, long dormant, bloom.

But "Auld Lang Syne" was not the point. She did not believe, she told herself, in "happily ever after"; it was not the way true stories ended, and all those tales of friendship and courtship left out the sad parts—the stories about disappointment, the parts about failure and fraud. Waiting, she thought about Lawrence, and she remembered the things that went wrong, the trouble he had been . . .

On Friday she made up the guest room. Airing it, then shaking out the blankets with their smell of camphor, she recognized how much time had gone by since she'd had guests, or entertained, or had what they used to call "sleepover dates." For the Sunday of his visit she planned a dinner party, intending for Lawrence to meet her good friends—the Wilsons and the Banners and Arturo—and wondering how he'd fit in. She reminded herself, if he tracked mud on the soles of his shoes or left dishes unwashed in the sink, not to complain.

She vacuumed; she tucked in the sheets. Then, patting the pillow, she froze. She understood that what she'd done was think about her daughter in preparing for his visit, and closed wounds were opening. *This is* not *about*, she told herself, *abandonment; this is* not *about departure but arrival, and he's coming for a weekend, and it isn't a big deal.* Old habits die hard, she reminded herself, and solitude was a habit she ought to learn to break. The wallpaper was peeling and would have to be reglued. *You're a grown-up,* Hermia assured herself. *You're a big girl now: behave.*

—

When he crossed the Bourne Bridge, it was raining; by the time he got to Truro, there was sleet. His cell phone did not function, and he called her from the phone booth by the post office, in the wet dark. She directed him toward the ocean, on the Pamet Road, and told him where to look for the sign to her driveway: two rights, and then a left.

He found it; it was five o'clock, and his headlights raked the house where Hermia was standing by the door. The trees were bare. Beneath the dripping overhang she raised her smiling face to his and offered him her hand. "Welcome," she said.

"How *are* you?"

"I'm happy you're here."

"It beats Geneva," Lawrence said, "where I stayed last night. Upstate New York. The Finger Lakes are the middle of nowhere. But *this*"—he extended his arm, expansive, pointing to the pine trees and the dune beyond—"is civilization."

Hermia studied him. "Why *did* you drive?"

"I'm not exactly sure. It felt like it would give me time . . ."

"They landed just up the road, the Pilgrims, and stocked up on water and berries. I'll take you there tomorrow, maybe, if the weather's better."

"It looks just the same. The house, I mean. I remember the driveway, that fence there, the woodshed . . ."

"A century ago," she said. "Come in."

He collected his bag and a bottle of Pommard and followed her through the door. The table had been set for two; there was a fire in the fireplace. The bookshelves were as he remembered them: narrow, crammed full of leather-bound books, with oversize art books piled high on the chairs and the floor.

"Should I take off my shoes?"

"No. Not, I mean, unless you want to . . ."

"My coat? Where do I hang it?"

She showed him. "Your quarters, sir."

He looked at her questioningly. Hermia smiled. "Separate cabins. Number 63."

"And you—you were 71."

"Welcome, world traveler. Fresh water, berries, a drink?"

"I clocked the distance coming here—it's just about a thousand miles. Not as the crow flies, maybe, but I did take some detours."

"Remember that song?" She did not hum it. "'If I go ten thousand miles . . .'"

"I think it's time you kiss me," Lawrence said.

She did so, then drew back. He smelled of exhaustion, the long day's drive. "Do you want a shower?"

"I want us to not be so nervous. I want to relax, a little."

"Mi casa, su casa," she said.

——

He did relax; he used the toilet, then washed his hands and face. They drank Pommard and sat by the fire together. The Hopper and the Motherwells, she told him when he asked, were sold, and what he was hearing in the kitchen on the CD player were the nocturnes of John Field. "I thought it was Chopin," said Lawrence.

"The Irish version of him, yes."

"It's beautiful here."

"You like it?"

"It's a beautiful house. You know that."

"Yes."

"I keep remembering," he said, "how long ago I came here, first . . ."

"In 1962."

"Most people on the planet weren't even *alive* then, Hermia."

She smiled. They talked about the weather and the coming winter, how isolated it could be, how inward-facing on the

Cape—but that was what Hermia loved, she explained, the silence of the woods and beach and how different it felt from the summer and the constant roar of traffic on Route 6. He talked about the Finger Lakes, the museum he'd gone to in Seneca Falls, the temples in the Valley of the Gods at Agrigento. "I made a photograph album from the trip," said Hermia, "but it's a disappointment—the album, I mean, not the trip."

Outside, the rain solidified, tapping at the windowpanes. "It isn't," Hermia said, "predicted to amount to much, the weather's supposed to improve." They spoke of the red cone of Etna at night. They remembered the little tour guide who sang, who called himself "Povarotti," and the way the captain of the MS *Diana* pronounced "Henglish." They tried to remember the names of the couple from Boston, the gracious white-haired gentleman and his deaf wife, those people who lived on Newbury Street, then Dick and Jane—remember them?—and the waiter who played the banjo up in the Elsinore Lounge.

The windows were small-paned, six over six, and where the panes remained intact, the blown glass had rippled and bubbled. When was this house built? Lawrence asked, and she said 1790, or thereabouts. "'Thenabouts,' I suppose, is the word, and it's been added on to, but the center section hasn't changed, this room's the original part. My father loved it here," she said. "He died outside."

He touched her arm.

"Well, not outside the house, in fact it was down in Hyannis, but this is where he crashed the truck and for the longest time I couldn't see that stand of pine at the first curve past the driveway without being haunted, a little, by everything he'd left unfinished—his paintings, my mother, the waste of . . ." Her voice trailed away. "I mean, when he died, he was younger than *I* am. Than both of us."

Lawrence changed the subject. "What happened to Vermont?"

"I sold *that* house. There was too much Battenkill under the bridge . . ."

He looked at her. She was wearing a loose black sweater and cotton pants with flared cuffs. "For a big-city girl, you seem to be spending your life in the country . . ."

She raised her glass.

"Have you noticed," he inquired, "how it's easier to talk about the things we did together than what we did apart?"

"I've noticed, yes." She drank.

"The way time flies and crawls," he said. "That's the thing I've been thinking about. I don't *feel* old, or as old as I look, and I'd guess that's true of everyone: these ancient wheezing hulks we are—not you, of course, you look terrific—still shocked by the face in the mirror and planning to play hooky or skip home from school."

"The school of second chances . . ."

"Right . . ."

An ember flared. They watched it. "There's dinner. I've made dinner."

"I'm not hungry yet."

The music in the kitchen ceased. They kissed. This time she moved her lips and tongue, and this time he held her closely and she did respond, pressing herself against him, and the two of them embraced. The furnace hummed; a shutter, somewhere, knocked against the siding. After some moments Hermia rose and led him wordlessly past the guest room she'd prepared, and past her own adult bedroom to the room of her childhood next to the porch, where decades earlier they'd made love standing up. In his mind's eye he was a boy once more and there had been no interval, no sundering. In his arms she was a girl again, eager and unweary. Sleet beat at the roof, tattooing the window. This time they used the bed.

—

Next morning the weather improved. At dawn there was a fine white glaze upon the branches of the trees, and everything looked crystalline; by ten o'clock it melted, and at noon the sky was clear. On Saturday they talked and talked, driving to Wellfleet and Eastham and looking at the beaches and walking dirt roads between ponds. At the Stop & Shop in Orleans they bought ingredients for the dinner party next evening, and she would not let him pay, so he purchased six bottles of wine. That night they ate in Provincetown, and he spoke about retirement and his fear he would miss teaching and how much he liked to teach.

"Please take this as a compliment," said Hermia, smiling in the candlelight across the restaurant table, with its red-checkered tablecloth, "but you were always a talker, and it's easy to imagine you behind the podium."

"Point taken," Lawrence said.

On Sunday evening her dinner guests came. Formally, she introduced him to Arturo and the Banners and the Wilsons, and they had a fine time together, eating fish pie and complaining about the horrors of a second term and the Republican majority. The Banners in particular were troubled, and said they were thinking of leaving, or refusing to pay taxes, but there was nowhere to go to that felt any better or any country, truthfully, that *wanted* Americans nowadays. "I was wrong," said Lawrence. "When we were in Italy in October, I was certain George Bush would be thrown out of office, but there were all those other people on the cruise—remember, Hermia?—who said their boy would win. In a town like Ann Arbor you never quite notice, and maybe that's true here in Truro also—you think America's *sane*."

"We get what we deserve," declared Jon Wilson. "The ones who vote for God and country are the ones who get sent to Iraq. I pray to the God I don't really believe in we survive for four more years."

Arturo pointed to her father's portrait of Hermia's mother and said, "It shouldn't hang so near to the fireplace, darkening. It's a fine fireplace, excellent draw, but anyhow there's smoke. I'm doing a show," he continued, "next spring—just Irene's face. Sketches, lithographs, one terra-cotta head I tried. And twenty-seven oils."

He was on the verge of tears, it seemed, then suddenly was weeping, and Joanna Wilson put her arm around the painter's shoulders. "I miss Irene so much," he said. "I think about how happy she'd have been to be here with us. Sitting in this room."

"We miss her too," said Hermia. "Everybody does."

She looked around the table at her friends and felt a rush of, if not pleasure, satisfaction: not, of course, at Irene's absence but at the presence of this company, those who had mourned her together and were telling stories about the scarecrow in her garden, the way she dressed it in Schiaparelli scarves and thrift shop Calvin Klein.

"It was the best-dressed scarecrow on the Cape," said Henry Banner, smiling, "and all the crows minded their manners. Rabbits too."

Lawrence felt a tightness in his chest. These people knew each other well, and had long shared memories; Arturo's wife, of whom they spoke, was someone he never had met. For dessert they were eating a strawberry fool, and he picked at his food while the others discussed Irene—her dream of visiting the Hermitage, her gift of mimicry, and how much she loved to dance.

"Remember the square dances," asked Susanna. "How she'd *skip* to do-si-do?"

Jon Wilson raised his glass. They drank. Lawrence attempted not so much to join in the discussion as to join in the shared sorrow, but the memories of Hermia's father and Arturo's wife remained abstract, incorporeal, and he focused instead on a painting of white birds flying over dunes.

After coffee and brandy the others departed. He helped her clean up. They stood side by side in the kitchen, a domestic couple—he rinsing off the plates, she stacking them according to her system in the dishwasher—and when the machine was full, she said to him, "Leave it, OK? We'll do the rest tomorrow."

The tightness in his chest, however, did not go away. At midnight Lawrence excused himself, saying, "It was a terrific meal. But I need to get some rest, I'm tired, dead on my feet."

"Poor dear," said Hermia. "Plum tuckered out . . ."

He joined in the joke of it: "I'm all used up."

"Not *all*, I hope. There's always tomorrow."

"No. Yes."

"Did you like them?"

"I liked them very much. Admired them, really. You've got excellent friends here, I think."

"Yes."

"Old friends. That's one of the things we can no longer do."

"Excuse me?"

"Make old friends, I mean. We make *new* friends, not old."

She smiled at him. "In my better moments, I think we're doing both."

They kissed good night. Then, wearily, he took himself to bed.

———

The party had been, Hermia told herself, fun: the meal was good, and Lawrence and her company did seem to get along. She was happy now, she told herself, happy, happy, and tomorrow she would ask him to extend his stay. She listened to the wind outside, and thought of her mother in Hampstead and what it would be like to bring her back to this house she would no longer recognize because, for years, her mother had recognized nothing at all. We wait and wait, thought Hermia, and sooner or later the thing we wait for does in fact appear: the statue moves, the painting comes down off the wall. She saw a statue move, a painting fall, and recognized she had fallen asleep; the image of her mother—washed and fed and put to bed insensate—and the image of herself when young, and then Arturo's wife, Irene, in portrait after portrait fused, were one.

Lawrence lay wakeful in the windy dark, counting backward from two hundred and attempting sleep. He pictured the buildings of Moshe Safdie, of Rafael Moneo, of Mies van der Rohe; he thought about his children and grandchildren and the woman in the next room no doubt also awake. His knowledge of her habits was old but incomplete. The word "choleric" came to him, and he made a chorus of it, repeating "choleric, choleric," emptying the word of meaning, placing it next to "caloric" and hearing the two of them rhyme. Noiselessly, he sang. He thought about "enfolded negativity" and a phrase the Smithsons used, in London, describing the interior space of their buildings as a "charged void"; he repeated the phrase: "charged void." Again he counted backward from two hundred and watched the clock register 1:11 and tried to make a pattern of it: time.

—

In the morning, when he woke, he knew he was at risk. The band of pain across his chest and taste of tin were what he'd felt in July. Over coffee he told Hermia—who came into the kitchen smiling, fresh-faced, wearing slippers and a beige terry-cloth robe—that if she didn't mind, he'd drive himself down to Hyannis for an EKG and maybe a stress test; it was nothing to worry about, not serious angina, but better safe than sorry. "What are you *talking* about?" she asked, and he said, "It's Monday morning, the third day of my visit, and I smell like fish." "All right," she said, "this isn't funny, will you be serious a minute?" and he said, "I probably shouldn't have driven, probably shouldn't be pushing myself, and if you have a doctor here, I think I'd better visit him, or the simplest thing is just the emergency room."

She drove him to Hyannis. It was December sixth. He said that, in Ann Arbor, he'd had to wait through the Fourth of July, and the timing was much better now; this time it was Pearl Harbor Day, or almost, and there'd be no need to wait. "I know you're trying," Hermia said, "to joke about it and keep me from worrying, and it's very impressive but not very funny; do you mind if we don't talk like this and talk instead about the way you feel?" So Lawrence did describe it: the shortness of breath, the ache in his chest, but repeated that he wasn't worried; he was catching it, he hoped, in time, and they'd warned him before it might happen again since the stent could be rejected, or, more likely, there was another problem in another artery and he shouldn't have eaten dessert. "It's not halfway as bad as July," he said, "and I was joking of course about dinner, the strawberry fool was superb."

She gripped the steering wheel tightly. She was trying not to cry. In the stretch of single-lane traffic past the rotary, they were caught behind a line of trucks, and she could not pass them and wondered if they should have called an ambulance, or 911.

He touched her wrist. "It isn't an emergency."

"We're almost there."

"That's fine. I'm fine."

"*Was* it the strawberry fool? Something you ate?"

He shook his head. The day was gray.

"Or—oh God, I hate to ask this—what we did together?"

"When?"

"On Friday night. Saturday. Yesterday."

"Listen to me, Hermia. You mustn't—no—don't blame yourself."

"There *was* heavy cream in the fish pie. And butter, oh God, butter everywhere. I'll *never* cook that way again . . ."

"Please," he said, "I'm being careful. That's all it is, a precaution."

"Promise?"

"Love, I want to live."

In silence they drove the last mile. The outskirts of town were blocked by construction, and a man with a *Drive Slow* sign he swiveled to read *Stop*. Traffic slowed to a crawl in Hyannis; she passed a row of buses, a cement truck, a stalled car. But it was as though all things had changed: he'd called her "love," and she who'd held herself aloof was desperate to help. His weakness enlisted her strength. At the emergency room entrance Lawrence waved and walked carefully in through the door while she went to park. It was ten o'clock. After some circling in the parking lot, she found a spot and got out of the car to join him. Then, locking it, swinging her handbag up over her shoulder and starting to walk to the hospital, she saw the world go dark.

Hermia leaned against the window of the Volvo, breathing deeply, standing, seeing black spots dance across the screen of her closed eyes. The air was cold. She was, she feared, going to faint. It was, she knew, a migraine, or the onset of a migraine, the announcement of it stalking her: a distant thing, then near. It *could not* be, she told herself, that he had come into her life to depart it on a stretcher; it *could not* be he'd joined her just to be taken away. What terrified her was recurrence: this hospital she had avoided—not needing more than an annual checkup with the family practice in Orleans and, routinely, a series of mammograms and Pap smears and once, when the test results were less than routine, a procedure up in Boston—for the decades since her father's accident. "Oh please," she heard herself saying, "oh please, it can't happen again, I can't lose this one also, not lose everybody. Please please just let him live."

And as though it was a prayer and her prayer had been answered, he was lying in a hospital bed, smiling at her when they let her visit in Cardiac Care, attached to tubes of oxygen and an IV and wearing a white smock. "The second time around," he said. "It may be a new blockage, or maybe the old stent's occluded."

"Don't talk. Are you supposed to?"

"Where Louis Kahn collapsed was in the men's room of, I think, Grand Central Station. He'd just come back from India, and nobody knew who the traveler was, and he lay there a long time before they could identify and then reclaim the body from the morgue. This great American architect, maybe the greatest of them all, and he's lying in a men's room where some passerby rolled him and took away his wallet . . ."

"Why are you telling me this?"

"Because I'm not planning to die," said Lawrence.

A nurse appeared.

"My new best friend," he said. "Meet Hermia."

"Pleased to meet you," said the nurse. "This one's a talker, am I right?"

"It's all those drugs you've been giving me. Valium? I'm usually the silent type—ask Hermia here. I've been silent forty years."

———

Hermia moved through the next hours, days, with a strange doubling sense of what was happening, had happened, as though the migraine that was not so much a migraine as the aftermath of terror had brought with it alertness and an equivalent lack of alertness. Everything mattered immensely and nothing mattered at all. The details to attend to—her car needing gas, the clothes she changed, a bowl of chicken noodle soup, the messages from the Banners and the Wilsons offering assistance, the telephone numbers Lawrence provided and the calls she made to Vail and Phoenix and a long conversation with his daughter in Chicago, the Monday night alone in the house—were unimportant and important both at the same time.

It was, she told herself, shock. It was minute by hour and hour by day, and all she wanted was for Lawrence to get well. He had mattered to her long ago and then he had not mattered much and now he mattered to her very much indeed. She could not bear to lose him, or to relinquish their shared space.

Except the space kept changing. It was the cubicle he lay in, first, with a blue curtain on an oblong rail they could use for privacy, and then the semiprivate room with a man from Barnstable in the next bed, who coughed and coughed, and then—when the procedure was over and the smiling doctor from Pakistan informed them they had found a blockage and removed it, inserting one more Cypher stent, this one a ninety-five percent occlusion but in a secondary artery, related to and a kind of sequel to what they didn't deal with before—a private room. The doctor was elegant, doe-eyed, and he seemed to assume she was married to Lawrence because he spoke to her with the deferential attentiveness reserved for family members when a patient is at risk. The doctor was a baby—they all were babies nowadays; how did it happen, she wondered, that doctors and lawyers and presidents all were infants now? "Your medical team in Michigan," the doctor said, "and we of course have been in touch, decided—correctly, in my opinion, correctly—the left anterior descending was more important; a lot of this, madam, is luck of the draw and where the plaque decides to lodge, so if there was an earthquake in July, you can think of this as a December aftershock, and if we had to do it all over again, if we'd had the entire picture, we might have considered a bypass, but anyhow it's over now and you did the right thing coming in . . ."

She sat with Lawrence. He slept. She held his hand and listened to him breathing, and when he was discharged the next day, she brought him back to Truro. The pots she'd left for cleaning an eternity ago were waiting in the sink, and the pans and unwashed glasses on the counter. Lawrence lay on the living room couch, beneath a blanket, while she set the house to rights.

He watched. He was weak, and sentimental, and told her he was grateful and loved her very much.

"Don't say that," said Hermia.

"Why? Why not?"

"Unless you mean it."

"I do," he said. "I *told* you . . ."

"We sound just like children."

"No. No, we don't."

"Remember what you called it, 'the school of second chances'?"

"It was you who said that."

"No."

"It was."

"Just listen to us arguing. We do sound like children."

"I love you very much."

XII
—
2004

Carefully, she nursed him. He said she did not need to, but Hermia insisted; she made him take his pills and brought him breakfast in bed. "You're spoiling me," he said, and she agreed. "I'm fine," Lawrence assured her, and she told him to lie back.

The weather remained cold and clear. He walked a half mile to begin with, and then a mile, then more. As December progressed, he found himself imagining the holidays in Truro and wondering if he should leave, or if they might travel together. The radio played Christmas music, Bach and Christmas carols; the announcer for Cape Cod Classical listed bake sales and charity drives.

Catherine called and kept in touch; so did the boys. His daughter offered to fly one-way to Providence or Boston and meet him there and share the drive back to Ann Arbor.

"I'm planning to stay," said Lawrence, "a little longer, maybe. If the lady of the house will let me . . ."

Across the room, Hermia smiled. The telephone was in the living room, and while he talked, he watched her: the severity of feature softened by increasing age and blurred by firelight. Her hair was down. She wore her reading glasses and a cable-knit brown sweater, and they were having their six-o'clock drink. He told his daughter he was getting better, feeling fine.

And this was true. At times—walking with Hermia down to the beach, or driving back from Provincetown, or unpacking groceries—he felt as though each minute of each day was a reprieve. He might, he thought, have died.

"It's day by day."

"You sound"—he smiled at her—"like an inspirational video. Some guru of the cherished moment."

"It's always day by day. Only sometimes we're more *conscious* of it."

"I love you," Lawrence said.

He said this to her often, as though trying the phrase on for size. It fit. The episode in Cape Cod Hospital had loosened something in him, and sentiment poured out. Love was unstoppably with him: he told Hermia he *loved* the house, the smell of her hair on his shoulder, oysters, Handel's *Messiah*, the feel of her forearm and hand. Often, he wanted to cry. He *loved* the *St. Matthew Passion*, the fading light at Pilgrim Spring, the scent of fresh-crushed mint. She reminded him that he had been self-protective and chary before, and he said, "That was then. This is now."

"You sound"—teasingly, she repeated the phrase—"'like an inspirational video.'"

He nodded. "Tonight let's have pasta and scallops. I'm cooking. There was a special on scallops at the Fish Market."

"Oh, excellent."

"And Scotty assured me these were actual scallops, not sea skate cut to shape."

"Sea skate?"

"Right: they have the same consistency. Some vendors cut up sea skate into what they sell as scallop chunks for maybe five times the price . . ."

"But that's illegal," Hermia protested.

"I love you," Lawrence said.

—

The Banners visited. The Wilsons visited. One evening they went to the movies and watched an action hero and his English girl-friend cavort. One afternoon they attended a concert, a benefit for Outer Cape Emergency Services, and the performers were good; they played Mozart and Schubert and then something atonal by a Russian. "I smell like fish," he said. "I promised to be gone by now."

"Oh?"

"I said I'd be leaving two weeks ago, and you should kick me out."

"I will," she said, "as soon as you begin to stink. It hasn't happened yet."

Lawrence was conscious of his children and grandchildren and therefore all the more keenly of Hermia's isolation. He bought presents for his relatives—fishermen's sweaters in Provincetown, a ceramic tea set from a gallery in Wellfleet, a compass and a set of paints for Andrew's children, Jack and Tim. Furtively, he sent these gifts from the post office in Truro, as though other attachments were unfair and evidence of family elsewhere might trouble her.

She was conscious of his restlessness, his sense that he should be at work but the work was over and had proved less important than earlier he'd hoped. He used to dream of consequence, an enduring reputation, and as a fellow of the American Institute of Architects had wanted recognition. Recognition had not come. Often, Lawrence doodled—on napkins or scrap sheets—cross-hatching buildings in perspective and drawing elevations of houses on the shore.

They were conscious of adjustment and the way their edges fit. He took an afternoon nap. She thought dawn the best time of the day. "Each sunrise is chock-full of promise," said Hermia, "with everything opening up." "You *are* an optimist," he said, and she said only in the mornings, not by night. She was, Lawrence told himself, both the girl he'd desired in college and the sixty-three-year-old he visited, and this juxtaposition of the strange and familiar confused him: which Hermia was spooning soup, which woman shared his bed? They talked of their journey to Pompeii and how long ago it seemed, how far in the receding past. "Can you believe," asked Lawrence, "it was just three months ago?" "If I'd jumped ship," she said to him, "I thought about it—did I tell you?—and finished the trip in Rome, we would have missed each other." "Is that," he asked, "our plain dumb luck or fate?" "Both, I think," Hermia said.

Their pleasures were quiet ones, cooking and reading and watching TV. The darkness was complete by five o'clock. He hated the war, as she hated the war, but that did not prevent their mourning the young dead. They talked about how much had changed, and also how little had changed since their own period of protest—Vietnam, then Watergate. It's not so much a question, they agreed, of *whether* but *when* the bill for oil comes due; they spoke of their parents and classmates and the inexorable forward march and then the triumph of time.

—

His sister telephoned. "How are you?"

"Fine."

"That's not what I've been hearing."

"I'm fine."

"And where *is* this anyhow, Larry? What sort of area code's 508?"

"Truro. On the Outer Cape. I'm here with an old friend."

"Which one?"

"You never knew her. Hermia."

"*That* Hermia? *The* Hermia?"

"Happy holidays. And thanks for having found me; you spoke to Catherine?"

"She's worried about you. An old dog performing his favorite trick."

"What a pleasant way to put it, Allie."

"Well, you haven't exactly been brilliant at this, have you?"

"At what?"

"At figuring out who to live with, or visit. At making romantic decisions."

"And you've been such an expert?"

"No. But promise me you're being careful."

"I am, I promise," Lawrence said—and wondered, was that true?

———

Each night, in front of the fire, they talked. "I want to know everything," he said, "*everything* about our years apart. I hate not knowing where you were in 1969. Or '96."

They tried for five-year intervals, but these were difficult to manage: one memory led to another. The house he built near Lake Champlain, for instance, and her home in Arlington were hard to keep distinct. The structures themselves were dissimilar, but the time frame was the same, and he had flown to Burlington and Albany while she was living nearby. His time lying ill on the island of Rhodes and hers in Nova Scotia seemed somehow the same journey, and her work at Harry Abrams and his at SOM belonged to the same past. Once he referred to Interlochen and the arts school at Cranbrook, and she asked him which was closer to Ann Arbor. Lawrence smiled. "You're being," he said, "a typical Easterner; not everything across the Hudson River is in another country, and you should visit me there."

They talked about the seventies and eighties and nineties and how they felt about the new millennium and what they did that night. Remember the millennium bug, asked Hermia, how everyone was certain the computers and the banking system would go haywire and the world was coming to an end? "It is," he said, "it was, it will, except not the way we imagined."

They talked about things that continue. She described her friend Anne Martineau and how the Prospect School had grown famous; the school itself had been forced to shut down for lack of financial support, but they'd kept extensive records, and the archive provided a resource for educators everywhere. So nobody was enrolled at Prospect now, but everyone studied the children who went there, the drawings and maps they produced. "You can't predict it," Lawrence said. "The law of unintended consequence is not the exception but rule."

They talked about retention, what stays or fails to stay. He spoke about his grandson, Jack, the way he loved to chart the stars, and wondered if there could be such a thing as a born astronomer, a person fascinated from the start by outer space. "Galileo, Tycho Brahe, and the rest; I'm not comparing Jack to Isaac Newton," said Lawrence. "It's just that everything about the night sky *speaks* to him. I've been looking all my life and can barely identify the Big Dipper, but this kid *knows* the constellations, his favorite toy's a telescope, and I wonder if an obsession like that will continue in his professional life or be like other hobbies and one day disappear."

"Some things remain," said Hermia. "They don't just fade away."

"It's short-term memory that goes." He reached for her hand. "I can remember everything about you, say, in April 1962, but who I met and what I did last year is hazy by comparison."

"Our waiter's name?"

"Darko. I mean before we met again. It's like the world was black-and-white and now it's Technicolor."

"You're spoiling me," said Hermia.

"I feel like everything went out of focus and now again it's clear."

They reminisced about Cambridge. When he returned for architecture school, said Lawrence, he missed her on a daily basis but had failed to understand it at the time. "Let's not rewrite history," Hermia said, and he admitted, "You're right, that's what I'm doing, but it could use some revision, my personal history could be improved." "Mine too," said Hermia. "Do you want a refill?" Lawrence asked, and she shook her head.

When the wood box by the fireplace required it, he brought in cordwood stacked beside the generator housing. She talked about her marriage and he talked about his marriages, and they agreed they might have chosen better or not made so many mistakes. They spoke about mistakes they'd made together and the ones they'd made apart. "I'm sorry I was jealous of Charette," said Hermia. "It was irrational really, but I never knew how truly crazy jealousy can make a person till I married Paul."

What happened to him? Lawrence asked, and she said he was killed in Sarajevo in the war. "It's strange," said Hermia. "I'd forgotten all about him, or at least I thought I had, but when the news arrived, I found myself dreaming all over again, unable to shake it, remembering everything, *everything*."

"You think you've closed the book," he said, "but then it opens up. In my case, though, whenever I run into Janet—it's a small enough town so that happens—I think, good Christ, how is it possible I shared a life with her; what did we have in common but a house and bank account?"

Two sons, she reminded him, and Lawrence said, "That's true. I loved and love them very much, but it's still as if I produced them with a nearly total stranger. And now they're grown-up strangers, and I see myself standing in the kitchen: making breakfast, making lunch for school, putting training wheels on bicycles or wiring the transformer for the train set in the basement, and I think the person in that picture is impersonating *me.* I must have been there, must have done the things I can remember having done with, *for* the children, but it's like another life. Or a dream of existence. You know . . ."

"I do," she said, "I know." "Most of the time I'm sleepwalking," he said, "but with you I'm wide awake. It's as though the rest of life has been, well, the rest of life." She spoke of how Arturo Tucci drew his dead wife's face obsessively, and modeled it. "There are stacks and stacks of paintings," Hermia said, "and plaster casts and maquettes made of clay, and it's as though she's still alive, alive to him at any rate, when you walk into the room." "You've been that way for me," he said. "For all these years I've kept you in a safe place in my heart."

She smiled. "The left ventricle."

"Right mitral valve."

"I want the whole chamber," she said.

—

On the morning of the winter solstice the front doorbell rang. The day was cold and gray. Hermia was doing errands in Wellfleet, then mailing a package at the post office, and therefore he answered the door. It was rare, he understood, for someone to use the front entrance, or ring; most of those who knew the house entered through the kitchen, and so Lawrence expected a stranger.

A young woman stood on the stoop. She was tall and black-haired, slender, somehow familiar. He wondered if he knew her or had seen her somewhere in Truro, but knew he would remember so striking a physical presence and they had not met.

"Can I help you?"

"Good morning. Are you the man of the house?"

She held, he could see, a petition: there was a clipboard, a sheet of paper with some signatures on it, a pen.

"Not really, no. I'm visiting."

"Are you a registered voter in Massachusetts?"

Lawrence shook his head.

"Is this"—she consulted her sheet, then gave Hermia's name—"her residence? Is she living here?"

"Yes."

"And can I speak to her?"

"She's not at home."

"Oh?"

He told himself that Hermia would not welcome a petition. "She should be back in an hour, maybe less."

"I'm sorry." The girl's disappointment was palpable, but there was also—he saw it in her face—relief.

"You could come back."

She shook her head. She was wearing mittens and a bright red scarf.

"You're lobbying for something, right?"

Again, she shook her head. Then, stamping her foot, she stepped away and he remembered where he had seen her: at the talent show in Ann Arbor, years before. But this seemed so improbable, he could not credit it; this girl was not that girl.

The canvasser withdrew. Her car had its lights on, idling, its exhaust a billowing thickness against the wintry gray. The car was an old Subaru, a battered Outback station wagon with a roof rack: white. There was no one waiting in the driver's seat or passenger seat; she'd come alone. Lawrence watched her drive away.

Oddly unsettled, he finished the *Times*. The news was bad. There were suicide bombers and scandals over prisoner abuse. Social Security was, the president warned, in trouble; it would be a disaster for our children unless we invested in private accounts.

Others disagreed. Lawrence folded the page for the crossword, then put the paper down. He noticed a crack in the left lower section of the six-over-six-pane living room window and went to examine it, tracing the line of the break. Had it been there earlier and he had failed to notice, or was the fissure new?

He heard a car engine, then saw it. The Subaru was retracing its path up the driveway, with Hermia behind; they must have met near the entrance and, unable to negotiate the single lane, the visitor backed up. Then she emerged, and Hermia stepped out of her car also, and the two women paused a moment, face-to-face.

—

She did not believe it. She could not believe it. A light snow was falling, breeze-eddied, and Hermia held her car keys and purse. She had been to Eccentricity and then the post office, waiting in line, deciding not to fill the tank but to do so with Lawrence, later, since there was a quarter tank remaining and she was anxious to return to him and uneasy now alone. On the Pamet Road she'd felt a strange—what was the word?—presentiment, a sense of something happening or about to happen, a shift in the sound of the engine or slight recalibration of the pressure in her ear.

She cracked the window open, and the sound changed pitch. These days all change was threatful, and she was feeling urgent and accelerated into the driveway and nearly hit the oncoming car, then braked while the stranger backed up.

Her first reaction was anger: this was *her* house, *her* drive. Her visitors were few, and rare, and this was not a car she knew, or delivery truck, so maybe it was just a tourist rubbernecking in Truro, or using the drive as a turnaround, lost; she assumed that once she'd passed it in the parking circle, the car would continue.

It did not. It stopped. It was not a meter reader, not a service call. A woman emerged from the driver's side, tall, black-haired, in a black woolen coat and red scarf, and stood and waited for her, shifting her weight on her feet. Her gloves too were red. She peeled them off, uncertain, and the way she peeled them—finger by finger, in sequence—was familiar.

"Patricia?" She could hear her voice change, break, but it was not a question—or, rather, the question was answered even in the asking.

"I should have called, I know. Or given you some warning . . ."

"Let me look at you. How is this possible?"

Her daughter held out both hands. "Could I come in? It's cold."

———

What followed was day after night. The two of them did enter, and Lawrence said, "Hello again," and Hermia said, "You've met?" Not really, Lawrence said, and introduced himself, and Patricia explained to her mother that she'd arrived a bit before and had just been leaving. She was deciding not to stay, or not this morning anyhow, which is why they'd almost crashed into each other at the mouth of Hermia's driveway, for she had nearly lost her nerve and driven off, and had only been pretending to be mounting a petition drive and asking for a signature. Because what if her mother had sold this house also, or moved, and after all these years some total stranger answered; how would, *could* she have explained herself, and what other reason offered for her presence at the door?

"Take off your coat," said Hermia.

"Do you want coffee?" Lawrence asked, "Tea?" and they all pretended that the visit was a normal one, a reunion after time away that did not entail disappearance and had not lasted for years. "Tea, please," said Patricia, and sat.

She told her tale. Haltingly, little by little, the history emerged. It had adventures in it, and people who were kind to her, and people who were less than kind, and dangers she alluded to but did not describe. That would come next. That came over time. As the afternoon progressed she did describe the places she had gone to and the people she had lived with and the farms she worked on—an orange grove in Florida, a cherry farm in northern Michigan—not as a day laborer, because she didn't have the back for it or stamina, but because she admired the migrant workers and had helped them organize, bookkeeping, cooking, laboring in a kind of solidarity with the unions and the workers; because the life of privilege and world of art and commerce from which she'd come had seemed to be the enemy and very far away.

That was the point, of course, the starting point at least, this anger she'd been harboring in Arlington in the picturesque house with a trust fund and the prospect of college and marriage and all those things the upper middle class can take for granted but neighbors up in Woodford or Sandgate couldn't dream of, much less take for granted. Her friends in Arlington had been the children of the rich, the country gentlepersons—"remember, Mom, that's what you used to call them?"—and then there were the others, the dropouts and the inbred ones with walleyes and a hundred-pound sack of potatoes in a trailer for the winter: two worlds so separate that when she tried to bridge them she felt she was doing splits.

Rueful, Patricia smiled. Her teeth were good. "It's one of the marks of distinction," she said, "one of the ways we could tell what side of the orthodontics track you come from or if someone took care of your teeth. I thought of pulling them, you know, as an act of solidarity; Rain did, remember Rain? She used to say the difference between us and the locals is only cavities, is crooked teeth, and so she had hers pulled. The last I heard she was on welfare, living with a shell-shocked vet, but nobody who knew him knew if what went wrong was Desert Storm or something else inside his head, and Rain and Ryan and the others are ancient history now."

She spread her hands. She was wearing a diamond ring. There had been, she told them, a sense of adventure, a belief they were inventing a whole new set of rules. "And we were all so certain everything would work out fine: munitions manufacturers and gasoline cartels and chemical monopolies would come to see the light. When I left, I felt desperate," Patricia said. "What was the word for it? 'Banishment,' 'exile'—and of course I knew that it was self-imposed.

"Except there was pride in it too. I'm twenty-nine by now," she continued, "old enough to know much better, but back then I was seventeen and telling myself: You close your eyes, it's night. You laugh, the world laughs with you. 'Give me your poor, your huddled masses, your weary' was our theme song: the Statuettes of Liberty just yearning to be free. Remember what we called ourselves: the G-String Quartet? There was all this music in my head, this certainty that everyone would start to sing and join the universal melody, putting down their briefcases and Uzis and chorusing, 'Joy to the world . . .'"

"It didn't work," said Hermia. "There isn't much joy in the world."

"Not a lot of music anyhow," her daughter said. "Sometimes I think that what I missed most was the music, not the guitar but piano, that silence in our living room I used to love to fill. And sometimes, on some dinky little mattress in the hallway of some boarded-up room, I'd sing myself to sleep with *Kinderszenen*—you remember *Kinderszenen*?—or a phrase from 'Für Elise' or pages from the Notebooks for Anna Magdalena Bach. You don't have a piano here, do you?"

"I couldn't bear to have one in the house," said Hermia.

"I'm sorry," said Patricia. "I deserved that, didn't I?"

"Yes."

Lawrence watched. The girl kicked off her shoes. Her toenails were dark red. Hermia wore glasses, as if her child's face were a small-printed text and she needed to read every word. Mother and daughter sat close together on the couch, and it was as though the adult and her youthful self had been conjured by a kind of stage-craft: two halves of the one whole.

From time to time he left the room—to carry in wood or tend to the kettle, offering tea and olives and nuts. That afternoon he went walking alone, and when he returned at four o'clock, it was clear his presence in the house had been explained. "We knew each other long ago," Hermia was saying, "and met again—it's embar-rassing to admit this—on a cruise." A *cruise?* Patricia asked. At least it wasn't a college reunion or some sort of dating service, Lawrence said. At least it wasn't on the Internet, added Hermia, with Google playing Cupid.

Next the girl described her history of doing nothing special, and how all that time—a dozen years!—you tell yourself that in fact it *is* special and the people you are with or not with matter, and the town you stay in or the road you travel is the only town and road. Patricia spoke about Anne Martineau, the memory of her failed commune in Pownal, a place Anne had talked about often, not romanticizing it but making it seem like a life choice. And therefore she herself had joined one for a year in Oregon, but it wasn't a success—the men discussing how to build a teepee, or who would fix the tractor, and the women performing the actual work. "We were always," she said, "a bonfire away from freezing, and laundry was a project, and the apples were blighted that sea-son; you raised a farm girl, Momma, but I wasn't any good at it and wasn't all that interested in the end."

"You should have called," said Hermia, "and let me know you planned to come. You could have written to tell me . . ."

"I know. I *should* have. I do know."

There were old scores to settle and explain. There was the question of her silence, her telephone calls that left no sort of message and letters that weren't really letters. "Do you have the slightest idea," asked Hermia, "how long I waited and how hard I searched for you?" Her face was stone. "I know," her daughter said. "It's inexcusable and I'm not making excuses, but the only way I could continue was by forgetting everything, or that you were waiting. Then little by little I *did* escape, I *did* forget, and it seemed harder and harder and then finally impossible to come back home. I never left the country, but the places I lived in did feel like different countries, not dead, but dead to you."

She talked about hunger, then anger, the way you think a safety net is strung until you end up on the floor and find the net has shredded and there's no one left to shelter you or to lend a hand. There had been music to start with, and protest songs, but it wasn't possible, or possible for *her* at least, to make people listen or pay attention. And when she did get a foot in the door, what they wanted—mirthlessly, she smiled again—were the other parts of her, not feet.

Then, when the music failed, she did a year or two of summer stock: disaster in the Poconos and, for one brutal winter, Minneapolis. There were towns she couldn't name and others she'd as soon forget where what she slept in were motels on the outskirts by abandoned mills, or railroad tracks, and what flourished were crazies, and rats. "This thing called poverty," she said, "is not as picturesque as I believed; I know it sounds ridiculous, ridiculously innocent, but the vow of poverty did seem attractive once. Sometimes I tried to blame you, Mom, for having failed to bring me home; sometimes I thought you should have tried, oh, *harder*, and then I tried to punish you for quitting hide-and-seek. It's a very long story," she said, and Hermia said, "We've got years of catching up to do; will you stay tonight at least?" Patricia said, "Yes, if you mean it." "Of course I do," Hermia said.

Patricia had thought about calling, she said, but every time she tried to call there'd been too much to say. She had driven to the Cape from Boston, not with any conscious plan but not on a whim either. She had arrived without a suitcase and could always turn around and had been half expecting to, but this was better, this was best, the meeting she dreamed of for years.

Lawrence watched. The girl borrowed her mother's black sweater. When Patricia shook her long hair loose, it was with Hermia's old insouciance, and at the base of her neck there was a butterfly tattoo. "Something *my* mother used to say," said Hermia, "every single winter solstice she declared the winter over; this is the shortest day of all and they're getting longer and soon it will be spring. So why have you come back today, what made you change your mind?"

"Frank," she said, "my prince."

"Excuse me, who?"

"I've met a man, my prince at last, the one I plan to marry. He has this way about him, this *certainty* that right is right, wrong's wrong. Black's black for him, white's white." She smiled. "We were at this fund-raiser for children of Africa, children with AIDS— well, *he* was there as an invited guest, and I was working the concession stand, you know, dispensing beer and spring water and T-shirts. And he bought a pair of candied apples and offered me one of them, handed one back, and I said I couldn't accept that, and Frank said yes, I could."

"Did you?" Lawrence asked.

"We argued a little. He won. And when my shift ended, we left the fund-raiser together—because I knew, and he did too, from the very first minute I saw him, *this* was the real thing."

Her face was radiant. "It *is*," she repeated, "it *is*. I knew it right away. We've been together now almost a year, and this is his engagement ring, and of course I want you all to meet, but I think—*he* thinks, *we* thought—I needed to do this alone. One night I told him who I was and where I came from, and he told me I should stand up and declare myself, and what's totally amazing, Mom, is his father *knew* you way back when."

"His father?" asked Hermia. "Who, what's his name?"

Patricia said, "Will. He knew you back at Radcliffe, when he was living in Cambridge."

"*Will*," said Lawrence. "What's his last name?"

When the girl offered it, Hermia laughed; they talked about coincidence and how the three of them had been friends.

"The *best* of friends," said Lawrence, "but then we lost touch, and what's he doing now?"

"Now he's retired," said the girl. "He was an entertainment lawyer and a big success at it; he told me how he played the guitar and wanted to play for a living, but wasn't good, or good enough, and so he went to law school and ended up dealing with music from what he calls the corporate side, the making of deals, not CDs. He was, I think, almost embarrassed by having made a lot of money and running a kind of empire; he said he thought of it as selling out. But he's the *sweetest* man, the kindest man, and once I finally met him—when Frank took me to his house—I understood, it's what I *felt*, I could come home. When I told him who you were and when he made the connection, he gave me—it sounds old-fashioned, saying it—his blessing. He sends you his best."

—

It was as though, thought Lawrence, their story was repeated in the younger generation: the girl and boy enacting what their parents failed to do. In the morning when he took his pills, he heard their visitor breathing softly in the room beside the bathroom, and he told himself he ought to leave and let the child and mother celebrate alone. Alone together, Lawrence thought, and again his eyes went wet. He understood how often he'd been self-absorbed, king of his own little island, the self, and how the gift to make to Hermia would be his own departure. He might have lived his life with her but had not been prepared for it, was careless and unready . . .

Therefore he packed his bag. It did not take him long. Hermia came into his room and watched; she was wearing her dressing gown and slippers and asked, "What are you doing?" He said, "I thought it would be better for you, the two of you, if I just left, if I leave you alone. Not forever, I mean, for a while." "You're used to this," said Hermia. "You've done this sort of thing before," and he said, "It's different now." He could be home for Christmas, he said; he could see Catherine, or Andrew, or John. "Don't go," she said. "I'm happy at last, don't just go and wreck it, OK?"

"Do you remember," Lawrence asked, "those arguments we used to have—I don't mean the two of us, I mean *everybody* used to have—about coincidence and conscious choice: free will and determinism?"

"Yes," she said, and sat.

"Well, I've been asking myself," he said, "all night and morning I've been wondering if this is an example of one or the other or somehow a mixture of both. I feel, I mean, as if we're playing out a set of parts that someone else has written, I feel like a character in an old play and trying to remember what to say."

She smiled. "'My lord, I do repent me . . .'"

"Not that line, no."

"''Tis time. Descend.'"

"Well, you're the English major."

"Don't leave me," Hermia said. "It's only a few days to Christmas, and I need you to come down the chimney."

"It's wonderful to see you happy. So complete."

She looked at him. He smiled at her. His dear face shone.

"Please stay."

BOOK TWO

I

I have a piece of paper and a pen and brush. I have a cup of water Daddy gave me and a watercolor box. My favorite color is pink. Sometimes my favorite color is purple and today it's only purple when I paint the water which doesn't have a boat on it but anyway is blue. Blue is what it ought to be but Daddy says if you want purple go ahead. Except hold very still for a minute, just one single minute, can't you, it shouldn't be this difficult. What's difficult, I ask him, and he says things that don't come easy but it's easy to hold still.

I do. I do so for seven eight nine. Then Mommy says that's excellent and do you want a butterscotch and would you care, my precious, for another piece of paper while we leave this one to dry? Daddy's working at his picture which is on not the table but easel because he's a slowpoke and squints. Squints is when you shut your eyes but not all the way so you see through them funny and draw. He has his pipe and whiskey and his bowl and fiddlers three. He is, he says, a merry old soul and calls for his fiddlers three. Mommy gives me paper and says don't forget to wash your brush and I don't and use yellow instead. This is what we always do and always do and always do and the trouble is, says Daddy, it's hard to not be cute. Don't flatter yourself, Mommy says.

Then she goes into the kitchen and I'm left alone and ask him how much longer and he says hold still. Our puppy Lance is short for Lancelot who was a great hero and this dog will be one too. I hold for one two three. My first picture is the water and the second is a ghost. In years to come I jump and jump and then am sitting still again and am a picture instead. This time it's in a chair. This time it's wearing my yellow pleated knee-length skirt and my Mary Janes. This time the puppy is Tigger, a golden retriever who sits in my lap. And there's a frame and I hang on the wall and stare at myself staring out.

II
—
2005

He stayed. It wasn't difficult: one closet, two bureaus sufficed. There were a few suits he would fail to wear, three boxes of books and two of shoes, a small crate of CDs. The house in Truro, Lawrence said, had art on every single wall, and books and music on the shelves, and he had no desire to compromise her space.

"It's not," said Hermia, "a *compromise*. Why would you call it that?"

"I meant the house," he told her. "Not what's happening with us."

"Just bring whatever you want to. Please."

He told her he had always traveled light. She urged him to bring furniture or anything he needed, but he repeated—with a gallantry she was beginning to think genuine—that everything he needed was here on the Cape, in her house. He did return to Ann Arbor to pack up his apartment and empty out his office, but it was oddly like the time so long ago when he departed college as a student, not a professor. There was little to keep him, said Lawrence, and little he wanted to take. The life he'd led without her was a life he left behind.

Hermia felt the same way. It was as though the interval—those decades they had spent apart, the marriages and children and illness and reunion—disappeared. She knew this wasn't true, of course;

everything that happened to them each alone *had* happened and *had* mattered and would continue to matter. He had had his career. They'd lived their separate lives. But sometimes when she looked at him, she saw the college boy she'd met when she was a junior and he was a senior and everything seemed possible. They both had been so young. Things changed but did not change. Now he was old and bent and white-haired, yet still Lawrence, always Lawrence, and she did not need to close her eyes to see him as she saw him then: lithe and leaning down above her in the narrow bed.

"It doesn't go away," he said.

"What?"

"Any of it. All of it. This terrific luck I feel."

"Don't let's talk this way," said Hermia. "It makes me nervous when you do."

"All right. What do you want for dinner?"

"Salmon." She smiled at him. "Grilled."

"With broccoli or spinach?"

"You decide."

He liked to do the shopping, and he liked to cook. Increasingly she let him, since she knew it gave him pleasure and a sense of purpose to run their household errands and fix what needed fixing—a rheostat or broken lamp, a window or door frame or lock. Lawrence was good with his hands. He said an architect does need to know the way a circuit box or furnace works, and if what went wrong was minor, he could be her handyman. "Let me be," he liked to sing, in his high-pitched, off-key warble, "your handy-man." He would take the car to Provincetown, or the hardware store in Wellfleet, and come back with a replacement part or quart of paint or fresh-caught fish and a bottle of wine. At night he set the dining room table, complete with silverware and linen napkins and candles, and busied himself in the kitchen preparing what she would declare was wonderful, delicious, and mean it—so glad she was to share the meal, so happy he was happy in her house.

—

They weathered the winter together. The sunrise was astonishing; she woke with the first light. In previous years, said Hermia, she'd gone into a kind of hibernation—burrowing into her blankets, sleeping longer, reading, listening to music, seeing only a few people and making a few phone calls and waiting, not impatiently, for spring. But now all that had changed. This winter was their wonderland, with beautiful weather and parties to go to and parties to give and walks to take and, when the snow was deep enough, to ski. Together they skied cross-country, carefully, not pushing themselves, or snowshoed from the pantry door if the drifts were high. The sunsets were astonishing; they drove to Sunset Hill.

Where the ice melted, sand gleamed. Out on the dunes, on windless days, while gulls circled above them or rode the white waves, she could remember what it felt like the first time she had brought him here, driving together from Cambridge in—when was it, 1962?—and showing him her parents' house that had been closed for winter. As though in a photograph album or some sort of amateur movie, she saw herself letting them in with the key beneath the woodshed overhang and noticing the things he noticed: the double chimney rising from the center of the shingled roof, the wide plank floors, the adze marks on the oak beams in the ceiling and the plaster walls, the six-over-six small-pane windows with their handblown glass. The original Cape Cod saltbox had been built in 1790, and what a succession of previous owners and then her parents added were extensions in the colonial style: the studio, the kitchen wing, green shutters with a heart incised, the library, the fireplace with its andirons fashioned by some sculptor she could not now name, the Oriental rugs, the chairs, the sideboard with its bottles and decanters.

The heat had been turned off. The toilet bowls held antifreeze, and the pipes were drained. She still could remember the way Lawrence looked when studying the oil by Edward Hopper, who had lived nearby, and the paintings by her father's friends, the ones he'd traded for his own, so there were paintings everywhere—her father's drawings, aquarelles, oils—or how he'd stopped to study the portrait of herself at ten, the one that eight years later was acquired by the Whitney. Then, in her childhood bedroom, because it was too cold to take off their clothes and there were mothballs on the coverlet, they made love standing up. "Do you remember?" she would ask, and he always answered, "Yes."

"What was I wearing?"

"Your parka."

"What color was it?"

"Purple."

"My God," she said, "the things we wore . . ."

"I liked it best"—again, the gallantry—"when you were wearing nothing."

"Boots."

"Yes, brown ones. With a zipper. And all the way up to your knees."

Now Hermia pictured their old acrobatics as though she were watching a dance danced by others, a game played by athletes they must once have been. In her childhood's summer bedroom or his college dorm or the backseat of his mother's Impala, in bathrooms or outside beneath a canopy of pines, in ten-minute spasms or all through the night they embraced each other fervently until they broke apart. They had been passionate together the way the young are passionate, and nothing in her life before had readied her for how they fit together or how she, holding him, felt. When she thought about their time at Harvard and the months of their affair, she could *see, touch, hear* and *smell* and *taste* them at their playful work: body with body entwined.

That passion was not spent. It was spent in the physical sense, of course; she could no longer manage, and he could not manage, the revels of the young. "Our revels now are ended," said Shakespeare in his retirement speech, and then he left London for Stratford-upon-Avon and, a few years later, died. But it was like *The Tempest*; it was everything restored, made whole, old treacheries forgiven and old arguments resolved. What had been lost was found. They were gentle together now, slow. It was strange to be so much in love with someone she had loved before and known so well and parted from and then spent more than forty years not knowing till they met again by accident, on the cruise ship *Diana*.

She came aboard in Marseilles. He joined the trip in Rome. Neither Hermia nor Lawrence had taken such a tour before, but both had been persuaded—separately, for separate reasons—to sign on. It was a coincidence but had not felt like one; it seemed inevitable, somehow, that they would find each other in the ruins of Pompeii. She could remember watching him, her lover from college days, and wondering if she should introduce herself or simply walk away.

"Time-lapse photography," Hermia said. "That's what I see when I look in the mirror."

"You're beautiful."

"Not any longer."

"You are."

"This weekend the Zuckers are coming down to Wellfleet. Helen called this afternoon. Do you want to see them?"

"Do you?"

"Not particularly, no."

"I like it best," said Lawrence, "when there's nobody here but us chickens. Spring chickens."

She laughed. "Let's rent a movie, maybe."

"*Barry Lyndon? Paths of Glory? Eyes Wide Shut?*"

"Don't you *ever* get tired of Kubrick?"

"The man who is tired of Kubrick," he said, "is tired of life."

"Is that a quote? And isn't it London, not Kubrick?"

"What do *you* want to see, darling?"

"Oh, anything, as long as it's in color. And not by Stanley Kubrick."

"*Lawrence of Arabia? The Muppet Movie? The Godfather?*"

"Whatever you want to watch," Hermia said. "Except let's just do it together and not invite the Zuckers. They're lovely people, yes, but I want to be alone."

"Greta Garbo, that's who I'll get us. *Ninotchka. Anna Karenina.* 'I vont to be alone.'"

Again, she laughed, considering him: this old man in her living room whom she had known when young. He had been twenty-one, she twenty, and though they both pretended to be grown-ups, they had in fact been children. They swore their love was permanent—"'Till a' the seas gang dry, my dear'"—yet courtship had been brief. "'Good night, sweet prince,'" she liked to say when Lawrence walked her to her dormitory door, and he would answer, "'Flights of angels sing thee to thy rest.'" They both had understood, of course, that "good night" means "good-bye," and "rest" means "death," but this was Horatio's meaning in *Hamlet*, not theirs; they were wishing each other sweet dreams.

It did not last a year. After graduation, Lawrence traveled, and Hermia remained behind, not living happily ever after or playing Sleeping Beauty or Cinderella with her prince, but living in some nursery rhyme like Humpty Dumpty or Jack and Jill without a happy ending. Neither felt ready for marriage, and although they promised each other they would be faithful forever, it had not ended well.

"Do you want to attend the reunion?" she asked when the invitation arrived, and he told her, "No."

"You're sure?"

He kissed her cheek. "This is the only reunion I want."

"We *could* drive up to Cambridge . . ."

"Why? They'd put us at separate tables. Or even in separate tents."

Her years at Radcliffe, his at Harvard, belonged to another existence; what once had been their future was the receding past. It seemed like only yesterday but also very long ago; time flies as well as crawls. Now Hermia was sixty-three, and Lawrence a year older, and they had no business, she knew, being silly and giddy together: the world is a serious place. There is poverty, famine, and war. There are people dying everywhere, and people falling ill. He himself had gotten sick; the trouble with his heart was real, and sometimes she feared losing him again.

But since their reunion on the *Diana* (the way he looked at her when finally she touched his sleeve), she had been an optimist. Now everything was excellent—her daughter come back after long years away, with no estrangement there either—and she reveled in his bluefish or swordfish or grilled salmon and the nightly bottle of Sancerre. She loved playing Scrabble or reading together, listening to the French Suites with the fireplace ablaze and snow falling silently, wetly, outside. Because he was proud of the new hallway dimmers, she kept the hallway dim. Because it proved his competence and no longer squeaked when closing, she closed the pantry door. All through the months of January, February, March— the long nights waning, the stacked wood dwindling—they sat together in companionable silence or watched the nightly news on PBS or, if the day was warm enough, went out to the bay to dig oysters and clams, using her shellfish permit and the rakes and buckets and waders she kept hanging in the mudroom, and she was happy, she told him, as happy as could be.

—

"Do you want to travel?"

"No."

"Go to New York, I mean, or Boston? Nothing elaborate," Lawrence persisted. "Just to spend a weekend in a city . . ."

"Do you?"

"Not if you don't want to."

"We might go to LA," she said, "and visit with Patricia there."

"*We?*"

"Certainly," said Hermia. "I wouldn't leave here without you."

"You're sure she'd want me?"

"Yes."

She wasn't sure, in truth. In truth she knew almost nothing about her daughter's present life, or the man she was living with in California and planning to marry in June. Patricia had grown self-sufficient in a way that brooked no meddling; not that it *would* have been meddling, just a mother taking part in preparations for a wedding the way mothers are doing all over America. She would have been happy to help. It would have given her a kind of satisfaction to deal with the food and flowers and help select the wedding site and music for the ceremony or shop for a trousseau. But when she offered assistance, her daughter said, "Don't bother, Mom, really. We can handle it; just come and be a guest."

So she was trying not to push the envelope—that was how Patricia put it, "push the envelope"—which Hermia supposed was some sort of Hollywood term from the Oscars, something to do with a daring extravagance, although it wasn't clear to her if doing so, *pushing the envelope*, was a good idea or bad. And in any case their telephone calls, an invitation to the wedding, and the suggestion that she, *they*, might fly to California this spring was better than the almost total silence of the last twelve years, the way Patricia disappeared and then, as if by magic, reappeared. When her daughter, arriving, had knocked on the door and said, *I'm home, I'm here again*, it was as if some god had given her, by sleight of hand, the gift once more of everything she'd lost. Lawrence had returned to her, and then Patricia too returned, if only for a visit, if only to assure her there had been no lasting damage, and she was living in Los Angeles and would be getting married. It was as though a phantom limb were once again the actual thing: the ache assuaged, the leg or arm restored.

Lawrence was opening wine. "It's getting darker later."

"Yes. We're almost at the solstice."

"If there'd been any sun today, it would be over the yardarm."

"Your health."

"And yours," he said. *"Ours."*

"It's almost a full moon, I think."

"I never can tell if it's waxing or waning."

"Just look at the calendar. Two days till full . . ."

They joked about the moon in June and how beneath it soon they would spoon; they joked about their world as an oyster—whatever *that's* supposed to mean!—and good enough to swallow whole, with just a taste of lemon. It's an expression, Lawrence said, like "happy as a clam," and she said, "I don't understand that one either," and they agreed it referred to the line of the shell, a kind of smiley face.

"Snug as a bug in a rug," said Hermia.

"As a pig in . . . clover, is it clover?"

"No, silly, that's a horse. Or cow. You *know* what pigs are happy in . . ."

In this fashion they amused each other and passed the time together. How could it happen, Hermia asked herself; why should she—a woman in her sixties—be so ready to believe in what for decades she'd dismissed: this boy-man she had slept with when they both were young now suddenly restored to her, her knight in shining armor once again? The things that had been lost were found. *In our beginning is our end.*

"'All shall be well,'" he assured her.

"Dame Julian of Norwich, right?"

He nodded. "'And all shall be well. All manner of thing shall be well.'"

———

It wasn't true. All was not well. Her mother lived in London, in the flat in Hampstead, and at ninety-three was senile—or suffering from dementia, or Alzheimer's, or a systemic breakdown: whatever it was they were calling, these days, old age. The language for it changes and the terms have changed, Hermia knew, but all of it means the same thing. Senile dementia means lying in bed or sitting in the padded chair while paid attendants spoon your gruel or sponge you down or fuss with and then compliment your hair. The patient was dying a slow, lonely death, and there was nothing she or anyone could do.

Her mother had settled in England with her second husband, and G. Edson Lattimer himself was long since dead. When he passed away, his widow declined to return to America, saying London now was home. Over the years she seemed more and more English: the stiff upper lip not so much stiff as curled, the cucumber sandwiches and jellied meat staling, the tea lukewarm, the gin neat. And later, when Patricia too withdrew, Hermia asked herself if there were a pattern or gene for departure—if daughters who were estranged from their mothers became, in turn, the mothers of girls who would leave.

In any case, things changed. Her mother grew incompetent, no longer able to fend for herself and staring at the wall. There was money for round-the-clock nursing, and she remained in the flat. Mrs. Lattimer—her second husband had been a good provider, and Hermia's father left paintings to sell, and the English are adept at caring for the elderly—lived on. As time went by, she wrote less and less often, and then no longer wrote or called, and for the last year had been wholly vegetal and did not speak a word. "Incremental aphasia," one physician explained. "We understand it as a symptom but can't pinpoint the cause." So Hermia relied on monthly bulletins from the accountant, who would append the nursing reports to his statement of expenditures, always writing, "Your mother appears to be holding her own," and promising to inform her if that were not the case.

On April 1 he reported decline, and that the doctors recommended hospice care, and the end approached. In April, therefore, she and Lawrence flew to Heathrow out of Logan, not going to California as they'd hoped but taking a taxi to the flat on Lyndhurst Road and sitting at her mother's bedside, where Hermia too fell asleep. During their ten days in Hampstead they did attend the theater once, and went to the Tate and the Wallace Collection and the Courtauld, but all she would later remember was her mother's hand in hers, the stertorous breath, and how on Thursday afternoon at five o'clock the breathing stopped.

There had been no change of pressure in her mother's hand. There had been no recognition, no flicker of alertness in the staring face. "She waited for you, dear," the hospice nurse assured Hermia. "Your mummy wasn't willing to depart this earth without a final visit. You can take comfort in that."

She had been an only child. She had no relatives in London and nothing to bring back with her except a necklace of old jade and gold and one of her father's aquarelles, the sketch made when they were first married of her mother in a bathing suit on the Truro dunes. This was before he embraced abstraction, when he was painting waves and trees, and the figure of the woman—brown and black against the scumbled dunes—was an image of youth gloried in and lost. Her father's reputation had been established by just such compositions, and what one critic called his "deployment of the figurative color field as plane." It owed much to Matisse. The hospice nurse was short and plump, with the singsong intonation of someone from the islands, and though Hermia understood that her solace had been practiced—*your mummy wasn't willing to depart this earth without a final visit*—she took comfort in the well-worn phrase of consolation nonetheless. There had been gold fillings in the nurse's teeth.

Lawrence offered comfort too, helping her pack and distribute belongings and helping with the funeral arrangements. These had been prearranged. The few elderly mourners were strangers who said, "You must be the daughter. We've heard so much about you. You have our sympathy, dear."

Hermia spent hours dealing with bureaucracy, signing forms in triplicate and meeting with lawyers and bankers and closing down accounts. Her mother's arrangements were "shipshape," as the accountant declared. She found herself wondering what the term meant: Is every ship well ordered on an outbound trip? By the time they themselves could leave London, she was eager to depart; the spring rains felt cold, not nourishing or full of verdant promise, and the formalities of burial were done. She was hoping, she told Lawrence, to put all this behind her—the snobbery, the pinched politeness—and resume their life together on the Cape.

He agreed. They flew home on British Airways, and were sitting in business class and drinking bad champagne. He said, "I liked the estate agent, the one with the pencil mustache—what's his name, Alistair Redmond?" and Hermia, looking out the airplane window, knew she was going to cry. She could not tell if she agreed or disagreed about liking Alistair Redmond; she understood it made no difference and was utterly beside the point and in the scheme of things irrelevant. But somehow her indecision on the matter of liking or not liking a man she knew she'd never see again became an occasion for tears.

Lawrence took her hand. His palm was warm on hers. He asked how she was feeling and what he could do, and Hermia tried to explain: it was absence, only absence; it was what she *wasn't* feeling that was causing her to cry.

—

Once back in Truro, however, she could not shake the pain. It would not be denied. She had not seen her mother in years, and had grown used to distance. Yet the grief persisted. She had become, she tried to joke, a sixty-three-year-old orphan with no parents to rebel against or attempt to please. "What did I do to deserve this?" she asked. "How could they leave me alone?"

Lawrence looked up from his book.

"Oh, I know it isn't funny," Hermia said, "but you've got to admit it feels strange."

"What does?"

"The fact we have no parents. The way, without half trying to, we're elders of the tribe."

Her father had died young. His death made the national news. In time what eulogists described as "his characteristic excess" and "an impulsive gesture" became part of her father's myth, the imprimatur required to consolidate his standing. But now the famous artist and her mother, the muse and intransigent model, both were gone, mere memory, and Hermia was mourning what she never had: the companionable presence of a parent at the kitchen sink, or sitting in the living room, crocheting or reading. Too, Patricia was a world away and getting ready to marry and perhaps already planning on a family of her own.

"So you," she said to Lawrence, "are the whole show nowadays, the only one I get to care for or complain to."

"It's why I'm here."

"Not really."

"Things are fine. We're doing fine."

"Poor darling," said Hermia, "not what you signed on for, is it?"

"I signed on for the ride."

The ride, she tried to tell him, was a roller coaster, full of ups and downs and level stretches and finally a swooping and precipitous decline. Whenever she opened the paper, it seemed, she found someone else she'd known or known about on the obituary page. This very week, in the *New York Times*, there had been an art dealer acquaintance of her parents, and a Radcliffe classmate, and a man she'd dated briefly while she worked at Harry Abrams in New York. On the *NewsHour* they showed photographs of soldiers, listing their names and how old they had been and the towns and states these children came from before being killed in Iraq. She could not help it; she thought of them as children, though a percentage of the dead—the career officers or members of the National Guard—were thirty and forty years old.

"They're all so *young*," said Hermia. "Just look at them. Nineteen, twenty, twenty-two . . ."

Watching, he stood at attention.

"Most of them sign up for money. Or because there are no jobs."

The roll call of dead warriors continued on in silence.

"Bring back the draft, that's what we ought to be doing," she said. "This war would finish in a heartbeat if any of the senators had children who were drafted. Or if awful Bush and Cheney ever went to war themselves . . ."

"I'd like to plant a garden."

"I'm being serious, Lawrence."

"Yes. What grows well here?"

"Don't change the subject, please."

In a gesture of submission, he raised his hands, palms out. "We're on a sand spit anyway. In case you hadn't noticed."

"Turnips? Parsnips? Potatoes?"

"The best are tomatoes. And, I think, arugula."

"At your service, madam."

"My handyman," she said, "my perfect, perfect gentleman"— and burst out again into tears.

—

The spring came late. Yet when it came it was decisive: gnats and mosquitoes, wet heat. She and Lawrence started working, spreading a truckload of topsoil and repairing what was once a fence and marking out the rows of vegetables and establishing a border of bright marigolds and herbs. The existence of a garden—the assumption they were making that they would be here to harvest it—was comforting to Hermia. And although it seemed—what was the word?—*unserious* to take pleasure in a patch of earth, she felt her mood improve. She planted carrots and squash. Their shared project (the weeding, the hoeing and thinning out and watering the first green growth) became a daily habit and a gift. She staked the early peas. When rabbits grew inquisitive, or birds alit to peck at seeds, she shooed them indignantly away. With Lawrence's help she fashioned a scarecrow, using torn clothes and a pillow for stuffing and old boots and a straw hat.

They walked the narrow trails of Bound Brook Island. There they found the Lombard cemetery, where Mary Lombard, dead of smallpox, had been laid to rest. In their fear of infection, Hermia knew, the elders of the village passed a law declaring no one dead of smallpox could be buried on town property. In 1859, Mary's husband, Thomas, interred her in the middle of nowhere on Bound Brook and, when he died years later, joined her so their two stones stood together upright in a clearing. "Will you stand by me?"—she took his hand, half serious—and Lawrence answered, "Yes."

Their walks became more leisurely, less brisk. They explored the shorelines of Corn Hill and Ballston Beach, Newcomb Hollow and Head of the Meadow and Pilgrim Spring. They attempted to swim in the ponds. The network of freshwater ponds between the bay and ocean grew warmer sooner than the harbor or the open sea, but even so the shallow bodies of water in Wellfleet—Williams and Higgins and Horse Leech ponds—were too cold to enjoy. Therefore they borrowed the Zuckers' canoe and went canoeing instead. Hermia was more adept at paddling and steering, so she sat in the stern, he the prow. Adrift in the clear waters, seeing cattails clustered to the shore, an osprey perched in the crook of an oak, she felt herself a child again immersed in noisy silence. A deer was standing drinking on a sand spit at the causeway. "It's beautiful here," said Lawrence, and she feathered her paddle and watched a fish jump.

"Was that a snapping turtle?" he asked.

"No."

"You're sure?"

She smiled and told him, "Yes."

III

He likes the carapace of bread, the hard baked crust of it, while I prefer the soft buttered center; between the two of us we lick the platter clean. This explains why we're happy together, Lawrence says. He prefers the dark meat of the chicken, I the white; it makes us a matched pair. We fit together hand in glove and toe in shoe and mortar in pestle and cock in cunt; we have a dozen ways of saying that our edges fit. That last phrase—the one after "mortar in pestle"—is his; he likes to pretend he can shock me and whisper sweet four-letter nothings in my ear.

But what shocks me is the truth of it, the flat fact of our intimacy, who for decades did not know at noon or night if the other one was wakeful or asleep. Who did not need assurance or the reassurance of company and broke our bread alone. I can remember playing with puzzles, turning and turning the thick wooden shapes—a circle, a square, a triangle, a rectangle—to fit within the slotted apertures of an upright painted box and which, when inserted correctly, would drop. Hey, presto, the key in the lock. The coin in the meter, the hard rubber plug in the drain of the tub, the cigarette, ashtray, and match. Or Patricia doing jigsaw puzzles, turning and turning the cardboard pieces so they nestle together and make a shared unit, a border of clouds, grass, or sea. For, ah, the little ecstasy of fashioning a shapely arrangement, of putting the pieces together—the stars aligned, the circle unbroken—so that what at first seems separate is joined.

Heigh-ho, the fiddle and bow. Heigh-ho, the cow and the moon. I feel myself a child again, a breathless panting baby who was, or so they told me, serious and would sit unattended for hours and seldom chortle or smile. What was I waiting for—pabulum, a drink? What kept me in my crib content with only a doll and a blanket and why need his company now? When Lawrence and I rhyme "June" and "moon" and "spoon," are we playing with language the way children play, or have we two together put off childish things? Am I fooling myself, is he fooling himself, are we where angels fear to tread now fooling each other by fooling around? I can remember when that expression meant the tentative rustle of flesh against flesh, a suction of fingers and lips. The years, the years.

IV
—
2005

When Patricia called to say, "Please come," spring was becoming summer. It was the end of May. She would be getting married, she informed her mother, at the Walt Disney Concert Hall, and they'd reserved a night three weeks from now, when the LA Philharmonic would be out of town. There had been a cancellation, and she and Frank had taken it, so the space was theirs. Patricia described the booking procedure and the hoops they'd had to jump through and the complications of rental, but said they loved the rooftop garden and the view. Her voice had been buoyant, elated. It would be a small affair—last minute, really, nothing elaborate—but there were fifty friends who would be part of the party, and on such short notice there wasn't much room to maneuver. "Imagine," she joked, "the Walt Disney Concert Hall, and *I* play Minnie Mouse."

"The Gehry building?" Lawrence asked when Hermia hung up.

"Yes," she said, "it's what they seem to want."

"There's a cathedral I'd like to see. By Rafael Moneo, it's just around the corner."

"Where?"

"In the same neighborhood, I think. They're planning to make it a cultural center."

"You admire Gehry, don't you?"

"I need to see the building. So far I've just seen photographs." He was trying, she could tell, not to sound impressed.

But it *was* impressive, wasn't it: the great gleaming downtown structure, the major architectural statement by a major architect that her daughter and her bridegroom would take over for the night. Frank Gehry's burnished steel plates and cones would make a fitting backdrop for the wedding, wouldn't they? And Hermia was happy for them both. Again she offered to fly out to help, and again Patricia told her no: "Just come and be a guest," she said, "just please enjoy yourself, Mom. I *wish* you two could stay with us, but it's just so crazy here we've reserved you a hotel . . ."

She dithered over what to pack and puzzled as to shoes. She asked herself how formal or informal she should be and whether she had time to buy a dress. There was nothing on the Cape, and the garden was exploding so she didn't want to spend a day in Boston shopping, and anyhow Patricia had assured her the ceremony would be casual. No bridesmaids or matrons of honor, she'd said. "There'll be no aisle to walk down, Mom. I'll give myself away."

Hermia's yellow silk still fit her, with the cowl neck and puffed sleeves. It flared below the knee. In Truro she'd not needed skirts or gowns, and what she owned was out of fashion and hadn't come around again, but there was a magenta sheath she might be able to wear. She packed her mother's necklace: the strand of gold and jade. The bridegroom's father, she reminded Lawrence, was a friend of theirs from college days, and had become some sort of mogul— music, the movies, why couldn't she remember?—but would no doubt expect them to be wearing what they wore when young: "bell-bottoms in your case," she told him, "and knee-length boots in mine."

"Don't be nervous," Lawrence said. "She's happy. And I'll be glad to see Will."

"Are you certain? It's been *forever* . . ."

"We don't change all that much. Some people don't, at any rate. Just look at you."

"Flatterer." She smiled at him. "They're living in his house, you know, till they find something of their own."

"To buy? To rent?"

"She hasn't decided. *They* haven't decided."

"Strange, isn't it—last month we were in London. Now we're going to Los Angeles. For such a pair of homebodies, we're pretty busily moving around."

"My mother died." Hermia straightened. "My daughter's getting married. Those seem like good reasons for travel."

"Of course they are. I didn't mean we shouldn't go. Only we're doing a good bit of flying."

"A pair of jet-setters . . ."

He touched her cheek. "My best guess is, Ma Kettle, we ain't seen nothing yet."

"Are you worried you'll feel out of place? I promise we'll see the Moneo."

"And the Richard Meier—the Getty Center. There's a lot happening there."

He went on about the architects, the way Los Angeles had changed and was transforming itself into a megalopolis, a city where art and architecture counted and the downtown was worth visiting. His time at SOM in San Francisco and the north-south split in California meant you couldn't like Los Angeles, or admit you did, but he looked forward to the chance to study the Gehry and the Meier and Moneo buildings firsthand. He continued in this vein until she realized he was humoring her, attempting to distract her from the fact of their exclusion from the wedding preparations. Ma and Pa Kettle, Lawrence joked, ride the stagecoach into town. He was being, she assured him, oversensitive; he didn't need to worry her feelings would be hurt.

—

It turned out he was right, of course; no sooner did they land at LAX than she wanted to go home. She missed her house, their garden. She had become, she told him, a country not a city mouse; she was Ma Kettle with a daughter here in La-La Land who was planning to marry a prince. It would be a fairy-tale wedding, but Hermia found herself thinking instead about the early peas and pole beans and the redwing blackbirds nesting by the pond.

At the airport there were hordes of children screaming, and women in stiletto heels, tan and impossibly thin. Beside the luggage carousel stood men in muscle shirts, with buzz cuts and goatees. One woman wearing leather pants was carrying a dog wrapped in fur and saying, "Precious, precious," and kissing the dog's snout. The dog kept its eyes closed. Lawrence put his arm around Hermia and advised her to breathe deeply, saying what she was feeling was jet lag and to blame it on the flight.

She tried. Their bags arrived. Patricia made them welcome— sending a car to the airport, arranging for flowers and a bottle of wine and bowl of fruit in their suite at the hotel. The hotel was near the site of the wedding; the bill had been prepaid. But Hermia had hoped, of course, her daughter would have found the time to meet them down at baggage claim—not send a driver wearing livery and holding a placard with her name on it. *Can't wait to see you, Mom,* read the note the driver proffered once they settled in the limousine. *We hope you're not too tired from the flight. Come just as soon as you can.*

The house in Brentwood, which she and Lawrence visited that afternoon, was huge. It was built in the style of a Moorish palace, with pink stucco walls and green roof tiles and matching conical turrets at the end of matching wings. The circular driveway was brick. The electrified gates were wrought iron, and there was so much grillwork it looked as though the owners were prepared to repel an attack. At the gate, they were quizzed and buzzed in.

Patricia and Frank, her fiancé, appeared on the front steps. The girl was radiant, gleeful, everything a bride should be, and she opened the taxi door with a flourish and kissed Hermia, then Lawrence, saying how long and how impatiently she'd looked forward to this visit and how happy she was they were here. Will himself was out of town, Frank said, and would be returning tomorrow; he couldn't wait to see them and sent his very best.

Hermia had been a child of privilege; there had always been a safety net and money for emergencies. Her father's death had multiplied—if only in commercial terms—the value of his art. Her mother, she now understood, had left a legacy behind. But nothing had prepared her for the scale of this enormous place, the lavish furnishings and tennis court and swimming pool and the trappings of Hollywood glamour that her daughter now appeared to take in stride. There were gardeners and maids—all deferential, smiling, speaking Spanish and wearing white shirts. An ornamental fountain graced the entrance hall, and orchids fluttered everywhere. The ceilings were vaulted and tiled. The chandeliers and sconces glimmered, and the marble gleamed.

"It's a *beautiful* house," said Hermia.

"Do you like it?"

"How long has Will been living here?"

"Forever," said Frank. "When he's not in Hawaii. It's"—he shrugged his shoulders winningly—"the house where I was born."

She liked him; she couldn't not like him; he was who her daughter loved. Frank took her needless coat and hat and hung them in a closet the size of the kitchen in Truro; then he offered them a cup of coffee or tea or a mimosa or Bloody Mary or fruit juice or wine or prosecco, whatever they desired, saying his father had prepared a red—a *crimson*—carpet for his old friends from

Cambridge. "He means it," said Patricia. "Will's instructions were precise. Last night he read us both chapter and verse: you're to make yourselves at home."

"At home" meant sitting on the patio while a woman called Maria served fruit and cheese and Frank ordered her, in Spanish, to bring drinks or remove them. It meant being told about movies and music and people she knew she should have heard of, whose names meant nothing to her but apparently were famous and very important to know. It meant nodding, smiling, at the guest list for the wedding and pretending she cared about celebrities who were absolutely A-list, so one of the problems with the concert hall was how to keep strangers—photographers and autograph seekers and the uninvited who got wind of it—away. "Security's an issue," said Patricia. "You just get used to it here."

Something had changed in her, Hermia saw. There was something in her daughter's face she had not seen before. When Pat-a-cake had been a child and they were hiding in the hills in Arlington (while Paul was attempting to find them, while she feared he would drive north with guns), the two had been inseparable. Nothing could pry them apart. They ate and drank in unison, speaking a secret language and knowing without needing to be told if one or the other were restless or wanted to watch television or do a jigsaw puzzle. At night they slept in a shared bed; all day they shared the living room, or sat at the plank table in the corner of the kitchen, and when they went for walks outside, they did so hand in hand. When Patsy learned the piano, and proved good at it, Hermia would listen to her daughter practicing, and she could tell without asking if the passage had been easy or difficult to master, if the melody was simple or a challenge to express.

It was as though, thought Hermia, great Nature had been wasteful when she made two separate bodies, because mother and daughter felt the same way—cold, hot, needing to pee or to sneeze—at the identical instant and with no need to discuss it. Breathing, they breathed the same air.

—

In Brentwood, however, it was as though she visited an affable, self-possessed stranger. "Try these," Patricia said, passing out jalapeño pepper crackers with goat's cheese and a rémoulade spread. "We got them at the farmers' market. They go brilliantly with olives."

"We'll take you there," Frank said. "It's the LA version of a traditional farmers' market . . ."

"You said you were born here?" Hermia asked.

He offered another mimosa. His parents, he explained, divorced when he was two, and a year later his mother's plane crashed in Guatemala, so he'd had a succession of surrogate mothers and his father married some of them, but now Will was living alone. Which is why he wanted company, and Lord knew there was room enough, and the two of them were in no rush to establish a place of their own. His father was hoping they'd stay in the house, and—Frank smiled—the rent couldn't be beat, and they were undecided as to precisely in which neighborhood to live. They would maybe move after the honeymoon, and he'd heard that Hermia and Lawrence had been in Italy together, so he wanted their advice about Lago di Como, or the hills of Umbria and Tuscany: where to travel on their trip. But first there was the ceremony and the preparation: it did seem to take up a good deal of time.

"He loves it," said Patricia. "He's astonishing at details. Mostly I tell him, 'Just say it with flowers,' but it turns out there are twelve different shades of freesia and he insists we choose."

"You said it would be casual . . ."

"Did I say that? I meant, I think, informal. My man is a stickler for details"—she rested her hand on Frank's knee.

"More prosecco?" he inquired.

The bride-to-be drank grape juice. She ate olives and celery sticks. She passed around a platter of vegetable pâté.

"Aren't you drinking?" Hermia asked.

"Not yet. It's a little early for me. But for you two it's three hours later . . ."

"And what will you be up to," asked Lawrence, "when you're *not* preparing for the wedding? When you come back from the honeymoon?"

Modestly, Frank said it was too soon to talk about his project and not what they came here to hear. Patricia pressed him, saying, "Baby, why not discuss it, why not tell them what you're working at and what's been going on?" He had his father's light brown hair, a long nose, bright blue eyes. He was wearing beige linen shorts and red sneakers and a purple shirt patterned with orange moons—ascending from crescent to full. He poured another round. "Bottoms up," said Frank. "Chin-chin." Then, after another demurral—"You must be tired from the trip, would you like to take a swim?"—he launched into a discourse Hermia failed to follow about reality TV as an explosive genre in terms of its potential, and how it was like documentary filmmaking, not so much in the mode of cinema verité as record keeping, and how he hoped to fuse the two for purposes of consciousness-raising. "It's an old-fashioned term, of course," and he used it tongue-in-cheek, "but *consciousness-raising* is as good a way as any to describe the project; think of it as a kind of high jump, or a pole vault maybe, where you keep raising the bar. Most of our reality shows today pander, don't they, to the lowest common denominator and what's worst about our culture, but there's no intrinsic reason that that has to be the case. The question is how high to go, how much you can manage to elevate what used to be called public discourse," and he himself was guessing the American public was ready—or at least he hoped so, and was gambling that his guess was

good—for a film-format (DVD and the Web, and what was starting to be posted now—*give us this day our daily blog*) discussion of
the way we live and what our aspirations as a nation consist of in the
year 2005. "These days what I've been asking myself," Frank said,
"is whether we are or aren't in a parallel situation to Rome's when
the empire crumbled, and does the act of posing the question itself
make the answer more likely to be in the affirmative: what's self-
fulfilling about the prophecy and what's inaccurate; who, in short,
are the barbarians at our nation's gates? But there's a difference, isn't
there, between an empire threatened by quite literal hordes on horseback or by someone half the world away in the hills of Pakistan or
maybe Afghanistan who got lucky with a pair of planes one bright
September morning; fortress America, this thing we're so busily
building, has had twin towers leveled, but it's not as if the nation
itself is threatened with invasion as was the case for Rome, or can—
unless we willingly *ourselves* destroy it—come apart."

Patricia was nodding, agreeing. Bougainvillea flared against the
garden wall, and there were lemon trees in pots. There were flowers
Hermia could not name, and multicolored roses in the flower beds.
Frank spoke about his project—open casting, docudrama—and the
thousands of hours of footage he'd shot (most of them, he smiled, so
dull you wouldn't believe it, you can't *imagine*, much of it just pure
plain tedious in the fashion of town meetings everywhere, but even
the Constitutional Convention, he was sure, had had its share of
windbags, men in powdered wigs and vests and pantaloons blowing
off steam and making speeches that posterity would come to reverence
and think of as our nation's sacred text). When it was happening in
Philadelphia, the convention we honor in history books was probably
as tedious as any congressional hearing today, and how he *wished* he
could have been there to record it, just for a single session be a fly with
a camcorder on the wall. Our forefathers were great talkers, weren't
they: axe grinders in the literal sense, and routinely argumentative,

a bunch of rhetoricians, which is one of the strange—maybe the strangest—things about democracy, how every kid with pebbles in his mouth believes his real name is Demosthenes and feels entitled to a podium—"which is what I'm studying, if you take the point."

"I'm not sure I do," said Lawrence. "I'm not certain I *do* take the point."

She watched him. Was he saying this to demonstrate attentiveness, or because he disagreed? Years before he might have argued, if only for the sake of argument and to stake out an alternative. But now he was being polite. Maria replenished the tray. Patricia said, "What Frank is saying is that history repeats itself because the people who write history repeat themselves, correct?"

"Correct," said Frank, "that's exactly right, and what I'm doing in these interviews is letting people ramble—uncut, so far, though Lord knows there'll be hours, *days, weeks, months!* to cut—about their dream of liberty and what the good life means. Dad used to say, perhaps you heard him back in the day, that everything he learned about the business model that provides all this"—he raised his arm, inclusive, gesturing at the pool, the lemon trees and tennis court—"he learned from having spent a winter in Des Moines. You remember, maybe, that time he spent in Iowa, when he came back to the studio executives and said, 'Don't tell me what will or won't play in Dubuque, I've *been* there, folks, I know. The Archie Bunker show.' So maybe, just maybe, in the middle of this endless-seeming public discourse, if we look long and hard enough there'll be a nugget or a kernel or at least a grain of truth." Frank wouldn't bet the farm on this, but he wondered if they'd noticed how a phrase like "bet the farm" or, come to think of it, "a kernel or at least a grain of truth" derives from our agrarian past, our history as farmers, and so for him the seminal text—again that word "seminal," planting a *seed*—is Crèvecoeur, not de Tocqueville, and *Letters from an American Farmer* in—he'd just been reading it again and therefore knew the date—1782. "Give me Hector St. John de Crèvecoeur," he said, "and I'll give you America's *roots*."

Patricia was holding his hand. He emptied his glass of prosecco, she her grape juice, and the sun was going down. "Are you cold?" she asked her mother. "Chilly, a little?"

Hermia nodded.

"Let's go in."

"But I haven't finished," Frank protested, "I was only getting started," and it took her a second to see he was joking and had finished with his lecture on Crèvecoeur and de Tocqueville and the business of public forums or what we call town meetings and the parallel or lack of parallels to ancient Greece and Italy in the present American scene.

"Can I show you my room?" Patricia stood. "There's something I want you to see."

—

They left the men alone. Her daughter led her through the butler's pantry and kitchen and the dining room—twelve plush chairs at a polished table—and the library and living room with floor-to-ceiling mirrors down a hallway to a bedroom suite that gave out on its own walled garden, with ornamental shrubs. The bed was king-size, strewn with pillows and an orange bolster and duvet; the carpet was pink tufted silk. A glass-topped circular table and two white wicker chairs were positioned in front of French doors. The girl busied herself with closing the doors, rearranging the chairs, and asking Hermia to sit. "I didn't really need to *show* you anything," she said. "I did want to get us out of there. And I've got something to tell you . . ." Then she fell silent.

"What?"

"Guess."

"About what?"

"You can't guess?"

"Frank? Will?"

"No."

"Are you all right?"

Patricia nodded.

"Is anything wrong?"

She shook her head.

"It's been a long day, darling. We started out from Truro in the dark this very early morning: five o'clock . . ."

"I thought you would be happy for me."

"Yes."

"Us. Happy for the two of us, is what I meant to say."

Hermia was weary from the trip. She allowed herself to feel it—the drive into Logan, the six-hour flight, the drive from the airport and then the hotel and the shock of her daughter's surroundings.

"Of *course* I'm happy for you, but this isn't twenty questions. I don't really know what you want me to ask."

"No."

She let impatience surface. "So we've been treated to a discourse on Crèvecoeur and docudrama and the existence of opinion polls. But I'm not feeling up to it—or anyhow not yet, not now . . ."

"Up to what, Mom?"

"This game you're asking me to play. Twenty questions."

"It's just you always used to know—you always *seemed* to, anyhow—exactly what was going on."

"Temps jadis."

"What's that supposed to mean?" Patricia shook her head. The butterfly tattoo on the back of her neck emerged from her black lifted hair.

"Long time ago. The operative phrase is 'used to know.' You changed all that."

"I'm pregnant. We're having a baby."

There was silence between them. "You're sure?"

Patricia nodded.

"Darling, that's *wonderful.*"

"Isn't it? Is it? I was certain you had guessed—the way you were looking at me earlier, when you asked why I haven't been drinking . . ."

"I'm sorry, no, I didn't guess. I *did* see something in your face."

"Not yet in my belly, I hope." She stretched her hands across it. "I don't want to show at the wedding."

"You're reed-thin, you'll be beautiful. How are you feeling?"

"Shitty." Tears were welling in her daughter's eyes. "Every morning, it's like *whoa*, what's going on inside me!"

"Does Frank know?"

She nodded.

"And is he excited?"

"I think so. I'm, yes, sure he is. Except . . ."

"Except?"

"I'm frightened, Mom. I *hate* the way it makes me feel."

She stood and moved to where Patricia sat and bent and hugged her shoulder. "Don't worry, darling. We all go through this. Went through it. You were a *bear!*"

"I was?"

"Impossible," Hermia lied. "A ton of bricks that kept on shifting inside me is what it felt like. You felt like. So sick to my stomach each morning: the works."

"I'm not sure what I'm doing here. In LA, I mean. Sometimes I think . . ."

The telephone rang. It was Will. Patricia said, "Excuse me," but she had to answer this, to take the call, he'd called two times already to make certain things were fine—and while she was assuring the man who would soon be her father-in-law that everything was perfect, and yes, her mother had arrived, and Lawrence too, and did he want to speak to them or wait until tomorrow, since she knew he was in transit and the cell phone was breaking up, and could he hear her? Did he want to call again? Should she try calling him instead? And of *course* she would give them the message, they liked the place, they *loved* the place, and tomorrow there'll be dinner at Osteria Mozza, yes, she'd made a reservation, eight o'clock, and she hoped his trip was worth it and they awaited his return and would celebrate tomorrow—"Fine, fine," she repeated, cajoling him while tears coursed down her cheeks.

Hermia watched with alarm. She heard her daughter chatter on: bright-voiced and attentive. It was the voice she'd heard, herself, the night Patricia told her she was getting married, was renting the Walt Disney Concert Hall, and how happy she was feeling and how very lucky she felt. It was the brittle voice of welcome she'd heard, the voice of admiration that half an hour ago had been praising Frank's docudrama project: the voice of an actress performing a part, but not one she wanted to play.

Patricia hung up. She blew her nose. "I'm sorry, I didn't mean to be this way, I'd planned to tell you earlier . . ."

"I hate to ask this," Hermia said. "I hate not knowing the answer. But have you ever been pregnant before?"

She wiped her eyes. She shook her head.

"Our bodies—of course you understand this—do scary things to us, darling. All these hormones, they kick in . . ."

"I know. And I *want* to be pregnant, I do. It just feels I'm going crazy, like you say my father was."

"*Paul* wasn't the one with the baby, Pat-a-cake. *I'm* the one who carried you."

"It's just that I never knew him. And I don't want to think I'll be *dangerous*, Mom. So you don't think I've inherited . . . ?"

Patricia, crying, was trying to stop crying. Hermia touched her daughter's cheek.

V
—

Mannerism, class, says the professor, is here exemplified in the work of the sixteenth-century Florentine master Jacopo Pontormo, whose agitated figures evoke what we may best describe as the body in extremis. Lawrence puts his hand on my knee and slides it up and squeezes as if to say, though wordlessly, remember our own bodily extremis last Saturday? I'm with him now, and he with me, we're sitting next to each other while the man at the lectern discourses on the human figure, its proportions and contortions and exaggerations, using a pointer to point out examples. There's an hour exam in Soc Rel 10, and a paper due on Friday on the influence of Ibsen in the early work of Joyce, but I've done *Dubliners* already so it's only *Stephen Hero* and in turn I squeeze his knee. The slide projector clicks, and it's *The Supper at Emmaus* from the Uffizi except it's upside down and from somewhere in the hall comes a brief bark of laughter and the professor apologizes as he's done three times already this morning and says the slide-carousel has been giving him fits all week. I need to sneeze. I spread my legs and Lawrence crosses his and *The Supper at Emmaus* is supplanted by the *Portrait of a Musician*, also the Uffizi, tempera on wood.

We fuck. In his room in Claverly behind closed doors we fuck.

I fuck, you fuck, he fucks, she fucks, we fuck, they fuck. This is called a conjugation, class, a declension I do not decline. In springtime, the only pretty ring time, and I'm mad about the boy. What happens next is what happens next and it's too soon to worry but I worry anyhow because still through the hawthorn blows the cold wind. What are you trying to tell me, he asks, and I say it's Shakespeare's song and Lawrence says, but what are you trying to say? I say let's take your car and go this weekend to Truro and I'll show you where I live. Tintoretto, the professor says, and El Greco too engaged in what we might call mannerist exaggeration, the focus on metonymy, synecdoche, the part representing the whole, and there are many others who incorporate such disproportion on the canvas or in stone. It's a matter of emphasis largely, I fuck, you fuck, we fuck.

VI
2005

Next day they returned to the house. Lunch would be served by the pool. Hermia was fretful; she had had trouble sleeping, and her dreams were sad ones, filled with babies crying. There had been a railroad station where she was supposed to meet them, greet them, making certain they got off the train. In her dream alarm bells sounded; there was a loud piercing whistle and billowing smoke and, everywhere, confusion. There were packages to claim or send, but they could not be found.

Lawrence too slept poorly. He said the jet lag got to him, and he had woken up at six and used the hotel gym. When he returned and had showered and shaved, it was not yet seven o'clock, and he told her he wanted to take a short walk. They were near the Gehry and Moneo buildings, after all, and he thought he'd visit them; did she want to come along?

Hermia said no. She ordered room service coffee and fruit and read *USA Today* and took—not something she could do so easily in Truro, where the tubs were small—a bath. By the time she dressed he was back in the room; it was, he told her, a beautiful morning and would be a hot day. The Walt Disney Concert Hall was just around the corner, and locked, but the cathedral stayed open and he'd spent minutes watching a processional of early-morning worshippers—the janitors and housemaids and faithful on their way to work—and getting a sense of the site. Rafael Moneo and Frank Gehry, Lawrence said, had very different aesthetics; the former preferred to adapt a building to its surroundings, blending in with indigenous culture and the local landscape; the latter established a sculptural space that challenged and confronted what was in place before. The second design mode, of course, was far more notable or at least noticeable as an architectural assertion, and earned wider public acclaim. But in some ways, Lawrence said, the Moneo moved him more. He was sitting on the bed's edge, twisting his neck and stretching his arms, and she understood he was talking at least in part about himself, his own expectations as an architect, and trying not to sound bitter. The work of his youth, though respected, had won no major prizes, and he was embracing his "outsider" status as if self-conferred.

"Have you met them?"

"Yes." He nodded. "It's a small world."

"Do you like them?"

"I'm not sure. Moneo is, I mean, very much the gentleman—European and a bit standoffish—and Frank's not easy to know. Not for me, at any rate; I've met him once or twice . . ."

His own career had been, she knew, spent in the academy, and although he'd been successful—a department chair and interim dean—it wasn't what Lawrence had planned. He had hoped to make a difference in the shared structures of community, but what he'd mostly done, he said, was attend committee meetings on New Urbanism and sustainable development and deal with the curriculum and salary issues and grievances and hiring and tenure. "If you're a baseball player or a ballerina"—now he was standing, doing torso twists—"you know you'd better start early; if you begin the piano or start in on theoretical physics at thirty, you likely won't have a career. But architecture and urban planning and design are professions where a man or woman makes their mark in middle age, at fifty or sixty, not before, because apprenticeship takes years to serve and commissions don't come to the young.

"This holds just as true," he continued, "for major reputations; it takes time to establish a name. Mies and Louis Kahn and Corbu and Frank Lloyd Wright—not to mention Aalto, Gropius, and Breuer—all did important work late."

"Late?"

Lawrence smiled. "It's why so many of us teach in architecture schools. And why first houses—think of Charley Gwathmey's parents' place or yours truly designing my own parents' homes—are commissioned by the family, or by a family friend."

"What did you think of it, really?" she asked.

"What?"

"Will's house. His *mansion*."

"The Taj Mahal meets the Alhambra." He shrugged. "I think what we're supposed to think—this man is very rich."

Last night she had not told him about Patricia's pregnancy, or how it made her feel. She herself had been unnerved—shocked even, although this morning in the bath she'd told herself she shouldn't be—by the girl's reaction. It came as a surprise. Her daughter seemed to fear she had inherited her own dead parent's paranoia and would lose control. After they left when she was two, Patsy never saw Paul again, but the air was fraught with menace and the specter of her father—wild-eyed and wielding a knife—had haunted her for years. And now that she herself would be a mother, she was worried—*terrified*—she would behave the same way.

In the palatial bedroom, watching a breeze ruffle jasmine blossoms, Hermia had offered comfort, assuring her daughter that what she was feeling was normal, and mood swings were part of the game. "This is what happens during pregnancy," she'd said.

"It's a hormone storm. Your father, darling, had the kind of illness that has nothing to do with gestation; it's a different thing . . ."

Beyond the French doors palm fronds waved, and the sun declined. Patricia sobbed, then calmed herself, then laughed and chatted happily while the four of them ate dinner ordered from a local restaurant—chicken in mole sauce and tamales and black beans and rice and salsa and the best guacamole, said Frank, in all LA. At nine o'clock she and Lawrence begged off and took a taxi back to the hotel. There were chocolates on the pillow and bottles of mineral water waiting by the bed. He had wanted to make love, but she said she was tired, and meant it, and they talked and lay together on the king-size mattress until he fell asleep.

—

"My God," said Will. "My God, it's you."

"It's us." Lawrence hugged him. "Hello."

"I can't process it. Not really. I mean, I've been expecting it and I knew you guys were coming, but I just can't process it. Look at you two. *Babycakes.*"

He kissed her hand, then cheeks. He was portly, ruddy, bald. He was wearing a Hawaiian shirt, with pineapples and palm trees, and a pair of knee-length shorts cinched beneath his belly with a rawhide thong.

"Will," she said. "How *are* you?"

"Better now you two are here. My eyes are going, baby, but you look terrific."

She laughed. He hugged her, then held her at arm's length and looked her up and down appreciatively and said time had been kind to her: "Welcome welcome welcome. No wonder my kid wants to marry your daughter; he's got something to look forward to," said Will. Barefoot, he ushered them through the front hall and the dining room and butler's pantry and the kitchen to the patio they'd occupied before. This time the table was set for five, and Maria, smiling, nodding, offered a pitcher of iced tea and one of Bloody Marys. Hermia sat.

Will pushed in her chair with a flourish and said again how well she looked, how nothing seemed to change. "How long has it been," he asked, "how long *exactly* has it been?" and he and Lawrence calculated: forty-two years—no, *less than that*, because there was that time in Greece they met by accident on the Acropolis and spent the night together in the Plaka. Dinner, dancing, could Larry remember? They did the whole handkerchief thing. Will capered in front of the table, circling it, right arm upraised: *Yasou, yasou, O-pa, oom-pah-pah.* And did Larry know, could he *believe* Nana Mouskouri was still singing, wearing her signature glasses and being a national treasure; it's the grandson, isn't it, of old Papandreou who'll be their next prime minister? At least it's not— who played that part, was it Anthony Quinn?—Zorba the goddam Greek . . .

She watched him carefully. Capillaries flooded the red delta of his cheeks. The hair she remembered, the blockish agility, the muscles of his forearm: all were gone. He had a pair of glasses strung from a black ribbon at his neck. But his voice was Will's voice still, his grin Will's grin, and she felt happy to see him: this affable, overweight long-lost companion from—where was it?—Irving Street. As undergraduates, she and Lawrence lived on campus, but Will was enrolled in Harvard Law School, and living on his own. In his basement apartment he threw a series of parties; once at his invitation she and Lawrence spent a weekend in the back room by the brick-walled garden. The space was dark and crowded, stuffed with books and records and hookahs and guitars, and she could remember the upright citizens of Cambridge walking by with umbrellas and dogs on a leash. The house was tall, brown-shingled, with a separate entrance to the basement, and the owners did not seem to mind, but the men across the street were palpably offended when she and Lawrence and Will and whoever he was seeing sat on the front stoop.

There had been beer and wine and dope: marijuana and peyote and, near the end, LSD. Those were the years of Joan Baez and curly-headed Bob Dylan and Odetta and their fellow student Tom Rush. Young troubadours were triumphing at the Bitter End and Newport and, on Mt. Auburn Street, Club 47. Will too hoped to be a singer, but some part of him acknowledged that he couldn't make it, couldn't hack performing or get noticed up on stage. So he had started law school—this after a couple of seasons of failing in second-rate venues, doing backup guitar work and kicking around with Jim Kweskin's Jug Band—and found he was good at it, and he liked the law and could have a career . . .

One night he threw a pass at her—"Hey, pretty baby, this last song's for *you!*"—but didn't seem to mind when Hermia rejected him, saying she was with his friend, remember, and not ready for a threesome. In truth, his approach was halfhearted, a dutiful flirtation, and they liked each other better later; the air between them cleared. In her senior year, while Lawrence had been traveling and Will was finishing law school, he invited her to dinner, twice, and once to an Odetta concert, and what they were now was old friends. "You make new friends—*I* do," said Will, "with regularity, on a weekly basis nowadays, it's part of the system, everyone's MO—but a person doesn't get the chance to make *old* friends. So I'm damn pleased you two are here, and the kids have found each other; it feels like we're getting it right."

Patricia and Frank emerged, as if on cue, and made them loudly welcome. They sat and passed around ceviche and cold salmon with a drizzle of fresh hollandaise and dill. There were lemon wedges and curried mussels, and Lawrence said you eat very well, don't you, in LA. Or at any rate in this house. This started Patricia talking about the food she planned to serve at the reception, and the problems with caterers and the wedding planner, and how she couldn't ask their friends to fly in for a Saturday and not offer something on Friday as well—particularly, anyhow, for friends from out of town.

It dawned on Hermia little by little that there'd been lengthy preparations and elaborate arrangements made; her daughter's insistence the wedding was modest had been a way of asking her please not to interfere. Will was saying how he'd never planned on staying here, never believed California was home, but by now it had been, hell, thirty-five years and he'd never leave. Except for the condo in Maui when he needed to get out of town. You get used to it, don't you, he said. You make your bed—he smiled self-deprecatingly— your *beds*, and sleep in them, and pretty soon what seemed like an experiment or maybe just a onetime thing becomes a habit and pattern and then it's who you are. "Do you play golf?" he asked.

Hermia and Lawrence shook their heads

"That's a relief," Will said. "I couldn't imagine it somehow and I *hate* golf: a good walk spoiled. But damned if I don't have to *pretend* like it interests me, *sound* like it matters—or had to do so anyhow for twenty fucking years. By now I tell my clients *no*, I can tell them whatever I want to, I don't have to play fucking golf."

"Are you still working?" Lawrence asked.

"Not really. Not worth mentioning. I drop by the office and crack the whip or pinch an ass or two—but it's not what we used to call *work*."

"Speaking of which," said Patricia, "I do want to show you the studio. His office. It's just the most amazing place . . ."

"Let's talk about you two," said Will. "How did this happen anyhow? Where?"

"On the good ship *Diana*," said Lawrence.

"Those ads for a romantic getaway," Hermia said, "expanded horizons and shipboard romance—in our case turned out to be true. There was a visit to Capri and Taormina and a tour guide with a megaphone in the ruins of Pompeii: the two of us together for the cruise. And by the time we docked at Valletta"—she smiled—"we had, as they say, bonded."

"Is *that* what you call it?" Will asked.

"I think," continued Hermia, "it's what we're feeling now, isn't it? The friends and lovers of our youth exist outside of time. Oh, I know it sounds pretentious and it's not exactly what I mean, but somehow meeting Lawrence then, and seeing you again today, makes me feel time's on our side."

Will laughed. "It isn't, baby, don't be fooled. Time's never on our side."

He talked about the way things change, how what we took for granted, once, is no longer ours to take. He discoursed on the alteration—perceptible, imperceptible, it makes no difference finally—of fashion or music or population growth or hemlines and computers and the ozone layer, all those dictators we love to install and after ten years overthrow. Those of us who inhabit the planet are changing its contours and constitution by the very fact of habitation, the existence of existence, so the species is bound for extinction, but not cockroaches, of course, only dear old *Homo non-sapiens* is doomed—and while he was making his speech (happily, half persuasively, topping off their glasses) she told herself, *This is where Frank comes from, this is why he's such a talker*, and looked at her beautiful daughter and saw she was fighting back tears.

—

The back-and-forth went on this way: two sides of the one coin. It was as though the celebration and the mournfulness required one another—a mouth turned up, a mouth turned down, two masks on one wall. The wedding planners came and went, the caterers arrived, and Patricia greeted them ebulliently, then as they left began to cry while Hermia massaged her shoulders and told her not to worry, not to be afraid. Will and Lawrence resumed their old friendship, it seemed, with scarcely a hitch in their stride. They went to watch the Lakers in Will's company's box at the Staples Center; they approved or disapproved of restaurants together, and watched DVDs in the basement theater, with its professional screen. They took saunas together, or swam. Upstairs, in their shared privacy, Patricia shook and wiped her eyes and swore she'd never felt like this and never wanted or expected to: "When will it get better, Mom, when does it ever end?"

"It doesn't end," said Hermia. "You always worry about your own child—unborn or born. A grown one, come to that. You'll always be my baby, baby, like the old song says."

"You mean it, Mom?"

"Of course I do."

"I'm *glad* you're here."

"It doesn't change," she insisted. "It's always just the same." But she found herself wondering, was that the truth; could her mother—locked in the flat on Lyndhurst Road, half comatose and wholly inattentive—have been worrying about *her*, Hermia, and hoping for a visit and hoping all was well?

She doubted it. Her mother had been nothing if not self-absorbed. There had been blood ties between them, of course, and a shared history, but the distance remained absolute. In the bright armature of egotism, her mother seemed to say: *I close my eyes, it's night.* And Hermia herself had tried (for the time her daughter stayed away, the twelve years of their separation) to live her life alone.

It did not work. At night in their capacious bed—with Lawrence asleep beside her, the lights of the hotel hallway a bright ribbon underneath the door and a *Do Not Disturb* sign hanging from the knob outside—she wondered how and in what ways she might have failed her child, her complicated darling. The girl who'd marched on picket lines and slept in migrant worker camps was living, now, in luxury. Still, she was fighting for air. She smiled at Frank and Will and gave efficient orders to the caterers and, when they came to rehearse, the musicians. As the date of the wedding approached, her smile grew more and more rigid, her laughter less frequent and feigned. When they were alone together, in the kitchen or the laundry room or bedroom, she questioned her mother in detail about her own father's behavior, how Paul at first reacted and then how he acted and when and how he changed.

"What was he *like?*" Patricia asked. "When did he start to lose control, and what did you notice? What did it take to persuade the police to take out a restraining order, and when was he hospitalized?"

"You know all this," said Hermia. "It's ancient history."

"I don't," Patricia said. "I need reminding anyhow: Was it voluntary on his part, and how long did he remain in Bellevue?—*Was* it Bellevue, or did you say Austen Riggs?"

"You're not Paul's daughter," Hermia said, "or not the way you fear you are. His jealousy, I think, had something to do with his own mother's death and having been abandoned."

"How did you escape from him, how did *we* escape from him? When was the last time you saw him, what did he write you and what was he doing in Sarajevo and did he ever go home?"

The past—so carefully avoided—had surfaced now again.

———

Alone with Frank one afternoon, Hermia tried to discuss this. "Are you worried?"

"Excuse me?"

"Concerned, I mean. Patricia doesn't seem—what's the right word?—*easy* about all this. Comfortable in her skin."

"No?"

"I have to admit it, *I'm* worried. A little, anyhow. You know we don't really know each other . . ."

"We will, now that you're here."

"Forgive me"—Hermia spread her hands—"I meant *Patricia* and I don't know each other now. All those years she was away and only a little in touch—the time in the Upper Peninsula, Minneapolis, Florida, wherever. She's told me how you met, of course, and how she feels you rescued her, and though I tried and tried to help, she must have been, oh, angry . . ."

"At who?"

She attempted a smile. "At me."

"Why?"

"*Why?*"

"I'm not sure I follow . . ."

"Is there anything I ought to know?"

"Like what, for example?"

"Oh, something she tells you she's worried about. Something in our history?"

"Such as?"

"Anything . . ."

He looked away. They were sitting on the patio; there was a tray of tea biscuits and tea. Maria had brought milk and lemon, sugar and porcelain cups; the others were taking a swim. Why was he being, Hermia wondered, so tight-lipped and unresponsive when the instant he climbed on his soapbox, he talked and talked and talked? How like a man, she thought—how much like Lawrence, even—to avoid the display of emotion, or all conversation about it; how like them to discuss the public, not the private life. And then she remembered that "not sure I follow" was the thing Lawrence said when Frank had been discoursing on his docudrama project, and maybe Frank was telling her to mind her own business, not his.

"All right," she said. "Forget I asked."

"De nada." He offered her tea.

—

"This is Vanessa, Mom."

"Hello."

"And this is Heidi. Elizabeth. This is Jeanette."

"I'm glad to meet you all."

"We've heard *so* much about you. Patricia talks about you non-stop . . ."

"A ladies' lunch," said Heidi. "She's not letting us be brides-maids, but she didn't insist that we couldn't have lunch."

"I'm starving," said Elizabeth.

"They do good salads here."

The six of them were sitting in the Campanile on La Brea Avenue, because it had been Charlie Chaplin's studio and there were pictures on the walls showing the glory days. The waitstaff, aspiring actors, wore black. Vanessa and Heidi were married, and Heidi had two children; Elizabeth was single and Jeanette in the throes of divorce. She attempted to keep all this clear in her head, to distinguish between them and remember—*Eloise and Sasha*—the names of Heidi's children, but it wasn't easy and she felt like an intruder, and while they spoke of Tom and Dick and Harry (no, that's unfair, thought Hermia, it's Timothy and Richard and Enrique), she watched her daughter behaving in public as though all were well and drinking white grape juice and water while the rest of the women drank wine.

Elizabeth and Heidi had just come from the salon, and their

hair was curled and blond. The bracelets on their narrow wrists and rings on fingers sparkled; their legs were taut, arms toned. Everyone's girlfriends and husbands and boyfriends were—so Patricia had explained to her—in the entertainment business: "It's what we do here, *everybody* does, and Frank's of course a part of it, though trying to chart his own way. What I worry about isn't any of that, it's not the world we're living in but whether I can live in it, the things I see behind my eyes, which is why I don't dare close them, the roaring—you know what I mean about *roaring?*—in my ears."

"Do you still play the piano?"

"No."

"Do you think music could be useful?"

"No."

"There's professional help," said Hermia. "I'm sure we can find therapists or doctors in this town."

"What a good idea." Her daughter stared at her, inscrutable.

"I didn't mean . . ."

"Of course not. And I wonder why I never *thought* about professional help—a *brilliant* suggestion, Mom." Her voice was thick with irony. "I should get involved with yoga, maybe. Or find a management guru and stress intervention expert. A crisis counselor."

"Darling . . ."

"Thanks a bunch."

Now, however, they were eating crabmeat in avocados and cold squash soup and fried calamari in a pesto sauce. Jeanette was talking about the divorce, saying, "It's my cross to carry, my very own personal challenge, and make sure you don't marry a lawyer because when settlement time comes around you'll be not so pleasantly screwed." The women discussed an actress who'd been fighting anorexia for years, but bulimia's a losing battle once you're past a certain stage, and now the question wasn't could she *act* but could she *live?* "What's the difference anyway," Vanessa asked, "between anorexia and bulimia; I know there *is* a difference, of course, but it seems like six of one and half a dozen of the other, can you be ano-rectic but not bulimic today?"

Hermia found herself remembering the lettuce in her garden, the blossoms that would soon be cucumbers and eggplant. "I'm sorry," said Patricia, "I'm not feeling well," and excused herself for the third time to find the ladies' room. Her friends looked at each other inquiringly, and Hermia said, "You know her better than I do these days. It's nerves, I think. Prenuptial nerves."

"And a stomach bug," Heidi proposed.

"*We've* had it at home this whole week long," said Jeanette.

"Now she tells us," said Elizabeth, and the women, uneasily, laughed.

——

The day of the wedding was all she could hope for: the June sky clear and cloudless and the evening mild. That Saturday at six, guests gathered on the rooftop, and Hermia—who had spent the afternoon with makeup artists and florists and a photographer and hairdresser and stylist while her daughter stood staring at herself unblinkingly in mirrors—shook hands and said how pleased she was to meet you, meet everybody, and praising the flowers and praising the view and saying how thrilled she was for Patricia and how lucky she felt to be here. There were curvilinear stairwells and noiseless rapid elevators and a sculpture by Frank Gehry in the middle of the rooftop garden and great burnished plates of steel she angled past, attempting to tell north from south, attempting to distinguish from the vantage of the balcony the outlying districts and hills.

Then Lawrence took her arm and they sat in the front row of ten rows of chairs. There was a jazz combo and a solo violinist who performed a Bach partita as the audience found seats. They played "Here Comes the Bride." While she tried to hear what the JP was saying (Frank had been resolute, insisting on nothing religious, no hint of worship discourse in *this* ceremony, please), and hearing the low noise of traffic and, overhead, a helicopter, and the young couple stood before her, hand in hand, smiling at each other and exchanging vows and rings, Hermia was swallowing the taste of sugared rum. They had had, at Will's insistence—"Try these, they're terrific"—mai tais and mojitos for lunch, and although she'd told herself she needed to stay sober, pay attention, she was also feeling urgently that what she needed to get through the event was, if not oblivion, heartsease and the glow of alcohol. "Salud y amor y pesetas," Will had proposed, "y tiempo para gozarlos." Therefore when the JP said, "I now pronounce you man and wife," her own eyes had been streaming and heart pounding and her attention wandering—those shoes, where did Patricia buy them and how did she find white shoes with red soles? that woman in the third row, on the aisle, was it Jeanette or Vanessa? that man in the dark glasses whom everyone avoided staring at, was he Brad Pitt? and that woman Will was kissing looked like, who? Faye Dunaway?— so what she would later remember were not the words of plighted troth, whatever "plighted troth" might mean, but a shaft of evening sunlight and rivets in the steel.

And then there was champagne and dinner and toasts and dancing on a polished stage where on other weekend nights she might have heard Mozart or Strauss. She danced with Frank; she danced with Will; she danced with Lawrence often. He was telling her this place *does* work, this space *does* function beautifully, and she asked him was he happy, and he said he was happy for Patricia and glad to be part of the party. His face was wet with sweat. They were congratulated, often, by wedding guests who said to Hermia it was such a pleasure to meet her and she must be pleased and proud. There was laughter and loud music and a pair of singers performing with the band. Men with earpieces, wearing suits, stood watch beside the doors. Hermia was thinking of her own rushed marriage decades earlier, its aftermath, its terrifying denouement, and how she was not only a mother but had become a mother-in-law and soon would be a grandmother. The mystery, she tried to explain to Lawrence, was how you know someone so *well*—raise and nurture them, *extrude* them from your body and watch them crawl and stand and learn to walk and understand their every like and dislike, milk or chocolate milk and which color they prefer for sprinkles on their ice cream cone—until the children too are grown-ups and a continent away. "It's not an accident," she said, "that we live on the eastern shore and she and Frank are here, two almost total strangers, a couple living just as far away as possible and still on the one shared landmass, or is it?" "Is it what?" asked Lawrence, and she knew that she was giddy, and the room was twirling, having drunk too much ("not"—Hermia giggled—"the room but *me, I'm* the one who drank too much"), and said, "I need to sit."

They sat. "Are you all right?"

She shook her head.

"Can I get you some water?"

She squeezed his hand.

"Not bad," he said, "for Ma and Pa Kettle. I mean the dancing . . ."

She tried to smile.

"What's wrong?"

"Let's just sit here," Hermia managed, "and watch the children celebrate."

"They're off tomorrow, aren't they?"

"Yes. For Italy—Lake Como, first."

"Do *you* want to get married?"

Again, she shook her head.

"This isn't a proper proposal. Right now, I couldn't get down on my knees."

"You're wonderful," she told him. "You've been taking such good care of me."

"We *could* get married, Hermia. We *should* get married, maybe."

"I haven't had much luck with it. And you haven't either. With marriage, I mean."

"Let's discuss it tomorrow, OK?"

"OK. We'll do a meeting."

"Have your people talk to my people."

She hiccuped. "I'll be sure to tell my people: take the call."

———

In the morning it was over and they went together to the airport. Frank and Patricia were leaving for their honeymoon, first stop Milan ("*Malpensa* Airport," Will had joked, "but try to think well of it anyway"), and Hermia and Lawrence flying back to Boston. They gathered for a farewell brunch at the mansion in Brentwood, but the bedecked tables held little she wanted, or could swallow, and she waited on the patio while wedding guests stopped by in twos and threes or groups of five and were offered mimosas and coffee and plates of pastry and fruit. A Hawaiian man wearing a chef's toque and spattered apron served up eggs, and there were trays of sausages and bacon and several varieties of ham. The sound system in the garden was too loud.

She tried to spend time with Patricia, but all they were able to promise each other was to stay in touch. Her daughter did seem self-possessed—regal in her slate-blue traveling suit and Dior scarf, with a matching set of Louis Vuitton luggage—and when she said,

"I'll miss you, Mom," the sentiment seemed genuine. "I'm *so* glad you and Lawrence came . . ."

"More soon," said Will. "You come back soon."

"Of course we will."

"Next time stay here"—he gestured, inclusive, expansive. "We'll squeeze you in."

"Twelve thousand square feet," said Lawrence. "Unless I miss my guess."

"Hey, you must be a *architect* . . ."

"A sus órdenes." He clicked his heels. "A pleasure, truly, Will."

"And for me, old buddy."

Patricia was wiping her eyes. When Hermia embraced her, saying, "Darling, have a wonderful time," it was as when, long years before, she had gone off to summer camp. Each line of comfort— *Be careful, stay well, enjoy yourself*—seemed fraught with risk. Lightly, she patted her daughter's stomach and cautioned Frank, "Take care of her."

A limousine arrived. At LAX they were delivered to separate terminals, the bride and bridegroom first.

VII

—

Who was that?

Who?

You h-h-heard me.

Yes, but I don't know what you're asking. Or who you're talk-ing about.

The man in the elevator.

Who?

Not Billy who runs it. The m-man in the suit.

I don't know.

Are you s-s-sleeping with him?

Paul . . .

Or Billy? Is it Billy?

No.

I didn't think so. Elevator men aren't your style. But the men in s-suits, with briefcases—do they excite you, briefcases?

Can we not do this?

What?

Not have this conversation. Every time a strange man rides the elevator we have an argument. Oh, I'm terribly sorry. Such a bore.

So s-s-sorry to repeat myself. How ever do you manage to endure such repetition?

It isn't boring. It's sad and wrong.

Variety is preferable, isn't it? It's what you prefer—like that man in the s-s-suit. What was his name, darling, tell me his name.

I don't know. I don't care.

Harry, Tom, and Dick-dick-dick.

Can we stop this now?

Stop what?

This inquisition. This terrible thing that you're doing. And not just to me, to our marriage. To you.

What was he like?

Who?

The man in the suit?

Can't we stop now?

The issue as I understand it is this, Mrs. Lattimer. D-darling. I myself am entirely willing to stop. To cease, as they say, and desist. But first you must do so yourself. It's the necessary precondition, isn't it, it's the without-which-nothing, the sine qua non, if your Latin is up to it, for any such agreement. M-mind, I'm not urging chastity. Just that you don't suck strangers off in elevators when B-b-billy's on his lunch break.

Paul . . .

Am I boring you? Am I repeating myself?

Yes, and yes.

How disappointing. How very d-dull of me. Let's change the subject.

Good.

The plumber. When did you last fuck the plumber?

STOP it.

Precisely my preference, darling. That's just what I want you to do.

I can't bear this. I can't bear this.

Don't cry.

Don't make me.

Nothing turns my heart to s-s-stone faster than watching you cry.

VIII

2005

In the morning they were home again, and the garden grew. There was damage to the hostas and the berry bushes but not to the garden itself; their fence had held. The smell of wind in the white pines, the sound of water past the dunes was a kind of balm to Hermia, and she tried to put uneasiness away. Los Angeles, she told Lawrence, was not her idea of a city; she had become a country mouse: Ma Kettle, farmer Jane . . .

"I'm happy to be back," he said. "But it was fine to see LA."

"And the wedding couple. Patricia. Frank."

"She looks just like you. Can you see it?"

"The way I *used* to look, maybe."

He took her hand. "Still do."

The summer had begun. Route 6 thickened with traffic, and the parking lots were full. They timed excursions into town, going early in the morning or midafternoon, when vacationers flocked to the beach. Wellfleet and Truro grew clotted with cars, the roads impassable—or nearly so—by ten. There were traffic jams in Provincetown; tour buses idled like gas-spouting whales, and motorcyclists roared. It was a trial to go grocery shopping; the post office had long lines. As did other year-round residents, Hermia complained about the sudden crowds (how rude these people were, how fat and loud and poorly dressed), but part of her took pleasure in the change of seasons, the way noise supplanted silence and heat displaced the cold.

In the garden, they worked hard. She and Lawrence mulched the root crops—parsnips, potatoes, and turnips—and harvested the peas and beans and, later, green tomatoes and Swiss chard. They hoed and thinned and staked. He maintained his regimen of pills—the Lipitor and Lisinopril, the metoprolol and fish oil—and walked early each morning before it grew too hot. They watched the eggplants grow. It was a constant labor, a pleasure to share, although she wearied of the zucchini and the pickles they preserved; increasingly she thought of Will, with his elaborate ceviche and watercress salad produced by the staff. Every evening they watered the garden; each night they ate what they raised.

His sister called. She had a meeting in Boston, and wondered if they'd come to town and join her there for dinner. Lawrence said no. Then, looking up at Hermia, raising his hands to shape a question and getting her nodding permission, he asked, "Why don't you come here to see us instead? You could rent a car. Or take the bus; I'll pick you up in Barnstable."

She arrived on Thursday night. She was white-haired, thin, and elegant; she wore a dark gray business suit and carried a brown roller-bag. To Hermia she seemed her brother's look-alike, so obviously his sibling that she felt astonished; she'd thought Lawrence one of a kind. But when they walked in from the car, they did so in unison, and the resemblance was strong. She had his skin, his coloring, his way of crinkling up his nose in thought, the same worry line at the eyes.

"I'm glad to meet you," Hermia said. "Meet you in person, I mean. It's been too long."

"You can say that again," Lawrence said.

"This is terrific," Allie enthused. "I *love* to see the way you live."

"Surprised?"

She turned to Hermia. "You understand, my brother here, he always was a rolling stone. And now you've got him planted."

"It was *his* idea to plant a garden."

"Really?" Allie asked.

They showed her through the house. She admired its low plaster ceilings, the paintings, the warren of rooms. Then they sat on the porch, catching up. She liked it here, said Allie; she herself was living now in Arizona, and this place was two hundred years older than any single inhabitable structure in the state. "You do 'old' better in New England, don't you, bro."

"Tell it to the Anasazi," Lawrence said. "They knew how to build to last. We don't really know the reason, do we, why they disappeared."

"Water," Allie said. He replenished her glass. "The absence of water. It's what they *didn't* have."

Lawrence and his sister reminisced. They spoke about classmates and friends, the games they'd played at summer camp and the Canadian couple—what were their names, the Hamiltons?—with blond twins across the street. They discussed his children, Andrew, John, and Catherine, and Andrew's children, and although he'd spoken with Hermia often about members of his family, these were old intimacies, nicknames, a past she did not share. They talked about their childhoods, their parents' "lives of quiet desperation"? "Whose term was that?" asked Allie. "Was it David Riesman?"

"No, Thoreau," said Lawrence. "*The Lonely Crowd* is Riesman."

During the course of the dinner—striped bass, Pouilly-Fumé, a salad from the garden—Hermia felt as though she eavesdropped on a private conversation. They discussed the way their father left, taking two suits and a briefcase and just up and disappearing, then the school they'd gone to in Scarsdale, cutting through the neighbor's yards—old Mr. Vanderhoven, remember?—and walking through snowdrifts when young. Dropping his voice, Lawrence declaimed, "We walked *hours* through the snow. Ten miles to school and back, just for the sake of our ABCs."

"And the Hamilton twins," Allie said.

"I think," he said, raising his glass, "I never really understood how much I wanted this. The chance to share. How"—he mocked his own sententiousness—"the love of a good woman gives meaning to one's life."

"Are you all right?" asked Allie.

"Why?"

"You don't, I mean, *look* well. You're white as a sheet."

"'And your friends, baby, they treat you like a guest,'" Lawrence sang. His voice was high-pitched, wobbly. "Who sang that? Gracie Slick?"

"It's getting late," said Hermia. "And you have an early flight."

"I do," said their visitor. "Ten a.m. out of Logan. Let me help you with the dishes."

"I'll do them in the morning. It won't take ten minutes tomorrow."

He clutched his heart, intoning: "'Live every day as if it's your last. Someday you're bound to be right.'"

"Whose line is *that*?"

"I'm not exactly sure. Breaker Morant? Oscar Wilde? He said almost everything, didn't he? Or everything that's not by Mark Twain."

"It's beautiful here," Allie repeated, "but I'm dead beat. If you mean it about cleaning up, I'll say good night."

They conducted Allie to the guest room, and she promised, "I'll be asleep in a heartbeat. See you at six." When Lawrence and Hermia were finally alone, he said, "A penny for your thoughts."

She stepped out of her skirt.

"Did you like her?"

"Very much." She unbuttoned her blouse.

But she remained in bed while Lawrence took his sister back to Barnstable, driving in the early morning to the airport bus. Then, waking, she did do the dishes and brewed herself a cup of coffee; she was better off, she told herself, with only him for company and nobody else at the table or in the living room. Allie had been fine, and fun, but Hermia turned to the window and made her Greta Garbo mouth: *I vont to be alone.*

—

That afternoon Patricia called. "Hey, Mom," she said, "we're in Lago di Como. It's the most amazing place. We're in Bellagio—not the Villa Serbelloni, the place that's a conference center, but just above it, in a hotel. And with this *scrumptious* view."

"I'm very glad to hear your voice."

"I've been trying to call. Reception's shitty everywhere, but can you hear me?"

She nodded. "Yes."

"We've been doing all the lakes. Lugano. Lago di Garda. But *this* one is my favorite. It's like Hawaii, a little, Frank says, with hills dropping down to the water—and with so much history. They say Pliny loved this place. Pliny the Elder, I mean."

"How *are* you, darling?"

"And they caught Mussolini just across the lake. Trying to escape and dressed up like a woman, in an army truck full of gold . . ."

"An army truck?"

"Uh-huh. With his mistress beside him, leaning against a pillow stuffed with jewelry. Made up and trying to look like two women going to meet soldiers, on a ride to Switzerland."

"How's Frank?"

"He's well. We're well." Then there was static; her voice broke. "That's what I'm calling to tell you."

"I'm so relieved."

"Wish you were here. We're having a wonderful time." She continued with the platitudes, praising the landscape and food, the view from the hotel balcony, the wonderful time they were having, and while Patricia faded in and out, half audible, Hermia asked herself if what her daughter said was truthful or, again, practiced dissembling, and could not decide.

—

"Will you marry me?"

"Oh, Lawrence . . ."

"I mean it."

She faced him. "You're being such a gentleman. You're doing, what, the *proper* thing?"

"You said we hadn't had much luck, remember, with our marriages? That we didn't seem to get it right. But that's because we married the wrong people."

She rested her head on his shoulder. She closed her eyes.

"It doesn't have to be," he continued, "the Walt Disney Concert Hall. It's no big ceremonial thing: I want to be your husband. I hope you'll be my wife."

Why, she wondered, was she afraid; what was causing her to shiver? He had signed his retirement papers; he would become "emeritus" in June.

"Hold me."

He did. He stroked her hair and said, "I'll get a proper ring. I'll bake a cake and carry you over the threshold."

She attempted to laugh. "I weigh too much."

"I'm serious, darling. Say yes."

"We've waited all these years. Now what's your rush?"

"Because before I die I want to get it right."

Again she shivered.

"I don't mean I'm planning to die. But when I do, I want to be your husband."

The sun was high. Wind rattled the scrub oaks and the ornamental grasses by the stone wall and the pines. In the distance she could hear a church bell, its chimes carried on the wind. "Dingdong," said Hermia.

"And we should have a honeymoon. We deserve one, don't you think? I want to take you to the Loire to visit château country. Not the *faux* châteaux in Hollywood, but the real castles: Chenonceaux, Chambord, Chinon, and—while we're at it—Chartres. The four *C*s."

"Ding-dong," she said again. "'The bells are going to chime.' Can you hear it?"

"What?"

"The song from *My Fair Lady*. 'I'm getting married in the morning'?"

"Does that mean you're willing?" he asked her.

"Yes."

—

So they did in fact get married, in the town offices in Orleans, with the Banners as their witnesses, and a justice of the peace with a white handlebar mustache. That night they went to dinner at the Wicked Oyster, the four of them drinking champagne. It was, said Lawrence, a course correction; it was getting things right only forty years later, well, more than forty, but who's counting—and he should have asked her back in 1962. "Would you have said yes?" asked Susanna Banner, and Hermia said yes, of course. They ordered fried calamari and fish soup and swordfish, and Henry talked about the time there were real swordfish boats on the Vineyard and in New Bedford, men with harpoons, and how Wellfleet was a whaling town back in the eighteenth century before the industry went belly up and the harbor silted in. "Do you remember that sign to the tavern?"—he raised his glass, reciting it:

> *Samuel Smith, he sells good flip*
> *Good toddy, if you please.*
> *The way is clear, and very near,*
> *'Tis just beyond the trees.*

Last week he'd walked to Great Island, said Henry, and the tavern site was only a sign now, level sand, no shiver-me-timbers or tankards to find, and nothing left at all. "'Look on my Works, ye Mighty, and despair,'" he said. "That's Shelley, 'Ozymandias,' the King of Kings, and what I'm trying to suggest is you two have the best of it, the chance to live your lives out here together while the sands drift in."

"Sweetheart," said Susanna, "that's enough, they've heard this before, we've all heard it before."

"No," Lawrence declared, "he's making sense. 'Live every day as if it's your last. Someday you're bound to be right.'"

"And I've heard that before," said Hermia. "He says it every day."

"To repetition"—Lawrence raised his glass—"to saying things often. I love you, for example. You'll hear it more than once."

When the waitress learned it was their wedding meal, she said, "Congratulations. Please let us serve you a cake." The four of them protested, but the waitress—curly-haired, wide-hipped, enthusiastic—said, "No, no, you absolutely have to, we insist."

Four men at the next table clapped. They too were in late middle age, and would be getting married as soon as it proved possible, and were optimistic that gay marriage in the state of Massachusetts would be legal soon. They put their arms around each other's shoulders—two by two, they said, like animals in Noah's ark. "Please have some cake," said Hermia, "it's more than four of us can eat," and the oldest slapped his stomach and said, "Darling, does it look like I need cake?"

There was general hilarity, and congratulations all around, and a third bottle of champagne appeared unbidden at the table. "This changes nothing," she wanted to tell him. "I thought of you as my husband since that first night in Malta, and you've been my heart's darling all along." "True?" he would ask, and she'd say, "Yes," and everybody in the Wicked Oyster would applaud. But it was hard to say such things aloud, and a restaurant table was not where to say it, and Henry Banner was telling a story about a princess and prince in Great Britain, and how the woman is supposed to say, "I offer you my honor," and the man is supposed to answer, "I honor your offer," and then he climbs on her and off her. Henry laughed. It took her a moment to follow the joke, which wasn't very funny, but Lawrence took her arm and kissed her cheek and said, "Better late than never. 'All manner of thing shall be well.'"

—

That Saturday Patricia called again. "Hi, Mom, how *are* you?"

"Darling," she said, "I've got news. Are you still in Bellagio?"

"*Certo. Cómo no?*" Her daughter giggled. "Or is that Spanish? We're having a wonderful time."

"How's Frank?"

"His Italian is better than mine."

"And how are *you* feeling?"

"You said you have news?"

"Yes. I did something I never expected. Because of the two of you, really."

There was static on the line. She tried to imagine Patricia: standing, sitting, inside or outside? "Where are you exactly?" she asked.

"On the balcony. You're breaking up."

"So what I want to tell you is—because of the way you got married, you two, though that isn't the main reason, it's only one of the reasons, but when we were in Los Angeles you gave me the idea. Or not the idea but the courage . . ."

Hermia trailed off. Why, she wondered, did this feel hard to do? Why should it be so difficult to tell her daughter she also was married? "Post the banns. The *Banners.*"

"Excuse me?"

"I got married yesterday afternoon. We wanted you to know."

"Mom!"

"I did. We did." She paused. "It seemed like so much fun at Disney Hall we thought we should give it a try."

"What, marriage?"

"You like Lawrence, don't you? You do think he's . . . appropriate?"

"The bee's knees, Mom," Patricia said. "The cat's pajamas."

"Is that a yes?"

"Cómo no! It isn't my business, really. I didn't ask for permission to marry Frank, did I? But if you want to know, the answer's absolutely yes. I meant it about the bee's knees."

"Whatever *that* means." Now both of them laughed. Patricia talked about Lago di Como, the restaurant on an island in the lake they were planning to visit that evening, and how tomorrow they were setting out for Venice, where Frank had made a reservation at the Gritti Palace, and how she'd been told it was the most beautiful city, the most romantic place on earth, and when Hermia asked about the pregnancy said everything was fine—"Congratulations,

Mom." They spoke for several minutes more about this thing called nuptial bliss and everything they soon would celebrate together; in unison, they wished each other well and said good-bye. But after hanging up she heard the false note ringing in Patricia's voice—that bright singsong insincerity—and asked herself if her daughter was happy and could not decide.

—

There was trouble down the road. In July, young men moved in next door—Eric Foster's grandson, she learned, with two of his friends—and started wrecking things. They used chain saws and played music at all hours. Cars idled in the driveway, then gunned up the hill while dogs barked themselves hoarse: pit bulls and a three-legged German shepherd mix. Although she rarely saw her neighbors, she could hear them shouting, screaming at each other. The loudly swearing twenty-somethings in the Foster place brought back everything she'd hated in her daughter's adolescence; before Patricia ran away, she had been visited by just such low-life thugs. They were, it was rumored, drug dealers; they seemed to have no jobs.

They had money, however, to spend on entertainment, and when the wind was easterly, she could hear them arguing about a video game that someone else won and how he'd fucking cheated and would have his fucking ass kicked and had always been a cunt. Tonight outside the Rusty Nail he'd better watch his ass. They wore tattoos and nose rings and strangely colored spiky hair, and when Hermia encountered them, she felt both angry and frightened; why had Eric Foster—that sweet, stooped, toothless codger, a retired fireman who delivered cordwood and would split and stack it for an extra twenty dollars—left his half-acre property to his daughter's disreputable son?

His name was Luke; he had a skull and crossbones and a dagger tattooed on his arm. She met him by the mailbox, once, at noon. He was slackly muscled, short, and with a beer belly already; he was, she learned, twenty-eight and had a daughter up in Plymouth with his, "excuse my French," bitch of an ex who was—Angie, he meant, not the bitch of a mother—the best thing in his life. He said she's going to be three on Saturday, she's the prettiest thing, and flipped his cell phone open so she could see Angie's picture, naked, playing on a blanket. There were dollar bills splayed out across the blanket and between the baby's legs.

Hermia said, "What a beauty," and he said, "Pictures don't show half of it," and he'd be seeing her on Saturday and bringing her a cake. "What kind of cake?" asked Hermia, and he said, you know, one with pink frosting and rabbits; then Luke gathered up the mail and turned to go. Hesitant, she asked him if he'd maybe be willing to cut back a bit on the decibel level, the roar of the music, and he said, "My bad, no problem," and smiled at her with his carious teeth. That night he played songs twice as loud and screamed about the fucking prick whose ass he'd kick tomorrow at the Rusty Nail; that Saturday he stayed at home and turned the volume up even higher on his boom box by the door:

> *Which one's the bitch*
> *To scratch this itch?*
> *Let's bait and switch . . .*

She spoke to the police. They said they knew about young Foster, they were keeping track of him, but he'd broken no town ordinance and was not a public nuisance, and there really wasn't anything the police or the sheriff could do.

"He's dealing drugs," she said. "I'm almost sure of it. How else can he support himself, because he isn't working and there are all these cars in his driveway coming and going at night. Just making a deal, driving off . . ."

"We'd need some evidence," they said. "We can't assume it's drugs."

She and Lawrence played their own music, setting up a CD player on the west-facing porch. But Mozart piano trios and Schubert lieder did not suffice as an answer to the loud cacophony, nor could she drown out their shouts. The dogs and motorcycles and the roar of power tools reminded her, who needed no reminding, of the boys in Arlington when Patricia was a teenager: their awful smell, their terrible hair. She was, she knew, being a snob. But she'd never forgotten and could not forgive the behavior of those who came for her daughter with cases of beer and electric guitars and later on lured her away.

At last she went—this time with Lawrence—to the Foster place. It was an ancient trailer with a lean-to built against the side, the whole thing propped on cinder blocks. It was five o'clock. There were refrigerators and old stoves and rusting outboard motors piled beside the woodshed where the old man once had kept cordwood. Dogs barked.

Luke met them at the door. "I'd ask you in, but Killer here don't like it."

"Killer?"

"Right, the pit bull. She's OK by herself alone but not so good with company."

"Is she OK with Angie?"

"If you don't mind me asking, lady, what's the reason exactly you're here?"

"Your grandfather was once my friend." She climbed to the cement slab up against the torn screen door. "My parents' friend."

"Yeah?"

"He and my father were very good neighbors."

"And?"

"I just thought I'd mention it. What being a good neighbor means . . ."

"You think you're being one, lady?"

"I'm trying. I'm trying not to call the police."

He stared at her unblinkingly. "This ain't your property," he said. "It's America, remember?"

"Yes."

"And I got my rights and one of them is to ask you—very politely, you'll notice—to get the hell off my property please. Before you fuck with my head anymore or tell me what and what not to do."

"Whoa," Lawrence said. "We're *asking* you. And one of the things that we're asking is maybe don't use that language."

"Get lost. Fuck fucking off, all right?"

This was said without intonation, with a dispassionate venom and a twitching, blindered glare: unseeing, blank, unfocused.

"Hey, wait a second," Lawrence said, "we're trying to be civil here."

"You too, old man," said Luke. "Fuck fucking off, all right?"

"What she said about being a neighbor is partly about manners. Decency."

"Decency?"

"So if someone says they knew your grandfather, you don't start cursing at them, right?"

"Did you even *hear* what I said, old man? Get out of here, OK?"

"Let's go." She touched her husband's arm. "Let's just leave him alone."

He shook her free. "You and your dogs don't scare me, boy. You want trouble, you'll get trouble."

"Want me to whip your ancient ass?" Luke stepped down to the stoop.

"No."

"No? So get the hell out of here, man."

"Excuse me?"

"*Excuse* me. Do you hear what I'm telling you, asshole?"

"Don't use that word again."

Luke turned to her. "Tell this pussy I'm kicking his ass."

"*Enough.*"

"I'll fucking well say what I fucking want to. Get off of my property, pussy."

Then Lawrence did something so rapid she wasn't sure she'd seen it. With his left hand he gathered the front of Luke's shirt and pulled him off balance and forward; with his right foot he swept the boy's ankles so that he was falling, and as he fell, Lawrence slapped at his face, his right hand stiffly extended. There was the sound of splintering, a gush of blood from Luke's nose, a cry of shock and pain. On the cement stoop he lay quivering, wailing— "My nose is *broke*, you son of a bitch"—and Lawrence took her arm and said, "All right. Now we can go."

—

So there was a serpent in their garden, and the snake had tape on the bridge of his nose. "How did you do that?" Hermia asked. "Where did you learn how to do it, I mean?"

"What?"

"The martial arts—isn't that what you were doing?"

"Karate. Jujitsu. I studied a little bit, over the years. In San Francisco and Ann Arbor."

"Oh?"

"Mostly as a kind of exercise. A form of discipline. And I was never very good at it, but it's like bike riding, you never forget."

"Apparently not." She smiled up at him. "My hero, my honor's defender."

"It was the front stoop that did it. And God knows what would have happened if he hadn't been so wasted and had tried to hit me back. Or moved first."

The next day, however, Luke called. "I'm suing."

"Excuse me?"

"Battery. Assault and battery, you've heard of it. And on my property besides."

"You can't be serious."

"Oh, Mrs., yes, I can. And I'm taking out what they call an injunction. A 'no trespass' order, just ask the police."

"I'll do that," Hermia said.

The Truro police were embarrassed. "It names you and your husband, ma'am, both."

"And what are we charged with?"

"Illegal trespass."

"This is absurd."

"I'm not saying," said Officer Castle, "you're in any legal trouble. Only that you'd better not ought to go down that driveway again."

"Who'd *want* to?" Hermia asked. "My husband was defending me."

"Against? You want to file a counterclaim?"

"No. All we want," said Lawrence, "is not to have the boy next door playing his boom box at all hours. And selling, I'm sure of it, drugs."

"Which is why," agreed Officer Castle, "he isn't pressing charges. I don't think he wants us too close to the house."

"Eric Foster's turning over in his grave," said Hermia. "Did you know him?"

The policeman nodded.

"He was a lovely man. And a good friend to my parents."

"To everybody hereabouts . . ."

"And that's another reason we were trying to be neighborly. But not, of course, planning to trespass."

Lawrence took her hand.

"I understand," the officer said, "and I'm sorry for your trouble, ma'am. With any sort of luck it's over now." His telephone was ringing, and he said he had to take the call. "Like that pit bull he keeps bragging on, his bark is much worse than his bite."

She hoped so. She heard what she hoped wasn't shooting, and night after night there were drums and horns and electric guitars; she and Lawrence tried to sleep while the shouting and screaming continued:

Which one's the bitch
To scratch this itch . . .

They talked about planting more trees. They talked about a cinder-block or wooden fence that would serve as a sound baffle at the property line. They talked about offering to buy Luke out, but when one day she saw him at the parking lot for the post office and, smiling, tried to approach him, he ignored her so ostentatiously she knew it wasn't worth trying; he would, she knew, say his people had been in Truro for years, for *centuries*, and who the hell was she to tell him what to do?

It wouldn't, she knew, be an issue in winter; in winter they'd keep windows shut. But this was August, not December, and while she worked in the garden or sat reading in the rocking chair on the west-facing porch, she heard the ruckus of his chain saw and the scream of video games, the constant rat-a-tat-tat of someone shooting something on a screen. She glimpsed him through the scrub oak trees and heard shouting and the dogs.

But Lawrence had defended her, and would again, and no one was under attack. She told herself she ought to keep the problem in proportion: Luke was not an actual threat. In Manhattan or Los Angeles she wouldn't even notice him, so wide was their remove. She wasn't afraid of him, really, but did hate the noise. Hermia put by jars of relish and strawberry jam. She replaced the screen windows with storms. Long after Adam and Eve left the garden, the light in their cottage burned on; long after the serpent left Eden, the apple trees remained.

—

"We're back," Patricia called to say. "We got here just this morning . . ."

"Welcome home. How was the trip?"

"I slept for most of it. The flight, I mean, not the trip. *Gorgonzola. Pepsi-Cola.* See how my Italian improved?"

"Are you at Will's?"

"Yes. Frank's still sleeping. He's such a *traveler*, Mom, he wanted to go everywhere. Do everything. It's been a lot to handle, traveling for two . . ."

Her voice faded away. There was that peculiar blankness in Hermia's ear that meant the reception was gone. She called and got a busy signal, pressed the redial button and heard it again, then hung up and the telephone rang. "What was I saying?" asked Patricia.

"You've been traveling for two."

"Yes, with little John here. Or Jane. Which means I've had no wine for weeks and none of the rich dishes they're famous for in northern Italy. And you?"

She smiled. "Marriage agrees with me, apparently."

"When will you come out again?"

"Whenever you ask us to, darling."

Again, there was a burst of static. "That's what I'm doing, isn't it?"

"*Is* it? I must have missed that part of the conversation; it's when the phone went dead."

"Will asks about you all the time, we'd love it if you came."

"Things haven't been terrific here," she told her daughter. "There's a kind of criminal next door. And somehow *he's* the one who's pressing charges . . ."

"What? Why?"

"Well, Lawrence broke his nose. My husband, the kung fu master—who knew?"

"Please come," said Patricia. "I need you, Mom."

"How quickly, darling? And for how long?"

"Tomorrow. For six months, OK?"

"You're joking, I hope."

"Not exactly." She managed a laugh. "The day after tomorrow will probably do. I think I'll maybe last that long."

"I hear you. We're coming. Take care."

IX

Mommy, what does "flogged" mean?

What?

This word here. In the book I'm reading.

Can you spell it?

F-l-o-g-g-e-d.

Which book is that?

The pirate book. A sailor kisses the cannon and holds it while he's flogged.

It's a kind of punishment.

For what?

For breaking some big pirate rule. For disobeying the captain's orders, maybe. The sin of disobedience.

Except what does it mean? And what did he do to deserve it, the pirate?

To be flogged means to be whipped—the way that people sometimes do with horses. But they use a cat-o'-nine-tails. Which is a stick with nine strings tied to it, and knots in the strings, and the sailor puts his arms around the cannon and his back gets whipped.

Does it hurt badly?

I don't really know. I never had it happen to me. And you won't, Pat-a-cake.

Is it only for pirates?

And slaves. I don't think there's much flogging now. And certainly not in Vermont.

Did Daddy ever walk the plank?

Not that I know of.

It's kind of like a balance beam. I could walk the plank backward, I bet. I did it yesterday, in gym.

Should we take a walk?

Where to?

You decide. The pond? It looks like a beautiful morning outside.

To Bailey's, please. Can I have butterscotch?

You may.

And when we do, can I wear boots?

Not sneakers?

Because it could rain.

Oh, not this morning, I don't think. It doesn't look at all like rain.

Does he get bloody, the pirate?

Who?

The pirate who gets flogged.

I expect so. Then they fix him up and put on a Band-Aid and he sails the seas again.

Let's go to Bailey's.

Fine.

X

2005

This time they stayed in Will's house. There was a guest wing by the swimming pool: two bedrooms and a bathroom with a sauna and Jacuzzi. Here the motif was Hawaiian. There were images of volcanoes, erupting and inert, and photographs of flower-bedecked women offering armfuls of fruit. There were paintings of sunset and dawn on the beach. Will himself was gone again, on his autumn retreat to Maui, but Patricia and Frank made them welcome, as did the staff.

It was astonishing, thought Hermia, how quickly she and Lawrence could grow used to luxury; the two of them slept late. The Mexican gardeners tended the lawns, the cook prepared their meals. Each day she set out laundry to be washed and ironed; each afternoon she swam. Lawrence, her inveterate tinkerer, could not repair the doors or lights because the doors were noiseless and the light fixtures worked. She let housemaids make their bed.

Patricia was now in her final trimester and had turned a corner, or so she insisted when Hermia asked. The first trimester had been hard, but she was growing proud of how her body looked. Frank didn't want to know, she said, the gender of their baby, and she was fine about not knowing since the amnio was clear. The swelling of her stomach, the thickening of her hair, her legs: these things were unsurprising, but she felt anyhow surprised. "Was it like this for *you?*" she asked, and when Hermia assured her that the changes she was noticing were what expectant mothers feel, she nodded smilingly. She was reading *A Farewell to Arms*. At story's end, Patricia said, "I don't believe it. The amount of gas they give her. So much excitement in the hospital over a Caesarean, and how Cat knows she is going to die and sees herself dead in the rain."

"What are you talking about?"

"The pregnancy. The way the world will kill you if you're beautiful and brave."

"It does seem romantic, doesn't it? *I* wasn't very beautiful or brave, yet managed to deliver you . . ."

"The novel takes place during wartime. The First World War. Things were different then."

"A whole lot of people get born in a war. It's more or less called the human condition."

"Still, Catherine Barkley *had* to die. That was how Hemingway wrote it."

"Yes, and he killed himself later."

"It's a ridiculous book," said Patricia. "She's a ridiculous woman. *Oh, darling, I'll be good to you. Darling, I promise to be good. Oh, darling, wasn't I good.*"

"He's very effective on landscape, though."

"Poor Hem," said Patricia. "Poor Frederic Henry. Poor everyone."

"Let's change the subject."

"She was slim-hipped, wasn't she, Catherine Barkley? But English, of course, and blonde. With all that hair."

"We've gotten better nowadays at giving anesthesia. Why don't you read something more jolly?"

"What? *My Family and Other Animals? Cheaper by the Dozen?* You can't believe the crap Will keeps on our bedroom shelf."

"Those are the books of his childhood, I'm sure. Like *A Farewell to Arms*."

Patricia was not mollified. "And she's such an excellent nurse. And so competent a drinker. I think maybe she's from Scotland—which would explain it, of course. Why can't *I* smoke and have bottles of wine and a bottle of brandy for lunch?"

"You wouldn't want them, would you?"

"Do *you* like Ernest Hemingway?"

"Not really, no. But why were you reading that novel?"

"To see what happened in the end to the beautiful Catherine Barkley. With her nursing prowess and how good she is in bed and all her long blond hair."

"I wish you sounded happier."

Her daughter's shoulders shook. She blinked back tears. "I know," she said, "I *know*. Why can't I, Mommy, what's wrong?"

—

An old fear seized Hermia. Her life, she thought, had been too good; she was hedged in by happiness and had been too healthy too long. She herself possessed too much to keep, and would therefore lose it; she had been too lucky for all this luck to last. Each day she read of drive-by shootings, women gang-raped in systematic fashion, children pressed into service as soldiers or forced to work in mines. Whole families succumbed to AIDS or cholera or lost their homes to earthquakes and flood; others had to beg for food or sleep in makeshift tents. The first week of November, it rained. Mist coagulated thickly and she could not see the tennis court, or even the end of the lawn. The pleasure of her time with Lawrence and their house in Truro and the presence of her daughter in this California palace—her great unearned good fortune would end soon. It could not be sustained. It was pride waiting for a fall and tables to be turned; the dark, she feared, was poised to swallow light.

She knew this was irrational. But when she lay in bed at night, she listened to her husband's labored breathing as though his breathing would stop. When in the brief bursts of sun Patricia dove into the swimming pool, she thought her daughter was drowning; when she closed her eyes and pictured Truro, she saw the house in flames. In the street, the noise of trucks or the clatter of garbage being collected seemed a kind of menace; in the house the sound of vacuum cleaners or the roar of kitchen equipment made her hold her head. Rain drummed at the windows and sluiced off the roof. Their luck was too good to continue, and Hermia grew superstitious: crossing her fingers and knocking on wood and avoiding sidewalk cracks. What she wanted, she told Lawrence, was not something new or different but only more of the same.

"You think it's luck," he said, "but maybe we deserve it."

"No."

"Well, *you* deserve it anyhow. You've waited a long time for this. To be a grandmother . . ."

"Have I?"

He took her hand. "Haven't you?"

She nodded.

"Well?"

"You know that old expression 'nothing left to lose'? I feel like—what's his name?" Hermia said. "Bobby McGee. Except for me it's everything."

"Why not change the terms of it?"

"Of what? 'Freedom's just another word for nothing left to lose.'"

"Why don't you tell yourself you've waited long enough, and it's your turn now to celebrate, and your—our—luck has changed?"

"Poor Janis Joplin. She died so *young* . . ."

"Let's take a walk." He was her comfort, her distraction. "After lunch let's take a nap."

—

They spent November as Will's guests in the house in Brentwood; near month's end, he returned. "How's my girl?" he asked "My *girls*. My mother and daughter and baby makes three."

The old swaggering ease was with him, and the carelessness of wealth. He brought back necklaces and skirts and shirts and kitchen tiles that read *Aloha* and *Mahalo*.

Patricia said, "I'm fine."

And this seemed true. When Hermia reached out to her, she said, "Don't worry, Mom, it's over—the anxiety, I mean. It's funny, isn't it?"

"Funny ha-ha or funny strange?"

"Funny strange. Like a switch turned on that was off, or maybe the other way 'round. But I'm not frightened now. . ."

Frank too seemed happily preoccupied—doing interviews and amassing what he claimed were thousands of feet of opinion. "Do you remember," he asked, "that advertising jingle for the Yellow Pages? 'Let your fingers do the walking'? Well, my slogan is a variation on the theme, 'Let your neighbors do the talking.' *Neighbors Talking* is the title—well, the *working* title—of the show." He was going door by door and street by street and neighborhood by neighborhood and asking everyone the same set of questions, a purposefully vague inquiry into how they felt and feel about what we call values. It's a catalogue of things to live for, ways to live, the series of expectations and implicit guarantees made explicit in the Bill of Rights: our pursuit not so much of liberty and happiness as of the right to bear arms, the right to congregate, the right to vote and worship, and you would be—"as *I've* been," said Frank— *amazed* at what Mr. and Mrs. America, the average Joe or Josette or José, have to say in their unforced conversation, their table talk, their pillow talk, their doughnut-and-coffee chitchat in the early morning or at the mobile lunch wagon selling tacos and enchiladas on a side street maybe or idling here across the way where gardeners buy lunch. "It's a wide net we've been casting, listening to people, and it's unclear what we'll catch. But mostly what I've felt these days is astonishment at language, how everybody and his brother, daughter, mother, has something to say when you ask and touch on what most nearly touches them, the food, the clothing, and the shelter, the staples of existence and the American dream in this no-longer-so-American century, when the wheel has come full circle, or appears to, and is poised to turn. Maybe *Good Neighbors Talking* is the title I should use. Because what these people tell me most concerns them is more than mere subsistence, a future-facing anxiety and hopefulness which all of us share"—here he patted his wife's stomach, smiling—"about what's *soon to come.*"

The phone rang. It was Henry Banner. He asked for Hermia, and when Patricia handed over the phone, he told her, "Please don't worry."

"What?"

"It's serious," said Henry, "but not too serious. And it'll be fixed."

"Excuse me?

"I'm calling to tell you," he said. "We're on your alarm list, right? Our number's a number the company calls when there's an alarm and you don't answer."

"Yes. You and the Zuckers and Jim Ford."

"Well, we're the ones they reached last night. After the fire department."

"*What?*"

"The fire. But it's going to be all right."

Her hands were cold. They shook. "I don't know what you're talking about."

"I thought you'd heard."

"No."

Lawrence approached. He stood by her, watching.

"Oh, I'm sorry," said Henry. "We're *both* sorry. There was a fire last night."

"In the house?"

"Not really, no. The generator housing, the one by the wood-shed. It was burning, but they stopped it just at the edge of the porch." He paused. "And your neighbor—what's his name, the Foster boy?—there was fire at his place too."

"*Luke.* Do they know how it happened? What happened?"

"We've had a three-day blow, you know. A full nor'easter, which is probably a blessing, since everything was soaked. *Is* soaked. But there was lightning."

"In November? Lightning?"

He coughed. "They think so, maybe. Possibly."

"It's been raining here also," she offered. "Awful weather."

Then Henry said it was too soon to be sure; there would be an investigation and, no doubt, insurance adjustors. But it seemed at least possibly—well, probably—the case that someone had siphoned off the generator, jamming it, or anyhow it sprang a leak, because they found a trail of gas from the woodshed straight across toward the house, and though no one was calling it arson just yet, they did have their suspicions, they needed proof, and it was too soon for formal charges but looked as though the tire tracks, the gas trail, and the jerry can all pointed to Luke next door.

There was a burst of static. The line cleared. "I know about this," Henry Banner resumed, "because this morning the police came by and asked if we'd go with them, so Susanna and I drove over, of course. And it's almost like he blazed a trail, it looks like he'd broken the padlock and poured out a path of gasoline with what he siphoned off, except it didn't work that way; the automatic shutoff for the generator worked, and the porch was just too wet to burn, thank heavens."

"Thank heavens," Hermia echoed.

Lawrence took her hand.

"What happened to your cell phone? The police said they tried it. I tried too."

"We went to the movies two days ago. One of Will's comedy remakes." She closed her eyes, remembering. "I think I turned it off."

Now relishing the details or—so it seemed to Hermia—the chance to inform her about them, Henry reported on what the police suspected, why they were questioning Luke, and where they'd found his footprints and a half-torn photograph of his daughter, Angie. At the Rusty Nail that night, they learned, he had been boasting, drinking, saying he was damned if he'd be kicked around by a pair of out-of-towners. "The truth of it," said Henry, "is your neighbor's one of those people for whom nothing goes according to plan, and so what happened next was his own tinder-box of a trailer—they still don't know exactly *how*, they're establishing that—caught fire. In the storm the power went out, though only for ten minutes, and the generator kicked in. Except the system fires up each week to test itself, and keeps a record of the test, and there was nothing wrong. At the end of the nor'easter lightning came, and the Foster place has a good deal of damage, though they put out that fire too, and his dogs are dead—smoke inhalation, they were locked inside—but because the firemen were on your property, they followed the fire straight back through the woods."

He spoke about the volunteer firemen in Truro, how quick they were, how good it was the hose could reach and the shutoff valve was working, since maybe another three minutes, maybe five, and it would have been a very different story, with your whole place engulfed. Now while Henry, consoling her, said how much worse it could have been and how if she believed in lucky stars she should thank her lucky stars, relief came over Hermia; she found herself smiling at Lawrence and squeezing his hard hand. Had Luke been drunk, or stoned, she asked, and was he badly burned? Not very badly, Henry said, and who knows just how drunk he was, or what kind of drug he was taking—crystal meth is what they're saying; he hoped they'd throw the book at him and put him away a long time. Those poor dogs.

She shook her head, trying to clear it. As though her fears had been confirmed, what had been shapeless terror now took a shape and name. Yet the image of that tattooed boy-man trying to burn down her house, *their* house, and failing to, and leaving clues, was somehow much less frightening than her day-waking worries or what she dreamed at night. The lightning strike seemed not so much an all-leveling storm as a damp book of matches; the vengeful fate she'd feared was just a botched attempt at revenge or siphoning off gas . . .

She thanked Henry Banner. "Should we come home?"

"I don't think so."

"To press charges?"

"You'll want to make an inventory. There's no doubt some smoke damage. And water damage to curtains and suchlike. But nothing important."

The sky was clearing, the wind high.

"We'll come back soon," she said.

"Don't feel you have to hurry. The nor'easter's over, the property's safe." He coughed. "Please give our best to Lawrence. And to your daughter. Everybody."

She thanked him and hung up.

———

Early that Wednesday they flew back to Boston, then drove out to the Cape. Patricia had urged her to travel, since Will and Frank were home, and she should make certain the house was OK.

"I'll come back," promised Hermia, "the second you say you need me," and her daughter smiled and said, "I know you will, Mom, thanks."

"Don't think about Catherine Barkley."

Patricia made a face. "Who's she? Travel safely. Then come back when the baby's born, OK?"

"I *did* want to stay for Thanksgiving."

"We'll celebrate when you get back."

"Take care of yourself," Hermia said.

"I will, I promise, Mom."

The flight was smooth, the drive familiar, and they booked a one-day rental for the Hertz. Lawrence spoke again about the Loire, and how he was hoping to honeymoon there, and maybe they could go this winter after the baby arrived. The storm had left large puddles in the parking lots, and on the turnouts on Route 6; wet sand had washed across the highway, and the tree trunks were dark brown.

At the rotary in Orleans they filed past men working with forklifts and stringing wire from poles. At the Stop & Shop they bought provisions—enough for a dinner and breakfast: salad and a wedge of salmon, coffee, milk. Then, driving through Eastham and Wellfleet and turning on the Pamet Road, she felt her fears returning, but the house had been—as Henry Banner assured her—spared.

At four o'clock, the late November light was fading, and there was a low shaft of sun. Inviolate on its slight rise, with its shingled cedar-shake roof and green wooden shutters with the hearts incised, the structure looked untouched. The six-over-six small-paned windows glinted at her wetly. The garden had grown in with weeds, and the last plants had been toppled by a killing frost. The woodshed and the generator housing showed, as Lawrence pointed out, dark traces of fire and water, but there was no major damage and she felt her spirits lift. Beyond, the scrub oak and pines rustled their branches; a few final leaves from the birch tree blew past. Their scarecrow stared up at them, bedraggled, its hat gone.

"Oh darling," she said, "how close we came, how close *he* came, that bastard."

"Yes," said Lawrence. "Was it crystal meth, you think, or crack, or heroin; what drugs was Luke dealing?"

"All of them, most likely." She shuddered. "And with those awful dogs."

The kitchen door squeaked open. She tried the lights; they functioned; she turned on the radio too. The theme music from *All Things Considered* came on, and she whistled along with the tune. Lawrence carried their bags to the bedroom, and Hermia opened the shutters; little by little the house grew familiar. "It feels so *small*," she said.

"By comparison with Will's place, everything feels small."

"I suppose that's it. We've gotten used to all those twelve-foot ceilings and the enormous rooms."

"We'll get used to this again," he said. "Do you want a drink?"

"Please. What are you having?"

He opened a bottle of Médoc, and they clinked glasses and drank.

"We're home," she said. "Your health."

"Happy Thanksgiving."

"What do they call this? A narrow escape? A reprieve?"

"They call it having a bad boy as neighbor. Who learned his lesson, probably. And who's probably going to jail."

"You certainly reconfigured his nose." She touched his glass again, smiling. "What would I do without you? Wherever would I be?"

"Right here," said Lawrence, "but not perhaps so, so . . ."

"Happily." She kissed him. "That's the word you're looking for. I'm happy to be home with you. I liked it there, but it isn't the same."

"No. Are you hungry?"

"Yes."

"And should I light a fire?"

"Maybe tomorrow," she said. "I don't think I could handle it this evening."

"You're right," said Lawrence. "I'll set the table." He turned off the radio, then turned on a recording of Mozart piano trios. "This salmon will take twenty minutes. Why don't you go and unpack?"

"I'll stay with you."

"It's early still by California time."

"But we didn't have lunch, did we? Peanuts on the plane don't count."

So she was standing by his side when Lawrence paled and dropped his glass of wine. She was watching when he gagged and coughed a half-choked hiccuping cough. His hands clawed at his chest. He fell.

It was, she knew, a heart attack; Hermia found the telephone and dialed 911. He breathed. Oddly, she felt calm. What terrified her had arrived; it no longer hovered namelessly, and she would do whatever could be done. In the next minutes, waiting, listening for sirens, sitting on the floor and holding his head on her lap and making him eat aspirin, saying "Darling, you'll be fine, you're fine" and stroking his lank hair while he gazed up at her mutely, and trying to remember if she should make him move or not move, speak or not, stand up or not, she prayed although he could not hear her and not as prayer really, *Don't, don't die, oh please don't die.*

His head was wet; his hands were wet; his breathing was rapid and shallow. She sat beside him, murmuring. He did not speak. She tried to make a joke of it: the fact that they hadn't had dinner, or lunch, the fact that they'd failed to unpack. "Tomorrow," she told him, "we'll get a turkey, tomorrow's Thanksgiving, remember, or maybe we'll go out to eat." Then after a brief interval, or perhaps it was not brief but long before she had expected it—yet what had she expected, what was time now but contorted, contracting as well as expansive, doubling back upon itself, not a straight line but spiraling, recurrent?—Hermia heard the ambulance, the thrum of its motor, but not of a siren, the EMTs who came like angels to the door, and bent above her husband, took his pulse and fed him air and, by the time she'd rubbed her eyes and taken her own first deep breath and picked up his wineglass and turned off the Mozart and found her coat and handbag, had placed him on a gurney and were bearing him back carefully into the idling vehicle, its rotating red beacon and white boxy shape into which she also climbed: *Don't die, oh please please please.*

They drove to Hyannis. His hands were cold. She sat beside him in the van, informing the technician they had flown from California and had arrived this afternoon from Logan. Now they were racing down Route 6, the siren on, when two hours ago the two of them had driven the other direction. "That could explain it," said Tom. His name was stitched in red above the pocket of his shirt; he had tattoos and a handlebar mustache and pomaded hair and was gentle with Lawrence, efficient, asking every few minutes how he was doing, how he felt, and if he wanted air or water or was feeling any pain. Lawrence shook his head. He was staring at the apparatus of survival and the implements of rescue clamped in layers on the metal wall, and drifting in and out of consciousness, or so it seemed, keeping his eyes closed and then opening them, seeing her, trying to smile. He smiled. Unbidden, uncontrollably, she felt a flash of rage at Patricia for asking them to come to Los Angeles, for telling her she needed help and then not truly needing it, for putting her and Lawrence, poor dear exhausted Lawrence, through the trouble of LAX and the cramped enclosure of an airplane cabin on long-distance flights. This was, she knew, unjustified, and knew it even in the instant of her anger, but nonetheless she blamed her daughter, blamed Luke Foster too, that pyromaniac, blamed Henry Banner for his call and Will for having travel agents who could find them tickets on the day before Thanksgiving when it should have been impossible to fly. The tickets had been free. Impossible to get such things, to have such perks, but Will explained there isn't any limit to what platinum status can do, or more importantly perhaps his playing golf with the corporate VP for public relations for the airline, and knowing who to ask. Smilingly, he handed her the tickets and apologized: first class was full, but at least these were two seats together by the bulkhead. So she had kissed his grizzled cheek and now was angry at herself for taking them, for kissing him, for thinking it made sense to fly back east to Boston, for all things that conspired to have the two of them here in this ambulance while time performed its trick again, extending and contracting, taking forever and no time at all, so that the trip to Cape Cod Hospital felt both endless and rapid to Hermia: forty-five minutes she would not remember or not with sequential precision as they passed the rotary and rumbled down the single lane past Chatham and Brewster, making their way toward Hyannis, and could not forget.

For Lawrence died. He died, she would say, in her arms. She was holding him, caressing him, was telling him she loved him, and he seemed to see and hear her and then somewhere on the journey was not there. His jaw dropped. He went blank. He stared at her unblinkingly; he saw, then did not see her; he breathed, then did not breathe. She screamed.

Tom busied himself with equipment, adjusting things and changing things and doing something urgent to her husband's mouth and chest. He leaned above the prone, strapped immobile body, blocking her sight line, working fast. The man was saying "Roger" into his walkie-talkie and then a series of numbers, a word that sounded like "infraction," but his speech was hurried, garbled, and she could make no sense of it. The ambulance pulled over and the driver joined him, jumping in and helping, holding the defibrillator, talking in a kind of code or shorthand while they ignored her utterly and bent above the body and their intervention (the four arms, four hands, the life-saving procedures and equipment) failed. Whatever the technicians were attempting did not work.

It could have succeeded, perhaps. It could have been avoided had the EMTs come sooner, or never need have happened had the two of them not flown across the country and not driven to the Cape without a chance to rest. She knew, of course, this was magical thinking; his death was an accident waiting to happen, not something she or anyone was able to prevent. The Lawrence who was young with her—so lean and lithe and passionate—then old with her—the liver spots on his dear face, the wattled neck—was not the man she used to know and sleep with and marry but a corpse. He died in the van in her arms.

Hermia repeated this phrase often later: to herself, to friends, to everyone, Patricia, Frank, and Will. Lawrence died in her arms. It wasn't true, exactly, or she never knew if it was true because she never knew exactly when he died: the moment he looked up at her, the moment she leaned forward and leaned down? It happened by Brewster, or Chatham, or perhaps outside of Orleans, in the single lane. It was, she said, astonishing, an absence where there had been presence only an instant before. In days and weeks and years to come she tried to remember the change in his face, the way his dear eyes saw her and then, staring, did not see her, the way he breathed, then did not breathe, the way his closed mouth opened and then shut.

What her husband was was dead. He had come into her life again and lived with her and made her happy and died. He stood on the deck of the MS *Diana* and they walked through Pompeii's ruins and the well-tended streets of Malta and after a few months of courtship moved in together cautiously and had a year together, or nearly, from December to November, in Truro and London and

311

Los Angeles, until they flew back east again and Lawrence died. The two of them were married in a civil ceremony with Henry and Susanna Banner acting as their witnesses; he was her old young lover and the man she cooked and gardened with and read books out loud and watched the *NewsHour* on television and listened to NPR with, and then he fell down and died. He fixed the kitchen door lock and installed the rheostat and grilled salmon and made the thick Provençal sauce with olive oil and garlic called aioli and painted the porch furniture and died. He told bad jokes and lay beside her in the dark and comforted her about her mother, her daughter's unbreachable distance, and looked across her shoulder at the gray sleet at their windows through the bone-chilling month of March, the beauty of May and June and July, the willow tree first yellow and then budding greenly, and died. "'Grow old along with me,'" they'd joked. "'The best is yet to be.'" But this was a poem only, a phrase by Robert Browning, and "the last of life" for her husband was an ambulance on the twelve-mile strip of one-lane road by Orleans, or possibly Chatham, or Brewster, where he looked up at her, and smiled, or tried to smile, and died.

The best was past, not yet to be. He did not grow old along with her; he collapsed at sixty-five. A century before, that would have made him old, not young, but sixty-five seemed young to Hermia in the year 2005. They would have had—they *should* have had—more time together surely. They had not shared the best of youth and middle age, and now they missed what could have happened in the last of life. Or, rather, Hermia told herself, what happened in the last of life was rapid and annihilating and impossible to gauge precisely on Route 6 by the exit ramp for Brewster in the wet November dark. She did not forgive him. She could not forgive him. Lawrence died.

XI

—

I see myself in windows and I see myself in spoons and the image is refractive of, if not nothing, very little: there's a woman of indeterminate age, except on my last birthday I turned forty-eight. And can remember, dimly, when that was the number of states we as a nation claimed until our President Dwight David Eisenhower of late lamented memory decreed it should be otherwise. To wit, five serried rows of ten and, if Puerto Rico joins us, fifty-one. How many Betsy Rosses must have been stitching flags! Shoot if you must this old gray head, sing hey-diddle-diddle, the cat and the fiddle, the cow jumped over Commander John Glenn who became a senator and Alan the Good Shepard who's a man I shall not want.

A long, slow season here. It's forty years, or feels like, in the wilderness and what have I done to deserve it and what have I failed to do, Lord? Why am I left thus alone? I understand, of course—no need to belabor the point—that solitude's elective and I might well choose alliance with the various doing-good doctors and doing-well lawyers who present themselves as candidates for this my hand and could for instance focus on volunteer work in the school in Pownal or the hospital in Bennington, Putnam Memorial outreach, or simply drive the van for Meals on Wheels. Instead I am waiting—oh, patiently, silently—to resume the old familiar ways, for my daughter to come home again and in the watches of the night await my chevalier. Why so pale and wan?

I'm a statue built of stone. I'm exactly the person you try not to notice in the supermarket aisles. The tall, stooping snaggletoothed lady with the shopping cart and bag of onions and macaroons and oranges and the box of Kleenex and the jug of Drano and the Jerusalem artichokes and bleeding hearts of palm. Or is it heart of bleeding palms? I'm a divorcée and widow and the mother of a daughter who has—deftly, so very deftly and utterly entirely hey presto—disappeared. I'm the thing in the garden birds settle on to preen and, flying off, beslime.

XII

—

2006-2012

She stayed in the house in Truro and then, at her daughter's urging, left, irresolute, and visited, and after two months in Los Angeles flew east again, and neither being there nor not-there was a comfort. Years passed. Hermia lived by herself.

She did maintain the house. It gave her something to do. She had the wood siding repainted and the hallway wallpaper replaced and the garden rototilled and the driveway graded and new gravel added and the lawn reseeded and, once it grew in, mown. She left Lawrence's clothes in his closet, but his shirts and jackets were too few to fill the vacancy. He had been proud of his light carbon footprint, and that lightness weighed on her; his books stayed where he stacked them on the shelves. His boots stood in the mudroom and hats hung on pegs in the hall. His photo by her bedside (squinting, sunlit, on the dunes in Newcomb Hollow, halfway down the path to the beach, wearing his old purple windbreaker and a Yankees cap) and a photo of them taken by Susanna Banner at the Wicked Oyster on their wedding night (both of them lifting flutes of champagne and laughing a bit tipsily—she could remember Henry saying, "Smile, and say suppository!") and a blueprint of the house he'd built for his mother and stepfather and a certificate of excellence from the AIA: these composed her framed mementos. She also kept a Wolf Kahn calendar he had purchased on arrival in December 2004, showing the year to come. The calendar was outdated, of course, but not something she could relinquish; the days and weeks were wrong but he had been alive for them, and had turned the pages—fields and barns and pastel views of trees and lakes and meadows—till November 2005. It hung on the back of the library door, affixed to a nail there, reproachful, and though Hermia knew she should remove or replace it, she could not bring herself to do so; time had stopped.

Time did not stop. She turned sixty-five, sixty-eight. On the anniversary, each year, of Lawrence's death she stayed in bed till one o'clock, unable or unwilling to get up and make herself coffee and toast and deal with the spurious diurnal urgency of groceries and bills and housekeeping and e-mail, although Internet was available in Truro now, and Patricia wrote her daily, and she Skyped with Bill. Her grandson at four years old was growing tall, black-haired and green-eyed like his mother, and wholly obsessed with Spider-Man. He dressed himself in capes and a Spider-Man face mask each afternoon when he came home from playgroup, and liked to pose and tumble in front of the camera, always saying "Look at me, *look*, Granny, this is Spidey's attack stance: watch out!"

She loved her daughter and grandson unreservedly; they gave her two reasons to live. Yet Hermia could not disguise resentment: Why should they thrive when she herself was suffering; why should they celebrate birthdays when she herself had no one with whom to clap hands and sing? She had preferred, she understood, the needy and frightened Patricia to the enameled young matron lounging on a patio. Therefore she stayed a continent away from those who were her family, unwilling or unable to depart the place where Lawrence died.

His children kept in touch. She had met them the one summer he had spent in Truro, and then again after his death. His daughter, Catherine, and his two sons, Andrew and John, came from Chicago and Phoenix and Vail and introduced her to their own families, her stepgrandchildren. They were concerned and kind and told her how much their father mattered, even at a distance, and how hard he'd tried to stay in contact, how it was clear he loved *her*, Hermia, and very clear to everyone how happy she had made him that last year. They invited her to visit, when she felt like traveling, and she thanked them and said maybe sometime in the future, but not just now, not yet.

His sons—John in particular—had Lawrence's way of walking, the right foot slightly splayed, the dip and nod of his head when he laughed or repeated a joke. Andrew had two sons of his own—a pair of towheaded charmers who played Frisbee and baseball outside for hours, then gorged themselves on doughnuts she bought at the grocery store in Truro, Jams. She was glad to know her husband's children, and his children's children, but they were affable strangers, not adults with whom she felt a connection or whom she needed to see. She had lived alone for years, and had gotten used to it, and had made her peace with it, and then she lived with Lawrence and had gotten used to company, *his* company, and now she could not make her peace with how he was not in the house.

Catherine arrived for an overnight stay and called her father "Daddy Cool"; she said everyone in Oberlin, when they visited Ann Arbor, thought Lawrence was "the bee's knees." This was the expression Patricia had used when Hermia informed her she herself had gotten married. It was such a strange and old-fashioned phrase she wondered if the compliment had somehow come around and was again in fashion: *the bee's knees*. She wondered, idly, also if it could be possible that her stepdaughter and daughter had met, had ever known each other and acquired each other's expressions, and decided that the answer must be no. Catherine reminisced about her father and how he worried over her, the ways he coddled her, and said she wished she'd spent more time with him and had known her father better these last years.

"He talked about you often," Hermia said.

"Oh?"

"He was very proud of you. And he always carried your picture in his wallet."

Catherine's eyes grew wet. "Dad seemed so, so *permanent.* I don't think I'll get over it."

"I know *I* won't." They hugged.

"But I think he *did* die happy. Your marriage was just what he wanted; you saw as much of him in that last year as I saw Philip in five."

"Oh?"

"Ten, maybe. He was never home."

Then she spoke about her own marital problems, her sense that her husband had married his work, was having an affair with tax shelters and right-of-way disputes and lawsuits on his clients' behalf, because every hour not in the office wasn't a billable hour, and billable hours were what he lived for, never less than seventy a week, and often more. What she got from him each Friday night was sleepy inattention, a set of shirts to take to the cleaner and dinner out at the all-you-can-eat buffet at Kittery's, the steak house down the road.

She continued in this fashion, saying she hadn't been unhappy and didn't really care if Philip had been banging his sexy secretary, who was in fact a Jehovah's Witness and engaged to a minor-league baseball player being recruited by the Texas Rangers. It turned out her husband had been having an affair instead with a lawyer in another firm, and as far as Catherine was concerned the two of them deserved each other. But she did envy Hermia what Lawrence so clearly had given, *attention,* and she hoped she didn't sound self-centered, except once in her life it would be excellent to have what the two of them had had for a year . . .

"This is what they mean by 'misery loves company,'" said Hermia.

But she was glad, as well, when Catherine left. She had not meant it when she said that misery loves company; she preferred to be alone. The Banners spent the winter anyhow in Sarasota, and the Zuckers were in Cambridge, and she found it difficult to deal with dinner invitations, refusing them by saying, "I need time." Jim Ford—the third of her neighbors on the "call list" in case of an emergency—was a widower who drank too much and got too easily maudlin and, which she could not excuse him for, voted for McCain and Palin in the election of 2008. She could forgive him for his sloppiness, his sentimental assertion that the two of them were soul mates, but she could not bear his politics, and told him so, and the breach between them—papered over with politeness, because when Jim was sober he was mannerly and decent—did not heal.

Now Hermia spent long periods with only the radio talking, and in the winters wore the down vest Lawrence used to wear, not changing clothes for days at a time, or washing her hair or putting on makeup or getting into the car. It wasn't all that difficult to *leave* the house; what was hard was returning alone. She did take walks, when the weather was good, on the Pamet Road or on the beach or past the burned-out shell of Luke Foster's place. Often, she came upon deer. From their penned-in enclosures, dogs barked. She waved at the mailman or cars driving past and saw herself reflected in the plate glass windows of the modern summerhouses if they were not boarded up. Dimly, confronting her reflection, she was astonished by the look of the creature she faced. How did it happen, Hermia wondered, that she had grown so bent and slow of gait; how had she suddenly or gradually but in any case decisively become a shapeless figure in a yellow slicker, white hair blowing in the wind and carrying a stick? When had she lost and how misplaced the satisfaction that she once would take in walking, dressing, conversation? Where had her happiness gone?

She knew the answer, of course. It was on the turnout on Route 6, by Brewster. It was there she had grown old and then she lost her way. She tried to read, or watch the news on television, or listen to the piano trios Lawrence so much admired, but none of this held her attention. She e-mailed her daughter, or talked on the phone, or Skyped with Spider-Man Bill. But more and more often she could not remember the purpose of the e-mail or the topic of the conversation or the reason she was talking or watching her grandson cavort. The widow with a walking stick was not someone she could recognize; the blockish person in a bathrobe or a yellow slicker was Hermia not-Hermia, from whom all joy had fled.

—

His sister, Allie, called. She was once again in Boston and with an unscheduled evening, and she wondered if Hermia would care to join her in the city or, if not, would welcome an overnight guest. She missed her older brother and wanted to talk about Larry and see how things were going and catch up. Hermia could think of no excuse to keep the woman from her door and said, "Why don't you drive down tomorrow and we can talk."

"Is there anything you want from Boston?" Allie asked, and she said, "No, just come ahead, we can have dinner here."

"Great," Allie said. "I've got a car."

"I could give you directions."

"Don't bother; there's a GPS."

"See you tomorrow," Hermia said, and hung up.

It was then she understood how far she'd traveled, standing still, and how there was nothing to cook with and nothing in the house it would be possible to cook. She shook her head reproachfully; aloud, she said, "Buck up." She could not remember the last time—two weeks, two months, two years ago?—that she had made a meal or set the table for a guest; time crawled, then raced, and neither the crawling nor racing was important and she did not have Allie's telephone number and therefore could not call to cancel or change plans. It was October thirteenth. It was Tuesday afternoon. The year 2009 had offered up a first flutter of hope, the pride of having elected a black candidate as president, but by October she was feeling defeated: the Sarah Palins of the world would be triumphant anyhow, and Jim Ford with his right-wing know-nothing politics was gaining ground each day. The summer had been long, and hot, but autumn was arriving, and the roads were traffic-free. Hermia no longer drove to Orleans, or only if it could not be avoided and she had to see the dentist or the branch manager of Cape Cod 5; she shopped instead in Provincetown and drove there in the fading light and bought—as Lawrence used to do—a wedge of cheese, a bluefish, and a bottle of Sancerre. In the checkout line she smelled herself: rank, not so much unwashed as stale, and noticed how the cashier noticed, and the boy who bagged the groceries, then carried them carefully out to the car. She fished through her cracked leather handbag and gave him a five-dollar tip.

All the next day, awaiting Allie, she fussed and cleaned and cooked. It was as though her sister-in-law might pass judgment on her otherwise, or disapprove of how she spent the time. She tried to account for her time. The floor he had collapsed on was the floor she swept and mopped, and the door the EMTs maneuvered him through on the gurney that last afternoon was the door she locked. There *was*, she knew, a quiet beauty to the house; there *was* a kind of comfort in the lawn and pines outside, but in the aftermath of Lawrence's death she had accomplished nothing to be proud of, or worth discussing with Allie, and she wondered why she felt so nervous at the prospect of a visit, so tempted to turn out the lights and hide in the root cellar where she would not be discovered. "Don't be silly," Hermia said aloud, scolding herself for the impulse to flee, and straightening her hair. From the kitchen window she watched a red fox loping past, making its way to the woods. At that instant came the clatter of a rental car, her sister-in-law in the driveway, and she knew it was too late.

"Hello."

"Hel-*lo*!"

"Did you have trouble finding me?"

"It's an easy drive, once you're out of Boston, and now they've fixed the rotary. The Cape is so beautiful this time of year."

"Let me help you with that." She reached for the bag.

"No problem, it weighs nothing. I'm glad to see you, Hermia."

"It's been a long time."

"Yes, too long."

They went inside. Lawrence's sister hesitated for an instant at the door, and then with a toss of her white cropped head stepped across the threshold, sighing, smiling, repeating, "It's been a very long time." They made small talk together and, over chamomile tea, caught up with each other's news—or, rather, with her visitor's news, since Hermia had little to tell—and were chatting easily about the weather, the traffic pattern on the Cape, the improved approach to the Sagamore Bridge, the Arizona border wars and how that region of the country, already hot enough, was heating up, and drying up, and Hermia was thinking what a pleasure after all it was to have a visitor. She offered sugar cookies and a plate of cheese. Then she realized to her fearful shock that she had forgotten the woman's name, or perhaps had never known it, and could not remember why her guest had arrived, or how she came, and that for fifteen minutes—*was* it fifteen minutes, or longer and, if so, how long, all afternoon?—she had been conversing volubly with a total stranger, not someone she had met before, or—since she *knew* they knew each other—in what way they had met. A white light danced above her eyes; she attempted to swallow. She put down her cup.

"Is everything OK? You look," the woman said, "if you don't mind me saying so, like you've just seen a ghost."

"Yes?"

"Yes." The woman nodded. "Do you miss him very much?"

"Who?"

"My brother. *I* do."

"Who?"

"Are you all right?"

She shook her head. She made herself speak. "I'm sorry, I'm not feeling well."

Her visitor was kind. She bustled to the kitchen and ran the tap and put cold water on a kitchen towel and pressed it to the back of Hermia's neck and spoke soothingly and offered her water to drink. After some moments the episode passed—was *that* the word, an episode, a seizure?—and she knew Allie's name again, knew this was Lawrence's sister who had arrived for an overnight stay.

The pressure in her throat released; she knew she would not faint. She swallowed and could speak. "Would you like to take a walk?"

"I'd love to," Allie said.

They went outside, in late-afternoon sun, and walked along the Pamet Road to Ballston Beach and stood on the top of the dunes, looking down at green-blue waves and the whitecaps unfurling offshore. A dog was playing Frisbee, jumping in the shining waves and returning the disc to its owners: a young man and woman in red. From her distance Hermia could not be certain, but it appeared to be a yellow field Lab, or maybe a golden retriever, shaking its coat free of water and barking in anticipation of another throw after each bounding retrieval.

"You remember," Allie said, "when I was here before, and you showed me the garden, I called my brother a rolling stone. But I never decided if that's supposed to be a good thing or a bad: 'A rolling stone gathers no moss.' I think it means keep on moving, keep being energetic like"—she pointed—"that puppy there. But some-times I think it also means something's wrong with a person, or missing, and you don't *connect* to things.

"Because that was how Larry seemed—always, I mean, discon-nected. Until you found each other and he moved here that December. It felt as if, for the first time really—and he as much as told me so—he'd found what he was looking for and wanted to stay put. I know I shouldn't speak this way, we don't really know each other, but I feel I understand, and you've nothing to feel bad about . . ."

"Except he died."

They stared at each other. "That's true."

"He died and left me here alone."

A wind arose; she shivered. The couple below her was kiss-ing. The dog barked and leapt and circled them, awaiting the next throw. Hermia squinted, shading her eyes, while again a white light hovered in the middle distance, its beam dancing, juddering, attempting to remember the name of the beach they looked down upon, the name of the golden retriever she had had when young—Trigger? Tigger?—and the name of the woman beside her who was wearing a green scarf. Something unsayable rose in her throat, a wordlessness emerging. She knew she was going to leave.

—

But it was hard. In 2011 she turned sixty-nine: four years older than her husband when he died. He should have been, she told herself, seventy; he should be reading on the porch or washing up the din-ner dishes, standing at her shoulder, or listening to Mendelssohn and Schubert and Ives and Dvorak and Brahms. From time to time she did sense Lawrence's presence, so actual in the air she breathed she held her breath, inhaling, and tasted the faint residue of garlic and white wine from the sauce he liked to make for pasta, or *moules marinière*.

In the bathroom she still smelled—or told herself she could—the odor of his aftershave, a bottle of Paco Rabanne. The week before Thanksgiving, Patricia came to visit and by the afternoon she left had hired caretakers who passed through every other day to cook and clean and take the garbage to the landfill, then a young woman who called herself a caregiver and wore clogs and dreadlocks to her waist and through the winter months of 2012 did Hermia's shopping and laundry. She protested she was fine, and able to manage all this by herself, but Patricia had insisted, saying, "The least we can do."

One day she went out walking. It was a late spring morning, and she wandered through the parking lot at Pamet Cove. There was a fishing trawler in the middle distance, and several motorboats and sailboats rode at anchor in the channel. *CAUTION—CUIDADO*, warned double strands of yellow tape across an open pit. The dredged hole was deep and wide, and there were clouds of midges swarming and a small four-legged creature she could not identify swimming back and forth and bumping up against the banks of mud. A Chris Craft idled at the landing's docking ramp, and two men were preparing for what looked like a day's outing; they had jerry cans of gas and rods and reels and fishing nets and gaffs.

She watched. A gull circled above her and dropped what it held—a razor clam, an oyster?—to the tarmac so it shattered, then swooped down to eat the meat.

One of the men approached her, and he was familiar. "Hello, Mrs."

She looked up at him.

"Long time no see."

He was wearing blue jeans and a red-checked shirt and Red Sox cap; the sun was in her eyes and she shaded them, looking up from her bench, trying to make out his features, trying to place his voice and name. He put out his right hand.

"It's Luke. Luke Foster."

Hermia stood.

"Been *years*," he said. "A long time."

"Are you living here?" she managed.

He nodded. "Ayup. With Angie. Down to Eastham."

"Angie?"

"Oh, she's growing up—you wouldn't believe it, how fast. She's eight now, plays the clarinet, and just *loves* school; she's the best thing I could hope for and much more than I deserve in His abiding bounty."

"Your daughter," said Hermia, remembering.

"Ayup. Returned to me by His everlasting grace when I was born again and gave up evil ways, thanks be to God."

"Excuse me?"

"Evil ways. Those were my words. *You* knew about them, and your *husband* knew, which is why I've come to shake your hand and ask your pardon and beg you for forgiveness; not a day goes by I don't remember how near I came to perdition, how I was led into temptation and succumbed to it and, but for the grace of my Savior the Lord, would have been a sinner all my days."

"He's dead."

"Excuse me, ma'am?"

"My husband. Lawrence. Did you know that?"

Luke nodded. "I heard about it, yes, I did. But I was in detox and not allowed to come pay my respects, and I was off the Cape for years and only just got back this last December. Thanks be to God."

She studied him. He took off his Red Sox cap and shifted his weight on the balls of his feet, rocking back and forth, arms at his sides as if awaiting inspection. He did indeed look changed. He had gained weight and lost his hair and his tattoos were fading; the threatful venom in him had been replaced by meekness, the vulgarity by piety. "Christ saved me," he said solemnly. "I was redeemed by our Lord."

"I—I'm glad to hear it."

"And I owe you an apology as well as a great debt of everlasting thankfulness; I pray for you nightly, Mrs., as well as the soul of your husband. Because it was a kind of hellfire or anyways a foretaste that I put you through, *myself* through too, and when that cookstove exploded and my dogs all died, I come *this* close"—he raised his hand and pinched his thumb and forefinger together and squinted through the half-inch aperture between them—"to perdition." Luke sighed. "Which is why I come over just now to give and get, not a blessing exactly, I don't deserve that, but to tell you that you changed my life, *He* changed my life, thanks be to God, and Angie's too."

"Where are you living?"

"Eastham." He waved at his friend in the Chris Craft. "With Angie's mom. We got divorced, but never did get sundered in His sight. 'Who watcheth over Israel'"—Luke laughed, a high-pitched cackle—"and if He can manage *that* job, well, one bush-league sinner like yours truly ain't a problem. She's my landlady now, not wife, but we do make a family and it's better so for Angie; I'm doing carpentry and house painting and plowing and suchlike and giving what I can."

"Good luck," said Hermia.

He smiled at her. "The fish won't wait, it's time to go."

"Yes."

"God's grace upon you, Mrs., and His everlasting bounty. The fish won't wait," he said again. "I must be getting back."

———

This conversation stayed with her; she talked about it with Patricia when Patricia called.

"I wish," she said, "I could take comfort in religion. Do *you* take any comfort in religion?"

"No."

"Well, Luke Foster does."

"Who?"

"My old neighbor. Young neighbor. He's a man transformed."

"Luke Foster?"

"Isn't it astonishing? I don't mean I forgive him, or can forget what he did to the house—or anyhow he tried to, which is the reason we came home. Which is the reason Lawrence died, or so I sometimes tell myself, and even though it isn't strictly true, I mean, it wasn't cause and effect and probably *was* unavoidable and would have happened anyhow, a heart attack's not caused by sitting on a plane and driving a car or something you prevent by sitting by the pool and eating bonbons the way we did. Oh, I know it wasn't really bonbons, you wouldn't serve unhealthy food, it was carrot sticks and celery and hummus we were eating, and that lovely Maria—how *is* she, anyhow?—give her my best, please, tell her I miss her, and also the gardener—wait, don't tell me, I remember his name, is it José? *José*—but every time I pass their house, old Eric's place, do you remember Eric Foster? No, of course you don't, of course you can't, though he was just the sweetest man, and always stacked the wood he cut, but it's a burned-out pile of wreckage now and I prefer it that way. I don't want, I mean, the noise next door, don't want to hear him holy rolling or whatever it is that born agains sing, oh, Jesus save me, *save* me, but I have to admit it, he does seem improved. And, come to think of it, he was using gas again, had a jerry can there with him in order to go fishing. You should have *heard* the things they said, those boys that stayed with Luke, so 'Thanks be to God, thanks be to God' is a different kind of menace, and—what was I saying, what were we talking about?"

"Are you all right, Mom?"

"Of course not. No. What sort of question is 'Are you all right?'"

"A serious one."

"No, it isn't. You know the answer already, you know I'm not all right."

"I'm coming to see you. We need to discuss this."

"We do?"

Patricia arrived on the first day of June. Hermia prepared herself and tried very hard to be ready—remembering to brush her hair and teeth and to wear the kind of clothing her daughter would approve of. She tried to remember the name of Bill's karate instructor (Sensei Peter? Sensei James?)—and tried to remember but could not the name of the girl with the dreadlocks, the one who came every Tuesday to "caregive," impossible word. She was pleased to see Patricia, very glad to share the house with her, the garden and the pathway to the beach. There was breakfast to prepare. There were lunch and dinner to eat.

Her daughter proved unstoppable, dispensing checks and dealing with the heating oil supplier, who was dunning her for bills not paid and billing her for repairs never satisfactorily completed, then having conversations with the cook and cleaning lady and the person with the dreadlocks. On the third day of her visit, she said, "Let's take a ride." Where they were going, it turned out, was not five miles away, a place called SeaShells that was, or so Patricia claimed, a retirement community, an overgrown motel with a view of dunes and Route 6A and, in the distance, the Provincetown campanile. It was awful, so utterly awful, that while her daughter smiled and chatted with the manager of the residence facility, Hermia sat in the cheap plush armchair in the bright yellow waiting room, watching patients stagger past or slumped in wheelchairs, staring or talking to themselves in a twitching wordless jabber, and knew she was going to cry. She could not help it; she wept. The tears poured down her cheeks, but she maintained her silence, her hard-earned independence, and only when Patricia emerged from the office, regal, shaking hands with the manager, did she extract a handkerchief and wipe her eyes.

"Are you all right, Mom?"

"No."

"What's wrong?"

"What sort of question is 'Are you all right?'"

"We need to discuss this."

"You said that before. Don't take me for an idiot or think I don't have eyes."

"I don't."

"Don't what?"

"Take you for an idiot."

"Then would you mind informing me just what we're *doing* here?"

"It comes highly recommended. You could have some company, professional attention. Would you like that, wouldn't you enjoy that?"

"I would not."

XIII

—

Sailing, sailing, over the bounding main. Well, it's not exactly sailing; it's a cruise ship called *Diana*, and we ply the Bay of Naples, and what does that expression signify in any case: a bounding main? Last night at dinner a bowlful of shrimp. Last night at dinner a bitter white wine and a bore at table discoursing on the reasons he calls Las Vegas home. It's Lawrence there across the room, the man by himself in the corner, or not by himself but eating at a table with two couples who arrived together and appear to know each other but not him. I do; I know and knew him from the instant he came up on deck: that diffident assertiveness, that way of being a part of the party and yet suggesting somehow he wishes he were not. The slope of his shoulders, the falling of his arms, the downward-facing dog; does nothing ever end and do we start again?

In a bar on the Piccola Marina. We dock there in the rain. But that was Capri and this is Pompeii; imagine the terrified people, the ones who watch Vesuvius and are on the instant enshrouded with flame and onrushing molten lava and the all-encompassing ash. Who flee to the sea but are boiled there alive, who stay chained to the cookstove or tending the cattle: master, mistress, slave. Oh, I am all of them, all of them, quailing as I move to touch his elbow and then to take his hand.

What are you doing here?

What are *you* doing here?

And then we stare at each other, the distance unbridgeable over more than forty years, and yet with grace abounding in the ruins of this city: hey-diddle-diddle, the fiddle and cat.

Do you want lunch? A coffee, maybe?

It's good to see you.

And *you*. You look wonderful.

No. No, I don't.

You're here alone?

Alone. And you?

Not any longer. Not now.

So we resume. Dr. Livingstone, I resume. I cannot help it, I'm giddy with language, the things we've not said and will say.

XIV

—

2012–2013

Patricia came back that autumn and would not take no for an answer, insisting things must change. She was efficient and rapid and accomplished—all qualities Hermia too had once possessed, but lately had somehow misplaced. The girl whom she had known so well was now an adult stranger; the child whose every mood she could anticipate had grown beyond her reach. She confessed to her daughter, "I'm tired," and Patricia said, "Of course you are; who wouldn't be; you need to get out of this place."

"And what if I don't want to?"

"Do you mind if I ask you a question?"

"No."

"Take the number seven hundred and subtract seven from it. All the way down, OK?"

"Are you serious?"

"Yes." Encouragingly, she nodded.

"Why should I? What's the point of this?"

"It's useful. And because I asked you to."

"Six hundred ninety-three. Six hundred eighty-seven—no, wait, eighty-six. Six hundred seventy-nine."

"That's good; now keep on going."

"Why?"

"It's a test people take. It's a diagnostic procedure for how well you handle numbers."

"Six seventy-two. Six sixty-five."

"All *right*."

"Six fifty-eight."

"Good going, Mom."

"Six fifty-one." But then the bright light ignited again, the searchlight up above her eyes she'd learned to live with, blinking. "Six sixty-five," she repeated, and could not remember the problem, or why her daughter was asking. "Six hundred."

"Excuse me?"

"Oh. *I* don't know. This is silly."

"No, it isn't."

"A grown woman doing subtraction. Or multiplication tables— two times two is, two times four is, two times eight makes, what, sixteen? Don't patronize me, will you please, I know what this is about."

"What's it about, Mom?"

"Subtracting by seven."

"We need to make certain you're well taken care of. We need to be certain you're safe. And I don't blame you, really, for not wanting to move into SeaShells, I wouldn't want that either."

"Good."

"So here's what we're going to do," said Patricia, and it was not a question. "You're coming to Los Angeles and will live there for a little while and stay maybe through the winter; we won't sell this house, of course, or put it up for rental, but you can't live here by yourself. And I can't permit it."

The enormity of this announcement took some time to sink in. Hermia drank tea. She stared at the dust-thickened pattern of sun on the living room bookshelf, the way the titles danced together and the swaying motion of the art books: Goya, Velázquez, Picasso, the trio of Spaniards her father revered.

"Besides, Billy would love it if you came. He misses you a lot."

"Billy?"

Patricia made a movement of impatience. Hermia balanced her cup. There was a shelf devoted to Matisse, and books on Henry Moore and Andrea Mantegna and Amedeo Modigliani. Someone had alphabetized them at some point in the distant past; when? Who? There was, she knew, somewhere in the state of Minnesota a corporation called 3M.

"How old *is* he?"

"Last week was his sixth birthday, remember? He knows his grandfather, of course; Will sees him all the time. But it would be wonderful if he had a grandmother too. And I can't stay away any longer—am leaving in the morning—and we need to settle this. I don't mean tomorrow, but soon."

There was a shelf of catalogues and a book about Venice and Cairo and the pyramids and a book about Uxmal and Chichén Itzá and Angkor Wat. Would she leave them; *could* she leave them? What about, she started to say, the girl with the dreadlocks who comes every Tuesday, why can't she live here with me and be a caregiver, ridiculous word? But she could not remember the name of the girl and did not want her company and understood, even while formulating the question, that the answer would be no. No one shared her space but Lawrence, and he was not available, was— Hermia pronounced this—"dead and gone." Patricia stood. Her mute abiding witnesses—the books, the paintings, the teacups, the rug—must keep their watch without her and consign themselves, *resign* themselves, to an eternity of waiting while dust motes danced their rumba in the slanting afternoon sun. "Six sixty-four," she tried again, and thought about her daughter and grandson and her son-in-law and Will and bowed her head in resignation, saying, "Yes."

"Excuse me?"

"Yes."

"That's *wonderful*. It's just what I wanted to hear."

"But give me a week, won't you?" Hermia asked. "I need to say good-bye."

———

She did. She made her peace with the kitchen, the guest bedroom, the upstairs space beneath the rafters where old coffeepots were stored, and toaster ovens and champagne flutes and highball glasses and telephones and suitcases and lamps. She bade farewell to the pantry and the library and dining room and chairs, the brown couch by the fire where Lawrence used to sit. He'd rested his feet on the ottoman, often; she said farewell to that too. Then she set about the business of packing—deciding what she could discard or could not live without in sunny California, La-La Land. She filled a steamer trunk with books and shoes and music and a jar of cayenne pepper and several packets of the saffron he particularly cherished and, in order not to lose the feel of him, his shirts. She packed her own clothes in two large suitcases and a duffel bag, remembering the climate required nothing heavy—no lined jackets or sweaters or winter-weight fabric—and while she was assessing what she needed from the living room (the portrait of her mother, the pillow her husband had rested his head on while reading, the foot-high orange-and-black bow-and-arrow-brandishing kachina doll her father had brought back from New Mexico for her thirteenth birthday, two alabaster oil lamps from Afghanistan, and a framed note from Lawrence, saying, *Te quiero*), she understood as not before this was a formal sundering, a severance, and she might not return.

"Don't worry," said Patricia. "The house has lasted two hundred years. And some of it much longer. It will do fine without us."

"I know."

"And we'll come back, I promise."

"Don't promise. You don't need to lie to me."

Her daughter was departing. The car she ordered had arrived, and the driver awaited her, courteous.

"I'm not lying, Mom."

"But you're promising what you can't deliver. I loved this place. I love it."

Patricia smiled. "Of course you did. Of course you do."

"I *hate* being treated like a child. Don't condescend to me, please."

The driver collected their bags. He took the duffel and the steamer trunk and suitcases she'd packed, and Patricia's carry-on; this was, her daughter assured her, an efficient way of moving, and Hermia's possessions would be waiting when she arrived in LA. She herself was being, she protested, managed, *handled*, and as though to prove the point Patricia changed the subject. "What do you think of Obama these days?"

"The same thing I've always thought. We don't deserve him."

"No?"

"He's a leader this country is lucky to have. The last best chance. Our best hope."

"In Hollywood he's still admired . . ."

"What's your expression?" Hermia asked. "The bee's knees?"

"But everybody else is doubtful, and everywhere else is—Frank's working on this—a whole other story. He's losing his constituency, both the independent voter and the liberal left. The president's getting no new voters, and losing a lot of the old. Not to mention the Tea Party."

"Why are we discussing this?"

Her daughter had an answer. "Because the world keeps turning. Things change, they always change. And that's why I want you to come to Los Angeles, to be part of it again, where we have excellent doctors and where they can take care of you. We can, I mean, take care of you."

"Remember when I said the same?" Hermia sneezed. "That there were doctors in your town and you should consult one—remember how angry it made you?"

"I do."

"So why is this different?"

"Because I was anxious. Depressed. And panicky. And I *did* see doctors and they *could* prescribe things, except I was pregnant and not allowed to take them. But what *you* have, Mom, is a medical condition they can diagnose and help us with . . ."

"What?" She blew her nose. "The ability to subtract by seven?"

"Let's not argue. My driver is waiting."

"You act," she said, "as if all it takes is money. Power. Willpower, maybe, I grant you that—*Will* power, ha!—and everything will be just hunky-dory. But it isn't, it won't be, it can't be; he's dead and gone, I tell you, and that can't be fixed."

Patricia hugged, then kissed her. "He's coming back," she said, "on Thursday."

"Who?"

"The driver. James." She pointed to the car—long, gleaming, black, out of place in the driveway—and said again, "I *wish* you would come with me. But it's only three more days, and I've booked your flight to LAX, and now you can finish your packing, OK?"

"OK."

"Promise, Mom? We're counting on it."

She crossed her fingers behind her back. "I promise, yes."

"Good-bye."

—

Hermia had three more days. She spent them in mourning, walking the rooms, walking the trail to the beach. It was late October, and the scrub oak leaves were turning brown, the beach plums growing sere. Seabirds clustered at the tide line or waddled away from her, preening. She had crossed her fingers, lying to her daughter—or not so much lying as hedging her bet. She might not go, she told herself; she could decide to remain. Yet she herself was seventy, and gone were the days of the rotary phone and girdles that her mother wore and garter belts and push-up bras and the A-line dress she'd worn to her first high school dance with Bobby—Billy?—Ehrman in his Nehru suit. In dancing class they'd learned to do the mambo and the cha-cha-cha and samba and what Billy called the caramba, thinking he was funny and repeating it and telling everyone, "Ca-rumba!" as they did their dip and twirl.

Her dance class took place on Saturdays, at eleven o'clock in the morning, and she watched Arthur Murray on TV. Her family's first television set had been a Philco, black-and-white. The screen was thirteen inches on the diagonal, and it took some time to start up and shut down, and often there was snow. This fall would turn to winter and winter would be fierce and then subside and in its turn be spring again, but she herself would know no such recurrence. The wind was cold. She would never again, she told herself, remain in Truro for Thanksgiving or endure in solitude the day that Lawrence died. "'That time of year,'" she told Lawrence, "'that time of year thou may'st in me behold . . .'" There was something more to tell him, but she could not remember the rest. There would have been thirteen more lines.

The conga line was noisy; they danced the conga and caramba and, at bar and bat mitzvahs, the hora. They did the bunny hop. What time of year, she asked herself, what time of year would usher in her own final days, and when would they end? "Which makes thy love more strong"—that was how the sonnet ended, or nearly—"which thou must lose 'ere long." Was it "lose 'ere long" or "leave 'ere long," and did it make a difference to the poem's meaning, and what was the difference it made? She had been young and then not young and then a grown woman and now an elderly woman and all of it was over but departure from the house. She had lived in it when young and then no longer young but old; for every season of her life the roof had been her roof, the bed her bed. She was crying, Hermia knew, but no one saw or heard her and therefore she let herself cry.

It was water far under the bridge. It was milk spilled so very long ago the flavor of it vanished and the stain had dried and evanesced and, looking at the carpet, she no longer could be certain it was milk. Coffee, perhaps, or wine, or some other liquid substance—is liquid a substance, she wanted to ask, or does that term apply to solids only, does the category, *substance*, refer to each and both? And although she knew the answer, it was nonetheless a question and could serve as a distraction while she stared at the carpet's smudged pattern, a floral arrangement worn thin. The lily entwined with the rose. The blossom disguising the thorn. The spring become the fall, the winter the summer again. How strange, she thought, that what had been misplaced is found; how improbable that she should be so open to emotion who had long been closed. A deep purple faded to lavender, nearly, a green stalk gone yellow with age.

There had been Fred Astaire. There were Fred Astaire and his sister, Adele, and Ginger Rogers and—what was her name?—Cyd Charisse. There were Gene Kelly and Donald O'Connor and a host of—what were their names?—hoofers: men dancing in top hats and tails. Billy Ehrman in his Nehru suit was sweating and had acne and could not keep the beat. She tried to lead but not let him know she was leading, because his self-esteem and self-regard had to be preserved. It was always precarious, provisional, and Hermia was unsurprised when thirty years later she learned that he had killed himself in Silver Spring, having been indicted and about to face a very public trial for embezzlement, having diverted funds systematically from the bank in Maryland of which he'd been vice president and spent them on a cashier and a retreat in Costa Rica. The wind raised the sand up in sheets. Turning her back to the chill gusts and doing dance steps now along her tracks above the tide line, she found herself remembering his clumsy two-step motion: *Bobby* Ehrman, it was Bobby, although by the time she read about him in the newspapers, his name was Robert and he had been wearing what even in the photograph she could see was a toupee. Hermia wiped her eyes. She loved this strip of beach, this sand and sea wrack and the sea. She would not see it again.

The Banners came over for one final drink. The three of them sat on the porch. "I think it's best," Susanna said. "To try California, I mean. You would have been welcome to visit us in Sarasota."

"Where?"

"In Florida," said Henry. "We're leaving soon. By Christmas . . ."

"Where?"

"You remember," said Susanna. "We do it every year."

"I've never been," mused Hermia. "Why ever would you want to?"

Sarasota was, they told her, a good deal less lonely than the Cape in winter; it had a museum and a concert series and nearby, in spring, spring training for major league baseball; their condo had palm trees and a courtyard and a swimming pool, but of course they had to share it with two hundred other couples and the house in Los Angeles was only for her family; it had, if you happen to like such things, deepwater fishing and golf. "Do you happen to like them?" Hermia asked, and Henry raised his shoulders and said, "Of course not, no." They drank and ate crackers and cheese.

"Will you empty out the pantry for me?"

"Excuse us?" asked Susanna.

"I hate to throw it all away."

"There's a lot here," Henry said.

"We ought to share it," Hermia said. "You think there's nothing left and then there's so much *stuff*, I shouldn't let it go to waste and can't just leave it here. For what, raccoons? The deer?"

So they called the Wilsons and the Zuckers, and she tried to call Arturo Tucci but his number did not work.

She tried again; again there was no ring.

"He's dead," said Henry Banner. "Remember? Arturo passed two years ago."

Hermia felt herself blush. "I know that, I *knew* it, I must have forgotten."

"We miss him all the time," Susanna said. "He was an original."

Briefly the old white-haired painter appeared; smiling, he stood at her side. She reached her hand out to touch him, but he was mere memory: an incorporeal presence who could not profit from the pantry shelves, the cans of peas and tuna fish and peaches in syrup with a Sell By date embossed above the label. Arturo had died, she reminded herself, in the fullness of time. But what was time's fullness; what did that mean, and could it overflow? She touched Henry Banner's arm instead, apologetic, shruggingly; she had not thought she'd kept so much, but there was excess everywhere.

"Should I give something to Luke Foster, do you think?"

"No."

"He'd like this toaster oven," Hermia said, irresolute, holding it open and snapping it shut.

"Don't think that way," Susanna said. "You don't want him near the house." Therefore she filled cardboard cartons with bottles of vinegar, oil, molasses, the various syrups they had once cooked with and the canned tomatoes and boxes of cereal and pasta and salt and gave them to the Banners and the Wilsons and the

Zuckers, dismantling—*that* was the word, dismantling—the pantry and all its contents until the shelves were bare.

———

On Thursday the driver appeared. His name was James, he reminded her; his car was freshly washed. He tipped his cap and carried her bags and said her daughter was a gracious lady and this whole trip had been prepaid, including tip, and Hermia was not to worry and should try to rest. She did. She closed her eyes and leaned back in the leather seat so as not to see the Pamet Road or the road through Wellfleet past the Marconi Station and the rotary at Orleans where he took the turn for Boston and particularly not the stretch of one-lane highway past Chatham and Sandwich and Brewster where the ambulance had driven Lawrence on the way to Cape Cod Hospital on that fateful day. There were bottles of water and wrapped candy in a console by her side in the backseat; in the seat pouch up ahead were magazines instructing her on what to see and where to go in Boston. There was a copy of that morning's *Wall Street Journal* and that Tuesday's *New York Times*. She asked James if he lived in Boston, and he said no, he lived in Medford, it was better for the children, so she asked if he had children, and he told her yes, ma'am, five of them and four still at home. "You're a lucky man," she said, and he touched his cap and agreed.

To her surprise he accompanied her; they both got on the plane. "Your daughter hired me," he said when Hermia asked, "for full-service delivery, ma'am. Door to door." She asked if that made her a package and was he making a joke? He shook his head. The flight was smooth, reminding her of her first trip with Lawrence, when the two of them flew out to meet her daughter's fiancé and renew old acquaintance with Will. That had been many years ago, and she tried to remember how long it had been and if she could subtract by seven; she busied herself with subtraction from the year 2012, watching people wearing earphones and working on computers and turning the pages of books. Fitfully, until the pilot announced the sights out of the plane window—the Rocky Mountains and Lake Mead—and said they might encounter turbulence and should keep their seat belts fastened, Hermia slept. Then, as before, she made her way to baggage claim with a companion by her side— although this time not Lawrence—and met a driver holding up a placard with her name. The man from Medford tipped his cap and said, "It was a pleasure, ma'am, good luck," and said that he would spend the night in an airport hotel and first thing in the morning fly back home. "Can't I go with you?" Hermia asked, and James shook his head and shook her hand and left. Then she and her new driver made their way past office buildings and hotels and oil derricks pecking at the steep brown hills like long-beaked birds; they crept along in traffic till the traffic emptied out and she was in a place called Hancock Park, where her family now lived. This house was stone, half timbered, not a third the size of Will's residence in Brentwood but also with wrought-iron gates.

"I'm *so* glad you're here," Patricia said, and Hermia said, "Yes." "Frank and I have lived in this house, now, five years"—Patricia counted them out on her fingers—"and you haven't visited *once.*" Hermia admitted this. "How was the flight?" her daughter asked, and Hermia said, "Fine." "How are you feeling, Mom?" she asked, and Hermia said, "Tired," and was informed Bill was at school and coming back with the neighbor's child's driver and Frank would be home by dinner. "Do you want to get some rest?" Patricia asked, "I'll show you around the place later," and she—feeling the weight of the journey, the weariness of travel, and a keen-edged sorrow that she was not here with Lawrence—agreed.

Her suitcases awaited her. She lay down on the bed. Here she was safe, she understood, and would be protected and not required to shop or cook or drive or do those things that now, in her great weariness, eluded her: make conversation, wash, or brush her hair and teeth. Therefore she closed her eyes and saw herself a child again, the blanket drawn beneath her chin, the stuffed chicken and the teddy bear she slept with up against her cheek, her mother saying "Night-night" and hugely departing the room. How did this happen, she wanted to ask; how was the old woman on a street called Rimpau in Hancock Park the creature who once lay in Brooklyn Heights with her blanket—her *blankety*, silk-lined and worn thin with rubbing—in a crib? Where had they gone, the years between, and what would happen next?

—

"I've found you an apartment."

"Oh?"

"Just down the street. Two blocks away. In a house you'll like, I think."

"Not here?"

Patricia coughed. "We hope you'll stay a long, long time. You're used to a place of your own, though, and this one isn't big enough for you to stay in forever."

"Forever?"

"Right."

"I just arrived, didn't I? Only this afternoon got here, I mean."

"Yes, but we're talking long-term, Mom. We're not discussing tonight. Or this week."

"I see."

"I'm sure you'll want your independence."

"I *had* it, Patricia."

The girl looked away.

"And right now I need to go home."

"Whoa. You haven't even seen the place. Three minutes away, it's a three-minute walk . . ."

"I've seen enough," said Hermia, "to know when I'm not wanted."

"Mom, you're being unreasonable."

"Runs in the family, remember? Call me a cab."

"Stop it. *Stop* it!"

"What happened to my daughter? Where did she go, I ask myself, the girl I used to know so well, the one who never left my side?"

"Mom . . ."

"The one who wouldn't practice, even, if I wasn't in the room. Those hours at the piano, Pat-a-cake, all those hours at the piano."

"I haven't left. I'm here."

She shook her head. She tried to clear it, but it would not clear. She saw herself in the living room mirror—wild-haired, gesticulating, puffy-cheeked—and understood the trouble she was making, the mad old woman she had somehow come to seem. Then even the anger that kindled her waned; even the tide of it ebbed. She could not quite remember why it was that she had grown angry, and what imagined slight, or actual, she had just received. Therefore what she found herself left with was—Hermia hunted the word—*uncertainty*, a sense of displacement she couldn't quite place: she was in the room, not in the room, and watching herself being watched. She blinked. She took her daughter's hand. "I'm sorry."

"Don't be, Mom. You're tired."

"Yes."

"And I didn't mean to surprise you. I thought you'd be happier, probably, off by yourself."

"Yes."

"We'll discuss it tomorrow. Or next week."

Bill came running through the door—long-limbed and breathless, ebullient. "*Granny*," he shrilled. "You're *here*!"

"Yes."

"In school today for show-and-tell I told that you were coming."

"How *was* school, darling?" asked Patricia.

"Good."

"What did you do today?" Hermia asked.

"Jonah took my cookie."

"Oh?"

"And didn't ever ask for it and didn't give me his."

"Really?"

"Really really."

While her daughter and grandson conferred, rehearsing what had happened and what failed to happen at school, she looked at the wall with its pattern of vines, its cluster of grapes and a light blue flower that might have been bougainvillea, or oleander, or perhaps a hyacinth, with hummingbirds flitting between them. She could not be certain. What did oleander look like, and why was the wallpaper hand-painted silk? Again Hermia felt herself drifting, both in the room and elsewhere, here and not-here at the same time. For it was hard to concentrate, difficult to muster the precise degree of attention and concern required in such company, impossible to care if Jonah did or didn't ask permission for Bill's cookie that he ate at lunch, or find and express the appropriate rage at the outrage committed in school. It was as though she had a cold, a muffling cloth around her ears and eyes and nose and mouth, as though thick air the others breathed came only thinly to her, and what she heard and saw and smelled was distant and befogged. "That's nice," she heard Patricia saying, but what was nice and why it was nice and whether it was nice before were matters of indifference . . .

Yet the boy was persistent, insistent: "I *told* them you were coming."

"Maybe she'll visit school tomorrow. When I drop you off, I mean."

"Would you want me to?" asked Hermia.

Bill nodded, then picked at his nose. His eyes were a deep green. "What did you bring me, Granny?"

"Bring you?"

"You know, a present. I always get presents from Will."

"But your grandfather knows what you like." She mastered herself. "I don't. Granny will get you a present when she knows, as *soon* as she knows, exactly the thing you most want."

Then there was silence between them. The birds in the wallpaper flew.

——

Each week she met with doctors. There were men in white coats, men in sports coats, women at desks and standing by examination tables, holding out clipboards and saying "No problem" and "How are we feeling today?" They asked about her diet and her habits of reading and exercise and when she first had noticed these symptoms of memory loss. "I can't remember," Hermia said, and laughed at her own joke.

They smiled. They wore transparent latex gloves and, when they removed them, washed their hands. They introduced themselves, always, when they knocked and entered, and announced what role they played, but Hermia could not distinguish between doctors and interns and residents and nurse practitioners, or why they came alone or came in pairs. They asked her to spell "world" backward.

"Excuse me?"

"The word 'world.' Can you spell it backward?"

"*D-l-r-o-w.*"

"Fine." They asked how long she planned to stay and what were the names of her physicians in Boston and at Outer Cape Health Services since they would need to requisition her current medical records and was her billing address the address they should use? She said, "I'm here because my daughter wants me to be looked at. No other reason," and they said that's very often the case. "What year is this?" they asked her, and she said, "Two thousand ten—no, twelve. 2012." "If you needed help in the middle of the night," they asked, "what would you do?"

They scheduled MRIs and CAT scans and X-rays and blood tests. They came from Mexico and India and Texas: impossibly smooth-skinned and professional and young. "Copy out this figure, please," they said to Hermia, "of intersecting pentagons." She copied out the figure, and they told her, "Good."

They probed her ears and throat and shone pinpoints of light at her eyes. They asked about her mother and the final years in London and if she remembered the details of her mother's final illness, how long it had lasted and when it began. She had had no practice giving answers to such questions. It was as though there *ought* to be an answer, a single correct way to respond, but Hermia could not find it; she read their name tags instead. *Jamilla, Kayla, Brian, Nadia, Thor.*

And she could hear them talking. They spoke about assisted care facilities and transient ischemic attacks and the prospect of supervised living, saying to Patricia that it was not yet strictly necessary but planning for the next stage was appropriate and it made good sense to start. They had no doubt displacement was a factor, and the lack of recognized parameters; at home she would no doubt react with greater certainty to the problems posed. Again, she filled out forms in triplicate and was reminded of that time in London—was it eight, nine years ago?—that her mother's books had been described as "shipshape" and they went to the Courtauld.

She thought of Lawrence at her side and found herself remembering the oil paintings in the rooms in Truro when it was her parents' house—the Olitskis and the Nolands and the Hopper and Hans Hofmann—and how her father used to say that paintings are painted in all kinds of weather and require no protection. They don't need a furnace or air-conditioning unit to withstand the change of temperature. "Think of Piero," he would say, "or Raphael; those guys didn't have any climate control, and I'm damned if I'm heating the studio all winter just for the sake of the paintings; they can take care of themselves . . ."

Meantime, she spent hours with Bill. She always had loved him in theory, of course, but now she loved her grandson in practice and enjoyed their time together every day. The boy was quick and smart and self-absorbed. He came to Hermia's room, saying, "Let's do a art project, let's use my favorite colors, OK?"

"What are your favorite colors?"

"*You* know."

"Are they still blue and red?"

"Exactly right. For Spider-Man."

"And what do you feel like drawing today?"

"A elephant," said Bill, and bent to the coloring book. In total absorption he bit at his lip, making certain to remain within the outlines of the creature he'd selected from the zoo's menagerie. They drew together or played Candy Land and checkers, and Bill always won. They built bright plastic Lego forts, and once the two of them had finished building and then knocking down a structure, Patricia tidied up. This business of tidiness was more and more an issue, because Hermia could not be bothered to put things in their proper place, and did not know their proper place, and there were far too many cabinets and drawers in the kitchen anyhow; in her own room she felt ill at ease, remembering and then not quite remembering what clothes she'd worn the day before, and where they were, and reaching for a blouse or skirt she finally remembered was in Truro irrevocably. Bill always knew the clothes he'd wear—the Batman pajamas or Spider-Man cape—but she herself could not keep up appearances; she answered when her daughter asked: why should she be bothered, and for whom?

"For Will, at least, when he comes for lunch tomorrow."

"Will? Why?"

"Because he's observant; he notices things."

"Things?"

"You, Mom; he notices you."

"Well, let him. I'm tired, so terribly tired, of putting on a face or putting on a smile or putting on the right ensemble; none of it matters, understand, I can't do it anymore."

"Do it for *me*, won't you please?"

"What? Keep up appearances?"

"Exactly right," Patricia said, and Hermia heard in this expression not so much the echo as the origin of her grandson saying, "Exactly right," and bowed her head: "I'll try."

XV

—

"Time-lapse photography, that's what I see when I look in the mirror."

"You're beautiful."

"Not any longer."

"You are."

"This weekend the Zuckers are coming down to Wellfleet. Helen called this afternoon. Do you want to see them?"

"Do you?"

"Not particularly, no."

"I like it best," said Lawrence, "when there's nobody here but us chickens. Spring chickens."

"Let's rent a movie, maybe."

"*Barry Lyndon? Paths of Glory? Eyes Wide Shut?*"

"Don't you *ever* get tired of Kubrick?"

"The man who is tired of Kubrick," he said, "is tired of life."

"Is that a quote? And isn't it London, not Kubrick?"

"What do *you* want to see, darling?"

"Oh, anything, as long as it's in color. And not by Stanley Kubrick."

He agreed. They flew home on British Airways, and were sitting in business class and drinking bad champagne. He said, "I liked the estate agent, the one with the pencil mustache—what's his name, Alistair Redmond?" and Hermia, looking out the airplane window, knew she was going to cry. She could not tell if she agreed or disagreed about liking Alistair Redmond; she understood it made no difference and was utterly beside the point and in the scheme of things irrelevant. But somehow her indecision on the matter of liking or not liking a man she knew she'd never see again became an occasion for tears.

Lawrence took her hand. His palm was warm on hers. He asked how she was feeling, what she was feeling and what he could do, and Hermia tried to explain: it was absence, only absence; it was what she *wasn't* feeling that was causing her to cry.

XVI

—

2013–2015

It was Will who found her. She was staring at the hummingbirds, the blue vines they were perched on and the seams of the wallpaper at which they flew. She was examining lines on the walls the wallpaper hanger disguised. He had been an expert, clearly, and had known just what to match with what and where to turn a corner and fold the scene over and start again; birds flew and flew and flew.

Hermia was trying to; she was lifting her arms at the wall. She was allowing them to drop and lifting them so rapidly she did feel like a bird—a form of exercise, she knew, that would be useful for her promised flight and elevate her brilliantly above the chandelier and thick rolled silk at the crest of the curtains and out the window when it opened if it ever opened in this house on Rimpau, where they kept her in a gilded air-conditioned cage. She drew the line at birdcalls and did not try to crow or caw, because in any case a hummingbird is not known for its music, nor, truth be told, its actual nature—which is fierce and quarrelsome, so if the bird were sizeable (the size, say, of a duck or, God forbid, an osprey or an albatross or condor) it would be the most ferocious of the feathered kingdom—was that the phrase, "feathered kingdom"?—and therefore she felt grateful for its lack of size, its unimposing stature, and had no wish to call attention to herself: only to lift and drop her arms and smell the sweetness emanating from the blossoms there beyond the window—bougainvillea, perhaps, or oleander, she could not be certain—and (quietly, quickly, so rapid in her movements that an eyeblink would cause those who followed to not follow her) escape.

"Hey, girl," said Will. His voice was loud.

"Hello."

"How are we doing this afternoon? What are we up to today?"

"The royal 'we'? The editorial 'we'?"

"Excuse me?"

"The first person plural—you and me?" She was adept at such banter, such—what was the word?—badinage. As might a hummingbird, departing, she fluttered her eyelids at Will.

"What I want to know," he said, "is what you're up to, baby-cakes. And what you're trying to do."

"Just getting some air," said Hermia. "Or trying to. Would you care to take a walk with me?"

He stared at her. He was no fool.

"No fooling," Hermia said.

"Sure," he told her, dubious. "Where to?"

"Once around the block, is all. Up and down upon the earth."

"Let's go." Will offered his arm. He was wearing Birkenstocks and a T-shirt with a picture of a bagel and the legend *Rock-N-Roll.* They had had lunch. He wore a two-day growth of beard, a pair of stained, torn khaki shorts, and his nonchalance seemed odd to her: a rich man in his seventies with the attitude of the failed folk singer and law student she had known when young. "I'll tell the kids we're out taking a walk."

She hesitated. "I need to help doing the dishes . . ."

"We're fine," Frank announced. "Go ahead."

The lunch had been gazpacho and a salad Niçoise.

"Behave, you two," Patricia said. "Don't stay out too late."

This was a joke, it seemed, an after-mealtime pleasantry, a daughter telling her mother and father-in-law to behave. Will laughed. They walked down the driveway and out to the gate. He pressed a round black button—how did he know where to find it? she wondered—and the gate responded silently and they waited for an opening and stepped out into the road. Behind them, the gates hovered and then again were in motion and, pivoting, clanged shut.

"Which way?"

"Oh, I don't care," said Hermia. "Whichever you prefer?"

Again Will took her arm. She wanted to tell him, was trying to say that everything that mattered once was safely lodged some somewhere she could return to and, if only in a kind of muscle memory, walk around and through the way they'd done this minute at the driveway's portal, the wrought iron gate ajar and shutting silently again, or how the lunch they'd just consumed was somehow also reminiscent of soups and salads earlier, the habit of consumption over years and decades and, because of the calendar, centuries, *millennia*, so that the present moment replicated, in involuntary recall, the past: his apartment on Irving Street in Cambridge still reeking of incense and marijuana and cigarette smoke, the narrow mattress on the floor where she and Lawrence used to lie, the time Will made a pass at her—"Hey, pretty baby, this last song's for *you!*"—and how she had refused him and they liked each other better afterward because they could be friends and not, as he put it, fuckbuddies. And now of course it was the case that in some form of sympathy or symmetry he courted her as his one son had courted her one daughter, although not in active courtship, not an invitation into bed but rather as agreement that the two of them would walk side by side, because they had in common old shared memories of Cambridge, Lawrence, and were easy with each other. So he took her to a concert at what must have been Club 47 and what was the singer Odetta's last name?—Felix, *Felious*, that was it—with her great booming strident severity, her deep-voiced unsmiling dignity, and how in her mind's eye he, Will, was still the overweight and high-voiced banjo-plucking twenty-four-year-old he'd been, was being as they walked beneath palm trees while a man across the street was leading his Jack Russell terrier on a green leash, the man's strides fast-paced, delicate, his upraised arm and fluttered wrist a cross between a greeting and gesture of retreat. "A neighbor?" she inquired. "Do you know him?" and Will shook his head. Then Hermia remembered the adults' disapproval, the way the men on Irving Street (those elders now her juniors, those middle-aged men she now thought of as young) had looked at her, their sidelong glance, the assessment of class, and all of this silent, implicit, but trumped by the beauty she'd been.

"You understand," he said, "I know it's not my business."

"What?"

"What you're going through, babycakes. Just how you feel."

"How *do* I feel, Will?"

"Shitty. That's obvious. You'd have to be dumb as a post not to notice."

"Congratulations, sheriff," Hermia said. "You got me dead to rights."

"Let's not play games. I loved him too. Your husband."

"Yes."

"So I know what you're going through, maybe."

"No."

"Try me."

She did try. While the man with the Jack Russell came circling back across the street, completing his journey and, producing a blue wrapper from the *New York Times*, knelt to collect what the dog, squatting, shat, she tried to tell Will how this stage of age was not what she had bargained for, although natural enough, Lord knows, and in the course of things inevitable, a fading in and out of focus, a glaze on the surface of things. He must be feeling it also, she knew: the world had slipped its leash. "See, see," she said, as the dog trotted on, and her husband's old friend smiled at her and put his arm around what used to be her waist and was—or so it seemed to Hermia—assuring her that he and all the family were there for her, were at her side, and ready for whatever would be coming at them up ahead or down the pike; she leaned against him heavily and dropped her head and closed her eyes.

In Vermont long years ago there'd been a month of pleasure with a lawyer up in Manchester who met her at the Equinox hotel and whose marriage, he assured her, was a marriage in name only. For a while she had been hopeful, had felt the first stirrings of yearning, but then his wife gave him an ultimatum: either divorce or fidelity, and he had had to choose. He had chosen the latter, of course. Or at least he had elected it until the storm blew over and his wife was mollified and he could remove the eye patch that covered his wandering eye. Then he took off his wedding ring and slipped it into his left coat pocket and asked, "Are you free this Thursday night? Julie will be in Boston, so we could get together, couldn't we, at the hotel?" And Hermia had answered—reaching out her own ringless hand and giving him her sweetest smile and articulating carefully—"To hell with you, my friend."

"Hey, girl," said Will. His voice was low.

"Hey, there."

"How are you feeling?"

"Fine. I'm fine."

"You've got to fight it, babycakes."

"Fight what?"

He had an answer. "Collapse."

—

So this she did. It was, it turned out, possible. She helped her grandson race his racing cars and build bridges and corrals. She watched the video of *Spider-Man* more times than she could count. She went with Patricia to see Frank at work—the two of them made welcome in the room in which he sat, his earphones on, while a girl with purple bangs and a T-shirt with a drawing of a cigarette across her breasts and a legend that said *Holy Smokes* responded to his orders, showing scene after scene and frame after frame of people talking soundlessly, people smiling, people nodding or shaking their heads, and marking them *A*, *B*, or *C*, in order, he explained to her, to rank the takes and sequence them and know which ones to keep. "Is this what they mean by the cutting room floor?" asked Hermia, attempting to make conversation, and he said, "Well, sort of," and turned back to the monitor. It was as though these people—her daughter and her daughter's husband and her dead husband's old friend Will—were somehow multiple: at one and the same time both people she knew and people she did not. For this too could surprise her: the daughter she had nursed was now her grandson's mother, the man she'd met in 1962 was now the mogul by her side, their behavior inexplicable although once she would have understood their every move, their motives. It was as if she shut her eyes, seeing over and over the same scene enacted, the face on a sidewalk or passenger train or behind her in a supermarket aisle she'd registered, or failed to, and while Patricia texted—her quick fingers beating out a rhythm on the keyboard of her iPhone, making appointments or canceling them—she tried to join the discussion and remember, failing to, the faces of the Truro policemen, the face of the private detective she had hired and then fired in his office back in Bennington, the photos on his desk. She tried to remember also, and could, the names of Mary Lombard and her husband, Thomas, who constitute—together with their young son James—the entire population of the Lombard family cemetery at the edge of Bound Brook Island, there exiled because of the smallpox and a fear that from dead bodies it might spread. *D-l-r-o-w* is the reverse of "world."

"I've got a surprise," said Patricia.

"What?"

"You remember how he planned to take you on a honeymoon? He talked to me about it."

"Who?"

"Lawrence. Your husband, remember?"

She did. And the surprise, Patricia explained, was that the family was going, or perhaps she ought to say they were going *en famille*, since it's how they would say it in France, to Paris and the Valley of the Loire for Bill's school vacation. "You're coming with us, Mom," she said. "I've bought the tickets already, Frank has business in Cannes, arranging for the European distribution of *Letters from a Farmer*, but he'll fly with us to Paris and then you, me, and Bill will visit all those castles because you never had your honeymoon and we owe it to you now." "What are you *talking* about?" Hermia asked, but her daughter would not take no for an answer, and they flew together to Charles de Gaulle Airport, but lying down, but cosseted, and then there was a driver and a hotel in the Place des Vosges and it could have been *exciting* and it should have been *delightful*, the words her daughter used. In the Hotel Pavillon de la Reine, however, Hermia wanted only to sleep, to try to imagine herself walking these streets with her husband instead. They spent two days. She took a bath. Frank left. Then the three of them were driven south by a man in a beret, sporting an earring and a black mustache—so broad a caricature of a French guide and chauffeur she thought he must be joking, or Lawrence would have thought so, and she imagined the jokes they would make—from restaurant to restaurant and hotel to hotel and garden to garden and moat to moat. Young Bill—*Guillaume*—admired the moats, the roiling carp, a drawbridge, and she remembered their guide saying that gravel and not grass or cobblestones was the preferred mode of—how do you say, madam?—*access* by coach, so a gentleman on rolling wheels could properly announce himself to the lady he was visiting and the lady could make herself ready or, if the combat promised to be martial and not amorous, the sound of an enemy comes *en avance*, the clatter of men on horseback and with their troops approaching. She slept. For she could not be bothered now to learn about François Premier or why he was called "Salamandre" or which of his mistresses lived in and were granted or removed from which château; they made a pilgrimage to towns called Tours and Blois and Chinon and villages called Villandry and Azay-le-Rideau and talked about how exciting it was, how delightful, how well they traveled together and then—she slept—flew home.

In June Patricia showed her an apartment in a house on Hudson Avenue, with a separate servants' entrance; when Frank asked about it that evening, Hermia agreed it might be fine, but not quite yet, not now. Why not, he asked, no time like the present, and his wife put her hand on his arm. Not just quite yet, said Hermia, OK? "A visit to Jo-jo works wonders," said her daughter, "and a manicure and pedicure while we're at it: I've made us an appointment for Thursday morning, Mom." On Thursday morning, therefore, they went together to the hairdresser and had manicures and pedicures and facials, and she felt, sitting in adjacent chairs, that things could be attended to and, by such attention, redeemed. "Frank wants you to feel settled," said Patricia, "and be taken care of when there's nobody around."

There were people, always people, and not nobody around. There were people speaking Spanish to each other, and using leaf blowers and irons and hedge trimmers and mowers and mops. In the kitchen, to be useful, she folded cloth napkins and put them away. She decided not to sweep. It was simple enough to be grateful to Will, to visit him in Brentwood when he sent over the driver, and be pleased to share a meal with him at a restaurant in Malibu called Nobu, where the fish was raw, or take a walk by the water or not get lost and walk to the village of Larchmont, which was ten minutes from the house, with a street of coffee shops and restaurants and an ice cream parlor Bill particularly liked, and a weekend farmers' market and a bookstore and drugstore and real estate office; it was simple enough to listen to Frank while he talked about his editing, his present interview project, and sit by the pool and stare at the water and—restraining herself with an effort, because nothing could be easier, nothing simpler to arrange, with pills perhaps and a tumbler of scotch and plastic bag around her head and stones piled in her housecoat's pocket—try not to let herself drown.

—

Remember The Flies?

> *I remember.*
> *That pretentious director? That terrible play.*
> *Except we weren't so certain then . . .*
> *Of what?*
> *That it was terrible. That Sartre was pretentious. Or maybe we were too . . .*
> *And what was his line from* No Exit?
> *"Hell is other people."*
> *He was wrong about that, darling. Hell is having no one with you.*
> *I turned to stone, it felt like.*
> *Stone?*
> *Yes, a statue. A thing on a pedestal, maybe.*
> *Well, this is called a second chance.*
> *A second act. After years of separation.*
> *Except let's get it right this time.*

We were so young.
So busy proving things. I was, at any rate.
What?
Busy proving independence. "Hell is other people."
Why did you leave me?
Did I?
Yes.
I don't remember.
No?
I don't remember it that way, I mean. We each have our version of how it happened.
Out there on the dance floor, awaiting a partner.
There must have been dozens.
No.
Dozens who wanted to ask you to dance.
Well, maybe.
I never left you, really. You understand that, don't you?
No. Well, maybe a little. Yes. No.

———

But then the pageant faded and the view dissolved and her lines got even sillier with the director yelling Cut and Smile Don't smile take twelve take five it's subtracting by seven take minus two take minus nine let's do this all over again. So once again she held Lawrence and was holding him, and this is what is meant, she thought, by the peace that passeth understanding: right through hell there is a path. Oh, the bliss of recurrence the first act repeated the chance for revision the exit line altered: *Don't go.*

"Are you happy here, Mom?'

"I did enjoy that trip we took."

"I don't mean *happy* happy. But you're not sorry, are you?"

"Sorry?"

"To be in California. To be here with me and Billy. And Frank, of course. And Will."

She pondered this. There was a time when happiness had mattered to her greatly—when its absence or its presence could organize the day. Lately, however, what she felt was neither happiness nor misery, delight or grief, but only a gray constancy: a wakeful sleep and sleep-beleaguered wakefulness. It was half a dozen of one and six of the other, she wanted to say, and day by week the line between them blurred; there were no *seasons* here. "It's not much fun."

"What?"

"Growing, *getting* old."

"You're not that old, Mom."

"Forgetful. Getting forgetful, I wanted to say."

"Was Dad like that?"

"Excuse me?"

"Was he?"

"Was he what?"

"Forgetful."

They were standing in the kitchen. Patricia had peeled carrots and was making carrot soup. She was wearing an apron and had her hair tied back and was the very picture of contented domesticity; there were onions and parsley on the chopping block and a cup of fat-free half-and-half waiting to be added to the mix. There were salt and pepper and a bouquet of herbes de Provence. The kitchen windows sweated mist; the forecast was for rain.

"No."

"Why don't you ever talk about him? Why should the subject be taboo?"

"Who?"

"My father. Paul Lattimer. Who was born in London and died in Sarajevo. With whom you lived for, what, three years?"

"I know where he was born and died."

"Well?"

"You've reached what I believe they call a rolling boil. The soup has, anyhow."

"Is it because you don't want to? Or because you can't?"

"There's nothing to say. We should never have married. Except the marriage *did* produce you, and that was a very good thing. Something I've always been grateful for and have never once regretted."

"Me either, Mom. Not lately."

"But did you ever regret it? When you were having those—oh, what do we call it?—uncertainties? Anxieties."

"What was he like?" the girl persisted. "Can you tell me?"

"He was a good dancer. He had the kind of English accent that persuades you of intelligence, and for no real reason. He insisted on a Pimm's Cup when we went to restaurants, and he liked saying 'jolly good' rather too often. Before the paranoia and the rage set in, he could be amusing. If memory serves, and it *does* serve, he wore a forty-four regular sports coat size; his waist was thirty-four. Is that sufficient for you?"

"No. Did you love him?"

"I can't remember."

"*Did* you?"

"No."

—

The pool was a temptation. It was a single-lane lap pool—not like the elaborate and curvilinear installation at Will's, with its parasols and lounges and dining area and barbecue pit. This pool was six feet deep. It was of uniform depth, and long enough for exercise; Frank did fifty laps in the morning and again, often, at night. When Hermia closed her eyes, she saw herself outstretched in it, playing Ophelia or *Death and the Maiden* or some sort of mermaid in some sort of watery grave.

At times she lay faceup; at other times facedown; at times she raised her arms. But she wasn't Ophelia or the girl in *Death and the Maiden* and not a mermaid unable to breathe; she was a grandmother taking a nap beneath the overhang in shade.

Her grandson was learning the crawl. He wore angel wings and did the flutter kick and held his breath underwater and could do the backstroke and the breaststroke and the dog paddle and crawl. He said, "Watch me, Granny, *watch* me," and did the dead man's float. Inside, at his table in the living room, Bill constructed pirate raids and space station battles and *Galactica* spaceships and forts.

She helped. Time passed. Hermia had a birthday, and continued living, as did those she lived with in the house in Hancock Park. Three thousand miles away the house she once called home stood tenantless, and silent, but in Los Angeles, not Truro, a roof was a roof was a roof. So it made no difference, finally, if she stayed with or not with her daughter; it was exile wherever she slept. In December 2013, she moved into the ground-floor space on Hudson Avenue, a modern sprawl with sod on the roof and solar panels everywhere; the owners were called Jacobs—she thought of them as JJJ—who were friends of Patricia and Frank.

"This place is far too big," her landlords said, "and we're happy to have you here with us and, frankly, the rent doesn't hurt."

Jim too was in entertainment, but his last three screenplays had been on spec, and the three before had failed to get greenlit, so they were feeling the pinch. This was how he put it, and he was glad to do Frank a favor, and Jenny had worked as a registered nurse for years until their kids were born and took all her time and attention but now were off at boarding school and college and there was too much room. So Hermia had her own apartment and hung her own clothes in the closet and hung the portrait of her mother on the dunes in Truro and the photographs of Lawrence and the note that read *Te quiero* on her bedside wall. She had a microwave and a half-size refrigerator and a rocking chair. In her daughter's house two streets away she watched the hummingbirds, immobile, flying nowhere in the dining room; in her apartment she watched cracks in the ceiling, their intricate pattern, and slept.

From time to time Frank visited, and he and Jim discussed the movies they had made or seen or were hoping to make. They talked about distribution arrangements for *Neighbors Talking* and how 3-D technology was changing the name of the game. They talked about vampires and gravity, a film about the southern wild, an opening up and closing down of not-so-much-technological-as-conceptual innovation, the prospects of a sequel to or remake of *The Graduate*, what was happening in Bollywood and China and recently to the careers of men like Werner Herzog and Judd Apatow and whether *Un chien andalou* would be worth watching again.

Their language was not language Hermia could follow—or, more precisely, she understood the words but not what they were saying—and she sat and smiled while Frank talked on and on and Jim nodded in agreement or, in disagreement, shook his head. She could remember Lawrence and his love of Stanley Kubrick, who was having a show now at LACMA, but not the names of films Patricia took her to, or Will was engaged in producing, or the Oscar contender DVDs that came *For Your Consideration* each afternoon to the door. Jenny brought them tea and petits fours or strawberries, and asked Hermia how she was doing and how she was feeling tonight. She liked to give her husband back rubs, and he rolled his neck and closed his eyes and said, "That's excellent. *Excellent*, babe."

Time passed. More and more she conjured forth the names and faces of her schoolmates and classmates in college but not anyone in Larchmont—not the girl at the ice-cream store counter or the druggist who filled her prescriptions or the waitress at the Greek taverna who greeted her familiarly and with such seeming pleasure when she and Patricia stepped into the restaurant for lunch. She read their name tags but failed to retain them; she forgot the names of neighbors and the staff at Will's. More and more she was remembering the distant past and not last week or month. What was vivid now (the contents of her high school locker, the taste of an egg cream at Friendly's, the look and feel and taste and smell and sound of Lawrence in her bed) all came from long ago and very far away. Those were the songs inside her head: "Long Long Ago," or "Auld Lang Syne," or "I'll Be Seeing You," or "When the World Was Young."

In California no one smoked, but when she closed her eyes, the room was smoke-wreathed and the men's hair glistened with pomade. It was Bobby Short at the piano, or Noël Coward on stage at Las Vegas; it was performers wearing tuxedos and caressing the microphone, singing "Ah, the apple trees!" while she and Lawrence danced. JJJ, whose house she slept in, wandered in and out of focus, but the touch of his hand on her knee in the darkened lecture hall in the basement of the Fogg Museum in 1962 was something she could feel there still, and how he whispered in her ear that Tintoretto and Pontormo were not what he wanted to study that evening, and could they meet at ten?

—

"Tell me a story, Granny."

"What kind of story?"

"A scary one."

"Do you promise to be frightened?"

"Yes. Will there be lions?"

"Maybe."

"Make it really, really scary."

The child was in the bathtub. There were bubbles everywhere. "Once upon a time," said Hermia, "there were lions and tigers and bears."

"Where?"

"Well, they're supposed to be in the zoo, of course. But the Man in the Yellow Hat forgot the key, or maybe Curious George borrowed it, and somehow all the animals got out and ran away."

"Where to?"

"Right here. You guessed it. Rimpau Boulevard."

Her grandson stared at her, speechless. His green eyes were wide.

"And they settled in the garden and got very, very hungry and looked around for something to eat. And who do you think they saw?"

"Me?"

"Yes, a boy called Bill. Practicing his dead man's float in the swimming pool."

"Was he alone?"

"He was. But something magic happened. The lion was sitting at the pool's edge with salt and pepper and mustard. He was licking his lips and saying, 'Nothing tastes as good as a nice little boy. Especially with mustard and let's say a sesame roll.'"

"*That* isn't scary."

"It is. Because his claws were *this* long"—Hermia reached into the bath—"and very sharp and ready to just carve up what it needed for breakfast."

Bill shivered. "What happened next?"

"This magic thing. Bill turned into a boulder. A rock, I mean, for breakfast. So Bill stayed that way for forty years."

"For forty *years*?"

"Or anyhow until the animals got tired of waiting and waiting for breakfast and they went back to the zoo. Where everything is managed better and there's meat at feeding time and nice clean water in the cages for the animals to drink."

"*That* wasn't scary."

"Yes, it was. Imagine being turned to stone for forty years."

And then she took the washcloth and scrubbed his neck and ears.

—

I have a piece of paper and a pen and brush. I have a cup of water Daddy gave me and a watercolor box. My favorite color is pink. Sometimes my favorite color is purple and today it's only purple when I paint the water which doesn't have a boat on it but anyway is blue. Blue is what it ought to be but Daddy says if you want purple go ahead. Except hold very still for a minute, just one single minute, can't you, it shouldn't be this difficult. What's difficult, I ask him, and he says things that don't come easy but it's easy to hold still.

I do. I do so for seven eight nine. Then Mommy says that's excellent and do you want a butterscotch and would you care, my precious, for another piece of paper while we leave this one to dry? Daddy's working at his picture which is on not the table but easel because he's a slowpoke and squints. Squints is when you shut your eyes but not all the way so you see through them funny and draw. He has his pipe and whiskey and his bowl and fiddlers three. He is, he says, a merry old soul and calls for his fiddlers three. Mommy gives me paper and says don't forget to wash your brush and I don't and use yellow instead. This is what we always do and always do and always do and the trouble is, says Daddy, it's hard to not be cute. Don't flatter yourself, Mommy says.

—

It was Patricia who found her. She was lying on the Jacobs' bed and holding a copy of *People* and trying to look at the pictures of starlets getting married and standing on red carpets and in bathing suits. She had been turning the pages, but they would not turn.

What she saw instead were apple trees in flower, and herself on a picnic with Lawrence, and the blanket they were sitting on that came from Hudson's Bay. It was orange with a dark red stripe, and he had brought cold chicken and a bottle of white wine. Then they were young and now are old, and it was unclear to Hermia which of the ages obtained, which world she inhabited, or why the pages stiffened in what used to be her agile hands, her fingers no longer pliable but rigid, her body now not lean but slack and no longer obeying instruction—*move, breathe*—so he was disappearing even as he loomed above her smilingly, lips pursed to kiss her breast.

First love and last love, she wondered, are they one and the same? Her father's portrait of her, hanging in the Whitney, was a study of the girl she'd been but had long since ceased resembling and in any case was canvas, not the fact of flesh. She could remember telling Lawrence, although perhaps she failed to say it and therefore he had failed to hear, that she loved him very much and this made her happy. While he was measuring his carbon footprint, he stood above the sunlit patch of meadow where she lay. There were creatures in the garden, scurrying, not hurtful, and she watched them through the six-pane window, where they performed or rested from their complicated dance. It was hard to keep them open, and so she shut her eyes.

What I need from you, my darling, is the certainty you'll live. And since you cannot promise this, since already you have broken that particular and deep-sworn vow, I need from you the certainty that when I die I'll find you and continue the—what?—conversation, this thing cut off untimely on the border of Route 6. For I am an old lady now, and querulous, I know it, and not the sort of person to stop traffic in the street.

But stop we did, by the side of the road, and they tried and failed to save you with the paddle, the defibrillator, the oxygen, and all those implements of mercy by which we are distracted and in which we pretend to believe. You won't believe me, darling, but I kept our Hudson's Bay blanket, our wedge of cheese and bread, and thou beside me in the wilderness; it does not end, not end.

Where she has had him buried is where she plans to lie. There is room beside her husband in the plot she purchased; there is their headstone and a lilac bush and cranberry patch sloping down to the shore. The walkways of the graveyard have been covered with crushed oyster shells; there are beach plums and *Rosa rugosa* and a stand of pines. The cemetery is well tended by a crew from Provincetown, men paid to rake and mow. Lawrence liked the view. Ten years ago she buried him, but it feels like yesterday, a day ago he died. Now Hermia will sleep beside him while their dust and bones commingle, because this is what she asked for and her daughter will comply.

There is a kind of humming she can hear in silence, a color she can see behind closed eyes. There is her immobility and all the races run. She is talking and not talking; she curls to herself like a wreath.

ACKNOWLEDGMENTS

Book One of this novel, in a different form, was published as *Spring and Fall* by Grand Central Publishing, New York, in 2006.

Chapter II, Book One, of this novel was published as "Spring and Fall" in *The Southern Review*, Summer 2006.

For details of and expertise on an architect's career, the author wishes to thank Douglas Kelbaugh, dean emeritus of the A. Alfred Taubman College of Architecture and Urban Planning at the University of Michigan, as well as Margaret McCurry and Stanley Tigerman of the Chicago architectural firm of Tigerman McCurry. Thanks also to my colleagues at and the staff of the Institute for the Humanities at the University of Michigan—particularly its director, Daniel Herwitz—for making me so welcome during academic year 2004–2005; it proved a safe haven and splendid place to work.

My title is a cap tip to Virginia Woolf's *The Years*, originally called *The Pargiters*. Beyond that, the books have little in common, and the true urtext of this fiction is William Shakespeare's late romance *The Winter's Tale*. To that great play, I owe my epigraph, my principal characters' names, and some of their behavior.

Mary Beth Constant was a splendid copy editor: firm of hand and light of touch. Again, I owe a debt of gratitude to my editor, Ed Park. And, as always, to my agent, Gail Hochman. They are a pair of pilots any author can be glad for; this one is doubly so as his manuscript—a trim little craft, he hopes, after a long sea journey—is guided into port. To everyone involved in the publication process, my enduring thanks.

For permission to reprint Samuel Beckett's "Gnome" (1934), the author is grateful to Grove/Atlantic, Inc.

ABOUT THE AUTHOR

© Rob Hess

Nicholas Delbanco is the Robert Frost Distinguished University Professor of English Language and Literature at the University of Michigan. He has published twenty-eight books of fiction and nonfiction. His most recent novels are *The Count of Concord* and *Spring and Fall*, while his most recent works of nonfiction are *Lastingness: The Art of Old Age* and *The Art of Youth: Crane, Carrington, Gershwin, and the Nature of First Acts*. As an editor, he has compiled the work of, among others, John Gardner and Bernard Malamud. The long-term director of the MFA program as well as the Hopwood Awards Program at the University of Michigan, he has served as chair of the fiction panel for the National Book Awards and a judge for the Pulitzer Prize in fiction. He has received a Guggenheim Fellowship and, twice, a National Endowment for the Arts Writing Fellowship.